Beyond Forgiveness

Also by Caro Fraser

The Pupil
The Trustees
Judicial Whispers
An Inheritance
An Immoral Code

Beyond Forgiveness

CARO FRASER

ORION

First published in Great Britain in 1998 by
Orion
An imprint of Orion Books Ltd
Orion House, 5 Upper St Martin's Lane, London WC2H 9EA

A CIP catalogue record for this book is available
from the British Library

ISBN 0 75281 453 2 (hardcover)
0 75282 128 8 (trade paperback)

Typeset at The Spartan Press Ltd
Lymington, Hants
Printed in Great Britain by
Clays Ltd, St Ives plc

For Gwen

Chapter One

In the name of love. Leslie Maskelyne had heard the phrase when he was listening to *Start the Week*. Or rather, not listening. Too hard to pay attention to the ramblings of these pseudo-scientists and psychiatrists that Bragg seemed to like so much. They spoke a kind of jargon, delivered in tones and fluctuations of speech which were not comfortable to Maskelyne's seventy-four-year-old ear. People spoke differently nowadays, it seemed to him. From what he saw and read, the world was growing increasingly foreign, full of strangers, the children quite unlike children as he remembered them, young people largely incomprehensible, the middle-aged confused and unsure of their place in the scheme of things. He knew his own place, all right. Either in that bed or in this chair, depending on whether it was a good or a bad day, watching the world turn as he stepped slowly, daily, away from it, taking his medication, pondering everything with the impatience of decline.

In the name of love. It still stuck with him. What one did in the name of love, the man had said. He had not bothered to listen to what the man on the radio thought was or was not done in the name of love, but had wandered off on his own little train of thought. What had he, Leslie Maskelyne, ever done in the name of love? Married Susan, had Stephen and Lydia and Geraldine . . . No, that wasn't quite right. That was not what the words meant. In the name of love. It had a certain grandeur, betokening sacrifice, or

1

nobility of purpose. Marrying Susan had involved neither of those things. While not exactly a marriage of convenience, the attractions had been largely financial. And the children. You could hardly call their upbringing an act of love, more a matter of duty and affection – and hope. Hope that they would turn out decent people, despite the fact that their mother had rutted with half the county, then run off with another man, obliging him to divorce her. Given their handicaps, they were, in their way, not good or bad, merely products of their class and conditioning.

In the name of love.

What about Ruth? It was the closest he had ever come to truly loving someone. But even then he had allowed practicality to get the better of him. A brief affair from long ago, its memory no more fragrant than the scent of withered flowers, was not heroic. The act of lovemaking, no matter from what passion it sprang, did not suffice. Something more, surely, was needed. A demonstration, a proof beyond the merely physical. He had done nothing for Ruth. Everything which had come of that affair, each painful and deadening consequence, was as loveless as anything could be. He was sorry for that. It was not his way to make amends, to feel remorse, but he would have liked something better to have come from his time with Ruth. He looked out at the gardens beyond his window. He liked the plurality – gardens. The rose garden, the kitchen garden, the stone terrace and the lawns which stepped down to the carefully clipped topiary hedge and spread out beyond, the water garden to one side, with its discreet nooks and bowers, more grass and flowers beyond that, the azaleas planted round the winding paths, which drifted eventually into the fringes of the wood, itself a garden when the bluebells came out at this time of year, blurring the shadows with blue. It was all very beautiful, as was the big house in which he now sat, a chairbound invalid, amid all the splendid fruits of his labours. He thought of the lifetime's harvest of stocks and shares in their fat portfolios, the sheaves of gilt-edged bonds. In his mind they almost glistened. Such a satisfying sheen they possessed. The companies, all the controlling interests, rose in his mind like lofty pinnacles, ghostly and glassy. It was a marvel, to have made such wealth. But none of it achieved in the name of love, he reflected. Of power and ambition, yes. But not love.

These thoughts flickered away as Leslie Maskelyne looked down at his hands, lying inert on the tartan rug which covered his withered knees, and saw the faint tremor which galvanised his knotted fingers as the pain began. It always began like a slow, dull glow in the centre of his being, then burning up through him with an unbearable intensity. He knew its pace now, could summon Mrs Cotterell to administer more diamorphine before the monster sank its teeth and talons in to the truest and most terrible depth. It was little enough, but such knowledge made him feel as though he was, if not mastering the beast, at least keeping it at bay. For that was how he now characterised it. In the early days, when the pain had not been intense or spasmodic, he had seen his cancer as some worm crawling through his body, devouring him unseen. But the onset of pain had transformed the laidly worm into a rearing, ferocious, unpredictable foe, something looming so large in his consciousness that he thought of it almost as a being apart from himself. He closed his eyes and reached out a hand to the brass bell which rested amongst his medicines on the table next to him, and rang it sharply, sitting forward anxiously in his chair until he heard with relief the steady tread of Mrs Cotterell's feet approaching the room.

Thereafter, the hours until midday passed in a haze, Maskelyne vaguely conscious of the sounds of the household around him, Mrs Cotterell's presence looming and ebbing, words from the radio, which he insisted should remain on at all times, trickling into and past his mind. In the early afternoon his mind began to clear and his body, miraculously cleansed of pain, reasserted itself. Mrs Cotterell had helped him into bed before administering his diamorphine, and now Leslie Maskelyne leaned over and slid open the drawer of the cabinet next to his bed, fishing around for his cigarettes. He drew one unsteadily from the half-empty packet of Rothmans, placed it between his lips and lit it, drawing gratefully on the smoke as it slid deliciously down into his lungs – what was left of them. He glanced at his watch, whose strap he had had to tighten by a couple of holes in the last few weeks.

3

Nearly one. He smoked for a while, recalling how appalled Mrs Cotterell had been that he should still continue the habit after his lung cancer had been diagnosed. 'You can't mean to go on doing that, knowing that it's killing you!' she had said. That had been after the consultant had told him he only had months to live. He remembered lighting a cigarette while he told her – as his housekeeper, it had seemed to him more important that she knew before his family. The very fact that she presumed to utter such a thing told him just how horrified she was. Normally Mrs Cotterell was, in a dignified way, the humblest and most unpresumptuous of creatures, to the point of teeth-gritting irritation.

'That is precisely why there is no point in stopping now, Mrs Cotterell,' he had replied. 'I might as well enjoy myself while I can.'

The doctor had agreed with him.

Maskelyne's glance turned to the window, and he noticed with annoyance that Mrs Cotterell had, yet again, drawn the curtain against the late April sunshine. Tapping ash into the heavy glass ashtray on the bedside table, he jangled the little bell and waited until Mrs Cotterell appeared.

'Please don't draw the curtains in the daytime,' he said mildly, gesturing with a thin hand for her to open them. Mrs Cotterell stepped over to the window and pulled the cord, so that the curtains slid slowly back. Gentle sunlight, stippled with the shadows of the creeper round the large window, spilled across the floor.

'Let's clear some of the smoke in here,' she said, and opened one of the windows at the side, settling it on its hasp, so that a breath of spring air flapped the blind for a moment, then subsided. The distant sound of the motor mower drifted up from the gardens. Leslie Maskelyne closed his eyes with pleasure at the sound. It was the herald of spring and summer. He could almost see Reg Fowler astride the thing, battered panama well back on his head, riding the lawns like some proud cowboy, putt-puttering past the yew hedge, while the boy clipped and mulched, performing the more menial tasks.

'Do you feel up to some lunch yet?' Mrs Cotterell asked, moving around the room, plumping the cushions on his empty chair, refolding the tartan rug, rearranging the bottles on the table. All quite unnecessarily. She was one of those bustling women who could not leave anything alone. 'There's some rather nice cold chicken. You could have that with some lettuce and tomato and a spot of mayonnaise. And I could make you a fruit salad.' She touched the petals of the cut flowers in the jug on the dresser, smoothed a hand down the curtain.

The thought of white chicken flesh disturbed Leslie Maskelyne's delicate sense of temporary well-being. His appetite was almost non-existent these days. He would have thought that Mrs Cotterell knew well enough by now that it was all he could do to eat his toast and fruit in the morning, and a chop or piece of fish in the evening. Perhaps it was part of her nurturing nature. Suggesting cold chicken to an invalid must be the next best thing to getting them to eat it, he supposed.

'No, thank you,' he replied. 'I might have something later.' He reached for the cigarette packet and drew out a fresh cigarette. How he liked the look of them in their pristine state, their white, crisp slenderness, the fragrance of the unlit tobacco, the cleanness of the filter before the first drag of smoke sullied it. For years he had taken no notice, just smoked the damn things. Now each one he regarded as a small work of art. His lighter snapped and flared. As he puffed, Maskelyne glanced up slyly at Mrs Cotterell, enjoying her dutifully suppressed disapproval. No doubt she regarded substituting a fag for a nice piece of cold chicken as downright immoral. 'There is something you could get for me, however,' he added. 'Some paper and envelopes from my desk.' He indicated the little writing bureau which stood against the wall beside the window, not far from his chair. It had a lid inlaid with rose-coloured leather, which folded down to form a writing surface at just the correct distance from him when he was sitting in the chair. In it he kept most of his private documents, which he had had moved from the larger desk in his downstairs study when he had become confined to his room. 'And a pen. I had one in the drawer here, but it seems to have been moved,' he added in mild reproof.

Mrs Cotterell fetched him some sheets of paper, a pen, and the bound volume of drawings by Leech on which he liked to rest his work when he was writing in bed. The habit annoyed Mrs Cotterell, for the leather spine was mouldering and rubbed the linen bedsheets with rust-coloured stains, but she never said anything about it. It wasn't her place.

'Thank you,' said Maskelyne, as he settled his glasses on his nose. Mrs Cotterell gave him a hesitant glance, wondering if he was going to ask for anything else. As she looked at him, she reflected for a sad instant on how dramatically his good looks, preserved even into old age, were beginning to shrivel away. Soon he would look like any other bony old bedridden man. Then he glanced up, gave her a small smile, looked back to his paper and began to write. Realising that she had been dismissed, Mrs Cotterell quietly left the room.

By the time half past one came, the motor mower had fallen silent, and only the sleepy chirrup of the birds in the trees broke the silence in Leslie Maskelyne's room. He had laid down his pen, and was lying back against the pillows, eyes closed. Down in the cool peace of the water garden Reg Fowler and his young sidekick, Gary, were lunching off cold pasties and cans of Tango from the village mini-mart. Twenty-five minutes later, the fanfare heralding the end of the lunchtime edition of *The Archers* roused Maskelyne from his doze. He blinked for a few seconds, then glanced down at the letter which he had written. He sighed and read it through again, then folded it, his fingers running a smooth crease along the thick paper as he listened absently to the shipping forecast. The afternoon play would be coming next. He hoped it wasn't going to be one of those socially aware ones, full of gritty reality and people snarling at each other in regional accents. Or a weird one with lots of special sound effects from the Radio 4 stereophonic workshop. He slipped the letter into an envelope, dabbled his fingers lightly in his water glass to wet the gum and seal it – his own mouth too dry from cigarettes and medication to manage this – and picking up his pen again, wrote on it in a slow, sloping hand, 'Ruth Owen'. He jangled the little bell.

When Mrs Cotterell appeared, he handed her the envelope. 'I wonder, Mrs Cotterell, whether you would be kind enough to deliver this for me when you are passing through the village. It's for Mrs Owen.'

Mrs Cotterell turned the long, thick envelope over in her hands, concealing, she hoped, the astonishment she felt. 'I'll take it down with me later, when the night nurse comes,' she replied.

'Thank you,' murmured Leslie Maskelyne, and he slipped off his glasses, pressing thumb and forefinger against the red crease left on the thin flesh, the ever-thinner flesh, of his nose, adding, 'Oh, and could you pick up two hundred Rothmans from the shop for me? I think I'm nearly out.' As Mrs Cotterell left the room, he leaned back against his pillows once more, smiling with satisfaction as the announcer informed him that the play that afternoon was entitled *The Suspect Household*, a drama based on a real-life Edwardian murder trial. Just the thing. But then, try though he might to ignore it, an unmistakable urge gripped his lower innards. With a mild groan, he reached out once more for the bell, this time to summon Mrs Cotterell to help him to the commode.

There were three ways of reaching the village from Hemwood House. One down the driveway at the front of the house to the main road, another at the back down through the woods, and the third by a dusty little track which veered away to the left of the woodland path and ran steeply away from the Hemwood House property into a series of grassy gullies, studded with rocks, clumps of shrubby hawthorns, and tangles of bramble and giant hemlock. In these gullies, known locally as the Dips, the village children played, building dens and forts with pieces of scrap material, hiding behind the rocks to ambush one another, slithering down the slopes on their backsides on flattened sides of cardboard boxes. From the strongest of the hawthorn trees a car tyre hung suspended at the end of a knotted rope, dangling over the deepest of the gullies. This route from the house was too steep and tiring for any adult to bother with, even though it was the shortest, and indeed, since the days when the Maskelyne children had played down there with the other children from the village, it was scarcely used, except by the paper boy. Today Mrs Cotterell took the path through the woods, enjoying the quiet coolness and the lulling coo

7

of the wood pigeons far up in the trees. The path emerged on the far side of the woods, a distance of quarter of a mile or so, then ran down past the scrap-filled back yard of the local garage and became a lane, flanked by the garage on one side and the pub on the other, leading into Church Road, the main street running through the village of Hemwood.

Mrs Cotterell stopped at the off-licence to buy Mr Maskelyne his cigarettes and exchange a few pieces of gossip, then carried on up the street to deliver the letter. Ruth Owen's house was at the end of the street just past the church, narrow and picturesque, its plaster exterior painted pink in typical Suffolk fashion, its door giving straight on to the pavement. Doris Cotterell often stopped off there for a cup of tea after leaving Hemwood House, sometimes picking up groceries that Ruth fetched for her at the supermarket in Sudbury. She and Ruth went back as far as the local mixed infants, had gone to dances together as teenagers up at the American air-force base during the war, taken holidays at Clacton-on-Sea and Walton-on-the-Naze in foursomes with their husbands back in the fifties. Doris thought she knew everything there was to know about Ruth, but that Leslie Maskelyne should write to Ruth was a marvel. She recalled that Ruth's daughter, Abby, used to play in the Dips with Stephen Maskelyne and his sisters when they were little, and in a village this size Ruth and Mr Maskelyne would know one another by sight. But beyond a nod of recognition . . . What would Leslie Maskelyne have to say to Ruth that required to be sealed up in one of those long, ivory-coloured envelopes – especially one that said, not 'Mrs Owen' on the front, but 'Ruth Owen', in that direct fashion?

After ringing the bell, Doris waited for some minutes. Eventually footsteps could be heard in the hallway and Ruth opened the door.

'Sorry, love, I was out the back getting in the washing. Come on through.' Doris followed her up the hallway and into the little kitchen.

Ruth was a tall, big-boned woman, still handsome at seventy. Although her skin was pouched and slack, blooming with fine wrinkles, the high cheek-bones and clear eyes testified to former beauty. Her height lent her poise, and her grey hair was soft and gently folded up behind her head with combs and pins, unlike

Doris's, which was crimped and curled in a nondescript, old woman's permanent wave.

'So,' she said, filling the kettle at the sink, 'how's life up at the big house? Oh – before I forget, there's that detergent and biscuits you wanted in the Tesco's bag over there by the door.'

Doris got up and fetched the bag, opening it to inspect the purchases. 'Much the same as usual,' she said in answer to Ruth's question. 'He doesn't get any better. Bad in bed, worse up.'

'Well, he's not going to get better, is he?' said Ruth with only the mildest sarcasm. It had occurred to Doris recently that, however obliquely phrased, Ruth's first questions were always about Leslie Maskelyne. She wondered whether Ruth encouraged her to drop in as frequently as she did just so she could hear about him, about the goings-on at Hemwood House. She thought about the letter, but decided not to produce it just yet.

'He's going to need full-time nursing in a few weeks,' Doris remarked, accepting the cup of tea which Ruth had poured for her, and taking one of the Garibaldi biscuits set out on a plate. She slipped her shoes off and settled back in her chair with relief. This heat played hell with her ankles. They were all puffed up by the end of the day, even though she took her water tablets regularly. 'I can manage his liquid diamorphine, all right – God knows, I was that nervous to start with – but, of course, I can't give injections, and that's what it's going to come to.' She sipped her tea reflectively. 'Mind you, at the rate he's going, they'll be hard pushed to find anywhere to put a needle in. There's that little flesh on him.' Doris gazed at the potted geraniums on Ruth's window-sill and sighed, oblivious of the expression on Ruth's face. Ruth brought her own tea to the table and sat down. 'I'll be glad, mind you, when that day comes,' went on Doris. 'He'll have to have one of those Macmillan nurses. Did you see that programme about them on BBC2 the other week? Marvellous, really. Then at least that'll save my legs. I'm up and down them stairs every fifteen minutes. It's not really what a housekeeper should be doing, nursing an invalid like that. At my age, I should have given up the job by now, but as he's only got a few more months . . .' She shook her head and drank her tea.

'Is he –' Ruth hesitated '– is he all right? I mean, in his mind? In himself?' Her voice sounded awkward as she asked this, and Doris was reminded of the day she had told Ruth about Leslie Maskelyne's cancer, which she had done in her customary conversational manner. The expression which had clouded Ruth's eyes then had been unfathomable, and though Doris at the time had interpreted the silence with which Ruth received the news as mere neighbourly concern, she now began to think that something more might be read into it. And into this question. Why should Ruth care what Leslie Maskelyne's mental state was? What was he to her? Her mind flew to the letter once again.

'Oh, he's well enough, in that way. He doesn't let it get him down. That's to say, he's got a certain outlook. He just takes it as it comes. I don't know what word you'd use –'

'Stoic,' said Ruth, staring down at her tea.

Doris nodded slowly, watching Ruth and thinking that she couldn't put off mentioning the letter any longer. Making an effort to sound mildly surprised at her own forgetfulness, she said, 'Oh – talking of how his mind is, he asked me to give you something.'

Ruth raised her head quickly and looked at her friend. Beneath hooded and wrinkled lids her deep-set blue eyes suddenly shone with a youthful intensity. 'Something?' Ruth echoed. Then she asked more slowly, 'What thing?'

Doris had got up to fetch her straw shopper. She padded back to the table in her support stockings, fishing past the box of Rothmans and then producing the letter. Ruth stared at it for a few long seconds before reaching out slowly to take it from Doris. She studied her own name written on the envelope, then laid the letter down on the table next to her teacup. She did not look at it again. Her expression was totally inscrutable, and Doris felt a prickle of annoyance. That was the one thing about Ruth which had always irked her, throughout a lifetime of friendship. She wasn't a confiding person. She would be friendly as anything, intimate, capable of having a right good laugh – and they'd had plenty of those – but there were always moments when a sort of shutter came down, when she blanked you out, and you knew that there

10

were private thoughts and feelings she was never going to share with you. Not ever.

'Aren't you going to open it?' Doris could not resist saying.

Ruth picked up her tea and sipped at it, her expression almost absent. 'Later,' she said.

'Oh, well . . .' murmured Doris with mild resentment. She was Ruth's best friend, when all was said and done. You would think, after all this time . . . 'Is there any tea still in that pot?' Doris asked suddenly.

Ruth rose to fetch the teapot. She could feel it in her limbs like a sort of fire, a prickling, intense impatience. It had been all she could do not to open that letter then and there. Or to strangle Doris. Ruth longed for her to be gone, so that she could be alone with her letter. Doris must have divined this, which was why she had asked for another cup of tea. What strange things friends were, thought Ruth, filling Doris's cup again, watching her as she took another biscuit from the plate in an infuriatingly leisurely way. When Doris had arrived, Ruth had been all set to tell her about what the doctor had said about her heart, about the need for tests up at the hospital, had really looked forward to a good half-hour of concern and sympathy. But the letter had changed all that. More conversation with Doris was the last thing she wanted now. She just wanted the minutes to go by until Doris struggled into her shoes, picked up her bag and was gone.

Ruth scarcely listened as Doris passed on the piece of gossip she'd picked up in the newsagent's, merely sipped her tea and waited, reflecting on the ability of time to stretch or shrink according to circumstances. Doris's second cup of tea was interminable. Ruth managed, once, to slide her eyes to the handwriting on the envelope, anticipating and then feeling the painful little lurch of her old heart, which had felt like some tender weight within a shell since her visit to the doctor's that day. Her name, written by him, after all these years.

At last Doris bent to squeeze her feet into her shoes, then rose reluctantly to gather up the Tesco's bag and her shopper. She did not want to leave Ruth alone with that letter, resented the intimacy between it and Ruth which so excluded her. Ruth and her letter.

Leslie Maskelyne's letter. The contents could be nothing routine or domestic. Leslie Maskelyne's life contained no activity now which could in any way concern Ruth, consisted of nothing except a swiftly dwindling future. And a long past.

'Right. Well, I'll be off,' said Doris, aware that Ruth had said almost nothing during the last ten minutes, but was merely waiting, burning for her to leave. 'I'll pop in tomorrow,' she added. 'I can pass on your reply to the letter. If there is one.'

Ruth merely smiled as she walked slowly ahead of her friend down the narrow hallway and opened the door on to the street. 'I'll have the kettle on,' she replied. When the door closed, she went back to the kitchen, where the letter lay on the table.

Ruth picked up the letter and opened it, thrusting her forefinger beneath the gummed flap and ripping the envelope quite violently. She drew out the stiffly folded piece of paper and stood for a moment, waiting for this heated feeling to leave her, longing for calm detachment. She thought briefly of the days – early summer days like these – when she had hoped for a letter from him, listening to the flap and rustle of the letter-box with the certain and futile knowledge that he would never write, yet hoping still. He never had written. Until now. What use was now, after so many years? What relevance did now have to the past? She unfolded the letter and stared at the few lines written there.

'*Dear Ruth,*' it said. '*There is something I wish to speak to you about, which cannot be said in a letter. I wonder if you would come and see me one day, perhaps for lunch? Send me a note via Mrs Cotterell telling me which day would be convenient, and I shall expect you about one. Best regards, Leslie Maskelyne.*'

It was the matter-of-factness which astonished her. The casual tone, as though they were accustomed to communicating, and now something had come up which was more important than usual. They hadn't spoken for over thirty years, not since the afternoon when he had left her standing under the tree down by the river, the midges dancing in clouds over the water, she feeling so utterly bereft it had made her dizzy, fiercely conscious of the last touch of his fingers upon her shoulder . . . God, the memory of that was so alive. Then there had been the weeks of waiting, summer fading into autumn, the passage of months, one after another, turning hope to a kind of dead acceptance. The months had become years. They had spoken once, but it hardly counted. She had been standing outside the produce tent at the agricultural show with some friends – 1975, had it been? A hot summer, anyway – when Leslie had walked by with some other people, and in the murmured exchange of greetings they had said hello to one another with polite formality. That was all. Their eyes had hardly met. Ruth remembered vividly the long time she had spent before the mirror later that day, staring at her forty-eight-year-old reflection, trying desperately to see what he had seen, feverish with hope that she had not so changed that he had been disappointed, hot with anger that she should even care.

As she thought of this, Ruth gave a faint sigh and stroked her withered cheek reflectively, still looking at the letter. She was well past caring about such things now. Old age was something of a relief, in that department. By the time she was going on sixty, she had grown used to seeing him around the village, or at church – perhaps five times in the year – and no longer cared what he saw. By then, everything that had existed between her and Leslie Maskelyne was a precious part of the past. She saw herself as she had been when she was his lover, and it was like looking at a different person, nothing to do with the ageing woman living off her husband's RAF pension and the money she made working part-time at the pub, worrying about her daughter . . . Leslie hadn't changed, though. Not to her eyes. On the occasions when she saw him he looked older, yes, but he remained essentially the same tall, good-looking fellow. Or he had been the last time she had seen him, and that was well over a year now.

She put the letter down and went over to her basket of washing, absently and automatically starting to sort through and fold. How did he look nowadays, though? She didn't think she wanted to see what cancer was doing to him. The things Doris said about needles and so on were bad enough. There was a part of her that wanted to preserve her memory of him intact, to keep the bright, sensuous recollection of that short-lived affair, now that the years had washed it free from pain. Seeing him again, talking to him, might erase all that, the remembered pleasure obliterated by fresh and present ugliness. It might be best, she thought, examining the torn gusset of an old pair of pants, if she didn't see him. Just ignored the letter. They had nothing to say to one another.

She sighed and went to drop the knickers in the pedal bin. They were past it. Things got old and useless, chuck 'em away. Walking back to the basket, she stopped suddenly. Was she thinking the same about Leslie, half-consciously? Perhaps. She picked the letter up once more from the table. *Something which cannot be said in a letter.* For some reason, for whatever reason – age, illness, incipient dementia – he wanted to see her. If she had received such a letter thirty years ago, would she have hesitated? Not for an instant. True, in those days she would still have had hopes and fears, but more curiosity would suffice for the present.

She fetched pen and paper from the dresser and sat down at the table. She hesitated, then pushed the paper aside and picked up Leslie Maskelyne's letter. Turning it over, she scribbled on the back, '*Tuesday the 28th.*' Then she folded it and put it into a fresh, smaller envelope, sealed it shut, and wrote his name on the front. It was as much as needed to be said, for the present. Anything more could wait until Tuesday.

Chapter Two

In the five days which elapsed between delivering Ruth's reply and that Tuesday, Doris was in mild emotional turmoil. She felt resentful towards Ruth for failing to confide in her, and yet quite excited by this turn of events. She knew that Ruth was coming up to Hemwood House on that day, for Leslie Maskelyne had told Doris in advance to prepare the drawing room on the first floor, opposite his room on the other side of the wide landing. He wanted it well aired, with arrangements of fresh flowers, and a table laid for luncheon. Something simple, he told Mrs Cotterell – perhaps poached salmon, that kind of thing. He knew very well that he would eat little of it, in any event.

It was all Doris could do, when she called in at Ruth's on Friday evening to pick up the bits of shopping which Ruth had done for her, not to come right out with it and ask Ruth what it was all about. She had almost persuaded herself, at one point, that as housekeeper at Hemwood House, she had a right to know. 'Housekeeper' was something of an elevated term for what Doris did, and it was a title she herself had coined. Doris had started at Hemwood back in the sixties, when the children were still young, doing the odd bit of cleaning. Over time her duties had increased, until she was going up to the house on a daily basis. She knew the house intimately, was familiar with its workings and the routine of its occupants, and came to think of herself as indispensable to the Maskelyne family. When increasing old age had begun to limit the amount of housework she could do, Leslie Maskelyne, now living there alone, had no wish to disturb the equilibrium of things by employing someone entirely new. So Doris had remained in his employment, doing a little nominal dusting and hoovering, arranging flowers, fielding telephone calls, and supervising the robust young cleaners, of whom there had been a series, in their performance of the more arduous household tasks. With the onset of his illness, Leslie Maskelyne was truly glad of her comfortable, familiar presence.

She sat in Ruth's kitchen on Friday while Ruth made the tea and, after glancing at Ruth's calendar and noting that she had not so much as marked the day on which she was to lunch with Leslie Maskelyne, could not help asking, 'Looking forward to Tuesday, then?'

It was, as between two old friends, almost an outright demand for information. Ruth merely glanced at Doris, and gave a small smile. 'Not particularly.'

'Hmm. You're not going to tell me anything about it, are you? No good getting old without getting artful, I suppose,' said Doris huffily.

Ruth sat down at the table with the teapot. 'Doris,' she said, in that kind, slightly patronising tone which Doris found particularly irritating, 'I don't know any more than you do what he wants to see me for. He's an old man, and he's ill, and no doubt he's got his whims.'

'I never even knew you knew him.'

Ruth shifted her gaze to the window. 'Only slightly.' And it was true. How deeply and passionately one could feel for someone, how intimately one could be connected with that person, and yet how little one might know of them. Doris thought she saw something in Ruth's expression that was very distant, almost sad. She knew that Ruth would tell her nothing more.

She sighed. 'Oh, well. I just wondered, was all.'

The weather was still warm on Tuesday, but Ruth put on a cardigan over the blue linen dress which she was wearing. The woods would still be that bit cooler at this time of year. She set off up the path in

16

good time, taking it slowly, anxious not to bring on one of her attacks of breathlessness. They frightened her, as did the squeezing pains in her chest, that the doctor said were to do with her heart. The pills she took seemed to have less and less effect these days. Lord knows, at her age she should be adjusted to the idea of her own mortality, but still the idea that her heart, which had beaten – so faithfully for so long, was finally wearing out, was starkly terrifying. She did not feel ready for frailty, for death. She might be an old woman – that was what the rest of the world saw – but inside she was still five, sitting on the back step of her mother's house, shelling garden peas into a bowl, still twelve and reading *The Wind in the Willows* up in the tree house, still nineteen and newly wed in ivory satin, slim and smiling, still thirty-six and lying with her lover in the grassy shade of these very woods, lost in pleasure. Still young in her mind. Still herself. Everything you had been, she thought, you remained. At seventy, you were the sum of all those parts, those people from the past, the child, the girl, the woman. Nobody was just old. But young people, when they looked at you, didn't see past your old skin, and your white hair, to all the things you had been, any more than they could imagine themselves ever being old.

After ten minutes Ruth paused to rest, glancing up into the green canopy, listening to the woodland sounds of birds and insects and the rustle of new leaves. It wasn't far from here that she and Leslie used to meet. She always remembered this part of the path, that huge chestnut with the strange twin trunks growing up. There had been a small clearing deep in the woods, and you turned off here to reach it. She gazed at the apparently impenetrable thicket, the springy brambles and tangled roots of bushes. Impossible to find now. She had a sudden recollection of sitting in that glade in the dappled sunlight, unfastening the buttons on the front of her dress, then raising her arms to let him lift the dress over her head. She had lain with him in the cool moss and grass, the sensation of the air on her naked skin adding to the eroticism of their adventure. Even though they were Leslie's woods, and even though the little place where they met to make love was far from the main path, well-hidden, anyone could have come upon them. That had added to the excitement, to the urgency of their passion.

Ruth felt her heart take three stiff little irregular beats, then flutter, causing a momentary fear to rise within her. She found she was holding her breath, and let it out slowly, then breathed deeply and regularly with conscious effort. Her heartbeat steadied. Not good for an old woman to recall such things. It was hard to believe that she had ever been so uninhibited, so totally swept along by the force of her own sexuality. But it had been like that from the beginning, from the very day when she and Leslie had first set eyes upon one another at that awful annual village tea party. She knew that Mrs Maskelyne, who had lived at Hemwood House in those days, had a son, but he'd been living abroad since the end of the war – South Africa, they said – and Ruth had never seen him. When she saw the tall, dark-haired chap lounging beside the door of the village hall, looking as though he'd rather be anywhere else than where he was, she had no idea who he was. Nor when they got talking ten minutes later, when they realised that they couldn't take their eyes off one another and they had to talk, or they'd just be staring . . . He'd touched her – accidentally, just a hand on her arm to stop the plate of biscuits she was holding from going on the floor when someone bumped past – and it was like some electrical connection, like they'd been wired up. That had been a moment. That had been a moment she could replay again and again over the years and it never lost its magic. He had bent his head – she was tall, but he was that bit taller – and said why didn't they go outside for some air, it was so crowded in the hall. And outside they had just talked. About what, Ruth couldn't tell you. Then he'd said something that made her realise who he was, but that hadn't mattered because the next thing he was asking to meet her. Up in the woods. Just for a walk and a talk. And they had. The very next day. Only they hadn't walked and they had scarcely talked. Ruth hadn't ever thought herself capable of behaving in such a way. But falling in love like that made you capable of anything. Everything.

Ruth set off along the path again. The steepest part of it was behind her now, and she could already see the edge of the wood, beyond which lay the gardens of Hemwood House. She had been widowed just one month when she had met Leslie. That had been part of the shame she felt, and that same shame had been part of the shocking, guilty pleasure. Her husband, Tom, had never made her feel the way Leslie did. Not even begun to. Theirs had not been a good marriage. She and Tom had been too young, and after sixteen years of turning into people who had almost nothing to say to one another, it would probably have ended, anyway, had Tom not died. So there was all that guilt and shame mingled up – guilt at not even grieving for Tom, and shame at being so ready, so willing, to be seduced by a good-looking stranger. It hadn't occurred to her that their affair should remain anything but secret. What would the village have thought of a woman in her thirties, newly widowed, having an affair with Mrs Maskelyne's son, whom she hadn't known five minutes? They could say what they liked now about the Swinging Sixties, but in those days thinking hadn't exactly moved on very much around these parts. So there could be no trips to the flicks, no nice dinners together, not even a drink in the Hemwood Arms. Not that Ruth had wanted any of those things. She had wanted only Leslie, and their times together in the little clearing in the woods. Throughout those three months she had imagined that Leslie wanted their relationship to remain secret for the same reason, to protect her respectability. How naive she had been. Ruth drew in a sighing breath at the thought. Or how stupid love had made her. Leslie, of course, had never meant for it to be more than a brief, clandestine affair, something to fill in the time until his fiancée – what had her name been? Susan? Sarah? – came back from her trip around America. Not that she had ever known anything about any fiancée. Until that day when he had left her standing alone beneath the trees, Ruth had imagined that somehow time would take care of everything, that loving one another as they did, she and Leslie just had to wait until people could become accepting of things. What a fool she had been. And how he had used her.

A few yards ahead of her the path emerged into sunlight, and Ruth paused on the fringes of the wood. Before her lay the house. The only time she had seen it was when Leslie had brought her to the edge of the wood to show it to her. In the years that followed she had never wanted to set eyes on it, and had never had occasion to. It was essentially a stark, imposing building, but the grey stones of its walls were mellowed by the green of old creepers, and the lines of the steeply pitched roofs softened by cushions of moss. A cluster of stone buildings to the left of the house, leading to the stable yard, gentled its lines, lending a pleasantly haphazard effect. The symmetry was that of the perfect English country house, clumps of oaks and yews studding the grounds against the backdrop of the April sky. The gardens, Ruth saw, were still meticulously well-tended, the lawns trim, the pieces of topiary snipped and shaved. This was the home of the man who had used her and discarded her, and had cared nothing when she had his child. What was she doing here?

No one in the village had any notion that Abby wasn't Tom's daughter. She remembered thinking at the time, when she'd been carrying Abby, that if anyone had any suspicions about her and Leslie, then they would come out now. But no one had said anything. In fact, she recalled how sick and tired she'd grown of hearing people express their maudlin wonderment that God had taken Tom from her, but given her baby Abigail in his place. If only they knew. But they never would know. And all that time Leslie had stayed well away from her. She had thought at first that when he knew she was pregnant – she recalled the note she had written, the way it had slipped from her hand and into the pillar box – that he would at least get in touch with her. But he hadn't. In fact, the next thing she had known, he was married. Oh, what she had felt the day she heard that news . . . So, after all that, what on earth was she doing here now?

She could find no answer. The equivocality of her feelings towards Leslie Maskelyne surprised her. She knew when he abandoned her thirty-three years ago she should have hated him, despised him. But when the misery was spent – and it had been, far faster than she had imagined – neither of those emotions was there. Perhaps it was her own pragmatism. He was so completely excised from her life, living not a mile away and yet in another world entirely, that feelings for him, about him, were pointless. Or perhaps it had been a form of self-protection. If she had dwelt on things, let jealousy and resentment, hatred and self-pity, eat away at her, she would have been destroyed. Was that why she now saw

20

herself and Leslie, the lovers they had been, as people quite unconnected to herself and the old, cancer-ridden man up at the house? So that nothing of that painful past need touch her any more?

She stepped out into the sunshine and carried on up the path, round the side of the house, to the front door. Doris let her in, staring at Ruth for a moment as though she were a different person from the one at whose house she called every other day for a cup of tea and her groceries.

'That walk's made you hot,' she remarked. Ruth put a hand to her face. It didn't feel hot, but there was the faint squeezing sensation in her chest and the lightest of tingles in her left arm, as though someone had brushed it with fire. She should take one of her pills now, she realised. Doris gestured towards the staircase. 'He's waiting up there for you. First room on the right at the top of the stairs.'

'I think I'll just wash my hands first, Doris,' said Ruth. 'My pills, you know.' She had told Doris about what the doctor had said about her arteries, and Doris had been concerned – but less gratifyingly so than she would have been, were it not for the business of the letter, Ruth knew.

Doris nodded and led her towards the cloakroom and bathroom on the ground floor. As Ruth followed, she glanced around at the light, elegant surroundings, so different from the cramped cottage in which she lived, and in which Abby had grown up, but felt no resentment, merely interest. The small bathroom where she bathed her face, then slipped one of her pills beneath her tongue, seemed to Ruth unnecessarily fussy, with roses in a porcelain bowl on the sill, little soaps in another bowl, and a pile of fluffy hand towels with a basket beneath to chuck them in. The brass taps and plughole gleamed, all was spotless and sweet-smelling, and it seemed to Ruth a little incongruous that so much domestic care should be lavished on this one little room, while Leslie lay wasting away upstairs. Then again, maybe he had a lot of visitors. Maybe there was a constant stream of people washing their hands and discarding the fluffy little towels after one wipe. At any rate, it gave Doris more than enough to do.

She emerged to find herself alone. For a moment she wished Doris were still there to accompany her upstairs, for the imminence of this meeting suddenly made her feel intensely nervous. She made her way slowly up the curved staircase, keeping a careful hand on the polished banister, and saw that the door of the first room on the right was ajar. As she reached the stop of the stairs she paused, and thought for the first time of how nervous he, too, must be. That made her feel better. She knocked lightly on the door to announce her presence, and then, without waiting for a response, went in, closing the door behind her. Whatever they were to say to one another, she didn't want Doris to know.

Leslie Maskelyne was sitting near the window, legs crossed, the morning paper on his knee, a pen in his hand. Smoke drifted up from a cigarette lying in an ashtray on the table next to him. He was wearing slacks and a blue cashmere sweater over an open-necked shirt, and had it not been for his gauntness and the fact that he was sitting in a wheelchair, Ruth would not have known he was ill at all. In the couple of seconds that passed before he spoke, she realised that he had gone to great pains to look this way for her, to look like his old, easy self. He cared what she thought. Or maybe he was just vain. Had he been vain? She hadn't known him long enough or well enough to tell. He reached out a thin hand and picked up his cigarette.

'Come and sit down, Ruth,' he said. His voice sounded as familiar as though they had last spoken yesterday, and she was surprised by its effect upon her. She might be seventy, but it sounded to her just as it had in the woods all those years ago, sensual, magical. He took a drag of his cigarette and watched her as she came towards him and sat down in the vacant chair opposite him by the window. She remained silent, having determined earlier that she would wait for him to initiate the conversation, but felt oddly disadvantaged, as though she had been summoned for an interview and was meekly awaiting the first question. In fact, her silence operated in her favour. It made her appear utterly composed in Leslie Maskelyne's eyes, and he thought, as he regarded her, how very fine she looked, despite her years. Her eyes especially were just as he remembered them, blue and calm, and

22

her skin, though withered, clear and soft. He wished she would say something – but why should she? It was astonishing that she had even accepted his invitation, all things considered. 'I'm glad you decided to come,' he added. Still she said nothing, merely turned her gaze away from him towards the window. He tapped some ash from his cigarette. Clearly he would have to say something which directly invited a response. 'You had no real reason to, I suppose.'

Ruth turned to look at him again. 'You wrote to me. It took you thirty-three years. But you wrote. And here I am.'

Her words instantly robbed the moment of any pretence. She was not going to allow them to be just two old people meeting again after many years. She was Ruth, she was the same woman he had lain naked with in the woods, and there could be no forgetting that. He looked steadily at her eyes, suddenly remembered her breathless little laugh of longing and disbelief that first time he had taken her, skirt around her thighs, back against a tree, and his heart seemed to turn over. Yet she was old, he was old. Why go back to that? Because it was all there was of them. Oh God, thought Leslie, was this to be crushingly embarrassing? After all, time had turned them into virtual strangers. There were conventions. He must choose his next words with care. Pausing for a moment, he stubbed out his cigarette, gestured towards the table in the centre of the room, and said, 'Would you care for some lunch?'

Ruth turned to look at the table, at the white linen and silver, the cold salmon and mayonnaise which Doris had prepared, the salad and rolls, the wine. She was hungry, she had to admit. And something had to be done to ease the tension.

'Yes, that would be very nice,' she said. She glanced at Leslie's wheelchair. 'Can I –?' She gestured uncertainly towards him.

'If you wouldn't mind.'

She wheeled him carefully towards one of the place-settings at the table, and went to sit down opposite. She thought of herself and Leslie as they had once been, how little she could have suspected that one day she'd be pushing him in a wheelchair, and the thought made her smile without wanting to. She glanced up and saw with relief that he hadn't noticed. Leslie was fumbling in a preoccupied way with his napkin, and as she watched his slow movements,

23

Ruth was struck yet again by the arbitrary nature of time. It should have been amazing, absurd, to find herself lunching in this matter-of-fact way with someone who had abandoned her, pregnant with his child, over thirty years ago. But it was not. They were simply different people.

'Yes,' said Leslie, as though to himself, 'thirty-three years. Much has happened to both of us. I scarcely know where to begin.'

He spoke so conversationally, with such mild cheerfulness, as though they were simply old friends who had accidentally lost touch, that Ruth could not help marvelling at his nerve. He passed her the salmon and she took some, thinking to herself, well, why not begin where we left off? Why not start with your wife, whatever-her-name-was, the one you dumped me and Abby for, and take it from there? Or go back to that last time in the woods, when you told me it was all over, not five minutes after you'd been inside me, loving me, holding me and murmuring those sweetly obscene things, the way you always did.

'Some bread?' she asked, offering him the rolls. He murmured something and shook his head, and she noticed that he had spooned only the smallest amount of salmon on to his plate, and a little salad. He was very ill, she reminded herself. He was dying. Still, that didn't make her thoughts uncharitable. Dying didn't make him a better person. Even so, she could not say all the things she had once wanted to, in that first year after he had left her. The situation would not permit it. She must behave like a polite old woman. There was nothing else she could do.

'How is Stephen?' she found herself asking. She remembered him only as a dark-haired boy with whom Abby had played down in the Dips in the summer holidays, when he was home from whatever posh boarding school they had sent him to, but it was something to ask.

'He's well,' said Leslie, pouring her a glass of wine, then a little for himself. 'Working hard. I don't see very much of him. The girls come over more often, of course . . .' Leslie glanced around the table in a troubled manner, and Ruth wondered for a moment whether he was in pain. But then he sipped a little of his wine and added, 'But he should be here next weekend.'

Ruth felt suddenly grounded in small talk. What were his daughters' names? They had slipped her mind, though they were on Doris's tongue often enough . . . Then she suddenly realised the reason for his faint awkwardness, or thought she did. By asking about his son, she had obliquely brought up the subject of Abby. Was that it? Well, what if it was? She felt a little spark of anger. What on earth were they doing sitting here like this, when the one thing they had in common was apparently too difficult for him to mention?

'Would you like to know about Abby?' she asked. Her voice sounded sudden and a little loud, she thought. As soon as she had asked the question, she was swept with a sudden sense of unreality. Ten minutes ago, they had been people who had not spoken properly for over thirty years. And now there was this proximity – something beyond the physical. Forget the polite old woman nonsense. When two people had been as intimate as they had been, there could be no recourse to formality. He looked up, then reached for his cigarettes and lit one. She knew suddenly that he wasn't going to eat any lunch, that he probably never did. The meal was a device, its conventions intended to protect them from confrontation, from too stark an exploration of the past. The fact that he had lit his cigarette showed that he, too, realised the pointlessness of it.

'I have seen her, you know,' he replied. 'I made a point of . . . That is, I used to see her around the village when she was a little girl. She came up to the house a few times with Stephen. And once, a year or two ago, she drove up here with some things for Mrs Cotterell.' He remembered that day vividly, the faint shock he had had, seeing the tall blonde getting out of Ruth's beaten-up Mini, looking so very like the Ruth of years ago. 'Very pretty,' he added.

Ruth drank some of her wine. It was very good wine, not a thing she tasted often. 'I see,' she said, and nodded, as though his words confirmed something. A question formed itself in her mind. It was inevitable that she should ask it. Whatever his purpose in inviting her here today, she could not go away without having asked it. Her heart began to beat uncomfortably hard at the prospect. 'If you were so interested,' she said in a low voice, looking at him through the haze of cigarette smoke, 'why didn't you answer my letter? Why did you never acknowledge anything?'

Leslie spread his hands, long, thin hands, the wrists bony and old in their encircling shirt cuffs. The tips of the first two fingers of his left hand were yellow with nicotine. 'Cowardice. I was a coward then, and am only slightly less of one now.' He paused, puffed on his cigarette. 'I am amazed that you don't reproach me,' he added.

Ruth gave a sigh. 'Oh, I do. I always have done. For what you are and what you did. But where's the point in saying it? What are you to me, after all?' To show she didn't care, Ruth picked up her fork and ate, while Leslie smoked and regarded her.

'I think I am,' he said carefully after a few seconds, 'what I always was.'

'You think so?' Ruth sipped her wine and smiled. 'Leslie, we are old. We made our mistakes, as everyone does, and the chances are all gone. All gone. Do you see that?' She leaned forward as she spoke. 'Now, if you asked me here today because you have a guilty conscience, because you're dying and feel you should apologise – don't. I haven't forgiven you – I doubt if I ever shall – but it doesn't bother me. I'm past caring.'

Leslie studied the glowing stub of his cigarette for a few seconds. 'I didn't ask you here today to apologise to you. I wanted to do something more. If you'll let me. Something to make amends.' She waited. 'I want to ask you to marry me.'

Ruth stared at him. The air around her seemed to hum, vibrating and pressing in upon her in some mentally stifling way.

'You must be joking,' she said. The pressing feeling died away, and her head cleared. 'I hardly call that amends,' she added. 'If you need someone to nurse you, you've always got Doris.' She spoke mechanically, her words at odds with whatever passed for thought at that moment. 'You don't even know me. We're strangers now, Leslie.' She wondered vaguely if his mind hadn't become a little wandered.

'You don't understand,' said Leslie. 'But I didn't expect you to. What I am suggesting is – is –' He glanced around and sighed, looking for words. 'Some form of adjustment.'

'Adjustment?' echoed Ruth. Her voice, the expression in her eyes, the attitude in which she now sat back in her chair, all suggested detachment. But inside she felt raw. Why not thirty-three years ago, why not then? She felt the foolishness, the injustice of it so deeply that she almost wanted to cry it out. But she said nothing, merely watched him light yet another cigarette. It had to be some kind of horrible joke. Why didn't she just get up and leave?

When Leslie spoke again, he did not look at her. She could tell that he felt embarrassed, awkward. Or perhaps even ashamed. 'Now that I am coming to the – the end, you see, I have started to look back on my life. As people do. And certain truths become clear.' There was a pause. 'I behaved very badly towards you. I know that. But at the time, I could see no – well, no other way of acting. I told you, I was a coward. I thought it wouldn't do, you know, to – to stay with you. I – God, this is so hard . . .' He raised thin fingers to scratch at his sparse hair. 'I was engaged to Susan –' Ah, thought Ruth, so her name *was* Susan. Yes. '– and it was very important at the time that I should marry her. Not just to me, but to everyone. Our families. There was money involved, and other things.'

'You mean,' interrupted Ruth thoughtfully, 'that it wouldn't have done for you to marry someone like me. Someone not quite your class.'

He seemed to wince at this. 'Don't. Please don't think –'

'Don't worry,' said Ruth with a sigh. 'I'm not getting at you. I'm just trying to let you see that I do understand it more clearly than you think.' She paused. 'And yes – you were a coward.' There was a silence, one so long that Ruth did not think he would speak again. She stared unseeingly at the largely untouched food on the table. She had no appetite now. At last he spoke again, and his voice was gentle, as though seeking to escape harsh judgement.

'But the worst of it is, you see, that I did love you. More than Susan. More than anyone else. Ever.'

She experienced a brief, flooding sense of elation, remembering again how she had lain with him in the clearing, amongst the grasses and ferns and splashes of sunlight. Then it faded. That was all past. They were old. What was the point of hearing it now? He had never said it then. So why say it now?

'So.' She spoke flatly, unquestioningly. 'So.'

Leslie drew a deep breath. 'I want to set things right for you and Abby. I don't want to disrupt your life, please don't think I would be so presumptuous.' She looked up at him, the ghost of a smile gleaming in her eyes. 'But I want to end my life by doing one thing I should have done long ago. For us. This is just between us. I want to provide for you, and to leave Abby something. I want you to marry me. To set things right.'

'When you say, "between us"–'

'I mean the way it always was. Between us.' His eyes, though yellowing and watery, looked suddenly intense. He leaned forward, gazing at her from the other side of the table. He had not expected to find himself speaking in this way, but the sight and proximity of her brought back emotions he had long forgotten. 'We can't be what we once were, but we can do this. No one need know. You needn't tell Abby, I need not tell my children. Nothing to do with them. Or anyone, except us.' She felt a little astonished by the fervour in his voice, making him sound as he used to when making love to her. 'Don't you know,' he went on, 'that I have thought of you for all these years? Thought of you in the same way? Are you going to say that you haven't thought of me?'

Ruth hesitated. She felt overwhelmed by a confusion of feelings. He didn't deserve to hear it, but how could she deny it? 'Of course I have thought of you,' she said.

'Then let us do this one thing. Together.'

Ruth struggled with the idea. His suggestion was absurdly impetuous – but, oh, how absurdly impetuous they had both been once, that first day together. She had been unable to resist him then. Why now? What he was proposing was the closest he could come to an act of love, she realised. And there was Abby, too. If this could make a difference to her, why not?

She hesitated, astonished at herself, then looked up at him. 'Just between us? Without anyone knowing?'

He nodded. 'Just as it always was,' he said softly.

She could be his again, and he hers, in the same secret way.

Suddenly it seemed to Ruth that the wrongs of the past did not matter. She looked at the man who had once been her lover and did not feel old at all. She felt romantic. And hadn't they both been that, once?

'Yes,' she replied. 'Yes, I'll marry you, if you want me.'

He nodded, and they sat at the table, looking at one another, experiencing a sense of rediscovery. It was not what either of them had expected from the day. With a sense of tentative intimacy they began, for the first time ever, to talk properly to one another.

Chapter Three

An hour and a half later, Doris heard the shrill jangle of Mr Maskelyne's bell. She crossed the hall to the staircase, and as she did so Ruth appeared at the top of the stairs and began a slow and careful descent. Doris waited, her eyes on Ruth's face.

'Well,' said Ruth, taking a deep breath as she reached the bottom, 'I'll be calling in again on Friday.' She said it with the nonchalance of a regular visitor, her expression thoughtful, distant. Doris stared at her. 'Though I expect I'll be seeing you before then,' added Ruth. 'You want your usual from Tesco's?'

Doris nodded. 'Some kitchen rolls, too, if you don't mind. I'm nearly out.' The bell jangled again impatiently, and both women glanced upwards.

'I hope I haven't tired him,' said Ruth. 'Don't bother to see me out. I'll expect you tomorrow around tea-time.'

Ruth closed the front door behind her. Doris paused in thought for a few seconds, then started up the stairs.

She found Leslie Maskelyne seated once more by the window, leaning back in his wheelchair with his eyes closed. Only a few seconds earlier, before he heard Doris's footsteps outside the room, he had been gazing out to glimpse Ruth as she walked away round the house towards the woods.

Doris glanced at the lunch table as she crossed the room, noticed the scarcely touched food and nearly full glasses of wine. Whatever today had been about, it hadn't been lunch.

Mr Maskelyne opened his eyes as Doris approached. 'Do you want anything?' she asked solicitiously, searching his gaunt face for grim, tell-tale lines of pain. But they were not there. His expression was tired, but placid.

'No, I don't believe I do, thank you, Mrs Cotterell,' replied Leslie. 'But if you wouldn't mind helping me back to my room, I think I'd like a nap. Then you can clear up in here.'

'Righty-ho.' Doris placed plump hands on the handles of the chair and wheeled it slowly across the carpet towards the landing. 'Mrs Owen was saying she'd be back on Friday,' remarked Doris, as she pushed open the door to Leslie's room and wheeled him gently in.

'That's right,' replied Leslie. 'She'll be coming every so often. We have some business to sort out. But not to lunch – not after today. Maybe just tea and biscuits.'

'I see,' said Doris, going over to Mr Maskelyne's bed and plumping up the pillows, smoothing the sheets. Her voice was mildly indifferent, but her soul fairly ached with curiosity.

Ruth came every two or three days over the following two weeks, avoiding the days on which Leslie's two married daughters visited him. In the beginning, Leslie received her in the same room in which they had lunched on that first day, but after a few visits he stayed in his room, mostly in his bed, and they talked there.

It was all a surprising and touching revelation to Ruth. The time she had spent with Leslie during their brief affair had taught her nothing about him, nor him about her. Passion had been too all-consuming. Now they talked. Their conversation was desultory, matter-of-fact, ranging over village goings-on, their children, mutual acquaintances, even touching upon the time they had spent together years ago. But this last was done obliquely, lightly, for when they talked about those times it was as if they spoke of strangers, and a certain delicacy was required. What absorbed them most, however, now that their pact had been made, was to discuss the practical aspects of their clandestine marriage. For Leslie, the significance of it all lay in its accomplishment, and a sense that he was redressing a wrong. The mild enjoyment he derived from Ruth's visits was a bonus, so to speak. He was essentially a selfish man. For Ruth, the matter was at once simpler and yet more complex. She did not fully understand why she was doing this thing – was it for herself, or for Leslie? – and there were moments when she felt outraged on behalf of her old self that she should so indulge him, allow him to ease his conscience. But he was dying, and there was a sentimental part of her that was touched by the idea of this token to past love. The other side of it was practical. He had said he would provide for her and for Abby. Ruth could not go on pulling pints at the Fox and Hounds on Wednesday and Thursday nights for ever. Money had always been tight, and a bit extra to make the remaining years more comfortable was a welcome prospect. But it was more for Abby than for herself that she cared. Abby was a single mother, living with her four-year-old daughter in London, and so far as Ruth could tell, her life was a precarious one, shifting from job to job, one flat to another, this relationship to that. If there was one person to whom Leslie Maskelyne owed something, it was Abby, and if this was the way that Ruth could ensure that it came about, then so be it.

So they discussed dates for the registry office, mused on the practicalities of Ruth driving them both there, how he would cope, whether there were steps. They fell into all of this very naturally, like elderly people planning a special trip or shopping expedition. It was not something they could delay. Leslie was aware that the grip of his cancer was tightening fast, and once when Ruth called in the third week he was too ill and deeply sedated to see her. Doris had already made arrangements for a daily nurse to start the following week, and now a cylinder of oxygen and a mask stood by the head of Leslie's bed.

In the meantime, Ruth had her own medical worries to contend with, but she did not tell Leslie of these, only Doris. The day before she had received Leslie's letter, her doctor had made an appointment for her to see a consultant cardiologist in Colchester. The day arrived more quickly than she could have wished. In a way, Ruth did not want to know the extent of her heart problems, would sooner just have carried on taking her pills in quiet ignorance, but the doctor had told her there were treatments which could help, and so she kept the appointment.

The consultant, Mr Munn, seemed to Ruth to be very young. He sat behind his desk glancing through Ruth's letter of referral and notes, a thin, quiet-voiced man, no more than thirty-five, Ruth would have said. A nurse sat in a chair near the window, hands primly folded in her lap, like a faintly bored duenna.

'Well, now, Mrs Owen,' said Mr Munn, looking up from her notes, 'let's have a little listen, shall we? If you wouldn't mind popping behind the screen and just slipping your top off . . .'

The nurse rustled the curtains round the little cubicle, and in there Ruth fumbled awkwardly out of her blouse and brassiere, slipped off her shoes and sat down on the bed like an obedient child. The nurse came and stood at the end of the bed. Ruth glanced at her, hoping for the comfort of a sympathetic smile, but the nurse did not meet Ruth's eye. Ruth could tell from her expression that she regarded all this as an unholy waste of time, having to act as a chaperone when there was clearly no danger of Mr Munn pouncing on some old girl like Ruth.

Mr Munn swept the curtain aside magisterially and arranged his stethoscope. His fingers were chilly and deft on Ruth's skin, their touch strangely delightful. She had expected to feel embarrassed in the presence of so young a doctor, but she was not.

'That's right . . . breathe in, hold it . . . now out again. Fine. And the back. Once more . . .' When he had finished, he left the nurse to take Ruth's blood pressure and went back to his desk. Ruth dressed and came out from behind the curtain and sat down again, waiting.

'Well, Mrs Owen, what I'd like to do next is a blood test, an ECG, a chest X-ray and a cardiac echo test. The blood test we can do today – the nurse will do that – and I'll give you a form to take up to X-ray to book an appointment. I don't know what their waiting-lists are like, I'm afraid. If what I think is wrong, then you'll probably have to come into hospital for an angiogram.' Ruth realised that her face must have registered anxiety, for Mr Munn gave a reassuring smile and added, 'It's nothing to concern yourself about. It's just an X-ray of the arteries. We inject a form of dye into them so that we can get a better look at the blood flow. You can probably have it done on a daycare basis.'

'You said, if what you think is wrong . . . What do you think is wrong?'

'Well, I'm concerned that the drugs your doctor has given you aren't controlling your angina as well as we would like. You've been taking them for six months now, but the attacks don't seem to be lessening. We may have to consider some other treatment to help your condition.'

Ruth nodded. He wouldn't be wanting to do all those tests, bring her into hospital and so on, if he wasn't fairly sure things were getting worse. Fear gripped her for a second. She had a vision of herself lying on an operating table, her chest bloody and open, her essential self exposed, raw meat.

'What other treatment?' She could see from his eyes that he didn't want to hypothesise further, but she would not relent. She needed to know.

'Well . . .' Mr Munn picked up his pen and drew a sheet of paper towards him. 'We might have to do what we call an angioplasty.' He sketched some lines. 'Say this is one of your arteries. If it's not too badly blocked, we insert a catheter, a little tube with a tiny balloon on the end of it. Then we inflate the balloon –' He sketched again, turning the paper towards her. '– and it pushes back the built-up material that's blocking your arteries, so that the artery is widened.'

'I see.' Ruth stared at the little diagram. It was quite amazing, the things they could do. But the idea of one of her own arteries, exposed to the air like slippery spaghetti, with a thing stuck up it, made her throat constrict. 'Does that always work?' she asked, looking up at the consultant.

'It depends,' replied Mr Munn. He glanced covertly at his watch and the nurse shifted restlessly in her chair. Ruth wondered if she was being tiresome. She didn't care. 'If the arteries are very badly blocked, we sometimes have to do a coronary bypass. But quite frankly, Mrs Owen, I don't think we need to discuss that at present. Let's have the tests done and see what we can see, eh?' His tone was firm, friendly and final, and he was already pulling forms out of a drawer. 'I'll just fill these in for you to take up to X-ray, and the nurse can do your blood test in the meantime.'

An hour later, as she walked across the hospital car park to the car, Ruth felt tired and baffled. The future, which had once possessed a certain solidity and clarity, was beginning to seem shadowy and precarious. She stood for a few moments, listening with some inner ear to the rhythm of her heart. Well, she was here, she was in Colchester. She might as well do it. They had discussed suitable days. She would drive to the registry office now and go through the notification-of-marriage business. Then she and Leslie could be married by the end of the week. The sooner that was out of the way, the sooner he could set about making some provision for Abby. And the sooner she could give her mind and attention to this dread business of her heart.

Ruth's old Mini puttered up the driveway to Hemwood House at ten past ten the following Friday morning. She and Leslie had arranged to be at the registry office in Colchester for eleven, and although it was only a fifteen-minute drive, getting him into the car and comfortably settled could be a slow business, and then there was parking at the other end, the wheelchair . . . Ruth wondered how he was this morning. He might be having one of his bad spells, the whole thing might have to be put off. How strange it was, she thought, as she waited for Doris to answer the door, that they had arrived so quickly at such a pitch of familiarity. From there to here. But then, it was human nature to adapt. And when you got past sixty, fewer things were left to surprise you. You took things as they came.

'How is he?' Ruth asked Doris as she stepped into the hall-way.

'Better than he's been for weeks, surprisingly enough,' replied Doris. 'Which is just as well, given this jaunt you're taking him on.' She knew that Ruth and Leslie were going somewhere that morning, but nothing beyond that. She, like Ruth and Leslie, had adjusted to the new pattern of relationships very quickly, but curiosity and resentment still simmered. She had regarded herself as part of Hemwood House and its doings for very many years, and it was hard not to feel excluded by this new-found intimacy between Ruth and her employer.

Ruth found Leslie sitting at his writing desk, dressed in a dark blue suit, pale blue shirt and a red patterned silk tie. The clothes, which must have been new only a few months ago, seemed to encase him, and his body looked even more spindly than usual. But his face was alert and cheerful. Doris was right. He actually looked better than he had done for some weeks.

Leslie capped his pen and put away the document which he had been writing. He had spent the last forty minutes or so drafting it. There were some things that could be done just as well without a lawyer. He knew the form. He was – had been – a man of business, after all. He would finish it later, then get Mrs Cotterell to witness it. Then it would really be a day of achievement, of setting past wrongs to rights. He looked appreciatively at Ruth. She was wearing a cream-coloured dress beneath a long linen jacket, and her smooth grey hair was swept up into a loose knot. She looked very smart, very discreet. He wondered for an instant whether he should have given her some gift, some piece of jewellery perhaps, to mark the day. But it was not that kind of arrangement, he knew. Afterwards he would come back here and she would return to her cottage. Life, what was left of it, would be unaltered. He had a sudden notion of how pleasant it would be if she really came to live with him here . . . And then the notion faded. Stephen and the girls would be appalled by what was happening, if they knew. If he and Ruth had done this publicly, there would have been ructions, arguments. Which was why they were not to know. This was between him and Ruth, and it mattered to no one else. As to the money which he was leaving to Ruth and Abby, his estate would be so large that it would scarcely be of significance.

'Right,' he said, and gave Ruth a smile.

'Will you be all right on the stairs?'

'Oh, I think so.' Leslie stood up. He was aware of how much resilience his body had lost over the past months, but today he felt possessed of a frail but vital strength. With Ruth holding his arm, he walked slowly from his room and downstairs, pausing for a few

36

breathless seconds on every fourth step. He had to rest at the bottom before crossing the hall to the front door.

Ruth had parked her Mini just at the foot of the front steps. She and Doris helped Leslie into the front passenger seat, and then the two women struggled to put Leslie's collapsible wheelchair into the back. It was a tight fit.

'You reckon you can manage it at the other end?' Doris asked Ruth. Their eyes met, and Ruth caught the faint hostility in Doris's expression. She wants to know where we're going, thought Ruth. She wants to know what all this is about, and in a way she's perfectly within her rights. But Ruth knew she could not even acknowledge the existence of any mystery, could not even explain to her friend that she could tell her nothing. It was just something that had to be.

'I think so,' replied Ruth. The rear door nudged the wheelchair a little as she closed it. She went round to the driver's side and got in, carefully smoothing out her linen jacket as she fastened her seat belt. As Ruth put the car into reverse and backed up slowly to turn round, Doris bent her knees a little to peer into the car and wave goodbye to Leslie. But he was talking to Ruth as the car roared gently off down the driveway, and did not notice.

When they reached Colchester, Ruth was able to find a parking space quite close to the registry office. Getting the wheelchair out of the car and unfolding it was something of a palaver, but she managed it at last, while Leslie looked on anxiously from the car. Ruth paused after her exertions, conscious that a bit of her hair was coming down at the back. Well, she could attend to that when they got inside. She looked through the car window at Leslie, and the incongruity of it all struck her yet again. From those stolen days of love in the woods to this moment with a collapsible wheelchair outside Colchester registry office. There was something cheering in the realisation that you never knew what was going to happen next, no matter how little of life there seemed to be left.

She helped Leslie out of the car and into the wheelchair. The ramp up to the registry office was gently sloped, but necessarily long, and Ruth found it hard going. As they got inside the doorway she felt the familiar sensation of breathlessness and a tightness across her chest. She thought briefly of the angiogram she was to have next week, saw for a moment her veins made transparent, little coloured rivers coursing through them. She leaned back against the wall and fished in her bag for her pills. Leslie watched her as she put one beneath her tongue. She hadn't told him about her heart, and there was a look of concern on his face. She tried to give a laugh, but it was light and breathless. 'What a pair of old crocks we are,' she murmured.

In his anxiety, Leslie glanced around. 'No chance of a fag in here, I don't suppose.'

Leslie sat in his wheelchair in the waiting room, while Ruth went to the Ladies' to fix her hair. She glanced up and down the empty corridor as she went. She had supposed that they would find a couple of witnesses easily enough, just people hanging around. But there seemed to be a dearth of convenient passers-by. While she was pinning up her hair in the Ladies', a girl came in. She stood next to Ruth at the mirror, peered anxiously at her face, then took out a dark red lipstick and began to apply it. She was dressed in a short white dress and strangely heavy black boots. Her hair was short and bleached, and she wore a nose stud. Ruth wasn't at all sure how, but she recognised her as another bride-to-be.

'Excuse me, but are you getting married today?' Ruth asked the girl, meeting her eye in the mirror.

The girl nodded and half-smiled at Ruth's elderly face. 'Yeah.' She looked back at her own reflection and put her lipstick away.

'I wonder if you and your . . . fiancé would mind doing me a small favour?' enquired Ruth. The girl glanced at her guardedly, and Ruth went on quickly, 'You see, I'm getting married today as well, but my –' She paused. Calling Leslie her fiancé sounded absurd. 'Well, anyway . . . the thing is, we have no witnesses. I wonder if you and your fiancé would mind helping us out? We'd be very grateful.'

The girl considered, then smiled. 'Course,' she said.

Ten minutes later, Ruth and Leslie exchanged their vows in the company of the registrar, the girl with the nose stud, and her husband-to-be, a short, stocky youth wearing a new suit and looking generally uncomfortable. Ruth noticed that he had the words 'love' and 'hate' tattooed on the knuckles of either hand.

It was over in moments. They signed the marriage certificate, thanked the registrar and the young couple, and then Ruth was wheeling Leslie back down the ramp. The sun had slid behind an ominous grey sheet of cloud. Leslie had lit a cigarette and they waited for a few moments by the car as he smoked it. He flicked the stub into the gutter. A spot of rain fell on the back of Ruth's hand as she helped Leslie into the car, and by the time she had collapsed the wheelchair and wedged it into the back, it had begun to rain properly. Ruth got in and closed the door, and sat still, recovering her breath after her exertions with the wheelchair. The smell of Leslie's recent cigarette hung in the air. She opened her handbag and took out the marriage certificate, handed it to Leslie.

Leslie considered it for a moment. 'You look after it,' he said. Rain pattered heavily against the windows. The atmosphere in the car felt snug, intimate. Ruth looked down at the piece of paper. 'I don't know why we did this,' she said after a moment. 'Why did we?'

He looked across at her, holding her gaze. 'Don't you remember?'

She thought for a moment, recalling with her mind's eye two lovers amongst the trees and grass, with air and sun upon their limbs. Had that really been herself and this old man sitting next to her? She folded the certificate up and tucked it back into her handbag. Then she started the car, flicked on the windscreen wipers against the rain, and they headed back to Hemwood, husband and wife.

It rained all the next day. Leslie did not know if it was the effort of the trip, or the weather, or what, but he felt quite dreadful. Not just unwell, but afflicted with a mood of horrible depression. The energy and sense of well-being of the previous day had entirely vanished. He lay in his bed, watching the rain drip, drip, dripping from the eaves. Absurd, he thought wryly, to feel the pointlessness of one's existence when there was so precious little of it left. You would have thought that would have given it a point. Once again he picked up the sheets of paper on which he had been writing. Really there was no need to be too complex about it all. He scored through his efforts of the previous day and reduced it to a simple statement. It should suffice, he thought, as he read it through again.

'I, *Leslie Arthur Maskelyne, leave to Ruth Owen, of Alma Cottage, Church Road, Hemwood, the sum of £100,000. To her daughter, Abigail Owen, I leave the sum of £100,000, together with the residue of my estate not otherwise disposed of.*'

It was generous enough. He doubted whether his will had been drafted so as to leave anything undisposed of, but he had added that just in case. It might provide the girl Abigail with an extra windfall, one never knew. Everything else would go to Stephen, Lydia and Geraldine in equal parts, though the house was specifically to go to Stephen. He didn't think the girls would resent that. They wouldn't have wanted to see Hemwood House sold. Besides, they were both living comfortably enough, Lydia with Marcus and the two children in a large house on the other side of Hemwood, and Geraldine with her husband Peter on their farm outside Sudbury. What would Stephen do with the house? Leslie hoped he wouldn't sell it. Then again, his life was in London. What need had he of a country house the size of Hemwood Hall? It might make a difference if he got married. Most brides would be more than happy to settle down and bring up a family in a place like this. Maybe Stephen would marry. He must have been seeing that girl Harriet for over a year now. He hadn't brought her down with him on his recent visits, though. Understandable, mind you. What girl wanted to spend her weekends watching an old man dying of cancer?

Leslie reached out for his cigarettes, glancing as he did so at the oxygen cylinder. What a fuss Mrs Cotterell had made about that, after the nurse had told them how inflammable it was. Might be better all round if he did blow himself up. A do-it-yourself cremation. Save them all the trouble of burying him.

Smoking, he picked up his pen again and copied the codicil out on to another sheet of paper, then dated both documents. Had to be careful about that, he knew. He glanced at his watch. It was nearly four, and Mrs Cotterell would be off in another half-hour. Her son,

Don, always came to pick her up in his van when the weather was bad. If he wanted to have the document properly witnessed, he'd have to ask her now. Then he suddenly remembered the rigmarole that had taken place in Walter Hubbard's office when he had remade his will a few years ago. Hubbard had called in his secretary, and they had both stood there while Leslie signed the thing, then added their own signatures. You needed two people. Well, Fowler would do. He jangled the bell by his bed, and Doris appeared a few moments later.

'Mrs Cotterell, do you think you could ask Reg to step up here for a moment? With you as well. I need you both to witness something.'

Doris sighed inwardly. All the way up here only to be asked to go back down again and fetch Reg Fowler. She'd last seen him out in the greenhouses, but he'd probably wandered off somewhere else by now, just to be awkward.

'I'll see if I can find him,' she said, and went out.

Five minutes later she returned, with Reg Fowler puffing in her wake, his feet soundless on the carpet. Doris had made him take off his boots at the back door.

Leslie smiled at them. 'Thank you both. I wonder if you'd mind putting your signature to something for me?' asked Leslie.

'Not at all,' said Doris, thinking, that depended what it was. Fowler merely nodded, then glanced, blinking with curiosity, round the room.

'Just a legal document. Something to do with my will. I'd rather the contents remained private.' Doris glanced at the two sheets of paper which Leslie had folded so as to conceal what he had written. She probably shouldn't go signing things when she didn't know what they were. But then, Mr Maskelyne was hardly likely to be getting up to anything underhand. 'I have to sign them first,' said Leslie, 'and then you both add your signatures as witnesses.'

Leslie signed the documents, and then handed the pen to Doris. When both she and Fowler had added their signatures, he slipped each piece of paper into an envelope and put them on his bedside table.

'Thank you, Reg,' he said, nodding to Fowler, who merely

41

nodded back, then went out and downstairs in search of his boots. 'Thank you, too, Mrs Cotterell,' he added, and leaned back against the pillows, feeling more enfeebled than he had in weeks. 'You'll be wanting to get off now, I suppose?'

'I will, if you don't mind. The nurse is here. I'll see you on Monday.' Doris gave him a smile and left.

Half an hour later, Leslie was aware of the pain beginning, a clawing, scraping feeling. He gasped against it, pulling himself away from the pillow, and reached for the bell, fighting for precious breath until the nurse hurried in to administer the oxygen. Lying there, the mask clamped upon his face, dimly aware of the hypodermic needle sliding beneath his skin, he wondered if somehow his mind had willed his body to keep going merely to achieve today's ends, only to lose momentum thereafter. He did not think, somehow, that the end could be far away. And oddly enough, he felt quite relieved.

Three days later, Ruth went into hospital for the angiogram. It was a long time since she had been a hospital patient. Afterwards, sitting up in bed in the ward with a cup of tea, it occurred to her that such places could be soothing, almost beguiling. The fears of the past few weeks were still with her, but here in hospital, surrounded by the magical technical apparatus of modern medicine, they were somehow allayed. The professionalism and authority of the nurses and doctors reassured her magnificently. Everyone looked so young, godlike in their competence. If there was anything badly wrong, surely they could put it right. Ruth sipped her tea, turned the pages of her magazine, and gave the neat, white bandage on her forearm a satisfied glance.

But six hours later, when Mr Munn made his late-afternoon ward round, the tranquillising effects of the hospital atmosphere had quite worn off. Ruth longed to be gone, to be in her own clothes and driving her Mini back to Hemwood, a healthy, normal woman. She did not want to be among the sick and bedridden any longer. Being confined for so many hours to this bed had made her feel vulnerable. The sight of Mr Munn approaching her bed in his white coat was now strangely intimidating. She wished he was in his dark suit, as in the consulting rooms. The white coat seemed to say, 'This is for real, Ruth. Medicine. Doctors. Illness.'

'Well, now, Mrs Owen,' said Mr Munn. He pulled a chair close to her bed and sat down, running his eyes over the notes he held in his hand. Ruth set her features in an expression of intelligent expectancy. Mr Munn pursed his lips. 'I have to tell you . . .' He paused, scanning the notes. Ruth felt her pulse quickening. Come on, come on, she thought. At last he looked up. '. . . that the results of your angiogram confirmed what I suspected earlier. It's not good news, I'm afraid.' Ruth felt a jolt inside, as though she had taken a small, frightening stumble. Mr Munn flicked the pages over. 'Three of the main blood vessels supplying your heart muscles are quite severely blocked. As I explained to you, I had hoped that we might be able to treat the problem with an angioplasty. But I'm afraid I don't think that's an option here.'

'What will you do?' asked Ruth. She wanted to sound robust, in command, but her voice was faint and helpless.

'It looks as though we'll have to consider a bypass. Coronary artery bypass graft surgery, to give it its full name. CABG. Commonly known amongst us doctors as a cabbage.' He smiled, but Ruth found she could not smile back. She swallowed and coughed slightly to give her voice more strength.

'What happens?'

'Well, we sew on a blood vessel between your main blood vessel and the blocked arteries at a place beyond the blockages, if you can imagine that. We'll probably take a piece of healthy vein from your leg, or possibly your chest wall. That way the blood can flow past the blockages.' He was looking at her, still smiling his reassuring, serious smile, trying to assess from her expression what her feelings might be. 'Don't worry,' he added. 'We have lots of literature to help you understand it. You'll be well prepared. It's really quite routine. And I think it's the best option we have of getting you fit and healthy again.'

'I see.' Ruth was trying to take in what she was being told, but panic had invaded her thought processes. Surgery. Slit open, hacked up, soft, pulsing tissue exposed to the air and the light. She tried to block out the images. 'How long would I be in hospital?'

'Oh, probably only a couple of weeks. And after three months or so you'll be good as new. You'll have to take it very easy for the first few weeks, of course. Is there someone at home to look after you?'

Ruth shook her head. 'No. I live alone. I have friends who could come in . . . There's my daughter, but she's in London. I suppose she might be able to come for a few weeks . . .' Ruth's voice wandered, her eyes absent. It was as though life had suddenly taken a sharp turning off-course. What if Abby said she couldn't come? In her mind, Ruth was already dialling the number, speaking to her, trying to make arrangements. She looked back at Mr Munn.

'How soon would it be, the operation?'

'That's hard to say, I'm afraid. We'll just have to put you on the waiting list, continue with your drugs in the meantime. It could be anything from six weeks to six months. The hospital will send you an appointment.'

'I see.'

Mr Munn had been leaning forward in a confidential way, elbows on his knees. Now he straightened up. 'But as for today, you're free to go. The nurse is looking out leaflets that will tell you all about the operation.' He stood up. 'There really is no need to worry,' he added, giving her a reassuring little smile. Ruth wondered what had registered on her face throughout the conversation. Fear? Probably. Yes, she was frightened. And worried. Worried about Abby, about disrupting her life, dragging her back here. But there really was no one else. Doris had her own family to think about.

'Well, thank you, Mr Munn.' She essayed a smile. 'At least I know the worst. Yes. Thank you very much.'

'The nurse will be along in a tick. And ring me if you have any worries in the meantime.'

When Ruth got home she tried to call Abby, but the phone rang unanswered all evening. Eventually Ruth went to bed. She passed a bad night, one in which successive dreams brought images of slicing blades, of incisions, of sopping bandages that could not staunch the endless blood, of rushing sounds and sliding sensations. At five she got up, still tired and feeling horribly overwrought. She made herself some tea and sat by the back door, the chill morning air on her skin, watching the dawn lighten and lift across the fields at the end of the garden. Then she had a bath, dressed, ate breakfast, put on the washing and hoovered the lounge. She was hanging out the washing when the doorbell rang. When she answered it, she was surprised to see Doris standing there. It wasn't like Doris to call round at eight in the morning. Doris's face was anxious, her mouth pursed up and her eyes large.

'I'm awfully sorry, Ruth.' She hesitated, but Ruth knew the instant before Doris got the words out. 'He died last night. Mr Maskelyne.' Doris held out an envelope. 'He left this for you.'

Ruth looked at the envelope wonderingly, then took it. She suddenly thought of the clearing in the woods, how empty it would be at this moment, just sunlight and shadows and soft wind among the grass.

Chapter Four

There was a symmetry about everything, Abby thought. Life consisted of phases, a series of unplanned events that drew her in and along, sometimes for weeks, sometimes months. Never much more. Just as one phase burned itself out, something new would present itself. She could kid herself that it was she, Abby, who steered things along, made the decision, turned the corner, whatever, but, in fact, it was always just a question of life walking up and offering her a fresh start.

Not that this was entirely new. Going back home to look after one's ageing mother for a bit was hardly a step forward, but it was different, that was for sure. And it had come at an opportune moment. She didn't want this thing with Rick to go on any longer, the bloody landlord was getting her down, and she was fed up with her job. Besides, Chloe was due to start school in September, and she didn't much fancy the idea of sending her to any of the crummy places round here. This was the ideal time to get out.

Abby had acted on her mother's phone call with the simple suddenness that characterised most of the things she did. Instead of going back to work after lunch, she had gone to the childminder's, paid her off, picked up Chloe, and had come back to the flat to pack. It was a Thursday, Rick would be out all afternoon, and by this evening they would be history.

Abby plucked clothes from the chest of drawers and the wardrobe, setting the metal hangers ringing, stuffing things untidily into the two suitcases lying on the unmade bed. They had so few belongings that packing took a little less than ten minutes. Then she paused, suddenly aware of the closeness of the little room. She turned and jerked up the sash window and leaned out over the peeling sill, bunching her blonde hair back over her shoulders to let the air cool her face, pushing her head out as far as she could and gazing around. Lorries and cars ground their slow way up and down the High Road in a haze of fumes. Looking down, she could see the afternoon shoppers wandering idly by, the little knot of schoolkids hanging around outside McDonald's, two coloured guys talking animatedly at the entrance to the bookie's. Raising her eyes, she could see in the distance the green trees of Parliament Hill Fields, and the sight reminded her of Hemwood, of the fields and woods and places she had not visited properly for ten years, and, where she would be in just a few hours. No coloured folks in Hemwood. No McDonald's, no bookie's, no traffic. Bugger all, in fact.

Chloe came in from the next room, blonde, barefoot and clad only in denim dungarees. Her small, soft arms were criss-crossed with green felt-tip, and she was eating an apple whose flesh was stained the same colour.

'Oh, Chlo!' said Abby, turning to look at her. 'Look at the state of you. Come on, let's get you cleaned up. We're going to have to get going in a little while.' She wet a flannel at the sink and started to rub her daughter's skin, while Chloe glanced with idle interest at the suitcases.

'What you got in there?' she asked.

'Our things,' said Abby. 'We're going on a nice train ride. To see Granny. Would you like that, going on a train to see Granny?'

The child looked at her impassively. 'How long for?' The idea of a train stirred her mildly, but she wasn't sure about the granny part. She knew she'd visited her granny before, but had no recollection of the visit, was unable to say whether it had been pleasurable or not.

'Oh, I don't know,' replied Abby vaguely, dabbing at the patch of green on Chloe's mouth. Chloe ducked away. Abby sighed and chucked the flannel into the sink, then sat back on her heels, contemplating her daughter. 'A few months, maybe.'

'How long's a few months?'

'Twelve weeks, something like that.'

'That's a long time, isn't it? Is Rick coming?'

'No, sweetie, he's not. Now, where are your sandals?' There was really no reason why they should go to Hemwood straight away. Her mother had said last night that they probably wouldn't take her into hospital for a month or two, at least. But now that the opportunity had presented itself, Abby wanted to get out of this shitty little flat as soon as possible. She particularly wanted to get away from Rick and the stash of half-empty vodka bottles located in what he pathetically thought were hiding-places round the flat. She'd had no idea of the extent of his drinking when he moved in with her three months ago. Amazing how people could fool you. He probably hadn't been drinking that much then, but now that he thought he'd got his domestic situation cosily sorted out, with Abby bringing in a wage and paying the rent, his guard had dropped. God, he was a dosser. Abby got to her feet and ruffled Chloe's curls. 'Go on, have a look in the living room for them. And put your T-shirt back on.'

Chloe pattered out, and Abby stood with her arms crossed, glancing round the bedroom. Rick was welcome to it. Welcome to the flat, the TV and video rental, the noisy bloody neighbours, and, most of all, to that fat Cypriot slug of a landlord. As for the job, she'd write to Dickman's when she got to Hemwood, get her P45 sorted out. The priority now was to leave. She glanced at her watch. Five to three. She'd checked the times of the trains at Liverpool Street, and they went every hour. If they left in the next ten minutes, they could catch the three fifty. Then bye-bye to all this. She slipped on her jacket, picked up the cases and her bag from the bed, and went into the other room to fetch Chloe. Chloe was sitting on the worn carpet, felt-tip pens scattered around her, trying to buckle her sandals. Abby bent down.

'Wrong feet, sweetheart.' She rubbed the little toes affectionately, swapping the sandals round and buckling them up. Then she picked Chloe's grubby T-shirt off the floor and slipped it over the child's head.

'What about my colouring things?'

48

'They can go in my bag.' Abby scooped up the felt-tips and the colouring book and put them in her straw shoulder-bag. Chloe got up, ready to go, as unperturbed by this abrupt departure as she had been by all the other sudden transitions in her short life. She had no sense of home. She was happy to be wherever her mother was, and if the flats, the streets, the infant friendships and the faces in the corner shops changed every four or five months, she did not mind.

'Can I say bye-bye to Sunip?' she asked as they reached the front door. Abby gave a sigh. She had been hoping Chloe wouldn't think of Sunip, the five-year-old son of the Indian couple who owned the off-licence down the street, and Chloe's special playmate. She didn't want people round here knowing she was leaving. Not that Rick or anyone would be able to find her, even if they wanted to, but it was best if they just got out without saying goodbye to anyone.

'Well, sweetheart –' But before she could say anything more, Chloe suddenly remembered her video.

'Mum, my *Aladdin* video! We forgot it!'

Abby had packed Chloe's half-dozen, well-watched videos, but *Aladdin* was still in the machine. It was a pirate copy that Rick had picked up down the market, and the sound quality wasn't all that good, but it was Chloe's favourite. She dashed back into the flat to retrieve it. When she came out with it, she had forgotten all about Sunip, and Abby guided her thankfully down the dark, narrow stairway and into the street. They headed for the station without a backward look.

When the train was clear of London, and the last straggle of back gardens and breakers' yards had given way to green fields, Abby lay back in her seat and closed her eyes. Chloe had her colouring book out on the Formica-topped table and was busy with her felt-tips, a can of Sprite and a bag of Walker's crisps at her elbow.

Abby loved these moments, the sense of freedom and escape like a rush of adrenalin. You could get hooked on it, she thought. People did. People who couldn't stay put in one place for more than months at a time. She was one of them. She loved impermanence, the knowledge that nothing need ever stay the same. That was why she kept so few possessions, never let herself get tied down by material things. As for people . . . She opened her eyes and stared out at the blur of hedgerows and trees rushing past. As for people, Chloe was the only one who mattered. The rest, including Chloe's father, were just characters who had come and gone in her life, and she didn't regret a single one of them. She thought of Angie, the big, ugly woman with whom she shared – had shared – the cramped office at Dickman's packing company until yesterday. She and Angie had formed a really nice little friendship, had plenty of laughs working side by side amongst the sheaves of invoices, Capital FM permanently on in the background. When she eventually realised that Abby wouldn't be coming back to Dickman's any more, Angie would probably be genuinely sorry. For a while. But it didn't matter. In the transitory nature of things, there wasn't a relationship in the world that mattered. If there was one lesson Abby had learned from her nomadic existence of the past ten years, it was that everything was purely down to chance. The amount of money you made depended on whichever job you managed to land. That in turn dictated what kind of place you could afford to live in. And everything else led from that. The people you met, the places where you shopped regularly and where your face got known, the pubs, Chloe's little playmates, the mums at whatever nursery. Your life could be any one of a thousand different stories, each with a different ending. Take some other job, and it would be simply another street, other people, other shops. Other lovers.

At this, Abby let out an involuntary sigh. The perceived wisdom was that it was women who wanted to settle down, wanted commitment, a steady relationship, and men who spent their time avoiding all that, staying free agents. Her experience was quite the opposite. Most of the men she took up with seemed to want to own her, to bind her to the routine of their own lives, stifle her independent existence with their needs and demands. Which was why she always got out in the end. It could be three weeks or twelve months, the feelings she had for them might be really warm and genuine, but there always came that suffocating point where she had to get out, be on her own again.

She glanced at her daughter, at the fair head bent over the colouring book. Probably the kind of life she lived wasn't fair on Chloe. It had been all right when she was a baby, then a toddler, but Abby knew that a point had to come where the child needed stability in her life, and that point was coming soon. Abby pushed the thought aside with a vague flicker of guilt. She would deal with that after her mother was better. When they went back to London she would try to find a job with some prospects, get a decent place, find a school for Chloe. She had formed similar tentative resolves in the past. None of it bore thinking of for long. The same house or flat, the same neighbours, streets, shops . . . maybe for years. Years and years. God. And there would be some man. Abby couldn't live without some man in her life. The idea that there might be someone out there, some decent, hard-working guy who'd want to be Chloe's stepfather, look after them all . . . She couldn't stand that. That had to be avoided at all costs.

And what, then? Abby asked herself. She was thirty-three now, still had her looks, but what about in fourteen years' time, when Chloe was eighteen and off her hands, and she was forty-seven and past it? The fact was, Abby admitted to herself, she had no idea what she wanted from life. She couldn't see further ahead than the next few months. It wasn't the proper outlook for a grown woman with a four-year-old daughter. Still, that was the way it was. Anyway, the next few months were taken care of, thanks to her mother. No point in thinking any further ahead. With this comforting thought, Abby closed her eyes once more. She began to think about Hemwood, recalling her childhood, the places she had played, the things she had done. Playing in the Dips with Stephen. That had always been the best. Her mother had said that Leslie Maskelyne had died the other day. So maybe Stephen would be back. She hadn't seen him since she was sixteen. Abby smiled, eyes still closed. Chloe turned to glance at her mother, noticed the smile, and then turned back to her colouring.

*

Doris rather enjoyed Leslie Maskelyne's funeral. Not in any celebratory sense, of course; she had been fond of him, and his death, after all, probably spelt the end of the job which she had held for so long. But it had given her considerable satisfaction to oversee the preparations for the gathering that followed the funeral. It had been rather like organising their Julie's wedding, ordering all the food, seeing the rooms were straight, making sure there were enough glasses and plates and napkins laid out. Lydia and Geraldine, Leslie's daughters, made vague attempts to assert themselves, but there was a sense that the house was still more Doris's territory than theirs, and they didn't interfere. Besides, much of their time was taken up in conversing with far-flung relatives who had travelled to Hemwood for the funeral, possibly in the hope that their extremely wealthy deceased relative might have remembered them in his will.

The subject of Leslie's will did not arise until late in the afternoon, when the guests had gone. Stephen was lounging on a sofa discussing the cricket with Lydia's husband Marcus, while Lydia and Geraldine helped Doris to clear up the last of the glasses and plates. Geraldine's husband, Peter, was trying half-heartedly to prevent his fourteen-month-old daughter, Arabella, from bumping into the furniture and grabbing at pieces of porcelain as she staggered round the room.

'Don't you think I should put her in her pushchair for a nap?' he asked his wife despairingly. Geraldine, a rangy twenty-seven year-old with her late mother's leonine good looks and brusque manner, glanced at her daughter.

'No point. She'll only get out. She's not at all sleepy.'

'Well, can't you look after her for a few minutes?'

'I'm still clearing up, Peter!' she snapped, and picked up a plate to make the point, then turned back to the conversation she was having with Lydia.

Peter picked Arabella up and sat down in an armchair with her. To his relief, she suddenly settled without a struggle against his chest, and put her thumb in her mouth.

'Couldn't you get a sitter?' asked Marcus sympathetically, glancing at his niece. Marcus was a portly, dark-haired investment banker who thought of himself as a good father, but who regarded time spent away from his children as a bonus.

Peter sighed and stroked Arabella's hair. 'Geraldine has never liked leaving her. She's always come with us wherever we go, right from the start.' Fine when she had still been in the slug-like early stages, reflected Peter, and you could cart her about in her Moses basket, but this toddler stage was something else. Arabella had shouted all the way through the funeral service, until Peter had to take her out of the church and let her run around, while he sat on a gravestone; watching her.

Marcus scratched his ear. 'Made a bit of a rod for your own back there, if you don't mind my saying so, old man,' he remarked. When they had first met, Marcus had been rather intimidated by Peter, who was an imposing six foot three, with a farmer's healthy good looks and air of vitality, the kind of man who looked effortlessly right even in baggy corduroys and a dung-splashed windcheater. Marcus, who had the fastidious vanity of many short, unathletic people, and a wardrobe of expensive suits and ties to bolster his ego against the threat of other men, had initially resented his brother-in-law. But over the past three years, that hostility had given way to mild contempt. He really thought Peter pretty feeble. From what Marcus could see, Peter let Geraldine walk all over him. She bossed him about, made him fetch and carry, corrected him loudly in public when he talked, and he simply took it all with a kind of good-natured doggedness. It always seemed to be Peter who got lumbered with Arabella, while Geraldine swanned about in that self-satisfied way of hers. Marcus would have sorted her out pretty sharpish if she were his wife. But then, Lydia was not like her sister. Where Geraldine was sharp-tongued, domineering and conceited, Lydia was much more passive, a listener rather than a talker. She had her share of the family's characteristics, thought she was elevated in some way by mere virtue of being a Maskelyne, and she was every bit as big a snob as her sister, but she wasn't any trouble. You had to hand it to Geraldine, mind, she was something of a looker, with her smooth, tawny hair cut to her chin, nice breasts and legs, but didn't she just know it. In those troubled moments when Marcus found himself lusting after his sister-in-law, aware that any pass he made would have met with a derisive slap on his plump face, he consoled himself by telling himself that he couldn't spend one week married to a bitch like that.

'So,' said Peter, ignoring Marcus and addressing Stephen, 'when do you find out how things stand? With your father's estate, I mean?'

Stephen sighed and pushed a lock of dark hair from his eyes. He resembled his father, had the same old-fashioned good looks, lean body and indolent manner. He twirled the empty wineglass which he held and wiggled his toes thoughtfully. His expensive black shoes lay kicked off next to the sofa. 'I haven't spoken to the solicitor yet. I'll be seeing him tomorrow. But I know the rough gist of how he left things. Essentially a three-way split, with extra for Lydia and Geraldine to make up for the fact that I get the house.'

Marcus manufactured a small yawn, trying to compose himself into an attitude of indifference, though secretly marvelling at the incredibly exciting fact that he was married to someone who was about to inherit something a little over a million pounds, after tax. Peter just nodded, fiddling absently with Arabella's pudgy, slack fingers as Stephen began to discuss the amount of money he estimated his father to have possessed.

Doris whipped the corners of a white tablecloth together and folded it expertly, glancing across at Stephen as she did so. To listen to that boy, you wouldn't think he cared tuppence that his father had just died. In fact, at the funeral, Lydia was the only one who'd given any sign that she cared in the slightest. Mind you, Geraldine had never been one for showing her emotions. Yet she'd been the one who'd been round every other day these last few months, spending long spells of time talking to Leslie. You couldn't say how members of any family really felt about each other. But Doris detected a certain shallowness about Stephen. A weak kind of lad, she had always thought, for all his arrogance.

'Stephen,' said Lydia, interrupting her brother abruptly, 'don't you think you could leave all that for today? Please? I don't really think it's appropriate, when poor Father has only just been buried.' Lydia's voice was slightly strained, her eyes still pink and small from weeping at the service.

Stephen shrugged and lowered his feet from the sofa. But he stopped talking. There was a long silence in the room. Stephen set his glass down on the table and planted his hands on his knees. 'Well, Mrs Cotterell,' he said, looking up at her and smiling, 'I think we all have a good deal to thank you for. Today, I mean. I don't know how we would have managed without you.'

Doris inclined her head slightly and added the folded tablecloth to the pile of napkins. Geraldine wondered with mild irritation why Doris bothered to fold everything so neatly, when it was all simply going straight into the washing machine. 'It was the least I could do. After thirty happy years of working for your father . . .' Doris's voice trembled a little, and everyone in the room hoped this wasn't going to get embarrassing. But Doris controlled herself and managed a smile. 'I really don't quite know what I'm going to do with my time, now that he's gone.'

Lydia began to snuffle again, and turned away to the window. Stephen stood up and strolled across to Doris. 'Why, I hope you're going to carry on here just as before.' His tone was effortlessly patronising. Doris looked at him in surprise.

'I wouldn't have thought you'd need anyone, now –'

'Well, now that the house is mine, I'll be staying here, on and off. I don't see why you shouldn't carry on as you have been – for the time being, at least. Once the estate is sorted out, I'll have to make some decision as to whether I want to keep Hemwood or not –'

'Oh, Stephen!' exclaimed Lydia, wheeling round. 'You can't be thinking of selling the house, surely?'

Stephen looked at his sister in mild exasperation. 'Lydia, at the moment I haven't made my mind up about that.' His tone implied that even if he did, it was none of her business. Again there was an uneasy silence.

Doris broke it. 'I'll be very happy to come up each day, if that's what you'd like,' she said to Stephen. It didn't occur to her to decline his suggestion. Working for the family was what she did. She had no idea, as yet, that Leslie Maskelyne had left her a legacy large enough to keep her and her husband in considerable comfort for the remainder of their lives. In truth, such a possibility had not even crossed her mind.

'Good.' Stephen gave her his radiant smile, but there was something in it which made Doris feel that she was being dismissed. She picked up the bundle of linen and some plates, and left the room.

An hour later, Doris was sitting drinking tea with Ruth. It was a bit after her usual time for dropping in, but she wouldn't have dreamed of passing up the chance of giving Ruth a detailed account of the funeral, who had been there, what they had worn and all that they had said. Ruth listened, not saying much.

'Why didn't you come?' Doris asked her. 'After you and him getting so chummy the last few weeks, I thought you might have.'

'You know I don't like funerals,' said Ruth. She could not explain to Doris that what had been between her and Leslie had been so private, so much theirs and theirs alone, that she could not share with others the business of saying goodbye to him. She had done that in her heart.

'No . . . well . . .' Doris sighed and finished her tea, then glanced at her friend. 'How are you feeling today? You look a bit peaky.'

'Oh, so-so,' replied Ruth. 'I just hope I'm not going to have to wait too long for this operation. Now that I know I've got to have it, I just want it over and done with.' In fact, she had noticed her breathing becoming more difficult over the last few days. Was that psychosomatic, a reaction to being told how bad her heart was? Possibly. This close weather didn't help.

Doris gave a small, theatrical shiver. 'Ooh, I couldn't bear to think about it, being cut open like that.'

Ruth gave her a dry look, then rose to take the teapot to the sink. 'Well, I won't know much about it, will I? Mercifully.' She turned the teapot upside down and shook the dregs out into the sink, not wanting to think about it, about her arteries choked with deadly matter like scale in a tap. Glancing across the garden, she saw that the day's warmth had given way to thunderclouds. A few large spots of rain already marked the garden path, and there was a distant rumble of thunder. 'So, what will you do now?' she asked Doris. 'Did Stephen Maskelyne say what he intends to do with the house?'

Doris wondered how Ruth knew that Leslie had left Hemwood House to Stephen. Had she and Leslie really suddenly become so intimate that he told her family business? 'He hasn't decided yet. He wants me to carry on in the meantime. I'm glad, in a way. I'm not sure what I'd do with my time, otherwise. It means I'll have to find another cleaner, though, now that Melanie's leaving.'

'When's her baby due?'

'Some time in September, I think. I told her she ought to take things easy, with those veins of hers . . . Was that your front door?'

'Was it?' Ruth went to the door and glanced down the passage. She heard a faint irregular knocking. 'You're right. I don't know why they don't use the bell . . .'

She sighed and walked down the hallway, careful not to move too fast. Even the short walk from the kitchen to the front door could bring on an attack of breathlessness, if she wasn't careful. When she opened the door, she found a small, blonde girl on the doorstep, her fist raised to knock again. Ruth did not recognise her at first. 'Hello, Granny,' said Chloe. She didn't remember the old lady who had opened the front door, but presumed that this was Granny.

'Hello, love,' said Ruth in surprise, as this registered. 'My, aren't you getting big?' She looked up and saw Abby a few yards away, paying a taxi-driver.

'I was four last December. Is this your house?'

Abby turned round and picked up the suitcases from the pavement. She came quickly towards her mother through the rain, which was falling steadily now, and gave her a kiss. 'Hello, Mum.'

'Hello,' said Ruth. 'I had no idea you were planning to come down so soon. You should have rung.'

'Yeah, well . . . I thought, the sooner the better. I hope you don't mind.'

'Of course I don't. Come on in, then.' Ruth ushered them in, and Abby set down the cases in the hall. 'I've no beds made up, but that won't take two ticks. I'll just make a fresh pot of tea. Doris is in the kitchen.'

Abby and Chloe went down the narrow hallway ahead of Ruth, and into the little kitchen.

'Hello, Doris,' said Abby, giving a faint smile as she bent to kiss her. 'How are you keeping?'

'Oh, fine,' said Doris, pleased that she had been here to witness this interesting domestic development. Ruth had told her that Abigail would be coming down from London to stay when she had the operation, but this early arrival was unexpected. Doris turned to smile at Chloe. 'Now, you must be Chloe. I've heard all about you.'

Chloe gave Doris a long, expressionless look, then turned to Ruth. 'Have you got any biscuits, Granny?'

'Now, you're not going to start on biscuits,' said Abby firmly. 'You'll have something proper to eat.' She began to open Ruth's cupboards. 'Have you got anything I can give her, Mum? She hasn't eaten properly all day. Just spaghetti or beans, something easy?'

'Well, I don't know . . .' said Ruth vaguely, fingertips against her mouth. She was a little taken aback by this sudden change of pace. The sight of Abby moving so briskly and decisively made her feel slightly dazed. The former calm of the kitchen seemed fragmented. This is not good for me, thought Ruth with sudden intuition. She must take control, she told herself. Abby could be so – so disruptive, if you didn't keep a rein on things. She stepped forward and picked up the packet of biscuits and handed it to Chloe. Then she said to Abby, 'We'll see about making Chloe something proper to eat in a little while. Doris and I are just having a cup of tea at the moment, so you can make do with that. Chloe can have a glass of milk. You come and sit down and stop messing up my cupboards.' Her voice was firm.

Abby gave a shrug and closed the cupboard doors, then sat down at the table. Chloe got up on her mother's lap, clutching a handful of custard creams. Ruth set about brewing a fresh pot, fetching a cup and saucer for Abby, her movements slow and purposeful. There was a brief silence in the kitchen, and Ruth felt rather pleased with herself.

'So,' said Abby, flicking her blonde hair back over her shoulders and turning to Doris, 'what's new in the exciting world of Hemwood?'

You forgot, thought Doris, what a forceful person Abigail could be. She'd always had one of those personalities. She wondered now if Abby's question didn't have something condescending about it.

'Well, we've had quite a day today,' replied Doris, drawing herself up in her chair. 'Leslie Maskelyne's funeral. It was very well-attended, as you can imagine. Stephen and Lydia and Geraldine were all there, with their families. You remember them, don't you? You used to play with them.'

'Yes,' replied Abby. Ruth passed her a cup of tea and Abby gave her a quick smile. 'So Stephen's got a family, has he?'

'Oh, no – not him. I meant the girls. Geraldine's married to a farmer over Sudbury way, and Lydia's husband's a banker. They've both got little ones. But no, Stephen's not married. Though he has a very nice girlfriend that used to come down sometimes. That was before Mr Maskelyne got really poorly.' Doris sighed. 'Yes, I left them all up there, talking about how much money they would all get.'

At this mention of Leslie's money, Ruth's mind turned to the document in the envelope which Doris had given her the day after Leslie died, and her heart gave a little jolt. All that money. She had never expected him to leave them both so much. It had even been enough to make her think of going private over this business with her heart. She'd have to look into that. She glanced at Abby, who was sipping her tea with a faraway look on her face. What would Abby make of her legacy, when she eventually found out? It would all take some explaining. Ruth tried to picture herself recounting to her daughter the events of thirty years ago, revealing to her who her father really was, and something inside her shrivelled with fright. And there were the Maskelynes, too. They never need know about the marriage business – that was between herself and Leslie – but there was the matter of these extra bequests to herself and Abby. Had Leslie made a copy of the document and left it with his will? Ruth had no way of knowing. If he hadn't, Ruth supposed she would have to approach Stephen Maskelyne at some point, tell him about it. That was another thing she didn't much relish doing. Thinking about these things made Ruth feel anxious, and added to that she suddenly felt tired. She always got tired in the evenings now. And there were still the beds to be made up. Oh, hell, Abby could do that. Ruth tried consciously to relax. She smiled at Chloe, who was steadily devouring custard creams as Abby and Doris conversed above her, discussing the funeral.

'Would you like to sit on Granny's knee?' she asked softly.

Chloe considered this, then smiled and nodded, slipping down from her mother's knee and into her grandmother's arms. Ruth settled the child on her lap, enjoying the feel of the bird-like body, the faint custardy scent, the soft hair under her own old hands. At least she would have Chloe's company for the next few weeks or so, and there was that to be thankful for.

Chapter Five

The following morning Stephen Maskelyne was woken by the sound of Mrs Cotterell letting herself in through the back door of Hemwood House. He lay in bed for a while, gazing at the grey light behind the curtains, listening to the steady patter of the rain, aware for the first time of how profoundly empty the house now was. His father's presence at Hemwood had always been such a solid thing, even during the last few months, as the dismal paraphernalia of oxygen masks and morphine and nurses built up around him. He had always been the core of things, and now suddenly he was gone, utterly. For a moment Stephen felt a slipping, childish sense of fear. He had loved his father, despite whatever impression people might have formed by his impassiveness at the funeral the previous day, and now he felt his absence more acutely than at any time, even that awful moment when they had lowered his coffin into that muddy hole. With his father's death, he himself had been moved one step further down the line of mortality, and he felt very alone. At least Lydia and Geraldine had their husbands and children. The preoccupations of bringing up the next generation probably helped to buffer one against the eclipse of the last.

This made him think about Harriet, and his guilt at not having rung her last night. By the time the others had gone he had felt too tired and dispirited. Stephen sighed and ran his fingers slowly through his hair. He and Harriet had been an item for twenty-two months now, a fact which rather surprised him. A mutual friend had brought them together, thinking they were well-suited. Stephen hadn't thought so, not at first. She wasn't his type. He tended to go for women who reflected well on him, sophisticated, cool women, the kind who gave nothing away. That was not Harriet. She was girlish, good-humoured, open and kind. You certainly couldn't call her beautiful, but she was very pretty, in a way that reminded him of a marmoset, with dark, soft hair cut short, and large, grave eyes. Did he love her? At times he felt that he did, but there were other times, times when his confidence was at its height and his ego in full bloom, when he was not so sure. But one thing was certain – Harriet loved him. She was good for him, he knew that. She was calm and reassuring, she was honest, and she did not allow him to deceive himself. But things that were good for you had a way of becoming tedious . . . Perhaps that was unfair. There was no real reason why they should not get married. Things had fallen into place. His father's money would provide a great cushion of security, a back-up to the money he earned at the agency. He thought himself a pretty fairish copywriter, but advertising was a fickle business. At least now the future was assured. And the house. They could live here, have children, he could commute to London . . .

Stephen got out of bed and went for a shower. He'd think about that kind of thing another time. The estate came first. When that was sorted out, then he could devote more time to Harriet, decide where they went from here. The most important thing at present was his ten o'clock appointment with his father's solicitor in Colchester.

An hour later, showered and breakfasted, his ego bolstered by the smiles and mild obsequiousness of Doris, Stephen discovered that he had quite shaken off his earlier feelings of loneliness and vulnerability. Far from regretting his father's absence, he now walked round the house with proprietorial delight. Possession lent a different aspect to each painting, each piece of furniture. He smiled as he went from room to room. The realisation that he was now a rich man in his own right, that this splendid house and its grounds were now his, made him feel properly grown-up. He

62

thought of the people whom he would invite here, seeing himself through the eyes of others in a new image, a man of wealth and cultivation. It did not occur to him that such an image would be largely a sham. Behind the mask of arrogance and ambitious intelligence which Stephen presented to the world lay a person of some immaturity. The tall, attractive man with the supercilious smile and apparently serious and considered view of life was, in reality, no more than an anxious, insecure schoolboy, a fact which few, apart from Harriet, properly appreciated. He was a person given to hiding himself. And now he had a new means of concealment, in the guise of a man of property.

He went into his father's old bedroom last of all. Doris, with some idea of reverence to the departed, had drawn down the window blinds halfway, making the room dim and gloomy. Stephen glanced with quick distaste at the empty bed, the oxygen cylinder and other trappings of illness still in place. The deep, sweet pungency of old tobacco smoke permeated everything. It hadn't mattered when his father was alive, had been a part of him, but now it seemed revolting, like the smell of death. He gazed around. The little escritoire in which Leslie had left the document setting out the legacies to Ruth and Abby was closed. It did not occur to Stephen to open it. Since his father had been a man of business, he presumed that everything of importance was with the solicitors. And so he left, closing the door behind him.

At Alma Cottage, Ruth was trying to adjust to the change in her life brought about by the sudden arrival of her daughter and grand-daughter. Abby's past visits had been infrequent and brief. After Chloe was born, Abby had been to Hemwood only once, for a weekend, around Chloe's second birthday. It wasn't because she and Ruth didn't get on, but because physical and temporal distance had become a habit. When Abby had left home at seventeen to exchange the dreariness of village life for a brighter, imagined existence in London, relations with her mother had been very bad for a while. Ruth had agonised over the life which she envisaged her daughter leading, and was at the same time forced to listen to Doris's tales of how well Lydia and Geraldine Maskelyne were doing, which

A-levels they were studying, and which smart parties they were attending. That had been a time when Ruth nursed bitter thoughts about Leslie. When it eventually became apparent that Abby was leading a more or less blameless existence in London, sharing a flat with some other girls and getting by on part-time work while taking a secretarial course, Ruth's recriminations died away, and relations had improved. As Abby got older, Ruth worried less. It was Abby's life, after all. If she chose to lead a peripatetic existence, so be it. When Chloe was born, Ruth took it stoically. The world was full of unmarried mothers, it seemed, and she must trust to Abby to look after herself and her child as best she could. That philosophy had hardened over the years. Ruth herself had always been independent, and she expected much the same of Abby. She had not anticipated that the day would ever come when they would both be living under the same roof again. But that day had come.

It was, so far as Ruth could see, going to be more of a nuisance than anything else, at least until after the operation. They sat together over breakfast, Abby thumbing listlessly through the local newspaper, Ruth drinking tea, while Chloe ate toast and jam and beat an irritating tattoo against the table leg with one sandalled foot.

'Don't do that, there's a love,' murmured Ruth. She glanced out of the window at the rain and sighed inwardly. On such a day she would normally have put her feet up, let the washing and housework go to hell, read a Mills & Boon and watched *Countdown*. But now there were mouths to feed, meals to plan, guests whose boredom would only make her feel guilty.

Ruth turned to look at her daughter. Even with her blonde hair uncombed and spilling over her shoulders in long, untidy curls, she possessed a restful, inert beauty quite at odds with her character. The face was grave, the eyes watchful, clear. Ruth watched as Abby rose to clear away Chloe's plate and cup, admiring her slow, graceful movements. Tall women moved like that, she thought. She, Ruth, had once been just as graceful, long-limbed and beautiful. No longer.

'What will you find to do with yourself?' Ruth suddenly asked Abby. 'You're going to find it a bit quiet here after London.'

Abby shrugged, flicking her hair back from her shoulders in a characteristic gesture. 'Look after you, of course. That's why I'm here.'

Ruth made a dismissive little noise. 'I'm not bedridden, you know. It's after the operation that I'll need looking after, and Lord knows when that will be.'

'No, but you should be taking things easy. I don't want us to make extra work for you. I can do the housework, get the shopping.'

Ruth felt surprised and relieved. 'What about Chloe?'

'There's still a couple of months of the summer term left. I'll go along later to that new nursery and see about getting her a place. She's never any bother, anyway – are you, sweetheart?' She gave her daughter, who had looked up attentively during this part of the conversation, a warm smile that quite softened her features. Chloe shook her head, then resumed eating her toast and jam.

'You want to find something to do, fill in the time while you're here,' observed Ruth. Then she sighed. 'You could take over my part-time job at the pub. I'm not up to it, frankly. You might meet a few old faces.'

'Yes,' mused Abby, leaning her hips against the sink. 'I could do with earning a few quid. There's the extra expense of our food, I suppose.' She hadn't really taken that into account before she'd left London. Naturally her mother couldn't afford to keep them all. Then she remembered something her mother had mentioned to her yesterday, after Doris had left. 'Didn't you tell me that Doris was looking for someone to clean up at Hemwood House?'

Ruth looked startled. 'Oh, you wouldn't want to do that kind of thing,' she said quickly. 'Not after office work.' She didn't like to think of her daughter down on her hands and knees cleaning other people's floors, especially the Maskelynes'.

Abby shrugged. 'I don't mind. It's a nice house, which makes a difference. And there can't be that much to do, since there's nobody in it.'

'Oh, but there is. Stephen said he'd be staying there, Stephen who you used to play with when you were little.' She was sure that this would put Abby off. She wouldn't want to go cleaning for Stephen Maskelyne, would she?

But Abby merely smiled thoughtfully and said, 'That makes no odds. I'll have a word with Doris when she drops in later on. Which reminds me – you'd better give me that list of things she wants from the supermarket.'

There was silence for a few seconds. Ruth could think of nothing to say. She got to her feet and went out of the kitchen in search of Doris's shopping list.

Abby turned round at the sink, resting her hands on the edge and looking out of the window across her mother's garden. The rain had stopped, and a glimmer of sunlight warmed the grass. She tried to remember Stephen as he had been when they were children, but nothing was distinct, just the recollection of his biscuity-brown hair and rather thin, long legs, a green zippered cardigan that he always used to wear. He had been eleven when they sent him off to boarding school, leaving only Geraldine and Lydia to play with. Not that Abby had ever bothered much with them. They liked things like ponies and books by Christine Pullein-Thompson, or dressing up their Barbie dolls. They were no good at building forts. She had seen Stephen only in the holidays after that, and it had gradually become different. She had a very clear recollection of one summer's day, when they were both teenagers. They met down in the Dips as usual, a few days after the beginning of the holidays, and everything had been wrong. The idea of playing their old games, or building anything, had seemed really stupid and babyish. They had just sat around, bored, and then they had a quarrel, a rude, sneering kind. Something had happened during that quarrel. Abby couldn't remember what. But their perceptions of one another had shifted irrevocably. And then, when they had roughly made up and were on their way down to the village to get some Cokes, he had kissed her. Or tried to. She had hated it so much. Not because she didn't like being kissed – several other boys had done that – but because she did not want things between her and Stephen to change, and she hated the passing of all their childish pleasures. They might have met again after that, she couldn't really remember, but it died away that summer.

What would Stephen be like at thirty-two? What would he make of meeting her again as his new charlady? She smiled at the thought. He probably wouldn't like it in the slightest, but Abby thought that she might find it amusing.

'We should get probate in ten days or so, and then it's just a matter of transferring assets. Of course, there is the valuation of the house, but we'll do our best to speed things up.' Leslie Maskelyne's solicitor, Walter Hubbard, scanned the pages of Leslie's will again. 'There are no complications that I can see – really just a question of waiting for things to fall into place. Will you be going back to London straight away?'

'No,' said Stephen, 'I thought I might take a week or two off from work, spend some time at the house.'

Walter Hubbard nodded. He was a small, neat man in his sixties, with an old-fashioned pencil-thin moustache, now as white as his hair, and a bright, searching gaze. It was the first time he had met Leslie Maskelyne's son, and he had, in his sharp way, made a swift and fairly accurate appraisal of his character during their twenty-minute conversation. Stephen reminded Walter Hubbard much of Leslie, particularly in his facial features and languid bearing, but there was a certain coldness in Stephen's manner quite unlike the gentle geniality of his father, and Walter suspected that this masked an insecurity, a lack of confidence. Stephen had asked a number of questions which had indicated his financial inexpertise, but they had been asked without candour, as though Stephen wanted to hide his ignorance. Yet he conducted himself with arrogance, as though very much at ease with the amounts of money he would now have at his disposal.

'Ah, yes, Hemwood House. Quite a place to look after, I imagine. Do you have any immediate plans?' It was a polite way of asking if Stephen intended to sell the house; Walter's nephew was a local estate agent, and Hemwood would be quite a nice piece of business to be able to put his way.

'No,' admitted Stephen. 'I don't know quite what to do about it. I'm not keen on selling the place, you know, but my business is up in London, and I don't know that I could justify the upkeep of somewhere so large, merely for the odd weekend.'

'What kind of business are you in, if I may ask, Mr Maskelyne?' enquired Walter politely.

'I'm in advertising,' replied Stephen, conscious that this had a somewhat emptier ring to it here in this provincial solicitor's office, than it did at drinks parties in London. 'On the creative side.'

'Ah.' Walter nodded. Nothing wrong with that, of course, but he guessed that Leslie had been disappointed that his son hadn't had the brains for finance, and that he had been forced to sell his lucrative business, instead of keeping it in family hands. He remembered the regret with which Leslie had told him years ago, at the time of drawing up this will, that Stephen didn't seem to be university material. Still, it took all types, and to judge by this young man's expensive taste in clothing and shoes, Stephen would have no trouble in finding ways of spending the profits of his father's hard word and ability. 'Very interesting work, I imagine.'

Stephen thought of the chocolate biscuit campaign which he and the other members of his creative team were having such a hard struggle with. God, he wouldn't mind giving that up. One phone call and he could be finished and done with DRS, the agency for which he worked. But if he did that, what was he, where was he? Work gave him status, friends to gossip with and go out with, someone to be. Then again, couldn't he now be – well, just a rich young man, able to have fun, do what he wanted? He tried to picture in a hazy way how he would spend his time, and with whom. He couldn't. Anyway, he wasn't entirely sure that there was enough money for him to forget about working for the rest of his life. These thoughts ran in a muddled way through his head, and he stared distractedly at the documents on Walter Hubbard's desk.

'Yes . . .' he said absently, after a few seconds. 'Yes, it's moderately interesting.' He frowned. 'Tell me, how much do you imagine my share of the estate will be worth, in the long run?'

'Oh, that's hard to say, Mr Maskelyne –'

'Please, call me Stephen. I like to keep things informal.'

Walter, who on the contrary preferred to keep all business relations formal, hesitated only momentarily before replying, with the smallest of smiles, 'In that case, you must, of course, call me

Walter. Well, as I was saying, I would estimate your share of the estate to be in the region, say, of one, one and a half million pounds. Your father had accumulated considerable wealth.' Walter eyed Stephen thoughtfully.

Stephen tried to make sense of the figure. Surely it was more than enough to enable him to pack in his job. But then, he still could not envisage how he would spend his time. There must be some sort of club of rich people, but how did one join? Certainly stewing away down in Hemwood wasn't the way. Nor, he suspected, was marrying Harriet.

'If you have the time,' said Walter, glancing at his watch, 'we could go through a few things. I must say, your father left his affairs in very good order. He seems to have sold the bulk of his portfolio and put the money into various bank accounts, so that once we obtain probate the estate should be very speedily wound up. There are, however, some outstanding items – perhaps you'd like to discuss whether you wish to retain the investments or sell them.' He paused, gazing searchingly at Stephen, who still seemed to be caught up in his own thoughts. 'Or it may be,' he went on, 'that you would prefer to instruct someone else in that regard. That would be perfectly understandable. At the moment I am acting merely in the capacity of executor of your father's will.'

Stephen looked up. 'No, no – I'd rather you carried on looking after things. It's all rather a mystery to me, you know, stocks and shares.'

He smiled, and for the first time Walter found himself warming to the young man. He put on his spectacles and drew the handful of share certificates towards him. Stephen tried to look interested, but his thoughts were elsewhere.

That evening Doris sat in Ruth's kitchen, sipping her tea as usual, checking through the groceries which Abby had fetched for her from the supermarket.

'I couldn't get that ham you wanted,' said Abby, 'so I got some salami instead. I hope that's all right.'

'Oh, well,' said Doris. She didn't think her Don would fancy salami. He didn't go for anything Continental. Still, she didn't like to say. She wished Ruth had done the shopping. Ruth would have known to get some corned beef instead. 'How much do I owe you?' she asked Abby.

'I've got the till receipt somewhere,' murmured Abby.

'Why have you got fat ankles?' asked Chloe, who was hanging on the back of Ruth's chair, swinging one leg and staring at Doris.

'Don't be rude, Chlo,' said Abby.

'Little girls shouldn't ask questions like that,' said Doris stiffly. She felt out of sorts today. Things weren't right up at the house. It had been pleasantly busy over the weeks leading up to Leslie's death, and now it was so quiet. She missed having the nurses to talk to. The day had seemed monotonous, now that there was no longer the fact of her employer's mortal illness to lend it importance. Stephen kept himself to himself, had been out all the morning and then spent most of the afternoon on the phone and watching cricket on television. And with Melanie gone, she'd had to do more dusting and hoovering than she was used to, and it had made her feet and ankles play up. 'What kind of a day have you had?' Doris asked Ruth.

'Oh, very nice,' replied Ruth, and looked as though she meant it. 'I've been quite spoilt. Abby's done all my bits and pieces.' She had enjoyed the day, knowing that Abby was attending to everything. All she'd had to do was read stories to Chloe, and that was quite restful and pleasant.

'Well, that's nice,' said Doris grudgingly. 'I must say, I'm run off my feet up there, now that Melanie's gone.'

'Oh, that was something I meant to ask you,' said Abby, looking up. She handed the receipt to Doris. 'There you go. Four pounds twenty-two. I was wondering if I could take over Melanie's job.'

Doris glanced at Abby in surprise. 'Cleaning?' She couldn't really imagine the lissom, lovely Abby with a bucket and a mop, scrubbing out toilets. 'Well . . .' She rummaged in her purse, then handed some coins to Abby. 'You'll have to owe me the eight pence. I haven't got change.' She closed her purse. 'It's not the kind of thing you're used to, really, is it? I mean, you're welcome, if you want to . . .'

Abby shrugged. 'It's something to do. I can't expect Mum to pay for all the food and so on.'

'It's not a lot of money, mind,' said Doris. 'Melanie was getting three pound an hour. Though I might be able to get Stephen to stretch it to three fifty. And it's only a couple of hours every morning.'

'Well, that's all right. It'll keep me busy while Chloe's at nursery. So, that's settled, then, is it?'

'Fine,' said Doris, still somewhat surprised, but relieved. The local supply of cleaners seemed to have dried up recently, and she didn't want to have to cope with all those rooms by herself. It would give her a bit of company in the mornings, as well – not that Abby was much in the way of a talker. For all her strength of character, she often had a closed-up quality about her, much like Ruth.

Ruth sat listening to this exchange, trying to ignore the creeping pains in her chest. It alarmed her that she should get them even when she hadn't been exerting herself. She tried to put it out of her mind, concentrating instead on the idea of Abby working for Stephen at Hemwood House. Working for her half-brother. The relationship was something she hadn't given any thought to for years, not since the two of them had played together as children. Then it had possessed a certain irony. Now – well, now it was rather different. Ruth had been thinking all day about the business of Abby working up at the house. She had the feeling that Abby wouldn't be quite so prepared to work as Stephen's cleaner if she knew everything. And there was the matter of the money. There was all that money due to her and Abby. She should do something about it. But somehow she couldn't bring herself to believe that piece of paper, despite everything that Leslie had said, despite all that had happened. She had taken it out a couple of times and looked at it, wondering if she should show it to a lawyer. She didn't know any lawyers. Really she should ask Abby. She was more worldly-wise, and would know what to do. But then she would have to explain everything, and Ruth didn't know if she wanted to do that just yet. Soon, but not just yet. She took two shallow breaths, felt the tight pain easing, and was suddenly filled with a terrible tiredness, even though she had done nothing all day.

'Well,' said Doris, 'I'd best be off.' She rose to her feet and put on her cardigan, wondering what to give Don for his tea, now that she'd no ham. 'That weather's taken a turn for the better,' she added, glancing out of the window. 'I reckon it's going to be hot tomorrow.'

'I'll see you out,' said Ruth, getting up slowly.

'What time do you want me on Monday?' asked Abby. 'I'll be dropping Chloe off to the nursery at nine fifteen.'

'You got her a place, did you?' asked Doris. 'Oh, of course, you said before. Well, let's say nine thirty, shall we?' She had to say she was surprised Chloe had got into that nursery. It had become ever so popular in the last year, since that new woman, Mrs Cantley, had taken it over, bringing in all her fancy educational notions. Quite a handful of the more well-to-do kiddies in the neighbourhood went there. It couldn't be cheap. No wonder Abby didn't mind doing a bit of charring and pulling pints.

When Doris had gone, Ruth came back into the kitchen to find Abby washing up the tea-things.

'What would you like for supper, Mum?' asked Abby, glancing round from the sink.

Ruth sat down heavily, resting her head on one hand. She smiled wearily as Chloe scrambled up into her lap, then hugged the child. 'Oh, I'm not that hungry,' replied Ruth. It was true. she had no appetite at all. 'You know,' she said thoughtfully, stroking her granddaughter's hair, 'I don't want you to feel you have to go out cleaning, just for the money. I mean, there is some money.' Maybe now was the time. She had broached the subject, so maybe now was the time to sit Abby down and tell her about the legacies, about Leslie and herself, about everything.

'Oh, it's not just the money,' said Abby. 'Like you said, it's for something to do. Same with working in the pub. I want to, don't worry.' She laughed, a nice sound, a rare sound. 'I don't want you dipping into any nest egg just for me. I do have a bit in the bank myself, you know. Enough for Chloe's fees this term. They haven't half ponced that school up, have they?'

Abby began to talk idly about the nursery. Ruth let the moment pass. It was something that would keep. For how long, she didn't know. Just a couple of days. But by then Abby would be working up at the house . . . Oh, well. Ruth just didn't feel up to talking about it, not just yet.

Chapter Six

Mrs Cantley, proprietrix of the Hemwood Rainbow Nursery, bared her long, white teeth in a smile and surveyed Chloe. Chloe looked back up at her, thinking that this lady was one of the biggest she had ever seen. Mrs Mountjoy, the lady at the sweet-shop down the road from their last flat but one, had been fat, but this lady was enormous.

'So this is Chloe? How perfectly lovely.' Veronica Cantley's voice was large – large in the same way that she was, robust and full-bodied. She had thick grey hair tied up in a knot at the back of her head, and wore a flowing, tent-like dress in a Liberty print of maroon and brown. On her feet she wore stout leather sandals, and several strands of ethnic beads encircled her firm, fleshy neck. The look was middle-class bohemian. Mrs Cantley laid a broad palm on top of Chloe's head and addressed Abby.

'And it's Chloe –?'

'Sorry?'

'For the register. Chloe's surname.' Mrs Cantley bared her teeth again. It was a rapid, rather frightening smile.

'Oh, it's Owen. Chloe Owen.'

'I'm so sorry I wasn't here to meet you myself when you came to enquire after a place for Chloe. I do tell Natalie to write things down, but she's a bit of a scatterbrain at times. Have you moved into the neighbourhood recently?' asked Mrs Cantley.

'Not exactly,' replied Abby. 'I've come back to look after my mother. She's not very well.'

'Ah. And she would be –?' Margaret Cantley had herself lived in the village for only eighteen months but she liked to feel that she had established herself as a significant member of the community, acquainted with everyone.

Something in Abby felt like telling Mrs Cantley to stuff her Gestapo-like interrogation, but she managed to resist the urge. 'Mrs Owen. Ruth Owen. She lives in one of the cottages just past the church.'

'Ah.' Mrs Cantley nodded, still holding her smile, eyes scanning Abby rapidly, taking note of the matter of the surnames and the absence of the wedding ring on the left hand. It was like being assessed by some terrifying, smiling robot. Abby knew what was going on behind that robotic smile, had been there many times before. Single mother, loose sort, daughter could be a problem child, have to keep an eye on her. Chloe stood between them, the flat of Mrs Cantley's hand pressing on her head, marvelling at the size of stomach that swelled beneath the Liberty print dress. 'Well, let me explain something of our method to you, Mrs Owen,' said Mrs Cantley, gliding over the problem of how to address Abby. She took her hand from Chloe's head and gestured around the room, where fifteen or so children were engaged in the usual nursery activities, helped by a couple of serious young women. 'We aim here to bring out the best in all our little people. We have a wide variety of stimuli, and I like to think that the children learn as they play. Naturally Natalie and Anna and myself are here to guide them, but generally we prefer to let the little ones explore the various activities which we provide and absorb information in that way. It's difficult at this age, I know, but we do try to foster a sense of mutual co-operation amongst the children.' At that moment a squabble broke out in the book corner, and someone began to cry. One of the helpers went over to break it up. Mrs Cantley merely raised her voice to carry on above the hubbub. 'What we are trying to do here is to reach the *spirit* of each child. I am a great believer in the philosophy that children are capable of being guided towards correct behaviour. No threats, no coercion – we simply appeal to their better nature. Most children would rather behave nicely than not – don't you think?' Mrs Cantley turned her smile on Abby once again.

Abby murmured something noncommittal. She had heard a good deal of half-baked stuff in her time, but this took some beating. She glanced round. There were the usual books, toys, puzzles, papier-mâché relief maps, easels and paints, so it would do to keep Chloe happy during the mornings. They had a hell of a nerve charging the fees they did, just to let four-year-olds muck about with sand and water and bang a couple of tambourines, but no doubt most of the mothers round here listened to this overweight airhead and thought they were getting value for money. A caring, sharing, learning environment. Still, there wasn't another nursery school for miles, so this would have to do.

'Now, Chloe, would you like to come and join the others?' Mrs Cantley's long wooden beads clicked and swung out from her bosom as she bent smilingly down to Chloe, who was picking her nose and staring with mild hostility at the other children. Don't, thought Abby, please don't decide to throw a wobbly, Chlo. But Chloe nodded, and headed slowly towards the easels and paints. Mrs Cantley straightened up.

'Perhaps you would care to stay for a while and engage in some of the activities with the little ones? Most of our mothers like to get *involved* during the first few days, so that they have an understanding of the environment their child is working in.'

'No, I'm sorry, I can't,' replied Abby, 'I work in the mornings.'

'Oh?' Mrs Cantley, still smiling, appraised Abby once more, gazing at the tall woman who, even in her scruffy sweatshirt and jeans, had the effortless poise of a model. She looked quite unlike the other mothers. Was she an artist, perhaps? She had that sort of undomesticated, unconventional look about her. 'May I ask what it is you do? I'm so interested in other people's work.'

Abby smiled. 'I'm a cleaner up at Hemwood House – starting today, in fact.'

To her credit, Mrs Cantley reacted to this with as much smiling interest as if Abby had said she was a neurosurgeon. 'Oh, really? Hemwood House? The late Mr Maskelyne's place, isn't it? Very sad about his death.'

76

Abby glanced at her watch. 'Well, I'd better be off.' She went over to where Chloe was being helped into a painting overall. 'Bye-bye, sweetheart.' She stopped and gave Chloe a kiss, then said goodbye to Mrs Cantley. Mrs Cantley smiled and waved her fingers, watching thoughtfully as Abby flicked her blonde hair back from her shoulders and left.

Abby walked back along Church Street. She saw no one she knew. As she passed the garage, she glanced up the lane which led to the woods and eventually to Hemwood House, but she did not take that route. She wanted to go through the Dips, where she hadn't been for over fifteen years. She carried on walking until she reached the church, then turned up the narrow, grassy pathway which lay between the church wall and a row of cottages. The path straggled past the graveyard and through the trees into the Dips, and as she walked along it, Abby felt a small tingle of apprehension, waiting for melancholy and sentiment to hit her. But she felt nothing like that. It was just the old path, smaller-looking now, of course, winding as it always had past the trailing bramble bushes with their green nubs of early fruit, past the big boulder where she and Stephen used to lie in wait to ambush his dopey sisters, through the clearings and bushes, up to where it met the path through the woods. The day was clear and still, like any day from her childhood, broken occasionally with birdsong. She glanced towards the line of trees bordering the dusty gully, and saw that a rope with a tyre tied to one end still hung from one of the branches. That pleased her.

She stopped to catch her breath as she reached the steepest part of the track. Thirty-three wasn't old, but the years made a difference. As a child she would have scrambled straight up without pausing. When she came to the main path, Abby slowed her steps until she was no more than strolling through the shadows of the trees at the very edge of the wood. She paused, pushing her hair back from her face with both hands, and surveyed the tennis court. Or what was left of it. Cushions of moss had spread out across the pitted surface of the tarmacadam where the trees overhung it, and drifts of needles from the two old Douglas firs lay heaped in one corner. The posts were still there, but the netting was long gone, and the markings were barely visible. She pictured herself and Stephen patiently batting tennis balls in high lobs back and forth to one another with heavy, wooden-handled tennis rackets, shouting this and that across the summer air. The memory was tinged with no sentiment, no particular sadness or happiness. It was just a recollection. She wondered whether Stephen would bother to resurface the tennis court, put up a new net, now that the house was his.

She carried on up the path, passed through the creaking iron gate set in the wall, and walked towards the house. Abby had just the faintest childhood recollection of Hemwood House. The only times she had been inside were on the few occasions when she and Stephen had come to snatch a drink of water from the scullery sink. Stephen had spent many tea-times down at Alma Cottage, eating toast and jam and watching *Huckleberry Hound* and *Blue Peter* with Abby in front of Ruth's fire, his shoes off and his feet propped up on the coal scuttle, but Abby had not enjoyed the same kind of familiarity at Hemwood House. It was not a place where chidlren played – not children from the village, at any rate.

Abby stood for a moment in the early summer sunshine, enjoying the tranquil beauty of the house and the gardens. How much some people had, and how little others. It was a thought which had never crossed her mind as a child. She had never consciously compared Stephen's life to her own – at least, not until he had been sent away to school – but now she could not help thinking how very different his life must be from hers. Then she reminded herself that she had no idea of who he was any more. Sixteen years was a long time.

She walked past the kitchen garden to the back door, which stood open. It led through a narrow, stone-flagged vestibule into the scullery, and then into the kitchen. Abby stood in the scullery for a few seconds, glancing round. The stone sink was still there, next to a washing machine and tumble-drier. She remembered how she and Stephen had had to hoist themselves up on the edge of the sink, feet off the floor, to reach the tap. She carried on through to the kitchen, from which came the sounds of Radio 2, and found Doris, in a floral wraparound pinnie, putting cups into a dishwasher.

'Hello,' said Abby.

Doris looked up quickly, put her hand to her breast. 'Oh, you did give me a start. I always used to hear Melanie coming.'

'Quiet on my feet, that's me.'

'I'll make us a cup of tea,' said Doris. 'Chloe settle into her school all right?'

'Oh, yes.' Abby glanced round the kitchen. It was large and high-ceilinged, with smooth beechwood cupboards, an Aga, an old dresser ranged with plates and jugs. At one end stood a scrubbed wooden table and chairs, and through the long, low window the pale sunlight fell in pretty oblongs on the stone floor. But it seemed to Abby that something was lacking. It did not feel like a place where things happened much, or where food was often cooked. There were no bunches of herbs, no bowls of fruit, no plants on the window-sill, no jars of pasta or strings of onions. The work surfaces were barren, and the shining sink looked clinically clean.

Abby and Doris sat down at the long wooden table and drank their tea. After ten minutes Doris decided that Abby was not, as she had suspected, going to prove very rewarding company in the way of gossip. Maybe it was something to do with the generation gap, but she didn't even have much to say about Mrs Cantley, and most people had a good deal to say about her. She sighed and got up. 'Come on. I'll show you where we keep all the things, then I'll take you round the house. Melanie always used to do downstairs at the start of the week, then work her way up.'

When the cupboards containing buckets, brooms, dustpans, disinfectant and Ajax had been inspected, Doris took Abby on a tour of the house. 'Study . . . dining room – that table needs a good waxing, but only every other week – downstairs sitting room . . . there's a special attachment on the hoover that you need for those curtains. All this porcelain is very precious, so mind how you go. Fiddly to dust. There's a lot more to do than you'd think, with all these knick-knacks and pictures, and all this furniture needs polishing. Then there's the floors . . . Now the billiard room, you don't need to bother with much, beyond hoovering – everything's been covered up for a while now . . .'

They came back up the corridor from the billiard room. 'It's terribly quiet,' observed Abby. 'It'll be like cleaning a museum.'

'Well, it was quiet enough when Mr Maskelyne was alive, but at least there was people to cook for, his daughters coming and going, the odd visitor, and more than enough phone calls. But now . . .' Doris sighed, standing in the middle of the hallway, looking around. 'I used to put a bowl of fresh flowers on that table every other day, even though Mr Maskelyne hardly ever stirred out of his room, but there doesn't seem much point now. It was *his* house, you see, and now that he's gone, all the life's gone out of it, too.'

'What about Stephen?'

'Oh, it belongs to him right enough, but he won't live here. He's young, got some job in London. What does he want with a place like this? Unless he marries that girlfriend of his, of course. Mind you, he's had that many girlfriends. Too choosy by half. You watch. He'll go all round the orchard and pick a crab in the finish.'

Doris had not bothered to lower her voice, and Abby guessed that Stephen wasn't in the house.

'Where is he today?'

'Stephen? Oh, he went over to his sister's last night for dinner. Geraldine's, that is. His car's not here, so I take it he stayed the night. They have a lot of family business to discuss, I expect. Like they say, where there's a will there's relations.'

Abby felt faintly disappointed. Not that she had any reason. Any encounter between them would be quite mundane. She was just the cleaner here, he was the rich owner of the place. They were all grown up now.

When Doris had taken her through all the upstairs rooms, Abby set about her work. It was peaceful, mindless stuff. As she squirted Harpic into the lavatory in the downstairs cloakroom, she made a mental note to bring her Walkman up with her the next day, give her something to listen to. She stared at the neat pile of clean towels next to the sink and at the little wrapped cakes of guest soap. Why did Doris bother? Habit. And maybe people would come, after all. Maybe Stephen would invite a whole load of friends down from London every weekend, throw wild parties. Then again, maybe not.

At half eleven, as she was getting stuck into the drawing-room fireplace surround with a cloth and a tin of Brasso, Doris came through. She looked disgruntled.

'Stephen's just rung to say he's going straight back up to London. Says there isn't enough to keep him here. He'll only be down the odd weekend. I told him, I said, what am I going to do with myself all that time? So he said, stay home if you like, just see the place is kept clean, I'll let you know when I need you again.'

Abby, kneeling by the fireplace, pushed her hair out of her eyes and shrugged. 'I don't mind letting myself in in the mornings. I know where everything is now.'

'Well, I don't know . . .' Doris settled herself on the edge of a Hepplewhite chair, letting her mild indignation die away. She gave Abby a thoughtful glance. 'Could you manage on your own? Seems pointless me being here when I'm not needed. I could ask Reg Fowler to keep an eye on things when you're not here, and set the burglar alarm at night. He may be as dim as a Naafi candle, but I suppose I can rely on him to do that much.'

'Well then.'

'I told Stephen, I said Mrs Owen's daughter is doing the cleaning, and he seemed to think that was fine. Said as long as it was someone who could be trusted.'

Was that all he had said and thought? wondered Abby. Was she just a name he remembered vaguely, someone from the village? Well, there was no reason why he should remember her in any special way.

'Don't worry,' said Abby. 'I'm happy here by myself. It's only a couple of hours every morning. Why don't you show me which key does what, and then drop them off down at Mum's this evening?'

'You sure you don't mind?' asked Doris. Truth to tell, she would be relieved not to have to come up here every day. The whole atmosphere of the house had changed, and she didn't think she could bear the quiet, with so little to do.

'No, really,' said Abby. She rather liked the idea of being alone in this house, without Doris's elderly presence, just the hush of the beautiful rooms for company. 'I'll just finish in here, then I'm off to get Chloe.'

Stephen drove down the M11 at a leisurely pace, feeling fairly contented with life. He had been doing a good deal of thinking about his new-found wealth, and the status it would bring him. Maybe he should seriously consider packing in work at the agency. It was beneath him, really, to be scratching around on mediocre accounts for an agency which was, let's face it, only moderately good. Certainly not among the top ten. Or what about raising his game there, buying in? Then it would have to be Dacre Roper Sweeting Maskelyne. Somehow that didn't sound as good as Dacre Roper Sweeting. That ran off the tongue. DRSM. That sounded better. Stephen slipped in an Ella Fitzgerald tape and hummed along to the music. Then again, maybe it took more than mere money to get on a par with those boys. Each one – David Dacre, Paul Roper and Roger Sweeting – had made it very big creatively in their own right. Stephen hadn't exactly proved himself. They might not want his money. He could just finish up with a humiliating rebuff. Possibly it wasn't such a great idea. Anyway, he wasn't that keen on any of them. In fact, David and Paul were condescending shits – to him, at any rate. No, better to chuck it in. He would find something else to do, now that he had the money. Set up his own agency, perhaps . . . But Stephen knew that he didn't have the drive or the personality to create a successful agency of his own. He wasn't that interested, anyway. So what *could* he do?

Ella Fitzgerald began to sing about taking Manhattan, and Stephen's imagination drifted to skyscrapers, Fifth Avenue, chic restaurants . . . Inspiration suddenly came to him. A restaurant. He could open his own restaurant. Now that was something he'd really like to do. A trendy place on the river, Butler's Wharf, with a first-rate young chef, someone beginning to make a name . . . He would decide the decor – or let Harriet, she was good at that kind of thing. It would be chic, exclusive. Jonathan Meades would give it a brilliant write-up. It would become the place to eat and be seen. Famous people would go there, celebrities, and he would meet them, get on first-name terms with them. That way he would join the rich people's club, but still be doing something with his talents.

Because he did have talents. Creative ones, that weren't being properly explored at DRS. Stuff the agency. Yes. He would become a figure, someone people wanted to know. Running a restaurant had cachet, especially if people knew you weren't really doing it as a commercial thing, more as an amusement. Like Sir Terence Conran.

Stephen wove this delightful fantasy all the way into London, and by the time he got to his Pimlico flat he was so excited that he wanted to tell Harriet about it immediately. He rang her at her studio.

'Hi. I'm back.'

'I thought you were going to ring from Hemwood? I stayed in all Saturday night.' Harriet laid down her brush and made a little 'relax' sign to her model, a slim young man in his early twenties, clad only in a pair of striped boxer shorts, and sitting on a wicker chair. He had a slender face, handsome in a foxy way, good-humoured, and his blond hair was rumpled. He leaned forward in his chair and rubbed his face with his hands.

'Sorry. Things got rather hectic,' replied Stephen. He told lies casually, thoughtlessly, not thinking of them as lies at all, more as turns of phrase.

'How was the funeral?'

'Glum. Family glum. Naturally. But I went to see Father's solicitor on Friday.'

'That would cheer you up, I imagine.' Harriet glanced at her canvas, lifted a thumb and smudged some colour. The flesh tones on the neck still weren't right.

'More than a little. Anyway, that's what I wanted to talk to you about. I've got some projects. Can you do lunch?'

Harriet sighed inaudibly. 'I'm working at the moment. I'm really getting stuck in, actually . . .' She sounded undecided.

'Come on. It's only twelve now. Carry on working for a bit, and I'll meet you just after one. That place round the corner from you.'

She smiled and gave in. 'All right. See you there.'

Harriet put the phone down and glanced at Charlie, who was stretching his muscular arms high above his head.

'Stephen?' he asked, dropping his arms down and leaning back.

'Stephen. I'm meeting him for lunch, so you can clock off in half an hour. Sit up.'

Charlie resumed his pose, one leg across the other, ankle resting on knee, his right arm on the back of the chair, the other lying loosely in his lap.

'This is a dog's life,' he said. 'Why am I doing this?'

'I don't know. Go and get a proper job.' Harriet picked up her brushes and began to paint again.

'I am a resting actor, darling. I don't want a proper job. What if an audition comes up? At least this is flexible, though the money you pay me is lousy.'

'Don't bother, then. I can get someone else.' Harriet gave a sweet, critical smile, narrowing her large eyes. 'Tilt your chin up a bit to the left.'

'Not with a body like mine you won't,' replied Charlie with a self-satisfied air. 'Anyway, this artist–model relationship is all wrong. I thought artists kept their models, slept with them, that kind of thing. Why don't you keep me?'

'I doubt if I could afford you, Charlie,' murmured Harriet.

There was silence for a moment, while Harriet painted. Charlie gazed at her. He hadn't really thought much about Harriet when he'd first started sitting for her, but recently he'd begun to find her something of a turn-on. She was so slight, with that slender neck and dark, cropped hair, big eyes. He wondered what her body was like beneath the baggy shirt and paint-splashed trousers. She always went barefoot round her studio, and these days he even found her small, naked feet erotic.

Suddenly he said, 'Why don't you sleep with me, then?' He uttered the words lazily, but there was nothing idle about his tone. Harriet knew a genuine proposition when she heard one.

She gave him an easy smile. 'Because I happen to be in love with Stephen. And I don't sleep with my models.'

'Oh, well,' sighed Charlie. 'The offer's there if you want it. Only you'll have to pay me double time.'

Harriet just laughed.

*

'I hadn't realised how much money he had,' said Stephen, as he tucked into his ravioli. 'Not really. Not until now.'

Harried leaned her chin on one hand and gazed thoughtfully at her salad niçoise. 'If he was so rich, why didn't he give you money when he was alive – help you out, like the time you wanted to set up that design consultancy?'

'I don't think he believed in making life easy for us. Or maybe he was just tight. Anyway, it's all there now, plus the house.'

'So, what are you going to do now, O rich one?'

Stephen put down his fork. 'That's precisely what I wanted to talk to you about. I've had this brilliant idea. I'm going to open a restaurant.'

'A restaurant?' She laughed. 'What do *you* know about restaurants?'

Stephen shrugged. 'Not a lot. But I'll get hold of people who do. What I've got is the money to put up for the capital investment. Look, I don't want to sit around writing crappy advertising copy all my life – I'd go mad. And I can't just moulder away down at Hemwood. I need to put the money to good use. Being rich is – is a sort of responsibility. A social responsibility.'

'What?' Harriet could not suppress her laughter. Stephen frowned, and she smiled at him fondly, thinking how much she loved that uncertain, boyish look of his, his way of appearing vulnerable and defiant at the same time.

'Look, being rich is inevitably going to change me. I'm going to be doing new things, meeting new people. Money does make a difference, you know.'

'Does it?' Harriet had stopped smiling. He was such a child. She could read this plan perfectly. Stephen wanted to be someone, and he thought that running a restaurant would give him an entrée to some world where he imagined he belonged. Oh, well, if he had the money, why shouldn't he do as he wanted? It was just that the way he spoke seemed to put some sort of distance between them, as though his new-found wealth would take him somewhere that she could not go. The idea frightened her. She needed Stephen in a way that she had never needed anyone before. People thought of her as a clever, independent woman, happy to work away at her paintings and make her own life, but that was far from the truth. Harriet simply wanted someone whom she could love without qualification, someone to belong to. Stephen, with his weakness and vanity and numerous other faults, had, to her surprise, turned out to be that person. Even his small failings brought out the protective instinct in her, and made her love him more. For the past few months she had nurtured the simple hope that he would ask her to marry him. She had imagined that, if anything, inheriting his father's money would make it easier for him to do that, and instead he spoke as though it would take him further away from any kind of domestication. She gave a shrug. 'Why do you need to discuss your great plan with me?' she asked, knowing it sounded petty, but unable to help herself. 'Why don't you just go ahead and do it?'

'Harry, you know I need you,' said Stephen, his voice tender, coaxing. 'I don't want to do anything without you.' He laid a hand over hers.

She felt a small, warm surge in her heart. 'Don't you?'

'What kind of fun is it going to be on my own? Anyway, I need your invaluable expertise. You can design the interior, decide on colour schemes, cutlery, everything.' He gave a small, reckless laugh. 'I'm so excited about this – it's going to be absolutely marvellous, I promise you!'

'Hold on – I'm not an interior designer. I just paint pictures.' She laughed, too, infected by his ebullience.

'I don't care. You'll do it brilliantly, I know you will.' He leaned forward and kissed her.

If only, she thought, if only he would ask me to marry him, make me feel I was properly part of his life, that we were going to do everything together. 'What about the house?' she asked, sitting back and looking into his shining eyes.

'We can live there at the weekends,' said Stephen, still riding his wave of enthusiasm. 'Have a place up in town so that I can keep an eye on the restaurant, and go to Hemwood at the weekends. And you can have loads of kids, and life will be wonderful'. Happiness at the prospect of his exciting new fortune encouraged Stephen to talk carelessly, aware that this was the kind of thing she wanted to hear. When Stephen was happy, he liked the people around him to be happy, too. It didn't have to mean anything.

'There are one or two other things to think about before we get to children,' said Harriet with a quiet smile.

Stephen looked down at the small, paint-streaked fingers curled beneath his, and felt suddenly cautious. He loved Harriet, he wanted her to get involved in this project, to keep him buoyed up and confident, and to inject her help and ideas, but he wasn't sure he was ready to marry her. In the car on the way down he had had some very pleasant daydreams about the kinds of women he might meet in his new life. He needed Harriet for now, but things could change. This restaurant – and the ones to follow, maybe in San Francisco, Paris – could turn him into a pretty important guy. Still, there was no harm in letting her think whatever she wanted. He probably would marry her in the end. Someday, when he was ready to settle down. He leaned across and kissed her again. 'How do you manage to read my mind?' he murmured. Harriet felt flooded with happiness. It was as good a way of saying he wanted to marry her as any. Almost. 'But,' continued Stephen, switching to a businesslike tone, 'first we have to get this project off the ground. What I need is a partner – someone with a bit of know-how.'

Harriet thought for a moment. 'What about Russell, that friend you were at school with? Didn't you say he used to work on the management side of one of those fast-food chains? You know, the American sort of things, I can't remember their name.'

'Fifth Avenue Diners.' Stephen made a face. 'It wasn't exactly the kind of thing I had in mind. I want this to be something exclusive, Harry – a Marco Pierre White sort of thing, not ribs and burgers.'

'Oh, Stephen, that's not the point. You just need someone who's been in the business. Who knows about things.'

'Hmm, yes, that's true. And Russell's a good man. It needs to be someone I can trust. He's an ideas man, too. I could work with him . . .' Stephen was beginning to warm to the idea. 'Yes. Clever girl. You're making yourself invaluable already. I'll give him a call. If he's keen, then I'll invite him down to Hemwood next weekend to discuss it. Rose might like to come too. That's his girlfriend. You'd like her.' Stephen motioned to the waiter for the bill. There was something rather grand about the idea of summoning people down to his large country house for the weekend to discuss business plans. Harriet could act as hostess, looking after everyone's creature comforts. He had a vision of Harriet and Rose wandering round the gardens at Hemwood House in filmy dresses and hats, while he and Russell sat over whisky, laughing and talking, men of the world. He thought he was going to enjoy being rich very much.

'Is that where we're going this weekend?' murmured Harriet. 'I'm glad you let me know.' But she felt happy, already a part of his new world.

Chapter Seven

A week later, on Monday morning, Abby dropped Chloe off at the nursery and set off up the path through the Dips to the house. She had left her mother still in bed. Ruth complained of not having slept well, and of having very little energy. Abby had made tea and toast and taken it up to her, and assured her that she need do nothing – Abby would attend to it all when she got home.

If there was any good thing to be said about her mother's illness, thought Abby, as she skirted the brambles, it was that it had had the effect of improving relations between them. They were gentler, easier with one another, Chloe moving between them with a happy neutrality, content at her nursery school and calmly accepting of her new life. Ruth took pleasure in the company of her daughter and granddaughter, now that she felt less like going out. Abby enjoyed the morning hours spent at Hemwood House, going about her chores in silence. She had abandoned the Walkman on her first day there alone, realising that it might prevent her from hearing the telephone or the doorbell. It was absorbing enough being the temporary custodian of so lovely a house. Abby had never in her life lived in anything but the most mundane surroundings. Now she had time to admire and enjoy all the costly objects, carpets, furniture and paintings which Leslie Maskelyne had collected throughout his lifetime. In the upstairs drawing room, on top of the piano, she had found a collection of photographs of Leslie's children in silver frames, and the sight of Stephen's face made her wonder how she could ever have forgotten what he looked like. She felt an unexpected tightening of her heart as she picked up the heavy frame and gazed at the picture. He must have been twenty or so when it was taken. The same boyish good looks, slightly sulky mouth, dark, expressive eyes, thick brown hair. She imagined that she would not find him changed at all.

Abby sang to herself as she walked through the woods. There was something to be said for getting away from the relentless grind of London. She could happily live this kind of life, for a few months, at any rate. She let herself in at the back door of Hemwood House and went through to the kitchen. She could see immediately that the place had been occupied over the weekend. A collection of dirty glasses stood by the sink, together with several unwashed pans and a number of wine bottles. Clearly whoever had cooked the last meal didn't believe in cleaning up as they went along. Abby opened the dishwasher. It was stacked full, but at least it had been set off the night before. She filled the kettle and plugged it in, then began to unload the dishes.

Stephen lay in bed, listening to the faint sounds from downstairs. Poor old Mrs Cotterell. She wouldn't be too pleased at having to clear up all the mess from dinner last night. Russell had got rather carried away with that sauce he insisted on making. Oh, well, it was what she was paid for. He glanced at Harriet, who was lying next to him on her stomach, the pillow bunched up against her face, wearing Stephen's pyjama jacket. She was still fast asleep. Quietly Stephen got out of bed. He badly needed a pee, and a hefty dose of coffee.

Abby had just dropped a tea bag into a mug and was about to pour boiling water on to it, when Stephen appeared in the kitchen doorway. He was wearing a rather grubby towelling robe and his face was unshaved, his hair on end.

Abby's heart gave a small leap of surprise. Then she said, 'Hello, Stephen,' as though she had last seen him yesterday.

Stephen stared at the tall, blonde woman who was calmly making herself a cup of tea in his kitchen. It must be the cleaner, he realised. She had a damn cheek, thinking she could use his Christian name, and smiling at him in that know-it-all way.

'I take it you're the cleaner?' asked Stephen. 'In which case, it's Mr Maskelyne to you.'

'Don't you know who I am?' asked Abby. Her voice was gentle, amused.

'I don't care, quite frankly,' replied Stephen. 'And when you've finished your tea, perhaps you'd be so kind as to make me a pot of coffee.' His head was aching. He didn't know if there was any aspirin in the house. Maybe Harriet had brought some. He glanced at the blonde woman again. At any other time, and in any other circumstances, he wouldn't have been so bloody rude to her. She was far too nice for that. The legs beneath that awful, cheap, denim skirt were long and slender, and the face was worth a second look any time. Still, she was just a cleaner. Why was she smiling at him in that way?

Abby eyed Stephen reflectively. The skinny boy she had played with had turned into a good-looking man, the face only slightly heavier than in the photo on the piano upstairs. Was he always this ill-tempered and unpleasant, or could it be that he was merely hung over? She sipped her tea, set down the mug, and said, 'I'm Abby. Abby Owen. Remember?'

'Abby.' Stephen sat down on the edge of the kitchen table. A hundred recollections and images flooded his mind at once. A sledge made out of a cardboard box bumping and sliding wildly down the steep side of the Dips, Abby, all thin legs and wild hair, shouting and waving at the bottom as he hurtled towards her. The two of them crouched in the magical, cramped confines of their den in the bushes, where they kept their secret stash of comics and gobstoppers underneath a packing case. The tyre in the gully. Ambushing Geraldine and Lydia with water-pistols. Making wine out of brambles and selling it to Mrs Cotterell and Abby's mother for pennies. Pretend cowboy shoot-outs from behind the rocks. And then another, later time, a summer's day when they were teenagers, when he had tried to express his pent-up adoration of her by kissing her, the culmination of months of adolescent yearning and fantasy cooped up in boarding school. And failing.

And hating her. This her. This same smiling, blonde creature. How on earth had he not recognised her? 'Abby,' he said again. Then he laughed, partly to suppress the faint, unexpected pain he felt at the recollection of how she had humiliated him when he was a teenager. 'Well, well,' he managed to say at last, recovering his self-possession, recalling his new position as master of Hemwood House. It had unnerved him, momentarily, to be made to feel a boy again. Not a comfortable sensation.

In an effort to rid himself of this sudden feeling of insecurity, he looked appraisingly at her. He noticed her cheap shoes, the frayed sweatshirt, her out-of-condition hair tied back in a straggling pony-tail. He saw, instead of his childhood friend, an example of the kind of young woman whom he wouldn't normally give the time of day to. So this was the person Abby had become. Well, that was what happened to childhood friendships. You grew up and everything changed. Things like class and money took over. No room for sentimentality here. It was nice to see her – but she had to understand who he was now. He wasn't a boy any more. Why did he find something disconcerting about her cool gaze? As though she knew what he was thinking, and didn't care.

'I thought the name rang a bell when Mrs C said Mrs Owen's daughter was working here.' He smiled and nodded, and Abby could instantly sense that he intended to keep things friendly, but distant. So this was the man who had taken the place of the boy. Frightened, but of what? 'What brings you back to Hemwood?' he asked, his tone that of a polite stranger.

'My mother's not very well. She has something wrong with her heart. I've come back to look after her for a while.'

'I see.'

There was a silence. Abby felt the urge to take Stephen by the shoulders and shake him, demand that he be pleased to see her, and not look at her in that condescending way. But she knew that this was what he was now, and she must accept it. She felt bitter at the realisation that he did not share her own delight at meeting again. She turned towards the sink. 'Did you say you wanted some coffee?'

Stephen put his hand inside his robe and scratched his shoulder.

He was glad to see that she accepted the status quo. It had all been a long time ago, when they had . . . He did not want to think again about that. The way she had turned then was exactly the way she had turned from him when he had tried to hold her, make her kiss him. How many years – sixteen years ago? God, an eternity. 'Yes,' he said quickly. 'I have some friends staying. Would you make enough for four, please?' He got up and went to the door. 'Anyway . . .' He paused, and she turned to look at him. 'Good to see you again . . . Long time, eh?'

She nodded and smiled. 'Yeah. Long time.'

He left. Slowly Abby filled the jug of the coffee-maker, spooned out the coffee, pressed the button, watched the hot brown liquid trickle into the jug. So there were to be no hugs, no pleasure, no conversations about old times. Of course not. She had been a daft bitch even to imagine such a thing. He was who he was, a rich guy with a life quite different from her own, and she was who she was.

Stephen went slowly back upstairs. He felt annoyed that meeting Abby again should have affected him so much. He had pretended otherwise. But it had.

Harriet was awake now, sitting back against the pillows, her dark hair mussed, yawning and stretching her arms. They looked small and thin in the sleeves of his pyjama jacket. He bent and kissed her, thinking how clean and perfect she was, and how unlike the tall, scruffy woman downstairs. He wouldn't mention it, he decided; he wouldn't tell Harriet that he had just discovered the cleaning lady to be a ghost from his childhood. It was the kind of thing that would interest her, but somehow he did not want anyone to make any connection between himself and Abby. That was in the past, over and done with.

'Come down and have coffee when you're ready. Abby's making some.'

'Abby?'

'The cleaning lady. Daughter of some friend of Mrs Cotterell's,' said Stephen idly. There. That had relegated Abby properly to her new place in his life. If it was to be a place at all. He might have a word with Mrs Cotterell. He wasn't really sure if he wanted Abby as a permanent fixture at Hemwood House. It made him feel vaguely uncomfortable, for some reason.

While Stephen showered and shaved, Harriet put on his pyjama bottoms and went downstairs to the kitchen. There was a smell of fresh coffee, and Abby was setting out cups. Harriet glanced at her as she came in. 'Hi,' she said.

'Morning,' murmured Abby.

Harriet sat down. After a minute or so Abby realised that she was expecting to be served some coffee. Wordlessly she poured Harriet a cup, and placed a milk jug and basin of brown sugar on the table. Idly Harriet picked up the copy of *Vogue* which Rose had left lying about and began to flick through it. From where she stood at the sink, scrubbing the pans, Abby took the opportunity to scrutinise Harriet. She guessed that this was Stephen's girlfriend. One of many, Doris had said. But she'd also mentioned the possibility of Stephen marrying her. Well, she looked just the right type. Fine-boned, classy. From out of nowhere, Abby suddenly felt a small pang of dislike. Harriet glanced up, met her eye and gave a quick smile. Embarrassed, Abby managed to smile back.

After five minutes or so Stephen reappeared. He was wearing chinos and a pale pink shirt, the cuffs rolled up. His brown hair was washed and shining. He barely glanced at Abby. Harriet smiled up at him.

'I recommend Abby's coffee,' she said. 'It's very good.'

So this girl knew her name, thought Abby. She wondered what Stephen had said about her. Abby poured out another cup of coffee and handed it to Stephen.

'Thanks,' said Stephen. He sat down, and just as Abby recommenced her pan-scrubbing, he said, 'Abby, have you got other things you could be doing? I think it would be nice if we could have our coffee in peace.'

Without a word, Abby laid down the pan and pulled the plug in the sink, letting the water drain out. She left the kitchen, fetched a tin of Johnson's wax and the bag of dusters, and went through to the long, silent dining room to begin the week's cleaning.

'I met Stephen today,' she told her mother that evening.

Ruth was fishing a casserole out of the oven. She had got up around ten o'clock, feeling much better, and had decided to cook something nice for their supper. Her heart hadn't troubled her all day, and the faint depression of the last two days had lifted.

'Oh, yes? It's a while since you've seen one another.' Chloe came skipping into the kitchen from the back garden, her hands and overalls muddy. She was digging a pond for Ruth down by the fence, so that Ruth could keep fish in it. Chloe liked fish. 'Come here, you,' said Ruth happily, grabbing at the little figure, hoisting her up to the sink. 'Let's get you cleaned up for supper. You're as black as Newgate's knocker.'

'Sixteen years,' said Abby. 'He's changed, really changed.'

'Well, of course he has.' Ruth dabbed at Chloe's face, wiped her hands, and set her down on the floor again. 'You get the knives and forks out of the drawer for Grandma, there's a good girl.' She glanced at Abby's morose expression. 'He's grown up now, not a lad any more.'

Abby gave a quick, small smile. 'I'm not so sure about that,' she murmured.

Ruth set the casserole on the table and began to spoon it on to plates. 'Well, things change, people move on. You want things to go back the way they were, but they can't.' She thought of Leslie, and wondered if this was entirely true. 'Have some of those carrots. Doris's Eddie picked them fresh yesterday.' Ruth moved Chloe's chair closer to the table and gave her a glass of squash. 'I never thought it was such a good idea, you taking that job up at the house.'

'Maybe you're right. He had some friends staying. It was as though he wanted to put me down in front of them. He asked me – no, he told me to make lunch for them. I said I was off at twelve, and anyway, it wasn't part of my job.'

'What did he say?'

Abby ate a mouthful of food and shrugged. 'Nothing. Nothing he could say.' She sighed, glanced at Chloe and smiled. 'You're tucking in, aren't you?'

Chloe had almost finished the chicken casserole that Ruth had given her. 'Can I have some more, Grandma?'

'Please,' reminded Ruth.

'Please,' said Chloe.

Ruth spooned out some more, gratified. 'She's lost her appetite and found someone else's, by the look of things. Oh, I was thinking, would you mind taking a couple of bags of clothes up to the church hall this evening? Mrs Cantley's got a jumble sale on Saturday.' Ruth wanted to change the subject. She did not like to think of emotional friction of any kind between Abby and Stephen, not now they were adults. It was worrying. Guilt, she told herself. Guilt at not having had the courage to sit down and talk to Abby properly. Soon, she told herself. Soon.

'Sure,' said Abby. 'Don't forget I'm working in the pub this evening, though. I'll take them up and go straight there.'

'Right you are, love.' Maybe she could persuade Abby to give up the job at Hemwood House. Much better that she and Stephen were completely at arm's length when Abby found out he was her near relation.

When Abby went up to the house the next day, she found that Stephen and his guests had left. She wandered through the bedrooms, pulling sheets and pillowcases from the beds and dumping them in a heap on the landing. She was going to have to ring up Doris and mention it to her. She wouldn't have time to deal with all this washing and still get on with the rest of her work. Suddenly the doorbell rang. Abby went to one of the bedroom windows and peered out. A smart, very shiny red Mercedes with a soft top stood on the gravel driveway.

Abby went downstairs and opened the front door. She did not immediately recognise the tawny-haired woman in the blue-and-white sundress standing on the doorstep. She had a white sweater slung over her shoulders, smart white sandals, and wore large sunglasses.

'Can I help you?' asked Abby.

Geraldine took off her sunglasses and surveyed Abby, who was barefoot, clad in old jeans and a T-shirt, her hair loose and untidy around her shoulders. Geraldine thought she smelt lightly of sweat.

'I really don't know. Is Mrs Cotterell about?'

'No. She's not here. She's having some time off. I'm looking after things.' In that moment Abby recognised her. 'It's Geraldine, isn't it?'

Geraldine gazed at her in a careful show of surprise. 'Do I know you?'

'I'm Abby. Abby Owen.'

Abby saw Geraldine's eyes narrow very slightly. 'Abby? Heavens, so you are.' In those few seconds, many faraway recollections came back to Geraldine, and Abby could guess what some of them were. There was a pause, then Geraldine smiled and said, 'How astonishing. So – you're working for Mrs Cotterell, are you?'

'I'm meant to be working for your brother, actually. Whatever.' She stepped aside to let Geraldine in. 'Sorry. Didn't mean to keep you standing there like that.'

Geraldine stepped out of the sunlight and into the coolness of the hall. 'I've just come to pick up some things. Stephen and Lydia and I had a bit of a pow-wow the other evening, and we've pretty well agreed who owns what.' Geraldine actually thought she'd come off rather well in the little bargaining session, and today she was in a very good mood. She glanced at Abby again. 'Tell you what, though. I'm dying for a cup of tea, if you're making one. Then we can have a lovely talk about old times.'

Surprised, but not showing it, Abby led the way through to the kitchen. Geraldine had been a snotty little cow as a child, but, as Abby was beginning to discover, time could alter people in quite remarkable ways.

The two women sat for some time over their tea and biscuits. It amused Abby to discover that all Geraldine's recollections of their childhood encounters were entirely positive ones. She seemed to have obliterated all memory of the water-pistol ambushes, or the time she and Stephen had stuffed gravel down the back of Geraldine's vest and then watched impassively as she tottered home, crying and leaking gravel over the back of her shorts.

'I must say, you make a better cup of tea than Mrs Cotterell,' observed Geraldine.

Abby noticed that she and Stephen and, presumably, Lydia, still clung to the formal mode of addressing Doris, a throwback to childhood. 'She's not exactly over-generous, is she?' said Abby, smiling. 'Water bewitched and sugar begrudged, my mother always says.'

'That's the way I have to take my sugar these days, I'm afraid,' said Geraldine, patting her wonderfully flat stomach. 'I go to the new gym at Sudbury. Have you been there?'

'Not me. Not my scene, I'm afraid. Too expensive.'

'Oh, you should try it, really you should. Not that you look as though you need it.'

Abby merely smiled and picked up Geraldine's empty teacup and took it to the sink. Geraldine glanced over her shoulder at Abby, then looked away with a smile of her own. She could afford to be nice to Abby. Things had changed quite gratifyingly since the days when she had been both afraid and envious of her. Afraid of her tomboyish, unpredictable nature and of the minor torments that she and Stephen devised to inflict upon her and Lydia. Envious of her prettiness, her long, shining blonde hair, and the way in which she could effortlessly charm the brother whose loyalties should have been to his sisters first, but weren't. But what was Abby now? She was still attractive enough, in a loose-limbed, mysterious Darryl Hannah fashion, Geraldine granted that. But the inexpensive, shabby clothes had not escaped her attention, nor the bitten nails and workworn hands, the out-of-condition hair. Abby hadn't exactly got on in the world, for all her looks. Here she was, working as Stephen's cleaner. There was a certain irony in that. Geraldine smoothed one manicured hand down a tanned arm, setting slender gold bracelets tinkling expensively against one another. She got up. 'Now, I'd better see about those things I came for . . .' Geraldine went off in search of her loot, while Abby washed up their tea-things – not worth putting in the dishwasher – and went back upstairs to collect the laundry.

She was in the scullery, trying to work out the programmes on the washing machine, when Geraldine put her head round the door. 'I'm just off. I'll probably have to come back on Thursday to collect a few more bits and pieces. Will you be here?'

'Yes. Until twelve.'

'Fine. And thanks for a lovely cup of tea. It's so nice to see you again. Do give my regards to your mother – hope the hospital doesn't keep her hanging about too long.'

'Thanks. Bye.'

Abby heard the front door slam, then the revving of the Mercedes. All in all, it had been a very civilised encounter. It was encouraging to think that at least one member of the Maskelyne family had apparently made it to adulthood without too many hang-ups.

A week later, Doris called round at Alma Cottage at tea-time in a state of high excitement.

'I've had a letter from Mr Maskelyne's solicitor,' she told Ruth and Abby, settling in her chair at the kitchen table and slipping off her shoes. Abby and Ruth looked at her expectantly. 'He left me something in his will. Mr Maskelyne. A legacy.'

'Really?' asked Ruth. She thought of the piece of paper that lay upstairs in the bureau, together with the marriage certificate.

Doris leaned forward and spoke with slow deliberation. 'Fifty thousand pounds. I couldn't believe it. I said to my Frank, I said, here, read this before I drop down in a faint. Fifty thousand pounds. We're going to take a cruise, buy a new car. I told Frank, we won't have to want for anything. He said, we'll have to invest it carefully.'

'That's wonderful,' said Ruth. She smiled and poured Doris her tea. 'You really deserve it, mind. All the years you've worked up there.'

'I never expected anything, Ruth,' said Doris. 'Truly I didn't. It never so much as crossed my mind.' She sipped her tea and shook her head. 'It's a great deal of money. I hope his children don't begrudge it.'

'Don't you worry,' said Ruth drily. 'It hasn't rained in their kitchen yet. I'm sure they can spare it.'

Doris sat over her tea for some time, talking about the money and what she would do with it, while Abby went upstairs to bath Chloe and put her into her pyjamas. Ruth found it hard to concentrate properly on what Doris was saying. All she could think about was the document which lay upstairs. Something must be done about it soon, if the lawyers were already contacting legatees like Doris. For herself she cared little, but it was important to her that Abby should get the money which Leslie had left her.

At last Doris rose, worked her feet back into her shoes, and took her leave.

'Lucky old Doris,' murmured Abby, coming downstairs with Chloe just as Ruth was closing the front door. Ruth stood in the hallway for a moment, silent. 'What is it?' asked Abby.

'I want to show you something. Go on into the kitchen. I'll be down in a minute.'

Ruth climbed the steep staircase slowly. Damn, damn, the tingling and tightness were beginning again. She went into the bathroom, took her bottle of pills from the cabinet, unscrewed it and slipped one beneath her tongue. What exactly was she going to tell Abby? She felt scared at the idea. She replaced the bottle of pills and went through to her bedroom. The dressing table stood beneath the window, an old-fashioned, kidney-shaped thing with a glass top and chintz frills. Ruth opened the drawer in which she kept her few scant pieces of jewellery, some pictures of her mother and father, Abby's first baby shoes, and other mementoes. She took out the envelope which contained the marriage certificate, hers and Leslie's, and the document. She stood there for a moment, holding it, keenly aware of the sound of her own harsh, laboured breathing in the silence of the room. There was, she realised, a coward's way out of this. Abby need not know everything. She need not know that Leslie was her father. How would that help anyone? It might just make for a horrible mess between Abby and Stephen and Lydia and Geraldine, anyway. Better to keep it clean and simple. The important thing was the money. Stick to that, she told herself. The fact that she and Leslie had married just before his death was sufficient justification for what he had written down on the piece of paper. Clutching the envelope, she went carefully back downstairs. Chloe was in the sitting room, eating raisins from a cup and watching her beloved *Aladdin* on a reconditioned video recorder which Abby had rented from a shop in Sudbury. Abby was in the kitchen, folding up the washing which she had brought in from the line earlier. Ruth sat down at the table, feeling as though she had just run a mile. She hated being so easily tired.

Abby glanced at the envelope which her mother was holding. 'What's that?'

Ruth opened the envelope and drew out both documents. She laid the marriage certificate to one side and unfolded the sheet of paper with Leslie's handwriting on it, then held it out to Abby.

Abby sat down and took the piece of paper from her mother. She read it. Ruth watched the look of slow astonishment spread across Abby's face. She read it again, then looked up at her mother. 'Is this real?' she asked.

Ruth made a small gesture of impatience. 'It's genuine, if that's what you mean. He wrote it. Doris and Reg Fowler witnessed it.'

'I can see that. Why on earth should old man Maskelyne do something like this? Why should he want to leave us all that money?' She laughed. 'It's got to be a joke.' But Abby looked at her mother's face and knew that it wasn't. There was a pause, and then Abby, her voice slow and serious, said, 'Why, Mum?'

Ruth slid the marriage certificate across the table. Abby unfolded it and read it through. She looked up at her mother and shook her head in disbelief. 'You were *married*? You and Leslie Maskelyne?'

'Is that so hard to believe? Old people have feelings, too.' She must be careful now, must not put a foot wrong.

Abby looked back at the marriage certificate. 'Mum, this is dated a month ago.' This was unreal, she thought. Her mother and Leslie Maskelyne . . .

Ruth shrugged. 'Oh, it went back further than that . . . We had been old friends for a long time, you know.'

'No, I didn't know.'

'He wanted to provide for me. This was his way of doing it. I think he had the idea that marrying me would make it – oh, I don't know . . . more binding, perhaps. He didn't want his family knowing, that was the thing.'

'They're going to know now.'

'No,' said Ruth quickly. 'No, I don't want to stir up a hornet's nest. And I don't want all the village knowing. It was just between me and Leslie, and it'll stay that way. The money is the only important thing.'

Abby shook her head again. 'I'm finding it hard to take all of this in. And the money . . .' She looked at both documents again. 'But why me? Why should he leave me anything? He didn't even know me.'

Ruth's heart beat a little faster. Abby was no fool. All it took was one little mental side-step . . . 'I suppose because you're my daughter, and I've always talked about you. He knew you had a hard life.' Ruth looked away. 'Leslie was a very generous man. He liked to help people. I think he got it into his head to help you.' She shrugged.

Abby frowned. 'But, Mum, it's a fortune –'

Ruth gave a short laugh. 'To the likes of you and me, maybe. Not to him.' There was a silence. 'The point is,' said Ruth at last, 'I don't know what to do about it. The money, I mean. That piece of paper. I don't think the lawyers know about it, the ones who are sorting out his will.'

Abby was still trying to make sense of it all. For whatever daft reason of their own, her mother and Leslie Maskelyne had sealed some lifelong friendship by getting married in secret, and now he had left them both all this money. It was extraordinary. It was wonderful. She tried to imagine how Stephen was going to feel about this when he found out. And Lydia and Geraldine. It would put only a small dent in their own fortunes, but they wouldn't like it. Well, stuff them. 'The thing to do,' said Abby slowly, 'is to show this to a lawyer.'

'I don't know any lawyers.'

'There's a place in Sudbury. I noticed it when I was picking up the video. I'll give them a ring, show them this. They'll tell us what to do.' A hundred thousand pounds. She began to think of all the things she could do for Chloe, and for herself. A house, a car. She could make something of herself, become truly independent, get an education, start a business . . .

Ruth's voice cut across her daydreams. 'Not the marriage certificate. I don't want you taking that. No one's to know about that.'

'All right, Mum, don't worry,' said Abby soothingly. 'It's all very confidential, you know. Even if they did know –'

'No. I don't see why even the lawyers should know. The other thing's a legal document. It's all they need.' Ruth's voice was firm, but becoming a little shaky.

'Fine, Mum, fine.' Abby reached out a soothing hand. She stroked her mother's hand for a moment. 'Why didn't you tell me about this before?'

'I don't know,' said Ruth. 'I thought maybe the lawyers – his lawyers – would have a copy. That we'd get a letter like Doris's. Leslie was a very thorough man that way. But when she came round . . .' Ruth shrugged.

'Anyway,' said Abby, 'I know now.'

'Yes,' said Ruth. 'You know now.'

Chapter Eight

Robin Onslow was a man who no longer expected life to offer him pleasant surprises. Thirty-six, divorced, trying to hold together a shaky one-man legal set-up and a bottle-a-day whisky habit, he would often look in the mirror at his receding hairline and feel that his grip on life was fading in just the same way. When his wife had left him eighteen months ago, taking the girls, life had changed. No doubt of that. But he had thought then that he remained essentially the same, a not unattractive middle-aged chap with a good sense of humour and a sociable outlook, despite the drain of maintenance payments and the daily worries of his small solicitor's practice. Then one day, not long ago, he had woken up after a particularly bad binge and realised just how far, without his noticing, things had gone steadily downhill. His flat in Sudbury was shabby and rarely properly cleaned, his meals came from the microwave or the chip shop, he hadn't bought himself new clothes in ages – he'd rather have a couple of bottles of Scotch than new shirts – and although his practice was still relatively healthy, clients had started to dribble away. Reliability, that was the key. He simply wasn't as reliable as he had once been. Some days he didn't get into the office before ten, mildly hung over, while his patient secretary, Jackie, who was underpaid and overworked, fielded calls and tried to deal with the more minor matters. Clients liked their solicitor to be on top of his job. They expected him, or her, to be made of finer moral stuff than themselves, rather like their doctor. It didn't do to be seen leaving the local at closing time the worse for wear. Robin told himself that he would make an effort, that he would cut down on the hard stuff, sort his life out – above all, clear up the backlog of cases and impatient clients. But days passed in the same frayed, frantic manner, and nothing seemed to change. And there were no nice surprises. Until this morning, at any rate.

She sat opposite him, close to the desk, but not so close that he couldn't observe her slim, tanned thighs in faded denim cut-aways. Her clothes, and the long, blonde hair which fell about her shoulders, combined to make her look younger than she probably was. Even though her skin and eyes were as clear as a child's, Robin reckoned her to be somewhere in her thirties. Something about the set of her mouth, and the very direct way in which she looked at him, told him she'd been about a bit. He looked back down at the document which she had handed him, and tried to focus his attention on it. Even after four Alka Seltzer and a cup of Jackie's extra-strong coffee, his brain felt cobwebby.

'It's . . . um, an unusual document . . .' Robin turned it over and glanced briefly at the blank reverse side as though there might be something there to help him. He looked up again at Abby, and found himself wishing that all his clients were as attractive, and that he had not put on yesterday's crumpled shirt this morning. 'You say that this – this Mr Maskelyne gave it to your mother shortly before he died?'

Abby nodded.

'And the will itself is being probated? Mmm. I don't suppose you know who the solicitors are, do you? No . . . well . . .' Robin tapped his teeth thoughtfully with his finger, frowning intelli-gently. Codicils, codicils. What were the rules about them? His brain struggled back to all the things he'd learned for his Law Society exams, and had subsequently forgotten. He'd never had to draft a codicil in his life. Plenty of wills but, extraordinarily, not one codicil. Strange, that. He had to say something. She was sitting there looking at him, waiting. Well, there were no quick answers to anything, anyway. Robin looked up. 'I have to say, Miss Owen, that this is quite a novel situation. Not the kind of thing we country solicitors normally come up against.' He gave a little laugh, leaning back and swivelling his chair slightly.

Abby met his gaze unsmilingly, her blue eyes anxious. 'I just want you to tell me if it's all right. If it's legal.'

'Well, let's hope so. It's certainly a large sum of money . . .' Enough to matter a very great deal, he imagined, to someone like Miss Owen. There was just something in the back of his mind, something nagging him . . . 'But I can't give you an instant answer, I'm afraid. You'll have to leave the document with me, so that I can consider it in greater detail and give you a proper opinion.'

'When would that be?'

Robin was about to say that he would write to her, setting out his views in a letter, and then abruptly changed his mind. Remote though the possibilities were of making headway with this long-legged blonde, one had to make the most of them.

'Why don't you call back early next week?' he said. 'I should have some answers for you by then.'

Abby had no real experience of solicitors, or the way in which they worked. She did, however, know men. She looked across the desk at Robin Onslow, at the pouched features which might have been attractive, were they not so bleared with tiredness and drinking, and the shabby clothes, and knew exactly the kind of man he was. She could tell, too, from his smile and his eyes, what he was thinking about her. Trust me, thought Abby, to walk into the office of a third-rater. It crossed her mind to tell him not to bother, to take the document and go to some other solicitor. But there was something about him which she did not entirely dislike. She felt he was probably honest, whatever else he was. And she was here now.

Abby shrugged. 'All right.'

'I'll tell my secretary to make an appointment for you for next Monday afternoon,' said Robin, folding up the document and leaning forward, trying to sound businesslike. 'Four thirty?' By seeing her at the end of the afternoon, there was always a possibility that business could be extended into a drink or two.

'Fine.'

Robin rose from his desk and showed her out, realising as he stood next to her that she was almost as tall as he was. God, he didn't half fancy her. Not ethical, but who cared? 'I'll see you next week, then,' he said. 'Goodbye.'

When she had gone, he told Jackie to make a note of Monday's appointment, then went back into his room and began to search the shelves for the appropriate volume of *Halsbury's Laws of England*. He stared at the gap in the shelf for some seconds before realising that he'd taken *Weights & Measures to Wills* home with him last Friday, and that, together with the *Oxford Companion to Classical Literature* and Chambers Dictionary, it was currently propping up one corner of his bed where the leg had come off.

On Thursday afternoon, Stephen was sitting in his studio and thinking about heading out of London for the weekend, getting down to Hemwood with Harriet, recharging his batteries. The city was baking in the early summer heatwave, lawns and parks parched, the traffic intolerable, the tourists worse. The chocolate biscuit campaign on which he was working had entirely lost momentum, partly because of the weather, and partly because Stephen spent most of his time these days thinking about his restaurant project. He no longer cared about flogging ring-shaped chocolate chip biscuits. He cared about securing the lease of the prime site which he and Russell had found down on the river. Stephen leaned back from the storyboard on which he had been working and closed his eyes. He could almost hear the gentle lap of water, the murmur of expensively attired guests on the restaurant terrace, the tinkle of cutlery and glass, soft music somewhere, as waiters flitted like moths between candlelit tables and river craft made their way up and down the Thames, the sun sinking low towards Chiswick . . . He opened his eyes. David Dacre stood in front of him, hands thrust into the pockets of his trousers, belly hanging over his belt, his rather protuberant blue eyes staring morosely down at Stephen.

'Came to see how you're getting on with the Frangos stuff,' said Dacre. Then he closed the glass door of the studio gently behind him. Stephen didn't like that. It smacked too much of the headmaster's study.

Stephen tipped his chair forward and yawned. 'It's coming – slowly.'

Dacre folded his arms, and Stephen didn't care for that much either. 'Actually,' said David, 'I came in last night after you'd left to have a look. If you ask me –' Which I bloody don't, thought Stephen, who didn't like the idea of David Dacre snooping around his room after hours. '– it's coming much too slowly.'

'It's the weather, you know,' replied Stephen. 'Not conducive.'

'I don't give a shit about the weather, Stephen,' said David. He began to pace around the room, slowly. When he reached the door again, he seemed suddenly to remember something. He put a hand on the doorknob. 'I don't like it when the client starts to bitch. So if you and Andy don't come up with something remarkably good by mid-July, I'm taking you off the account. And then we'll have to think seriously about rearranging a few things round here.' He left as abruptly as he had come.

Stephen stared at the open door. Bastard, he thought. Rearrange a few things – was that some kind of euphemism for the down-sizing euphemism? Or was Dacre threatening him with the sack? Where was all the creative camaraderie on which the firm so prided itself? Stephen sighed and wondered why didn't he just leave right there and then. Why didn't he just dump Dacre and his fucking Frangos and have done with it? Because the time wasn't yet right. He wanted to get his father's estate sorted out first, get the money in the bank, secure the restaurant site, give Russell a bit of a toe up the arse. Then he would bid farewell to DRS and Frangos for ever. There was, however, one thing he would do, right now. He rolled down his sleeves, plucked his leather jacket from the back of his chair, and glanced at his watch. Four fifteen on a sweltering Thursday afternoon. Sod Dacre and the rest. For Stephen, the weekend started here. He slung his jacket over his shoulder and left.

Harriet gave a tiny start of annoyance and fright when the doorbell rang. She had been deeply immersed in her portrait of Charlie, which was going well, far better than she had dared to hope at the outset. Charlie himself merely blinked with the languor of a cat, then shifted his body and stretched his limbs as Harriet got up, wiping her hands on her shirt.

She padded down the polished wooden stairs to the street door, and opened it to find Stephen standing there.

'I am working, you know,' she murmured in mild annoyance, letting him in and putting her face up to be kissed.

'Then stop,' said Stephen, following her up the stairs. 'I've come to take you away for the weekend. I've had a shitty week at the agency and I thought we could make an early start.'

'Stephen, I've got a deadline. The exhibition's in six weeks, and I can't just chuck days away.'

Stephen followed her into the studio. When he saw Charlie, he felt momentarily startled. He had heard about the fellow whom Harriet was painting, some actor she knew, but he wasn't quite prepared for this. Charlie was standing beside Harriet's easel, snapping the elastic waist of his boxer shorts against his very flat, brown stomach, staring critically at the portrait of himself. The atmosphere in the studio seemed overpoweringly suffused with young masculinity.

'Stephen, this is Charlie. Charlie – Stephen. And,' added Harriet, giving Charlie a mock glare, 'you know I don't like people looking at things until they're finished.'

'Yeah, but this is me, isn't it? I'm entitled.' He stretched out a hand to Stephen, shaking his brown-blond hair back from his face and smiling. 'Hi. Nice to meet you.'

Stephen shook Charlie's hand hesitantly. There seemed something incongruous about this exotic creature lounging half-naked around Harriet's studio.

Harriet draped a cloth carefully over the almost-finished portrait and sighed. 'Well, it was about time to call it a day. Glass of wine, all?' She went over to the fridge and fished out a half-full bottle of wine.

Stephen did not feel particularly comfortable for the next fifteen minutes. He sipped his wine, listening to Harriet and Charlie's idle conversation but barely contributing himself. He felt relieved when eventually Charlie drained his glass and said he'd better be going. Stephen watched as Charlie picked up a T-shirt and a pair of Levis from the back of a chair. The boy shucked the jeans lazily over his lean hips and slid the T-shirt down across his torso with magnificent nonchalance. He did it, thought Stephen, just as though he'd spent a long and very pleasant afternoon having sex. Charlie put on his shoes and bent to give Harriet a quick peck on the cheek.

'Want me tomorrow?' he asked as he straightened up.

Harriet sighed and glanced at Stephen, then smiled up at Charlie. 'I think not. Let me give you a call on Sunday.'

'Check,' said Charlie. He raised a hand to Stephen. 'Bye.'

'Bye,' grunted Stephen. When Charlie was gone, he knocked the rest of his wine back and regarded Harriet, who was curled up in a round wicker chair. 'Do you always kiss your models hello and goodbye?' he asked.

'I kiss *all* my friends hello and goodbye,' said Harriet sternly, running her fingers through the short ends of her hair.

'Hm.' Stephen looked away, then back at her again. 'Doesn't it make you randy, having some half-naked Adonis sprawled out in front of you all day?'

Harriet threw back her head and laughed. 'No!' She laughed again and got out of the chair and came towards him. She leaned down and took his face between her hands and kissed him. 'The only thing around here that makes me randy is you.'

'Why don't you paint me, then?' asked Stephen, who was half-serious. He thought he'd make a good model.

'Because I wouldn't get a lot done, that's why,' said Harriet and kissed him again. If he wanted to possess her so much, why didn't he just marry her? Life would be so much simpler. 'Now, do you want to set off this evening, or go tomorrow?'

He sat her on his knee and examined her face in the intent, serious way which she so loved. 'Tonight,' he said. 'Let's find dinner on the way. Then we shall have a blissful and untroubled weekend alone together.'

'Wonderful,' said Harriet.

As she came through the fringes of the woods on Friday morning, Abby saw Stephen's dark green BMW parked at the back of the house. Her stomach tightened with nervousness. She had told herself that if the opportunity arose, she would have to mention the business of the legacies to Stephen. It was only fair. Besides, she would need to know the name of the solicitors dealing with old man Maskelyne's estate, so that Robin Onslow could get in touch with them. But, in a way, she had hoped she wouldn't see him, that he would stay down in London and the matter could be dealt with impersonally. The new, adult Stephen was a stranger, a man who bore a passing physical resemblance to someone she had once known, nothing more. She did not want to have to repeat the experience of talking to him again. It had made her unhappy. But he was here, and she could not let the matter pass without saying something.

It was ten before Stephen got up, leaving Harriet still dozing in bed. He showered and dressed before coming downstairs, anticipating that Abby would be in the house, going about her chores. He had thought about her often since they had last met, in a troubled way. He knew that he felt a deep, yet detached fondness for the person he remembered from his childhood, and yet he did not know quite how to deal with the woman she had become. She had a claim on his affections which he could not bring himself to acknowledge. He was uncertain how to behave towards her, overly conscious of their disparate positions. At the same time, though he barely admitted it to himself, she had had a disturbing effect on him. Meeting her again had evoked recollections of the sexual feelings which he had begun to harbour towards her in adolescence, and which she had so cruelly repulsed. All in all, he wished that Mrs Cotterell had found someone else – anyone else – to do the cleaning.

They collided in the narrow hallway leading from the kitchen to the main hall, Abby with a plastic bucket in one hand and a squeegee mop in the other.

'God, sorry,' said Stephen, stepping aside. 'Hello,' he added.

'Hello,' said Abby, and stepped past him.

Stephen went on through to the kitchen, relieved that she didn't apparently intend to hang around talking. If only they could keep it this way, maintain a polite distance. He didn't think he could handle anything else. The sudden sight of her had aroused some powerful, indefinable emotion in him, and it seemed important to him to stifle it.

He was spooning coffee into the coffee-maker when she reappeared in the kitchen doorway a few moments later.

'May I talk to you for a moment?' said Abby.

'Of course,' said Stephen, his heart sinking at the prospect. Yet she didn't sound as though she simply wanted to chat about old times. There was something very composed and intent about her. 'Sit down and I'll make us both a coffee.'

'No, I won't, thanks. No coffee. It's just I have something to tell you. Something you ought to know.'

'Oh?' The slight nervousness in her voice set Stephen at his ease, made him feel a little more in command of things. 'What might that be?'

'Your father left my mother and myself some money.'

Stephen was mystified, but only momentarily. Then he thought: Ah, somebody, somewhere feels they're due something that they're not getting. Well, well. 'I'm afraid not,' said Stephen. He smiled slightly and shook his head, pressed the button to start the coffee-maker. 'I am one of the executors of my father's will, Abby, and I do know the contents. I'm afraid your mother and you aren't mentioned anywhere.'

'No, you don't understand,' said Abby, and sat down at the kitchen table. 'It's not in the will. It's in another document. One he gave my mother before he died.'

Stephen turned to stare at her. 'What are you talking about? What document?'

'Something your father signed, saying he was leaving us each a hundred thousand pounds.'

Stephen felt suddenly angry. This sounded like some elaborate joke. Was she trying to con him? 'Don't be stupid! My father never even knew you, or your mother.'

'Don't call me stupid, Stephen,' retorted Abby. What was he getting so upset about? It was only money, only questions of fact. Why should he get emotional about it? Abby stood up. 'I'm not going to argue with you about it. I just thought that you and the rest of your family should know. Though I suppose your solicitor will tell you about it soon enough.' She turned towards the door, then added, 'Who is he, by the way? My solicitor needs to get in touch with him.'

'Walter Hubbard,' replied Stephen, his anger draining away. She was talking about solicitors, so she must be serious. It wasn't some try-on. But why on earth would his father leave Abby and her mother money? He badly wanted to see this document, to make sense of Abby's bald declaration. 'What – what does this thing say, this document, whatever?'

'You'll see it soon enough, I imagine,' said Abby coldly. She had read something of his thoughts. What a prat he had turned into. She closed the kitchen door behind her.

Half an hour later Harriet came down, wearing a sleeveless dress and sandals, her hair still damp from the shower. Stephen was sitting in the kitchen, going through the post which had accumulated during his absence. It included two letters from Walter Hubbard concerning the estate, but neither made any mention of Abby or her mother, or of this mysterious document.

Harriet poured herself a coffee and looked in the fridge. 'Stephen, there isn't so much as a croissant in here. I'm going into Sudbury to get some things in for the weekend. We can have salad and stuff for lunch, and then –' Harriet closed the fridge and came across to the table with her coffee, '– I intend to lie in the sunshine for the entire afternoon with a very silly book and a cold drink.'

'Do you mind if I don't come with you?' said Stephen, looking up from his letters. 'I have to make a few phone calls. All this stuff . . .' He put Walter Hubbard's latest missive down on the heap of correspondence.

'Of course I don't mind. I hate shopping with you. You just moan. But if there's anything in particular that you want me to get, you'd better tell me now, because I don't intend to go near Tesco's for the rest of the time I'm here.'

When Harriet had gone, Stephen poured himself another coffee and stood staring reflectively out of the window. The knowledge that Abby was somewhere in the house lay like a shadow on his mind. Their brief encounters so far had been strangely unpleasant, and he knew it was largely his fault, that his own uncertainty had led him to behave as he had. He should apologise for the way he had spoken earlier. He didn't want some great blossoming friendship – that was out of the question, such relationships lay in the past, in childhood – but he did want affairs in Hemwood to run smoothly. If there was some question of a legacy owing to Abby or her mother, then it must be handled without any animus. He would go and find her now, while Harriet was out, and speak to her.

He went out of the kitchen and through to the hall. Over the hallway and the landing of the floor above, a glass dome was built into the roof, and summer sunlight fell through its leaded panes on the polished wood of the floor. Stephen hadn't a clue where she might be in the house. Then a sound from the staircase caught his attention, and he looked up. Abby was halfway up the flight of stairs, on her hands and knees, rubbing at the heavily carved balustrade with a duster, her hair falling about her face, her short skirt riding up her thighs. She paused in her work and turned. When she saw Stephen standing there in the middle of the hallway, she stood up, brushing her hair out of her face. She came down the flight of stairs towards him.

'Did you want something?'

Stephen took a couple of steps forward, then hesitated. 'Yes. I wanted to speak to you.' He hesitated. 'Look . . .' She was very close to him now, and he could smell the faintly acrid tang of her sweat. It gave him a curious feeling, evoking a memory of sitting very close to her in the shrubs in the Dips, giggling, hiding from – from whom? Someone. Lydia and Geraldine? Big boys from the village? 'I'm sorry for the way I sounded earlier. I was just a bit taken aback. And the truth is –' Her familiarity, her strangeness, suddenly impelled him to honesty. His next words surprised even himself. 'The truth is, I find it hard to know how to behave towards you. Do you understand that? I mean, you're you, but everything is so different . . .' This was not what he should be saying, he knew. It was too intimate, too personal, leading everything in the wrong direction.

Abby nodded. She stood there, duster in one hand, damp stains in the armpits of her skimpy T-shirt, and Stephen suddenly had an overwhelming urge to reach out and unfasten the little row of buttons at the neck and – no, just to take it in both hands and rend it from top to bottom. He could almost feel how easily that thin stuff would part. And then to touch her. As these thoughts rose into his mind, he meant at first to push them away, bury them. But he didn't. He just let them come. He stared at the light film of sweat on her upper lip and waited for her to say something.

Abby stood gazing at his face, watching the emotions travel across it like the shadows of clouds over landscape. His uncertainty, anxiety, and desire were all there for her to read. She knew exactly what he would do, and wondered whether she should stop him. She could simply tell him he needn't worry, turn around, go back upstairs and carry on polishing the banister. But she didn't. She thought with fascination of all their closeness in childhood, the innumerable times that their bodies had collided, their limbs brushed heedlessly against the other's, and of giggling whispers and innocently intimate spells of concentration, when they had bent close-headed together over a game, or a comic. How things changed, and how much they stayed the same.

Without really thinking of anything, Stephen reached out and touched her face, drawing his fingers slowly down one cheek. Abby closed her eyes, lips parted, and lifted her face slightly, as though towards sunlight. It was a gesture that made her look very vulnerable, childlike. He raised his other hand to the other side of her face and held it lightly. She could feel his fingers trembling very slightly. He stood looking at her, touching her. Her body was inches away from his, arms at her sides, entirely submissive. Something in him wanted to draw the eroticism of this moment out for ever. With one finger he traced a line above her upper lip, and she made a faint sound, eyes still closed. He let his hand drop down to her breast, holding it lightly, stroking the nipple with his thumb. He felt his senses drowning in some giddy heat. Still she did not open her eyes, but parted her lips further. He leaned towards her and touched her mouth with his, kissing her at first lightly, and then more deeply, drawing her against him. It was exactly as he had wanted it to be when he was sixteen. Exactly.

The false barriers he had constructed all melted away in that moment.

He did not know for how long they kissed, was conscious only of the soft and wonderful sensuality of it, her body moving against his, their hands kneading and stroking at one another's clothes.

Suddenly Abby stepped back, leaving him feeling instantly empty and exposed, his arms still foolishly raised from holding her. Her face was expressionless, her breasts rising and falling lightly as she fought to bring her breathing under control. From the moment he had touched her, Abby knew that she should not be letting it happen. This was not the way back. There was no way back. This kind of thing could only lead to confusion and hurt.

'Stephen, forget that happened,' she said. The sudden desire which had washed over her moments ago had left her trembling slightly.

'I don't –'

'It's stupid.'

'No –'

'Please. Forget it.' She struggled to make her voice level and hard, then took a deep breath. 'I'm going to finish my work. Your girlfriend will be back soon. I don't think there's any sense in . . .' She looked away, unable to finish.

Stephen looked at her helplessly, aware of the ache of wanting her and, at the same time, some new, unnamed pain in his heart. Abby turned around and went back upstairs, leaving him standing in the dappled sunlight in the hall, dazed. He did not know how or why any of it had happened. But now she was behaving as though it was nothing, as though it had never been. He would have gone after her, but something made him afraid. Pride. Was it pride? He recalled the blankness of her expression, entirely at odds with the eagerness of her kiss, the response of her body to his. What was that all about? Control? A wish to turn the tables? She might think there was nothing there, that it was just to be forgotten, but he couldn't. Something had been started.

The thought of Harriet, smiling, loving and compliant, flickered into his mind, and he brushed it aside angrily. Realising that he was still simply standing there, that Abby had disappeared upstairs minutes ago, he turned round and went back into the kitchen. Confused thoughts crowded his mind, but the clearest and most insistent image was of kissing her, the feel of her, and he could not let it die away.

Abby did not go near the kitchen again, nor any of the rooms where Stephen might be. She put her cleaning things in a cupboard in one of the upstairs bathrooms and left the house at twelve. She walked through the fringes of the woods, her straw bag over her shoulder, feeling the house behind her, watching her. Stephen watching her. God, how stupid to let that happen. Stupid, pointless, daft, dumb . . . She turned off down towards the Dips, out of the coolness of the trees and into the dusty glare of midday. The steep little track wound away below her. She skittered down as she had in childhood, arms stretched out, setting the tall grasses rocking at either side. Then she suddenly lost control and fell backwards, sliding down the last few yards on her bottom and her heels. When she stopped she simply sat there in the dust, gravel between her toes and sandals, then put her hands over her face. She felt something inside her letting go. She thought that she might cry, but instead a wave of recollected sensuality swept over her, the same overwhelming, melting feeling as when Stephen had touched her, moved against her. She sat on her haunches, thinking, remembering, reliving it over and over. Why was she doing this, when she herself had said that they should both forget it ever happened? It was only sex, something senseless and animal which had touched them both at the wrong moment. Then she looked up at the blank blue of the sky and realised she would be late to collect Chloe. Enough. She would not think of it again. There was nothing there for either of them, not for her or for Stephen.

By the time she reached the main road, other mothers with children from the nursery were already passing by. Chloe would be waiting, the last. Abby broke into a gentle run, and reached the school slightly out of breath. She went into the coolness of the hall and saw Chloe sitting on a small wooden chair in a corner. Mrs Cantley was busy tidying art materials away on the other side of the room, and when she saw Abby she put them down and came towards her. Her face wore a calm, righteously stern expression, one which Abby remembered from the faces of teachers in her own youth. At that moment Chloe caught sight of her mother and raised small, plump arms to cover her face, then began to cry.

'What's wrong with Chloe?' asked Abby. She wanted to go to her, but Mrs Cantley's imposing figure was in the way, and it was clear she had something to say to Abby.

'I'm afraid we have had a little difficulty with Chloe today.'

'What kind of difficulty?'

Mrs Cantley took a deep breath. 'She was in the lavatories with two of the boys, indulging in some extremely silly, not to say offensive behaviour. It was rather a case of – I'll show you mine, if you'll show me yours.' Two spots of colour had appeared on Mrs Cantley's plump cheeks. 'I don't know how else to put it. Genital exhibitionism seems a little too strong.'

'Well, all children do that kind of thing at one time or another, don't they?' said Abby, feeling anxious and relieved at the same time. She didn't want Chloe to get into trouble, but at least this wasn't anything important. 'Besides, it wasn't just her.'

'I'm afraid the boys say that Chloe was the instigator. That it was her idea. And so I have spoken to her about it, explained to her that we do not regard that kind of behaviour in little girls as either appropriate or seemly. Then I put her on the thinking chair in the corner, so that she could reflect a little on what she had been doing, and see that it was wrong.'

'You mean you punished her, and not the boys?'

'We don't "punish" here, Mrs Owen. That is not our philosophy. We merely detach the troublemaker from the rest of the group and explain that they cannot be allowed to rejoin the others until they understand that their behaviour is antisocial.'

Emotions pent up in Abby for the last hour and a half now found direction. 'They're four-year-olds, for God's sake!' she exclaimed, careful not to raise her voice too far, not wanting it to carry to Chloe. 'And what do you mean – you don't "punish"? Of course you do. I don't care how you dress it up, but when you sit my daughter in the corner away from the rest of the children, of course it's a punishment. She sees it as one, and so do the rest of them.

118

And all this nonsense about the "thinking" chair! Do you know what the children really call it? What my daughter calls it? The naughty chair. Now don't you think that's a bit more honest, Mrs Cantley? And while we're on the subject of honesty,' went on Abby, spurred on by the defensive, wary look in Mrs Cantley's eyes, 'did Chloe admit that she started this game in the toilets?'

'No,' replied Mrs Cantley stoutly, 'she denied it. Naturally. And I would not dismiss this as a mere game –'

'Naturally? Why do you take the word of the boys and not hers?'

'I know Colin and Francis very well. They are truthful boys. And I must say, Mrs Owen, that I have not always found Chloe to be entirely straightforward. I have caught her out in fibs more than once.'

Abby took a deep breath, and then counted to ten. There was no sense in laying into this woman. She didn't want to lose Chloe her nursery place. It would mess life up completely. Anyway, they would only be here for another couple of months. Best just keep a lid on it. Oh, but the temptation just to let rip was great, so great. Abby glanced across at Chloe, who was sniffling watchfully.

'Well,' Mrs Cantley,' said Abby evenly, 'perhaps there's no point in discussing this further. Come on, Chlo.' She stretched out a hand towards Chloe, who rose and came towards her.

Mrs Cantley, who had been anticipating the possibility of a full-scale row, felt suprise and mild relief. She inclined her head, fingering her wooden beads. 'I am prepared to say no more about it. I'm sorry that you do not agree with our methods here, but I usually find them most effective. Happily, it is very rarely that any child has to be ostracised from the rest of the group. I only hope it won't happen again with Chloe.'

Watch it, lady, thought Abby. Don't push it. Controlling an impulse to slap Mrs Cantley's large, puddingy face, Abby took Chloe's small hand and led her out into the sunshine. She had entirely forgotten about Stephen. Her mind was taken up with thoughts of giving Chloe some kind of treat to make up for her rotten morning, and of mending the puncture in the paddling pool.

Chapter Nine

Throughout the weekend Stephen found he was unable to rid himself of thoughts of Abby. She was there like a soft light at the back of his mind in everything he did, from the mundane business of cleaning his teeth to the absorbing pleasure of making love to Harriet. He felt guilty about letting her exist in his heart like a third presence at such a time, but he couldn't help it. She was becoming a fixation.

On Friday afternoon he spent half an hour with Walter Hubbard, dealing with minor matters relating to the estate. Stephen told Walter what Abby had said, hoping the solicitor could throw some light on it, but beyond expressing mild astonishment, Walter could offer little advice.

'I must say that it sounds quite unlike your father. He was normally most meticulous in his affairs. I can't imagine him making a codicil without consulting me, but one never knows . . . Do you know the name of her solicitor? I really think we must clear this up as soon as possible.'

But Stephen knew nothing.

On Saturday evening Stephen and Harriet dined with Lydia and Peter. Marcus and Geraldine were there, too, and again Stephen brought up the conversation he had had with Abby. Simply saying her name aloud gave him a pang of furtive pleasure.

Harriet looked across at Stephen in surprise as he spoke, noticing the sudden animation in his eyes. This was the first she had heard of any conversation with Abby, any document. It must have happened on Friday morning, while she was out. She wondered why he hadn't told her about it when she returned from shopping.

'That's perfectly absurd,' said Lydia. She took a small sip of her wine and dabbed at her mouth with her napkin. 'Why should Father leave money to Abby and her mother? The woman's making it up.'

Stephen shrugged. 'That's what I thought. But apparently she's got a solicitor involved. There must be something in it.' Even as he spoke, the memory of her skin, her mouth, was vivid in his mind.

'Perfectly absurd,' repeated Lydia, her voice cold and dismissive.

'I'm afraid not,' said Geraldine quietly. She leaned back in her chair, glancing around slowly at the surprised faces. 'In fact, I know exactly which document Abby was talking about. I found a copy.' She smiled, enjoying the effect of her announcement on the others, then waited a few seconds for the flurry of expostulations and questions to die down. 'It was in the little escritoire in Father's bedroom.'

'What does it say? Why didn't you tell me?' demanded Stephen.

Geraldine shrugged. 'I was going to. In fact, I was going to show it to you after dinner this evening. I came across it when I was picking some things up on Thursday morning. I wanted to show it to you before giving it to Walter Hubbard.'

'You've got it here?' said Lydia.

'It's in my handbag, in the hall. Peter, would you fetch it for me?'

Meekly Peter went to fetch the handbag and gave it to Geraldine, who opened it and took out the document. Lydia reached out quickly for it, but Stephen grabbed it first. Harriet, watching, could suddenly imagine all three as children. Stephen scanned the few simple lines, then passed the paper to the impatient Lydia.

'What on earth was he doing? What *did* he think he was doing?' said Stephen.

'You'd better ask Abby,' said Geraldine. 'Or her mother.'

'Someone put him up to this,' said Lydia angrily.

'It's a quite astonishing amount of money, I must say. Still, it's probably not legal,' said Geraldine.

'It's not just the money – it's a point of principle,' said Lydia. 'If there's a way of fighting this, then I think we should.'

'You might finish up just throwing good money after bad,' said Marcus, who had scanned the document and was now passing it across to Peter. 'Legal costs, and so on.'

'That's true,' agreed Peter nodding.

Stephen and Lydia both raised their voices in dissent, but Geraldine lifted a hand and cut in.

'For God's sake, let's not squabble about this. The best thing to do is to show it to Walter Hubbard on Monday and see what he has to say about it. We're not lawyers. What do we know? Here you are, Stephen.' She took the document from Peter and passed it to him. 'You can sort it out.' She paused, then added, 'Abby was always your special chum, after all.'

Harriet wondered if she was the only one to notice the slight flush that these last words seemed to bring to Stephen's face.

Later, in the car, she brought it up. 'That business with Abby – the document. Why didn't you tell me about it on Friday?'

Stephen glanced at her quickly, then back at the road. 'I don't know. I forgot, I suppose.'

They drove the short distance home in silence, Stephen immersed in his private thoughts of Abby.

Abby had deliberately not thought about Stephen all weekend. It hadn't been too difficult. As long as he was out of her sight, she told herself, he was safely out of her mind. When she arrived at work on Monday morning, she saw that his car was still in the driveway, and felt a moment's unease. But even if she had to encounter him, she decided, she would behave as though nothing had happened between them. The kiss was a mere accident, the result of associations now in the past. She wanted nothing from Stephen now. When she had the money, she would put as much distance between herself and the Maskelynes as she could.

She found Harriet drinking coffee in the kitchen. Harriet gave Abby a small smile, but said nothing.

'Have a nice weekend?' asked Abby.

'Yes, lovely,' murmured Harriet. 'This is a wonderful place to relax.'

'It is nice,' said Abby, hunting in the cupboard beneath the sink for some bleach. 'Murder to clean, mind.'

There was a few seconds silence. Harriet, for some indefinable reason, felt slightly embarrassed. 'Actually,' she said suddenly, 'we should have gone back to London last night. But Stephen has to go and see his lawyer this morning.'

'Oh, yeah?' said Abby. She straightened up, Harpic in hand. She could imagine what that was about. She wondered if Stephen had told Harriet. 'Right, well, I'll be getting on. Nice to see you again.'

'Yes, you too,' said Harriet. Then she added, 'Don't you want a cup of tea before you start?'

'No, ta. I'll get one later.' She didn't want to increase the risk of seeing Stephen by hanging around in the kitchen.

Half an hour later Stephen went in search of Abby. He had persuaded himself that he wanted to talk to her only to tell her about the copy of the document that Geraldine had found, and which he was taking to Walter Hubbard that morning. It was less than half the truth. He would have found any excuse to speak with her, to look at her.

Abby was in the upstairs drawing room, lifting a series of little figurines from the broad mantelpiece and dusting beneath each one. Her hair was tied back with an elastic band, and she was wearing her faded denim cut-aways, a pink cotton vest and battered trainers. She had spent much of the weekend sunbathing in Ruth's back garden, and was sun-tanned, her shoulders faintly red and peeling. Stephen stood in the doorway, watching her for a few seconds.

'Hello,' he said.

She turned, glanced at him, then carried on dusting, wishing he had not come looking for her. It just made it worse. Well, it was too late now, and it had been her fault as much as his. She sighed inwardly.

'I just wanted to tell you that Geraldine found a copy of the codicil. The one you told me about on Friday. It was among some things of my father's.'

'Oh?' She turned to look at him again. 'So you accept now that it exists, do you?'

'I never said I didn't,' replied Stephen. 'I'm taking it to my father's lawyer this morning on my way back to London.'

She put down her duster and went over to a table near the window, where paper and some pens lay. 'You'd better give me his phone number,' said Abby.

Stephen crossed the room, pulling his address book from his jacket pocket. He read out Walter Hubbard's number and Abby scribbled it down. Then she wrote Robin Onslow's name on a separate piece of paper and handed it to him. 'I'm sorry, I don't know his phone number. He works in Sudbury. No doubt your Mr Hubbard can find it easily enough.'

She was as close to him, he realised, as she had been on Friday. He could almost smell her skin, wanted very badly to reach out and touch her hair. He would have given anything not to want her as he did.

'Tell me,' he said suddenly, his voice soft, 'what happened on Friday – didn't it mean anything to you at all?'

She looked up and met his gaze. 'For what it was – yes. But beyond that – no.'

'I don't know what you mean.'

'It meant something. At the time. But there's nothing beyond it.' She went back to the mantelpiece and picked up her duster.

Stephen stood by the table, unable to think of anything to say. She was so cold. He felt he wanted to hurt her in some way, just to force emotion from her. How could she have kissed him as she had, and now behave with such distance? Control. It must be all about control. Well, he knew a thing or two about that, as well. He turned and left the room, closing the door needlessly behind him. At the sound, Abby stopped what she was doing and stood motionless for a moment. Then her shoulders drooped, and she leaned her head against the cold marble edge of the mantelpiece, closing her eyes against the lie she had just told.

*

Walter Hubbard was not in his office when Stephen called.

'I'm afraid he's in court all day, Mr Maskelyne,' Walter's secretary told him. 'Can I take a message?'

Stephen handed her the document in its envelope. 'Please give him this. Tell him that I'll be at my London number this evening. He can call me any time after eight.'

Harriet was waiting downstairs in the car, thumbing through the *Guardian*.

'That was quick,' she said, glancing up as Stephen opened the car door. 'What did he say?'

'Not there. I told his secretary to ask him to ring me this evening when he's looked at the thing.'

Harriet studied Stephen's face musingly as he started the engine and pulled away quickly from the kerb. 'You're really pissed off about this, aren't you?' she said thoughtfully.

'What makes you say that?'

'The way you've been over the past three days. You really don't want her to have any money, do you?'

'Rubbish. I don't care. Why should I?'

'I don't know,' said Harriet. 'You tell me. Maybe she did something unspeakable to you in the dim and distant past.'

Stephen glanced at her, saw that she was smiling, and said nothing.

Robin Onslow was not feeling on top form that Monday. Despite all his resolutions, he'd had a heavy weekend, boozing with chums on Saturday, and then last night supping just a little too much on his own. He hadn't meant to, but somehow when you were by yourself, staring at the telly and flicking through the Sunday newspapers, it was hard to tell how much of an effect the stuff was having. That wasn't the only reason he was feeling down. He gave a gaping, creaking yawn as he glanced at his watch. She'd be here in ten minutes, and then he'd have to tell her the worst. He'd got the relevant pages of *Halsbury* marked. The volume lay to one side of his desk, and beneath it the thin, new file he had opened. The codicil – no, you couldn't call it that – the document was the only piece of paper in it, apart from the time sheet, and the file wasn't going to get any thicker after today. He didn't think he'd have the heart to charge her for the brief piece of research he had done.

It had not occurred to Abby that there could be any doubt about the codicil. She imagined that there were simply a few formalities to go through, that Robin Onslow would speak to Walter Hubbard, that things would be sorted out with the usual lawyers' delays, and that would be that. She felt her first misgivings only when Jackie showed her into Robin Onslow's cluttered ofice, and she saw his face. Beneath the brightness of his greeting his expression was uneasy, and in his eyes she thought she could already read the faintest trace of apology. She sat down, her straw bag on her knees.

'Would you like a tea or coffee, Miss Owen?' asked Robin.

'No, thank you.' She shook her head. She wanted only to hear whatever it was he had to tell her.

'Well,' said Robin, drawing the file towards him, 'let's get on, then.' He took a deep breath. 'I've had a chance to consider this matter properly, and I'm afraid I have to tell you that things don't look very good.'

'Don't they?' said Abby faintly.

'Unfortunately, the document which Mr Maskelyne executed is not a proper codicil.'

'Why not?' asked Abby. Oh, poor Mum. She didn't much care about herself – more about Chloe – but Ruth had been banking on this legacy so much. She had a right to. Whatever this lawyer was about to say, Leslie Maskelyne had wanted her to have the money. 'It was signed and witnessed and everything, wasn't it? What's wrong with it?'

Robin gave a small cough and flicked open the textbook. 'There's nothing wrong with the attestation – well, there isn't a proper attestation clause, as such, but I'm presuming all the formalities were observed . . . No, it's far simpler than that. You see, to be an effective codicil, the document would have to refer specifically to Mr Maskelyne's will.' Abby was gazing at him with sad, blue, uncomprehending eyes. 'It would have to say something like, "This is a codicil to my will dated such-and-such." It should mention the will. To show that it's a further testamentary disposition. That it's part of the will. Without the will, you see –

without being a part of it, the document is nothing.' There was a pause. 'And that is the legal position. I'm awfully sorry.'

'But it says there – it says that he wanted my mother to have the money. And me. He's written it out himself. He *wanted* it to happen!'

Robin sighed. 'I know. But he didn't realise that he had to make it clear that it was a further gift under his will. It's bad luck, more than anything else. But, as things stand, neither you nor your mother has a claim against his estate.'

Abby sat back in her chair. She lifted a tired hand and ran her fingers through her hair. 'I see.'

There followed a silence of some seconds. Robin regarded her sadly. He really wished he could have given her better news. Judging from the look of her, she could have done with the money.

'Well,' said Abby, 'that's it, I suppose. How much do I owe you? Or will you send me the bill?'

He shook his head. 'I didn't do more than open a few books. Well, one, in fact.'

'Hmm.' Abby smiled in spite of herself. He looked so rueful, you'd think someone had just taken a hundred thousand pounds away from him, instead of her. 'Great to be able to charge just for opening a book.'

He smiled back. 'It's knowing which book to open that counts. Anyway, I don't intend to charge you. This one's on the house.'

'You can't run a practice with that attitude, you know,' said Abby.

Robin shrugged. 'It would probably cost me more to have a bill made out, frankly.'

'Well, that's very kind of you.' She sighed. 'Now I have to go home and break the bad news to my mother.' She hesitated and looked at him hopefully. 'You're sure there's no point in taking it any further?'

'We could pass the document on to the executors of the will, wait and see what they say. But their lawyers will tell them exactly what I've told you, and you have to ask yourself whether Leslie Maskelyne's family are likely to pay out money when they're not legally obliged to. Especially large sums like these.'

'Oh, the family already knows about it. Mr Maskelyne's son is seeing his lawyer today. I very much doubt whether they would part with a penny if they didn't have to.'

'We can still make a formal approach, you know, through Hubbard and Harrison. In view of the fact that Mr Maskelyne clearly wanted you both to have the money, they might feel inclined to pay you – well, something.'

Abby hesitated. The idea of going cap-in-hand to Stephen and his sisters wasn't one she relished. If she and her mother were not legally entitled to the money, Abby didn't want charity from the Maskelynes. But could she really afford to be so high-principled? Her mother needed money, if she wanted to have her operation quickly, rather than wait on an NHS list. 'Do you think it's worth it?' she asked Robin.

He shrugged. 'You've got nothing to lose.'

Except my pride, thought Abby. She nodded. 'All right.'

'Fine. I'll write to this fellow Hubbard, and let you know what he says.'

Abby stood up. 'Thank you.'

Robin grasped her hand, which was cool, slim and strong. Should he ask to see her again, have a drink with him, or dinner? Somehow the circumstances didn't seem quite right. 'I'm sorry it had to be depressing news,' he said, moving to open the door of his office for her.

'You can't miss what you haven't got,' said Abby, giving him a brief smile. She slung her straw bag over her shoulder and left.

Ruth was lying upstairs on her bed when she heard Abby come in. She sometimes wondered whether it was worth the bother of coming all the way up those steep stairs for a rest, when it made her so out of breath. She might as well stay downstairs, only there wasn't anywhere really comfortable to lie. The sofa was too short, and she couldn't get the kind of rest she needed sitting in an armchair. She liked to get flat to ease the pressure in her chest. Gently she swung her legs off the bed and sat up. From downstairs she could hear the reedy sounds of Chloe's new *Beauty and the Beast* video.

She heard the front door open and close, and then Abby called up from below. 'Mum?' Her voice sounded faintly anxious.

Ruth would have called back, but it took too much puff, hurt her chest too much. She pushed her feet into her slippers and made her way slowly out of the room and along the short landing. Downstairs she could hear Chloe's voice, little and far away, saying, 'Granny's having a lie-down.'

Abby came to the foot of the stairs and watched Ruth make her careful descent. How slowly she moved these days. Her face looked puffy and rather grey, too. Abby's heart sank at the thought of what she had to tell her mother. There was no putting it off. Ruth had known she was seeing Robin Onslow this afternoon.

'What have you been doing with yourself?' asked Abby, taking her mother's arm to help her down the last couple of steps. 'Taking it easy, I hope.'

'Oh, I've been lying around all afternoon like a churn a-drying. I'm good for nothing else.' She paused at the foot of the stairs and looked expectantly at Abby. 'Well, how did you get on, then?'

Chloe tugged her mother's hand. 'Mum, guess what Colin Webster can do. He has a drink of water and then he shakes his tummy, and you can hear it all sloshing around inside. It's really good.'

Abby looked down at Chloe, smiling and nodding absently. 'That's nice, love.' She glanced at her mother, who had gone ahead into the kitchen to put the kettle on. With Chloe still tugging annoyingly at her hand, Abby followed her through. 'Chloe,' she said, 'you go into the other room and watch your video. I'll read to you after.'

'I want my tea,' whined Chloe. 'I'm really, *reeally* hungry, Mum.'

Ruth handed her a couple of bourbon creams. 'Off you go,' she said shortly. Chloe went obediently, clutching her biscuits. 'Well?' asked Ruth. 'What did the solicitor chap say?'

Abby sat down. 'There's something wrong with it. With the document. He says we don't have a legal claim against the estate.' Her voice was dry, matter-of-fact.

Ruth stopped in the act of spooning tea from the tea-caddy, astonished. 'What's wrong with it?' She set the caddy down and came over to sit down at the table, shocked, her eyes fastened on Abby's face.

Abby shrugged. 'It's not a proper codicil. It doesn't mention the will, like it's supposed to.'

'But it's all written out, clear as anything! I don't understand . . .'

'I know, I know. But according to the law there's something not right about it. Mr Onslow said we could always apply to Stephen's lawyers, but we don't have a legal claim.'

'Apply? What – ask them for the money?'

'Something like that. Maybe he thinks Stephen and Geraldine and Lydia will feel some sort of . . . oh, I don't know – some sort of moral obligation, because their father wrote it out that he wanted us to have the money.'

Ruth's eyes left Abby's face, her gaze travelling aimlessly round the room as she pondered this. 'I don't like to do that . . . Even though it was what he wanted . . .'

Abby got up and went to her mother, bending down to hug her. The gesture made tears spring to Ruth's eyes, and she tried to blink them away. 'I know it's a disappointment, Mum. I'm really, really sorry.'

Ruth gave a shaky sigh. 'Oh, it's more for your sake and Chloe's that I care. And the fact that he wanted to help me. Little enough, God knows, after all this time –' She stopped, then hurried on. 'I was hoping we'd get it, you know. Especially after this came today from the hospital.' She pushed Abby's arms gently away, then went over and fetched a letter from the dresser shelf and handed it to Abby. 'They can't take me until after September. That's where the money would have been nice, to go private and just get this operation over and done with, not to go on waiting and waiting. I get that tired and breathless, I wouldn't care if they cut me open from top to bottom tomorrow . . .' She shook her head. 'I can't believe the document's no good. But that's the law for you. More tricks than a tinker's dog.' She went to finish making the tea, drying her eyes and trying to come to terms with the reality of what Abby had told her. There was to be no cosy retirement, no easeful last years. Every little fancy of what she might do with the money must evaporate like mist.

'The solicitor says he'll apply to Mr Maskelyne's estate and see if they're prepared to give us anything.'

'I don't want charity.' Ruth shook her head.

'If they give us anything, we'll take it. I want to see you well again.'

Ruth said nothing. Abby began to take the tea things out of the cupboard. How long was she going to be in Hemwood now? Maybe until Christmas, at this rate. When she'd come here, she'd imagined that she wouldn't have to stay more than a couple of months at the outside. Stephen wouldn't have mattered. She would have seen him once or twice, and then probably never again. Painful though the idea was, that would probably have been for the best. Now she had no idea of how things would turn out. She set out the cups and saucers, then absently poured Chloe a glass of milk. If they were still here in September, she'd have to send Chloe to the local school. How much would she mind suddenly being uprooted from yet another school, another set of friends, and whisked back to London and a bewildering new chapter in her life, when Ruth was well enough? And what was that new chapter to be? Abby didn't have a clue. For once in her life, the prospect of a new beginning and an uncertain future failed to excite her. The false hopes raised by Leslie Maskelyne's money had allowed her to make plans which were now nothing, so much dust to be blown away. Well, she would think about that later, when her mother was better. The only thing to do was to get on with the present. She went to the kitchen door and called through, 'Chloe, do you want fish fingers or macaroni cheese for your tea?'

'Fish fingers,' called back Chloe.

When Abby turned around she saw that her mother was leaning against the sink, weeping, her shoulders shaking.

Quickly Abby crossed the kitchen and put her arms around her with awkward pity. 'Mum, don't,' she murmured. 'Forget about the money. It doesn't matter that much, you know.'

Ruth could not explain to Abby that it was not for the money that she wept. It was for the sudden, silly memory of sitting in the car with Leslie after their wedding, the smell of his cigarette about them, the rain on the windscreen. He had been so satisfied that day, so full of a sense that he had done something important. She wept now because all his last efforts to touch her life had finally failed.

Stephen was alone in his flat when Walter rang him that evening. Harriet had gone home earlier to do some work and prepare for Charlie the next day.

'Oh, Walter, thanks for calling. I really thought we should clear up this business of the codicil as soon as possible.'

'Quite,' said Walter, who was settling back in an armchair in his house in Colchester with a drink. 'Well, I have some good news for you. The document which your father left in addition to his will has no testamentary effect whatsoever.' He paused, wondering whether he hadn't perhaps expressed himself rather infelicitously. 'Well, perhaps one shouldn't say "good news" exactly. But, at any rate, the estate is not obliged to pay any money to the two Owen women.'

Stephen picked up the phone and wandered across the room. He was very much surprised, but beyond that he wasn't quite sure what he felt. 'Really? I'm no lawyer, but when I read it, I imagined that it would be quite valid.' He listened for a couple of moments while Walter Hubbard explained to him the point of law which Robin Onslow had spelt out to Abby that afternoon. 'I see. Well, well. Father didn't know as much about these things as he thought, did he?'

Walter was slightly surprised by the note of satisfaction which he detected in Stephen's voice. 'No, I suppose not. I imagine he would be disappointed to find his wishes thwarted by a legal technicality,' replied Walter thoughtfully.

'What do you mean?'

'Only that, whatever the validity of the document, he did express himself very clearly. It is always within your power to give effect to his wishes.' Walter did not feel he was venturing too far. He had been Leslie's lawyer, after all, and he had liked Leslie Maskelyne a good deal more than this jumped-up young advertising executive son of his.

There was a pause of some seconds before Stephen spoke, and when he did it was with a tone of false bewilderment. 'I'm afraid I don't see how, on behalf of the estate, I could possibly justify such a thing. I have my sisters to consider. You say that Mrs Owen and her daughter have no claim against my father's will, based on that document?'

'None,' conceded Walter.

'Then I don't see what I can possibly do. You and I are the executors of my father's estate, and as a lawyer I imagine *you* have to stick to the clear letter of the law. I have to consider the interests of my sisters, and I don't imagine they would feel any more inclined than I do to start handing out hundreds of thousands of pounds to people who aren't even entitled to anything.'

'I see,' said Walter. He took a sip of his drink, feeling suddenly tired. What a shit this young man was, to be sure. 'Very well. Am I to take it that this is to be the family's line, should these women apply to the estate for money?'

Despite everything he had said, Stephen could not help feeling a vague sense of guilt. He knew that Abby's mother was unwell, and, after all, his father had clearly meant them to have something. Maybe he should make some gesture – not as much as his father had left them, but something. Then he remembered Abby's impassive face this morning, the tone of her voice. She would know from her own lawyer by now that the document was as good as useless. If he offered her money, she might think that he was trying to buy her in some way, and he was damned if she should think him as weak as all that.

'Yes. That is to be the line.' In a moment of self-revelation, Stephen realised the unmistakable pleasure he felt in knowing that Abby had lost out, that the money she had imagined would be hers was now denied her. Control. Now he had a little bit of it himself.

Chapter Ten

Stephen spent the next week plagued by contradictory emotions. Despite the perverse pleasure he took in knowing that Abby had been humiliated over the matter of the money, he found he was filled with an obsessive longing to see her again. There was no pretext that he could think of, beyond the business of the money. In the end he realised that it would have to do. He persuaded himself that his attitude when he had spoken to Walter Hubbard had been wrong, that it was unfair not to give some effect to his father's wishes. The amount which the family could offer needn't be so large as his father had intended, but it should be generous. In his new frame of mind, quite forgetting the way in which she had behaved at their last encounter, he imagined that Abby would be grateful, softened by his unselfishness. He could easily convince Geraldine and Lydia of the rightness of his thinking. What was important was that he should go down to Hemwood and sort it out as soon as possible. He would speak to his sisters and, of course, he would have to see Abby. This weekend, in fact. He wouldn't take Harriet. She was busy trying to get everything finished in time for her exhibition, anyway.

He thought this all out as he idled his time away in the studio, trying in a half-hearted way to come up with the ideas which David Dacre wanted within the next three weeks. He no longer cared about his work for the agency, but until there was some movement on the restaurant project, which was currently hanging fire until Russell got the lease sorted out, Stephen didn't feel confident enough just to jack it all in. The familiarity and regularity of the place, and the company of his colleagues, provided a necessary bolster for his ego. Until he had created a new world for himself, he was not strong enough to leave the safety of his existing one.

In the middle of the week Walter rang him, and told him that Abby's solicitor had written to him, formally applying to the estate for some money on the basis of the document.

'Good God, a begging letter,' said Stephen. 'Well, as a matter of fact, I've been coming round to the idea that perhaps we should give them something. I'll talk to my sisters about it at the weekend and let you know.'

He drove down to Hemwood late on Friday evening, filled with a sense of subdued excitement. The fact that the prospect of seeing Abby again could generate such a feeling was not something he liked, but he was helpless. In the deep silence of the house, he poured himself a drink and paced about the rooms, creating various scenarios, working out things he would say to Abby. He had no idea of the sense of any of it, except that he wanted her. Above all, he wanted her to feel for him with the same intensity. He created in his mind a new and perfect Abby, submissive and loving, and told himself that if he could just hold her again, touch her, then she would respond as she had before.

After calling his sisters and telling them that he would see them the next evening, he went to bed and slept badly, waking every two hours or so to the same intense thoughts, then drifting back into troubled dreams.

On Saturday morning Abby stood in the back doorway of Alma Cottage in her dressing gown, a mug of tea in her hand, watching the early sun burn away the mist which pearled the fields, lifting it, warming the trees and the grass. It was the promise of another hot day. She went back into the kitchen where the washing machine was chugging into its final spin. Above her she could hear the sounds of her mother in the bathroom. Chloe sat at the kitchen table with a bowl of Coco Pops.

135

'What are we doing today, Mum?' asked Chloe.

'I don't know,' replied Abby vaguely. 'What would you like to do? Go swimming?' She regretted this as soon as she'd said it. The place at Earl's Colne would be heaving with people on a hot Saturday.

'Could Emily come?' Emily was one of the girls at nursery school whom Chloe had befriended. In fact, Chloe claimed her as a best friend, something which worried Abby vaguely. Until now, Chloe had always been matter-of-fact about friendships, but if she was going to start forming strong attachments, things could be difficult when eventually they left Hemwood.

'We'll see,' said Abby. 'It depends what Granny wants to do. And I've got some shopping to do this morning.'

After she had hung out the washing, Abby had a bath and put on an old blue sundress, one of only two dresses which she possessed. It had a white patch near the hem where she had accidentally splashed some bleach once, but it was loose and comfortable. It had been so hot recently that even her T-shirts and shorts felt uncomfortably close on her skin. She brushed her long hair, then held it back from her face and regarded herself in the mirror, wondering if she should have it cut off. It was such a bother in this heat, and there came a time when you got too old for long hair. Then she let it fall back over her bare shoulders, deciding that that day had not come yet.

Ruth was in the kitchen, scanning her *Daily Express*.

'Do you want anything while I'm out?' Abby asked her mother, glancing in her purse to see how much money she had left. Now that old man Maskelyne's money was probably no more than a fading dream, they needed to be careful. She had a decent amount saved up in the bank, but she had to make sure that what she had would last them for the next few months and beyond, at least until they got back to London and she found a new job.

'No, love. Not unless they've got some of those nice doughnuts in.' Ruth got up from the kitchen table and fumbled in a drawer for her own purse. She took out some coins and handed them to Abby. 'That's for Chloe's sweets.'

'You don't need to bother, you know,' murmured Abby.

'You know I like to. Off you go.'

Abby left the house, and Ruth sat down again to finish the crossword. Five minutes later the doorbell rang, and there was Doris on the doorstep with two jars of home-made rhubarb jam and seven back issues of *The People's Friend*.

'I got these up at the old people's home.' Doris handed Ruth the magazines. 'They'd finished with them, and I know you like the stories. Any tea on the go?' Doris followed Ruth into the kitchen and began to tell her about the cruise which she and her husband were planning in the autumn with part of Leslie Maskelyne's legacy.

Ruth had no sooner made a fresh pot of tea and sat down with Doris when the doorbell rang again.

'Honestly,' muttered Ruth, rising slowly from her chair, 'I'm up and down like a dog at a fair this morning.'

Doris got up and motioned to Ruth to sit down. 'Sit yourself down. I know you get out of puff. I'll go.'

Ruth sat down, wishing that Doris did not take such active pleasure in her own spryness these days. Still, that was friends for you.

When Doris opened the door, she was surprised to find Stephen standing there. Stephen himself looked somewhat startled to see Doris.

'Oh, hello, Mrs C. I – ah – I wondered if Abby was here.'

'Well, I don't know, I'm sure,' replied Doris. 'You'd better come in.'

Stephen stepped inside and followed her up the narrow hallway, ducking his head to avoid the lintel as he came into the kitchen. Ruth looked up in astonishment at the sight of the tall, dark-haired young man. She hadn't seen Stephen for some years, and he reminded her instantly and painfully of Leslie as he had been when she first met him.

'Hello, Mrs Owen,' said Stephen, holding out his hand to shake Ruth's. 'I just called by to see Abby.' He already sensed that Abby wasn't here, and wished he had stayed on the doorstep. Somehow the sight of Mrs Owen, older and heavier now, but still much as he remembered her, made him feel like an overgrown schoolboy.

'Oh, I'm sorry, Stephen. She's just stepped out to fetch some things from the corner shop. She'll not be long.' Ruth paused and smiled at him. 'Well, you're a stranger and no mistake. It'll be a few years since you used to sit at this table with your biscuits and juice, you and Abby.'

'Yes, it is,' murmured Stephen, wondering how he could make his escape. He didn't really want to stand around in this poky little kitchen, smiling and being polite to two old dears. 'Maybe I should call back –'

Ruth flapped a hand at him. 'You sit down and make yourself comfortable. She won't be five mintues. Tell me how you're getting on in the world.' To Ruth, Stephen was still just a lad, and his sisters still girls.

Reluctantly Stephen sat down, placing his car keys on the table before him like a talisman, murmuring polite responses to Ruth's questions as Doris fussed around with cups and the teapot. He hoped Abby wouldn't be too long. As Doris passed him a cup of tea which Stephen desperately didn't want, a small girl, blonde and very pretty, appeared in the doorway, wearing only a vest and knickers and clutching a banana skin.

'Who are you?' she asked Stephen, with a curiosity so bald and genuine that the question sounded entirely polite.

'This is Mr Maskelyne, lovie,' said Ruth, holding out her arms to Chloe, who scrambled on to her lap. 'He used to play with Mummy when she was a little girl.'

'Did you really?' asked Chloe. Anything that her mother had done as a child fascinated her.

Stephen stared musingly at Chloe. He'd had no idea that Abby had a daughter. 'Yes,' he replied absently, nodding.

'What did you play?'

'Games,' replied Stephen, searching in his memory for names to give to those spellbinding, endless hours of invention and play. 'We built houses – dens, you know. And we had a rope swing. I don't really remember much else.' That wasn't true. But it was all beyond description. He gave Chloe a smile. 'What do you play with your friends?'

Chloe started to roll the banana skin damply against her knee, and Ruth took it from her and put it on the table. 'My friend Emily and I play at being ponies. Starlight ponies.'

At that moment, to Stephen's relief, there came the sound of the front door opening and closing. Abby appeared in the doorway with a carrier bag full of shopping a few seconds later. She stopped in surprise at the sight of Stephen sitting in her mother's kitchen, a cup of tea and his car keys on the table before him.

'Hello,' said Stephen, giving her an uncertain smile. The sight of her, the fact of her, was arousing in itself.

'Hello,' said Abby, setting the bag down.

'Stephen just dropped by,' said Ruth, who had been quite delighted by this unexpected visit. 'He's just been telling Chloe all the things you and he used to get up to when you were little.'

Abby nodded guardedly, glancing from Stephen to Chloe.

'Actually, I just wanted a word with you, Abby,' said Stephen, trying to sound businesslike. 'It's about that matter of –' He hesitated. '– that matter we discussed last week.' He met Abby's eye, hoping for co-operation.

Abby nodded again, still saying nothing. It was only then that the business of the legacies occurred to Ruth. She had been so busy treating Stephen like a long-lost friend of the family that she had quite forgotten that he was one of the prime movers in all matters concerning his father's estate. I must be getting old and stupid, thought Ruth. She eyed Abby and Stephen, and wondered if that was what he had come about. Well, if he wished to discuss it solely with Abby, so be it.

'Come on,' she murmured to Chloe, slipping her off her knee and on to the floor. 'Time we got you dressed. We'll leave you two in peace.' She smiled at Stephen. 'Lovely to see you again, Stephen. You stop by any time you want.'

'I'd best be making a move,' said Doris. She smiled and said goodbye to Stephen, then followed Ruth and Chloe out.

There was silence in the little kitchen, except for the fretful buzz of a wasp against the window. Abby simply stood, combing long fingers idly through her hair, waiting for Stephen to speak. Again he felt that sense of control slipping from him, the intensity of his own feelings contrasting with the coolness of her manner.

'I thought I should come and see you,' said Stephen. 'We don't seem to have made much of a new beginning to our friendship, do we?' Abby gave a dismissive shrug and turned to pick up the bag of shopping, taking things out and putting them on the table. Stephen watched, filled with impatience. 'Look, let's get out of here. I don't want to talk here. It's so – so stifling. Let's go for a walk.'

Abby hesitated, a packet of cream crackers in her hand, considering this. 'All right,' she said. 'I'll just put these things away.'

He waited while she put away the groceries, watching with hungry fascination the graceful movements of her arms, the straps of her dress grazing her sunburnt shoulders, the light enmeshed in her fair hair. He did not want to feel any of this, but there was a kind of luxury in being so powerless in the face of his own desire. She glanced at him to show she was ready, and he followed her to the front door. They stood together uncertainly in the hot sunlight. Stephen glanced up and down the street.   'Where do you want to walk?' asked Abby.

'I don't mind,' said Stephen, then said, 'Let's go to the Dips. I haven't been there in years.'

They walked the short distance to the church and then turned up the lane which petered out into a grassy track at the far end of the graveyard. There was no sound here except the light rustle of the wind in the trees and the high cawing of the rooks. Abby paused to pluck a long, feathery stalk of grass. She held it before her like a wand as she walked, sometimes touching it to her mouth, not looking at Stephen.

They walked for a little while in silence. The track wound through the trees and up a short way, then down past bushes and into a clearing studded with clumps of bushes and boulders. Stephen had to stoop to avoid the low branches of a hawthorn. He held the branch back for Abby and she passed through into the clearing.

'The thing is,' said Stephen, 'I wanted to talk to you about the money.'

'Don't,' Abby said quickly. In that moment she felt that she couldn't bear the thought of discussing it with Stephen. She didn't want to hear it from him. If they were going to give her and her mother something, then they could do it through the lawyers. 'I really think we've got better things to talk about.'

Stephen was nonplussed. Maybe he didn't have to use the matter of the money as a way of getting through to her. Her mood was very different from that of the other day – softer, less chilly. If she didn't want to talk about it, so much the better.

'What things?' He longed to reach out and touch her, but the moment wasn't yet right.

She sat down on one of the rocks and smiled. 'Important things. Like when we were children. All the things we did.' She gave a faint sigh, but was still smiling. 'I thought when I met you again that day – you know, up at the house – that it would be just like old times. That we'd talk about those things. And that way –' Her smile faded a little and she glanced away. '– we'd become like we once were.'

The guilelessness of her words surprised Stephen. He realised that she was speaking from the heart, and it had the effect of creating an unexpected and instant sense of intimacy.

'Important things?' There was a light note of amusement in his voice.

Abby glanced up at him, then looked away again, tracing a pattern in the dusty earth with the heel of her sandal. 'I thought they were. It was everything once – absolutely everything. All the dens and the games. Still . . . maybe you're right. I suppose they don't matter any more.'

'I didn't say that,' said Stephen. 'I think we're what matters. You and I.'

'No.' She shook her head. 'Because nothing can be the way it used to be.'

He stepped near to her and touched her shoulder with light, tentative fingers. The touch of his hand was like a warm current, and she felt in herself that same instant weakness of desire as before. He continued to stroke her shoulder. Stephen knew how little it would take, how easy it would be to capitalise on her sentimental affection. It just required the right words. They need

141

not be false – the urgency of his need amounted to a kind of love. In that moment he wanted her so much, he would say anything. He crouched down awkwardly, to bring his face level with hers. She did not look at him at first. Her head was bent, hair falling across her face in a fine curtain. Then she looked up and into his eyes. For the first time, it seemed to her that she saw the person she had always remembered.

'I've always loved you,' said Stephen slowly. 'I never knew that until now. You don't think that way as a child. Yet I must always have.' He paused, his eyes fastened on hers. 'Only we're not children any more. What I feel for you has nothing to do with games, or make-believe.'

She looked steadily at him, and he could almost feel their minds moving on the same track, as though to some hidden rhythm. 'What about Harriet?' she said. 'Don't you think about her?'

'Whenever I try, all I think about is you.' That, at any rate, was true. 'You, and how cold you've been since that time in the house when I kissed you.'

'Cold?'

'What else?'

She looked away, unable to tell him how little she had trusted him, then. And now? She didn't know. He put out a hand and turned her face back towards his and kissed her softly, steadily, drawing her to her feet. When she pulled away from him after a moment, her features were softened with desire, and her body was warm and totally responsive to his. 'Oh, Stephen, I don't want to do this,' she murmured.

'What?' he whispered. 'Make love to me?'

'Start something that can't be finished. That hasn't got any purpose.'

Stephen bent his head and kissed the side of her neck, feeling her shiver with pleasure. 'Nothing has any purpose. The whole damned universe hasn't any. Just pretend it's the way it was when we were children. We believed in each other. We enjoyed every-thing. We took each day for what it was.'

She said nothing, merely stroked the hair at the nape of his neck, gazing blankly over his shoulder into the scrubby silence of the

Dips. 'Come on,' he said. 'Come with me.' He took her hand and set off, and she followed, dragging her feet a little in the dust, as a child might, climbing the steep little track to the green shadows of the woods.

An hour later, they walked back the way they had come. Stephen stopped at the churchyard wall.

'I won't come all the way back with you,' he said.

'Why not?' Abby turned to look at him.

'If I do, I shan't be able to kiss you goodbye.' He smiled at her. 'Come here.'

She lifted a hand to brush her hair from her face, smiling at him with the slow confidence of love, and leaned forward to be kissed. 'When can I see you again?' she asked.

There was a fractional hesitation before Stephen replied. 'Tomorrow. Tomorrow afternoon. Come up to the house.'

She nodded. Then she turned and walked down the grassy lane, pausing at the bottom to look round. But Stephen was already making his way up the path, his back towards her.

Stephen went back to the house, showered and changed, then drove to Peter and Geraldine's farm near Sudbury for lunch. He put on some Delius and thought all the way there about making love to Abby in the woods. He marvelled at the ease of it. She had given herself to him with a willingness which now, on reflection, had a touch of unseemly eagerness. His sense of achievement, of personal gratification, obscured any notion that Abby had come to him on equal terms. His upbringing was such that he still harboured the hazy idea that women should not want sex in the same way as men. They should be persuaded, should gradually succumb. It was not within his comprehension that any woman might simply take what she wanted, returning it through simple pleasure. It had been too easy, he told himself. He was acutely aware that the obsessive nature of his feelings for her had subtly diminished. He had wanted her, and now he had had her. And could have her again, he told himself, any time he wanted.

When he arrived at the farm, Stephen saw Marcus and Lydia's

Land-Rover parked outside, and could hear the voices of Oliver and Tobias, their sons, in the garden at the back. That was handy, at any rate – he could tackle both his sisters together, and get the thing out of the way.

Geraldine was pleased at Stephen's unannounced arrival for lunch, but it was not her way to show it. 'You might have rung,' she said, shaking water from the lettuce leaves she had been rinsing. 'I hope there's enough food to go round.'

'I'm not terribly hungry,' said Stephen, picking up a couple of cherry tomatoes from a bowl and eating them. 'I really came for a talk. Hello, Marcus.' He nodded to his brother-in-law. 'Where's Lydia?'

'In the garden, trying to stop the boys from fighting over the swing-ball,' said Marcus. His forehead and nose were red and peeling, and he looked hot and uncomfortable even in his open-necked shirt. He had spent yesterday at Lord's, had drunk too much Pimm's, and had fallen asleep without his hat on. Added to which, England had been bowled out for a hundred and forty. It didn't improve his temper to see Stephen looking, as ever, tall, cool and relaxed.

'Stephen, would you take this quiche? The table's laid in the garden. Here, you'll need an extra knife and fork, and a napkin. Marcus, you can make the salad dressing.'

Stephen, giving Marcus a superior little grin, did as he was told and took the things out into the garden, which was secluded from the nearby farm buildings by a semicircle of ancient trees. Lydia was at the other side of the garden, intently refereeing a swing-ball match in the hope of encouraging fair play between her sons, who would far rather have been left alone to cheat and bicker. She waved to Stephen when she saw him, but remained where she was, arms folded. Stephen noticed that she was wearing the same blue checked summer dress that she seemed to have been wearing year in, year out. Didn't the woman ever buy any new clothing?

Geraldine had put the table in the shade of one of the trees, spread it with a pretty blue-and-white checked cloth, and had carefully arranged matching napkins, plates and cutlery. Whatever

Geraldine did, thought Stephen, as he set the quiche down, it always had to be perfect. Nothing was ever casual, or untidy. He sometimes wondered how it had ever come about that his sister had married a farmer. It must drive her mad to have to live in close conjunction with so much dirt and noise and smell. The house and her own appearance reflected an altogether different lifestyle. She behaved exactly like a moderately well-to-do woman of leisure, lunching with friends, playing tennis and going to the gym, helping with various local charities, and going on shopping trips to buy Arabella expensive clothes which she did not need. She led a life which might have been more fitting for Lydia, whose husband earned a considerable amount and could afford the kind of things that Geraldine liked. But it was Lydia who dressed like a farmer's wife, who wore dowdy clothes and no make-up, and drove a mud-splashed old Volvo instead of a red Mercedes. Geraldine played no part in the life of the farm, which she vaguely disliked. She regarded as something of a triumph the fact that she had recently managed to persuade Peter to employ a farm manager to oversee the more physical and arduous tasks around the farm, leaving Peter free to attend to administration and paper-pushing. Peter had to admit that the EC had generated more than enough for him to do in that department, but at the same time he missed being physically involved with the day-to-day running of things. There were times when, crossing the yard, he would stop and watch with envy the cowmen herding the Friesians through the slather of mud and dung and into the fields, or a distant figure lurching atop a tractor over rutted expanses of brown earth.

Peter now crossed the lawn from the direction of the farm, raising a hand and calling out a greeting to Stephen. He knew, deep down, that he and Stephen were not kindred spirits, but he tried to be friendly and hearty whenever he saw his brother-in-law. He always hoped for the best from people, despite regular disappointments.

'Stephen! Hello! This is a nice surprise. Down to see Hubbard, are you? Where's Harriet?'

Stephen sat down in a wicker chair, lounging back and crossing his legs.

'No, just came down to see Gerry and Lydia. Harriet's still in London, painting away.'

Peter settled himself into a chair opposite Stephen, its frame creaking beneath his weight. 'So, when are you two going to tie the knot, then? No excuse now, you know. You've got the house, plenty of money.' In his attempts at bonhomie, Peter constantly made infelicitous remarks and asked tactless questions.

'I haven't got any money yet,' replied Stephen, deciding to ignore any mention of Harriet. 'God knows how long it's going to take Hubbard to wind everything up.'

Geraldine came across the lawn with a basket of bread, a bottle of wine and some glasses. She handed the bottle opener to Peter, called to Lydia and the boys, then went back inside to fetch the rest of the luncheon things. Stephen watched in silence as Peter wrestled with the corkscrew.

'So, what are you and Gerry planning to do with your share of the estate?' he asked.

'We haven't really discussed it yet,' said Peter, setting the bottle of wine on the table. 'There's some land I wouldn't mind acquiring, so that I can expand the dairy herd –'

'Nice to hear you disposing of my money already,' said Geraldine, approaching the table with plates and salad and catching the end of what Peter had said.

Peter glanced up at her, his face uneasy. 'Well, as I said to Stephen, we haven't exactly sorted things out yet . . .'

'In that case, I think you'd better refrain from making too many plans for the farm. I might have ideas of my own, you know.' She spoke lightly, but there was an edge to her voice. Peter said nothing, but poured everyone a glass of wine. Marcus arrived at the table with the salad dressing, dark circles of sweat staining the underarms of his pale blue shirt. Stephen glanced from Peter's face to his sister's. He could just imagine Geraldine deciding to keep the money for herself. The farm had dominated her life ever since she had married Peter. She might despise it, but it was the source of such money as she had, and no doubt she would welcome a little financial independence. Peter, on the other hand, in that naive way of his, probably imagined that her first priority would have been to

146

invest it in the farm. Poor old Peter. Since there was already a little acrimony in the air regarding the estate, Stephen decided he might risk generating some more.

'Actually, it was about money that I wanted to talk to you, Gerry,' he said.

'Oh?' Geraldine passed plates and food around.

'Where's Arabella?' asked Peter suddenly.

'Asleep,' said his wife. 'What were you going to say, Stephen?'

'I think we should give Abby and her mother some money.'

Lydia, Oliver and Tobias had left their swing-ball game and now came and sat down. Lydia paused in the act of tearing a piece of French bread in half and stared at Stephen. 'You're joking! Walter Hubbard says the thing that Father wrote out isn't worth the paper it's written on.'

'That's not the point,' said Stephen. He leaned forward and drank some of his wine, then sat back, watching Lydia's face. How well he remembered from childhood the way she would carefully hoard all her money in her piggy bank, taking it out now and again to count it into neat piles of copper and silver, frugal with the amount she spent on comics and sweets, and never, never on any account lending any to her spendthrift sister and brother. There were people in the neighbourhood who thought Lydia a no-nonsense, practical kind of a woman, with her sensible clothes and haircut, her lack of pretension. But Stephen reckoned she was just mean.

'Of course it's the point! We're not legally obliged to pay them anything. I thought the whole thing was highly suspicious from the outset, and –'

'I agree with Stephen,' said Geraldine, her mild voice cutting clearly across her sister's irate tones.

Lydia looked at her, then at Stephen. Two against one. 'Really? Well, perhaps you would explain to me why we should start giving away money to the likes of the Owens? I think I can guess Stephen's motives. He's probably smitten by the way his childhood sweetheart has grown up – aren't you?' She gave Stephen a wry look.

'Bollocks,' said Stephen amiably, though he felt mildly disconcerted. 'Sorry,' he added, following Lydia's frown in the direction of the boys, who were gorging themselves on bread and quiche. 'It's just that Father wanted to help them out, and I think we should. Besides, in spite of the fact that their lawyer has told them that the document is useless, they've actually made a formal application to the estate for money.'

'Cheek,' said Geraldine.

'But don't you see?' said Lydia. 'It's obvious they put some kind of squeeze on Father before he died. Well, maybe not Abby, but her mother must have.' Lydia looked round the table, satisfied that she had the attention of everyone, including Marcus and Peter. 'If you want to know, I've been talking to Mrs C, and apparently Ruth Owen had taken to visiting him during those last few weeks. Alone. Just her and him.'

'Really?' asked Geraldine in surprise. 'But I visited Father regularly, and I never saw her. He never mentioned her.'

Lydia gave her sister a small, triumphant smile. 'You see – you were up there every other day, and you had no idea. She was very careful only to go to the house when none of us were around. Mrs Cotterell told me. Now, I'm not saying anything against Ruth Owen – I scarcely know the woman – but I'm pretty sure she must have had some sort of – oh, I don't know, some kind of hold on Father to make him write out a document like that. In fact, I'm convinced she must have persuaded him. It all fits. The date on the document, the visits. Well, it didn't work out the way she wanted it to, and I'm heartily glad of it. So why you think we should give them anything, Stephen, is beyond me.'

Stephen sipped his wine and said nothing for a few moments. He had known nothing of this. Had Abby's mother been doing something underhand? It made sense. It would explain why his father had written the document in the first place. Mrs Owen was all friendliness and smiles, but that could conceal any amount of cunning. People would stoop to a lot of things for money. And Abby – why should he think any better of Abby just because she let him make love to her? Quite the opposite. He nursed his glass, and then said, 'Maybe you're right. I don't know. But it just seemed to me that if it was what Father wanted –'

Lydia, sensing that she now had the high ground, cut in. 'Stephen, don't let sentiment get in the way. You and Abby were friendly when you were little, but that's not a thing you should take into account now. People change, I regret to say, and I very much doubt if she's turned into a particularly nice woman. Not if she's picked up any of her mother's underhand ways.'

'Well, if what you say is true, it does put rather a different complexion on things,' murmured Geraldine, looking troubled.

There was a silence. Stephen shrugged and sipped his wine, aware that both his brothers-in-law were watching him, waiting to hear what he might say. 'I don't really care one way or another, frankly,' he said at last. 'I was merely interested in giving effect to Father's wishes. But if you don't feel the Owens should have anything, so be it.' The fact was, he didn't care. The matter of the money had been a mere pretext, a device to make it easier for him to seduce Abby. In the end, it hadn't even been necessary.

Chapter Eleven

It was Sunday afternoon. Robin Onslow was standing in his office, hands on his hips, gazing at the untidy stacks of files which heaped the floor around his bookshelves. 'We're going to have to have a complete clear-out, get rid of all the dead wood,' he said to Jackie, who had come in specially, on the promise of overtime, to help straighten out the office. He knew that his practice couldn't continue amid the current shambles of unfiled correspondence and unattended cases. His new resolutions about drinking less and taking better care of himself had put him in an attacking mood.

'I'd start with your desk, if I were you,' said Jackie, nodding towards the shallow swamp of paper and books that littered its surface. 'Get that clear, and then we can make a start on these.'

'All right,' sighed Robin. 'Make us both a coffee, would you?'

He sifted through the letters, slinging some into his out-tray, others into the bin, ramming stray books on to the shelves. It was only when he picked up a copy of *Archbold* that he saw Abby's file, forgotten since the week before. Robin picked it up and opened it. Inside lay Leslie Maskelyne's document. Well, she might as well have it back, useless as it was. He really should have given it to her the last time she was here, only it hadn't occurred to him. He would post it to her. No, on second thoughts, he would put it to better use. He hadn't liked to ask her out last time, under the circumstances, but there was no reason why he shouldn't use this as a pretext. Her phone number was on the back of the file with the rest of her details, so Robin copied it down on a scrap of paper and put it in his pocket.

'Tell me. Tell me what it is and I'll try to make it better.' Abby, sitting up in Stephen's bed, bent to kiss his back and stroke his hair. The blinds were half-drawn against the strong afternoon sunlight, making the room dim. 'I know there's something wrong. Tell me.' She had sensed his remoteness before they had even made love.

Stephen, his face resting on his folded arms, sighed and said nothing. How could he tell her? What was there to say? She leaned down to kiss him again and he could feel her nipples grazing his back. He turned over, and she slipped down beside him, nestling against him. 'I don't know how to say it,' he said at last. Abby pulled away from him to look into his face. 'There's just something – something not quite right about this.' He stroked an idle finger down the length of her arm and across her stomach. The expression in her eyes was tentative, showing the beginnings of fear. Only yesterday he had told her he loved her. How could he explain to her now that his fleeting obsession had run its course, that he already wished he'd never started it? When she had been cool, remote, he had wanted her so badly. Now that he had made love to her, now that she had shown him by every word and gesture that she was his whenever he wanted her, he felt quite dispassionate. He glanced from the bed to where her cheap sundress lay over a chair, her battered sandals kicked off beneath it. With enough money spent on her, Abby could be made to look all right. She was pretty enough for that any day. She would pass muster with any of the elegant women he knew. It wasn't just a question of the way she dressed, or spoke. That had turned him on initially, like the faint smell of her sweat. No, it had to do with Abby herself, the kind of life she had led and the person she had become. She had lain beside him here this afternoon and told him much about her life, recounting people and incidents with thoughtless frankness. He had listened in an after-sex drowse to the awfulness of it, as her voice murmured on. With every word he felt more remote, filled with distaste at having got himself into this. His obsession of the past few days had melted away with possession of her body. He was bored and disgusted.

Abby watched his face as he lay thinking. 'What do you mean – not quite right?' Her voice was wary.

He affected a little smile, not looking at her. 'Maybe it's just the mood I'm in.' Then he sighed, glancing at her. 'I'm a complex person, Abby. I say things I mean, and then I discover that everything's changed. The thing is –' He leaned up on one elbow, moving away from her to pick up his watch from the table by his bed. '– I can't help feeling there's something almost . . . well, incestuous about this.' She gazed at him blankly. Stephen swung his legs out of the bed, reached down for his boxer shorts and began to pull them on. 'You know.'

Abby sat up, pushing back strands of blonde hair from her face, her heartbeat quickening. 'No, I don't know.' She waited, her eyes questioning, watching as he put on his trousers and began to button his shirt.

Stephen sat down on the bed again, fastening the last button. He leaned across and stroked her cheek. It was the tiniest act, yet overtly patronising. 'I keep thinking about us as children. And it makes this seem somehow . . .' He shrugged, unable to find the word. 'We were like brother and sister, weren't we? I feel that we've violated that, in some way.'

The words were new, but to Abby the tone was all too familiar. The tone of someone easing themselves away, extricating themselves delicately from a situation they no longer wished to be in. She felt her stomach turn over, then right itself again. She had no idea what to say next. She had given herself to a number of men, had spent time and affection on them, but she had never loved any one of them, not even Chloe's father. And now she did. Now she felt that part of her soul had been handed over to this callous, so-familiar stranger. She had expected him to behave like the Stephen of her childhood, with loyalty and love, but suddenly she saw that he was just another man, after all. Just another man who had had his afternoon's fill of sex and was now about to put on his jacket before leaving. How could she have forgotten the way he had spoken to her when they had first met again, just a couple of weeks ago? That was the reality. The rest was just a sham.

'Stephen –' she said, her voice weak.

Taking his cue, he leaned down and kissed her. 'Don't,' he said. Again he sighed, helpless, hopeless. 'Look, I'm just as confused as you are. Don't take everything I say too much to heart. I have to go back to London now. Let's just leave things as they are. Don't spoil things.'

They were the right words, beautiful, damningly spoken. The ultimate, kind get-out. With an option to return for another bit of sex should his oh-so-complex personality permit it.

Abby sat back in Stephen's bed, pulling the sheet up across her breasts, feeling humiliation burn within her. There was nothing she could say that would not be demeaning or demanding. She felt cheap, as he meant her to. It would not have surprised her if he left a couple of twenties on the dressing table. Instead, as he picked up his wallet and car keys, Stephen said, 'I don't know when I'll be back down again. I'll let you know. Or Mrs Cotterell.' Then he touched a finger to his lips and left the room.

Abby left the house ten minutes later and walked slowly along the path towards the woods. It was almost half past six. Little clouds of gnats hung beneath the leaves, unseen animals scuttered in the undergrowth, and the air was still and cool among the trees. Abby felt as though some dead weight lay within her. So this was what love could do. Yesterday and this morning she had felt a kind of inert happiness, sure that what she felt for Stephen must be returned, must be as enduring and simple as when they were ten. She was not a particularly practical person, was not given to calculation. Abby lived for the moment, for the day, and she had given no thought to Stephen's motives. Only now, as she wandered slowly along the track, plucking the odd grass from the wayside, did she begin to consider what had really happened between them. He had wanted her, and she had been fool enough to believe it was deeper than that. Why, then, could she not just shrug it off, as she had done with past encounters? Why did she keep replaying that last conversation, seeking for stray crumbs of hope in certain things he had said? Because she was in love with him, and rational thought, reasoned argument, simply could not touch what she felt, could not begin to assuage the ache within her.

She felt she could not go through the Dips that day. Instead, she followed the woodland path down past the pub and garage to the main road. Arnold Macey, the publican of the Fox and Hounds, was standing shaking towelling bar mats into the summer air. The nicotine and beer smell of the pub's interior wafted out to Abby.

'Abby – just the girl,' said Arnold. He dropped the stub of his cigarette, grinding it out beneath his foot. 'You wouldn't be able to do a shift for me this evening, I don't suppose?' he asked hopefully. 'Only Lorna's gone to see her sister in Castle Hedingham. She's poorly.'

Abby had to drag her mind from Stephen with an effort of will. She didn't like to leave her mum with Chloe this evening, on top of this afternoon, but she needed any extra money she could make right now. They couldn't be sure that the Maskelynes were going to give them anything. Well, she had been the one who'd told Stephen she didn't want to talk about it. Maybe the subject was dead for ever, along with a few other things.

'Yes, I think so. I'll just check with Mum.' It would keep her mind occupied, anyway. Better than a blank evening spent nursing uncertainty and hope over Stephen.

Arnold nodded. 'How's she getting on? Still under the doctor, is she?'

'She's still waiting to hear when she can have her operation.'

'Ah. Well, give her my best.'

At Alma Cottage Ruth was playing picture lotto with Chloe at the kitchen table.

'Your daughter's got a lucky streak. I reckon if she fell in the sea she'd come out with a pocketful of fish.' Ruth glanced up and winked at Abby over Chloe's head. 'Have a nice time at Marjorie's? How's her baby?'

Abby had told her mother she was going to see an old school friend that afternoon, and had in fact dropped in to see her on the way to Hemwood, to ease her conscience.

'She's lovely. They're calling her Prudence.' Abby bent and kissed Chloe. 'You had your tea? Good.' Abby poured herself a glass of orange juice from the fridge. 'Arnold's asked if I'll work a shift for him at the pub tonight. Do you mind putting Chloe to bed for me?'

'You know I don't. Come here, buttercup.' She snuggled Chloe on to her knee. Ruth didn't like to think of the emptiness of the cottage in a few months' time. Once she was rested and well, Abby would go back to London with Chloe. How often would she see her granddaughter then? 'I'm going to miss this little lady when she goes,' murmured Ruth, kissing the small, blonde head.

Chloe wriggled on her grandmother's lap, turning her face up to look at her. 'Why can't we stay here and live with you, Granny?'

Abby leaned against the sink, watching her mother and her daughter, sipping her juice. Ruth thought she looked unusually listless. Perhaps it was the heat.

'You and Mummy have to go back to London when Granny's all better,' said Ruth with forced brightness. Just saying the words gave her a pang. Chloe said nothing, then slipped off Ruth's knee and ran out into the back garden. Ruth looked at her daughter. 'I wish you could stay. I keep thinking it might have made a difference if it had been all right about the money.' There was a pause. 'Do you think it would have?'

'I don't know,' said Abby, and shrugged. 'It might have. I might have found something to do round here. Chloe likes it. Who can say? Still, we're here for the time being.' She rinsed her empty glass under the tap. 'I don't know what's going to happen about the money, anyway.'

'Was that what Stephen came to see you about yesterday?'

'Partly.' Abby sighed and shook her hair back from her shoulders. 'But we got talking about – oh, other things. So I don't know.'

Ruth gazed at her daughter's inscrutable expression, and a sudden fear gripped her. What if there was something going on between Abby and Stephen? There couldn't be. They hardly knew one another – well, not properly, not as adults. And he was as good as married to that artist in London, so Doris said. But anything was possible. I should have told her, thought Ruth. When I told her about me and Leslie, I should have told her then. Coward.

155

'Have you eaten?' asked Abby suddenly.

'Yes,' said Ruth, aware that the intensity of her thoughts had increased her heart rate, made her chest tight. If only she could summon up the courage to say something now.

'I'll make myself some cheese on toast before I go out.' Abby glanced at her watch. 'Arnold will want me in half an hour.'

Ruth sat watching Abby as she moved around the kitchen, trying to find the words. Just as she was about to speak, the phone rang.

'I'll get it,' murmured Abby, and went into the hall. She knew that, from now on, every time the phone rang she would go to it in agonised hope. 'Hello?'

'I'd like to speak to Abigail Owen, please.'

Of course it couldn't have been Stephen, but still her heart dipped in disappointment. 'Speaking.'

'This is Robin Onslow – you came to see me about a document of your mother's last week.'

'Oh, yes,' said Abby.

'The thing is, I forgot to return your document to you when you were here. It's still in the file.'

'Oh, I see.' Abby sighed. She couldn't care less about the thing. 'Could you send it to me?'

Robin had already anticipated this. 'Well. I'm reluctant to trust original documents to the post . . .'

The thing wasn't worth this fuss, thought Abby. 'Oh, well, I'll come and pick it up,' she said. 'I have to come up to Tesco's in the week. I'll get it then.' She hesitated. 'By the way, I don't suppose you heard anything – about the money, I mean?'

'I'm afraid not,' said Robin. 'But maybe I'll have some news next week.'

'Yes. Maybe,' said Abby. From the way Stephen had behaved, she no longer expected anything.

It was eight o'clock when Stephen got back to London. He went round to Harriet's studio, hoping she would be in, anxious for the sight of her calm, loving smile, the reassurance of her ignorance of what he had done. He wished he had never laid a finger on Abby. He would speak to Mrs Cotterell, ask her to find some other

156

cleaner. He would stay away from Hemwood for a few weeks. With any luck, by the time his father's estate was wound up, Abby's mother would have had her operation and Abby herself would have gone back to London. He need not see her again. He marvelled now at the force of the physical obsession which had gripped him. Even now, as he drove through the fading dusk across Hammersmith Bridge, he felt a stir of desire at the recollection of her in his bed that afternoon, but he stifled it. She was common, she was easy, and he had been mad. From now on he would focus on the restaurant project, marry Harriet – maybe – and forget about this tawdry little episode.

The next morning Russell rang him at eight, with news of another possible location for the restaurant near Chelsea Harbour. 'You have to see it, Steve,' said Russell. 'It's a bit more than the Chiswick option, but worth it. Much better location. Besides, we could wait for ever before we get the lease on that place sorted out.'

Stephen agreed to meet Russell there at ten. He wouldn't bother to ring in at work. He could show up late. Nothing much happened on Monday mornings, anyway.

When Stephen eventually arrived at the office just before lunch, he felt elated. The place in Chelsea was perfect, a badly managed and underused wine bar that Stephen, with his father's money, would transform. He could see it now, one of the most elite restaurants in London, written up everywhere. Sir Terence, eat your heart out.

As Stephen sauntered into the studio, Andy looked up from his drawing board with a rapid, hostile glance. 'Where the fuck have you been?'

'Planning my future,' said Stephen, smiling, and slung his jacket over the back of his chair.

'Well, the present is here, mate, in the shape of David Dacre effing and blinding and demanding to know where you are. The Frangos people are threatening to pull the account because we haven't come up with anything. He said he wants to see you as soon as you get in.'

'Oh, yeah?' Beneath his lightness of tone, Stephen felt uneasy. He poured himself a cup of coffee and went out as nonchalantly as he could. In the thirty seconds it took him to climb the back stairs to the floor where Dacre had his office, he reminded himself that he had no need to be afraid of anyone like Dacre. He didn't need this job any more. The restaurant was rapidly becoming a reality. In a few weeks the estate would be distributed, and he would be out of here. He could do without David Dacre pulling his string.

None of this made any difference to the nervousness which he felt as he went into David's room.

'Where the fuck have you been?' demanded Dacre, as soon as he saw Stephen.

Stephen took a leisurely sip of his coffee. 'Is it office policy for everyone to greet me with this question on a Monday morning?'

'It's bloody nearly Monday afternoon,' said Dacre. 'We don't pay you to take Monday mornings off, Stephen. We pay you to be here, working. You have a job as a copywriter, and that's exactly what I expect you to be doing on a Monday morning. Writing copy. For your information, we are about to lose an important account because you and Andy, you pair of tossers, can't put together a decent campaign even when you're given six months to do it.'

Stephen shrugged. 'I don't know what was wrong with the first lot of stuff we submitted –'

'It was crap!' shouted Dacre. 'I sometimes wonder why we ever gave you a job here in the first place!'

Stephen felt his heart start to thump. He hated it when anyone hinted at his inadequacies, the ones he couldn't even acknowledge to himself. He put down his coffee. 'David,' he said quietly, 'you are an uncouth, overweight, overbearing slob, and you can take the account and your job and shove them both right up your extremely fat arse.'

He walked out quickly, remembering David Dacre's reputation for occasional physical violence. There – it was done now, thought Stephen, as he loped downstairs, pulse still racing. He was a free man. He hadn't really intended to jack in his job at DRS until the estate was wound up, but what the hell? The money was as good as in the bank. He would never have to work for anyone else for the rest of his life.

*

Abby found she had to go into Sudbury on Monday afternoon to get a new prescription made up for her mother, and decided she might as well call in at Robin Onslow's office on the way back. It was almost half past five when she got there, and he looked surprised and pleased when Jackie showed her in.

'I had half a mind to tell you to keep the thing, you know,' she said, as Robin fished the document from the file and handed it to her. 'It's not as though it's worth anything to me.'

He shrugged. 'Always best for clients to keep the originals.' Abby slipped the document into her bag. 'Oh, by the way – I had a call from the Maskelynes' lawyer this afternoon.' Abby looked up quickly, hopefully. Robin shook his head. 'Not good news, I'm afraid. They say they're not prepared to pay you or your mother anything. Let's see – how do they put it?' Robin riffled through his notepad. 'Oh, yes. They decline to entertain any applications based on a clearly invalid document. I'm awfully sorry.'

Abby shook her head and gave Robin a small smile. 'I didn't really expect anything, you know. Why should they pay out money when they're not obliged to?' Nonetheless, in her heart she was deeply hurt and angry with Stephen. He knew about her mother's illness. It wouldn't have cost him much to give effect to just one-tenth of his father's wishes. How could she be in love with anyone who behaved with such sincerity one moment and such falseness and cruelty the next? Well, she was, that was the answer to that. He didn't love her, he had lied, and he didn't care what happened to her or her mother.

Despite what she said, Robin could see the disappointment in Abby's face. He thought again how very pretty she was. His heart gave an unexpected little tumble, and he suddenly felt as nervous as a sixteen-year-old. 'By the way, I'm just about to finish for the afternoon. I wonder – would you – that is, I wondered if you might like to go for a drink somewhere? Unless you have to hurry back, of course.'

Abby was only mildly surprised. She knew just from the way he looked at her that he fancied her. She was used to that with men. She gave him a considering look. The last thing she wanted was some middle-aged solicitor coming on to her over a vodka-and-

159

tonic. But there was something about him that she liked. He had the appeal of a small boy trying to behave like a grown-up. And she had felt the need for company quite badly over the past few weeks. There was something lacking in the pedestrian conversation of her mother, Doris, and the nightly clientele of the Fox and Hounds.

To Robin's surprise, she nodded. 'All right. But since you wouldn't charge me anything for the work you did, you'll have to let me buy.' He grinned, and she added, 'I only hope you don't have expensive tastes. I'm not the wealthy woman I thought I was, remember.'

Robin told Jackie to lock up, and he and Abby went downstairs into the street, which was still hot in the late-afternoon sun. Robin was careful to choose a pub that was not one of his regular haunts, one at the end of the High Street with a small garden at the back. Despite his protests, Abby insisted on paying for their drinks, and made him take a five-pound note. She sat outside at one of the small tables while Robin went inside to the bar. From where he stood, waiting to be served, Robin could see her through the window. She lifted her chin, tilting her head towards the afternoon sun, as though drinking it in. She was as gorgeous as he remembered, but she should do something about her clothes. Legs like those could do with something better than cut-off denims and beaten-up trainers.

He came out with their drinks and sat down. Abby said, 'Cheers,' and sipped her Bacardi and Coke. 'Do you always drink doubles?' she asked, eyeing his glass. Robin followed her glance. He'd been careful to make up the difference with his own money. He thought he had put so much ice in it that it wouldn't be obvious. Ordering doubles was automatic, these days. Triples, when it was late on a Saturday evening. You didn't get the stuff into yourself fast enough, otherwise.

He shrugged, then smiled, somewhat abashed, and she smiled back. Suddenly he felt transparent, as though she knew everything about the way he lived, about his divorce, his slipping practice, his drinking. And how much he liked her. She had the kind of look that said she could read anyone.

'So tell me about yourself,' he said quickly. It sounded lame, but he wanted to divert the subject away from himself. 'Have you always lived in Hemwood?'

'Only when I was younger. I live in London now, but I've come back to stay with my mother for a while. She has to go into hospital for an operation, and I'm here to look after her. Help her convalesce.' She sighed. 'That's why we were banking on that money. She's had to give up her part-time job, and she hasn't got much to live on.' At the thought of her mother and the money, and then of Stephen and the wretched futility of her feelings, tears suddenly stung Abby's eyes. She shook her head to get rid of them, then drained her glass quickly.

'That was fast,' observed Robin. 'I don't know if I'm going to be able to keep up with you.' It was a relief, at least, to know she wasn't one of those women who lingered over a single drink for three-quarters of an hour.

Abby blinked and looked away, pretending to screw her eyes up against the sunlight. It was so shitty, so unfair. The things she could have done for Chloe and for herself with that money. Stupid old man. Why couldn't he just have gone to a lawyer, got the thing done properly?

There was silence for a moment, and Robin swirled the ice cubes in his glass, then drained it. The euphoric glow of the day's first double spread through his veins. Probably shouldn't offer to buy the next one straight away. They'd only just sat down. His mind drifted back to the document, the reason why she had to come to him in the first place. 'Tell me about this fellow Maskelyne,' said Robin. 'I'm curious. Was he very rich? He must have been worth a few bob or two, to hand out the odd hundred thousand here and there as an afterthought.'

'I'll say,' replied Abby. 'Money everywhere. And he had this huge place, Hemwood House. Must be worth a fortune. It's where I work. Cleaning.'

'Oh. Right.' Robin nodded and stared into his glass at the melting ice cubes.

'Not that I knew him very well,' went on Abby, leaning forward on her elbows, shoulders hunched. Robin tried not to stare at the tantalising line of cleavage where her T-shirt fell away from her breasts. 'In fact, I didn't really know him at all. Only to say hello to. You know.'

'So –' Robin hesitated, wondering whether it was impertinent to ask the obvious question. He decided it wasn't. 'So why did he want to leave you that money? If he didn't know you. And if you don't mind my asking.'

Abby shrugged. 'I don't know. Well – I do, sort of . . .' She remembered how insistent her mother had been about not mentioning the marriage, how much she didn't want anyone to know. Would it matter if she told Robin Onslow? He was a lawyer, after all, and lawyers were supposed to keep things confidential. It couldn't do any harm. She looked up at Robin, at his pleasant, rather pouchy face, the sparse hair carefully combed to make it look as though there were more of it. He was a bit of a sad guy, but she liked him. She wouldn't have come for a drink with him if she didn't. And she trusted him. Daft, when she hardly knew him, but she did, instinctively. 'I'll tell you something,' she said suddenly, 'if you promise to me that you won't tell anyone else.'

He looked up. 'You may have bought me a drink, and a large one at that, but I still regard you as my client. Everything is in the strictest confidence.'

'Right, well . . . Like I said, I didn't know Leslie Maskelyne very well, but my mum did. She doesn't want anyone to know this, see, but something happened just before he died. And it was because of that he wrote that codicil. Or the thing that's not a codicil.'

'What? This sounds intriguing,' said Robin.

'Well, she didn't go into details – I didn't ask her to – but apparently she and Leslie Maskelyne had known one another a long time. Maybe they were lovers or something – I don't know. Anyway, they were very fond of each other, and just before he died they got married.' She shrugged. 'Sounds odd, I know. But he wanted to provide for her, you see, and he thought that this was a kind of binding way to do it. He didn't tell anyone because he didn't want his family getting their knickers in a twist.' Abby tilted her glass, watching the remains of her drink slide in a little puddle along the side of the glass. 'Old people. They've got quirky ways, I guess. Maybe keeping it secret had some special significance for them.'

'So he married her? Very romantic.'

'Yeah. She showed me the certificate. And that's why he wrote out the document. I asked her why he'd included me in it, and she said that he knew I was a bit hard up, and that since I was her daughter, he wanted to help me out.' She looked up and smiled. 'There. The secret is out. For what it's worth.'

'Hmm.' He nodded towards her empty glass. 'Fancy another?'

'All right. I better make it my last, though. I'm not used to drinking, these days. And I have to get back.'

Robin went into the pub and stood at the bar, waiting to be served. Interesting little story – pity the old chap hadn't had the sense to consult his lawyer and get the codicil right . . . Suddenly, in the middle of his musing, Robin's mind stopped dead. The implications of what Abby had told him came home to him with mind-jolting force. The old man had made his will, and then he had remarried. Which meant . . . Robin might have forgotten much of the law he'd ever learned, but not all of it. If he was right . . . but was he right? The barman came up and Robin gave his order, his mind working furiously. Damn, damn . . . He couldn't go back out there and tell her unless he was absolutely sure of his facts. And then there was the document. What about the wording? Was it sufficient? He wasn't sure, blast it. He simply wasn't sure. On impulse, he turned and went out of the pub into the street, and headed towards his office at a brisk jog. He arrived badly out of breath, his heart going like a piston, just as Jackie was locking up. She stared at Robin in astonishment as he puffed up the stairs.

'You all right?' she asked.

'Fine. Forgot a book,' he gasped. 'Off you go. I'll lock up.' He went into his room and fished around on the shelves. *Williams on Wills*. There it was. He didn't need the forms volume, just this one. He hauled the book off the shelf and set off again, locking the door behind him. This time he didn't run up the street, but walked wheezily instead. He managed to remember the drinks on the way through the pub, and emerged in the garden clutching two glasses and the book.

163

'Service is slow in there,' remarked Abby. 'I wondered where you'd got to.'

Robin sat down, smoothing his hand over wayward strands of hair, and recovering his breath. 'I went back to the office to get this. I think you said something five minutes ago which could make a considerable difference to your life. I want to check in here to make sure.' He took a quick slurp of his Scotch and opened the book, realising that his fingers were trembling a little. 'Revocation, revocation,' he muttered, riffling through the index. 'Here we are.' He found the page. The relevant passage was very short. He read it to himself, looked up slowly at Abby, turned the book around and pushed it towards her. Abby set down her glass. 'Read that,' said Robin, pointing to the passage.

Abby read aloud hesitantly, tucking her hair behind one ear as she bent over the book. '*A will unless it is made in expectation of a particular marriage is revoked by the marriage or remarriage of the testator.*' She looked up, her face a blank. 'I don't get it,' she said.

'It means that when this fellow Maskelyne married your mother, his will was automatically revoked. The one he made leaving everything to – well, his children, whoever. It's nothing. It's meaningless.'

Abby gazed at Robin, trying to comprehend his excitement.

'But what difference does that make? So his will's a dud. So what? His kids will still get everything, won't they?'

Robin's expression was boyish and excited. This was giving him a buzz better than any amount of whisky. 'Give me that document. The one from the file.' Abby pulled it from her bag and unfolded the piece of paper. Robin laid it on the table and scanned it, muttering. 'Dated . . . no attestation clause, but that probably doesn't matter . . . two witnesses . . .' He flipped through the textbook again, just to make sure. 'Here we are . . . *The maker must intend that his document shall take effect as a revocable ambulatory disposition of his property which is to take effect upon death.*' Robin pondered for a moment and then looked up at Abby. 'I wouldn't stake my last fiver on it, but there's a possibility that that document' – he pointed at Leslie Maskelyne's carefully worded single paragraph '– operates as a will. And if it does –' he took a deep breath '– it means that you, Miss Owen, would stand to inherit Mr Maskelyne's entire estate.'

Abby stared at him. 'Don't put me on,' she said. She took a long drink of her Bacardi and Coke and gave a small laugh, and shook her head. 'That can't be right. How do you make that out?'

He held up a hand. 'I may be wrong. I often am. Which could explain why my practice is going down the pan. But since Leslie Maskelyne's old will is revoked by his marriage to your mother, then, on the face of it, I can't see what's to stop this document operating as a will.' Robin picked up the document and read aloud, *'To her daughter, Abigail Owen, I leave the sum of £100,000* – and now listen, this is the important bit – *together with any residue of my estate not otherwise disposed of.'* There. Estate not otherwise disposed of. If I'm right, you get the lot. The house, money, everything.'

Abby frowned and shook her head. This was unreal. Sitting in a pub garden in the sunshine, and being told this. 'But that can't be right. He never meant that. When he said –'

'The law doesn't care,' broke in Robin. 'Remember how it was before, when he had meant you and your mother to have the money, but didn't make the document a proper codicil? The law didn't care about his intentions then. He simply hadn't got the formalities right.' Robin leaned back in his chair and drained his second drink. 'This time, there's a good chance he has got it right. Without even meaning to.'

Chapter Twelve

Doris and Ruth were sitting in the late-afternoon sun in Ruth's little back garden. Instead of tea, they were drinking home-made lemonade and eating some seed-cake which Doris had bought the day before at the church sale.

'That Geraldine asked me if I'd like to do a bit of cleaning for her, now that I'm not working up at the big house, you know,' remarked Doris, after a general lull in the day's gossip.

'Did she now?'

'Well, I said to her, those days are past for me, thanks to the bit of money your father left me. And she seemed quite surprised, said she thought I'd like to keep busy.' Doris helped herself to more lemonade. 'It's nice, this. Tart, mind. But nice.' She took another slice of cake and shook her head. 'No, I wouldn't work for that one even if I needed to. She's a bring-me, fetch-me, carry-me sort of creature. I can't be doing with her.'

'I was never particularly fond of either of those girls,' murmured Ruth in agreement. 'Always thought they were better than everyone. Not like Stephen.'

'That Lydia! She lords it round the WI like I don't know what, carping and complaining if everything's not just to her liking. She'd grumble to be hung and then say the rope was too tight, that one would.'

'I dare say,' murmured Ruth in assent. She shifted a little in her chair, plucking at the bodice of her dress. The air seemed heavy,

166

and she had to take long, shallow breaths. All day she had felt slightly unwell, though there had been no chest pains.

'I know you always had a soft spot for that Stephen, but I don't trust a man who's that charming,' went on Doris. 'Too sweet to be wholesome, as my mother would say.'

Ruth was suddenly swept by a wave of nausea. She passed a hand across her brow and murmured, 'Do you know, Doris, I'm feeling a little giddy. I think it's this heat. Do you mind if we step inside for a while?' She rose, and Doris put out a hand to help her. Ruth lifted her head. 'That's Abby back. I can hear the car.' She and Doris went into the kitchen.

Abby came up the hall with her purchases. 'Are you all right, Mum?' she asked with concern, seeing her mother standing unsteadily in the middle of the kitchen, Doris supporting one arm.

'I think I just need to lie down on the sofa for a few minutes. Then I'll be fine.' Abby took her other arm and helped her through to the sitting room, where Chloe was playing on the floor with a Barbie doll and a one-legged Action Man. Ruth sat down on the sofa, slowly and heavily, trying to get her breath. 'It's just the weather,' she assured her daughter. 'Just a bit close.' She lay back, closing her eyes.

'Is granny all right?' asked Chloe.

'She'll be fine. You come out and leave her in peace,' said Abby.

In the hallway Doris glanced at her watch, then said in a hushed voice, 'I don't like to leave her, but there's my Don's tea to get. She seemed fine when we were out in the garden . . .'

'Probably just the heat, like she says.'

'Probably.' Doris nodded. 'Tell her I'll look in first thing tomorrow.'

'I will.' Abby showed Doris out, then went back into the sitting room. Her mother's head was propped at an awkward angle against the arm of the sofa, and Abby fetched a cushion and slid it gently beneath her. 'Mum,' she said quietly, 'do you want one of your pills?'

Ruth nodded without opening her eyes. 'They're in the kitchen drawer.'

Abby went into the kitchen. Through the back door she could see

167

Chloe finishing off Doris's seed-cake. She went back through, shaking one of the pills into the palm of her hand, and handed it to her mother. Then she knelt down next to her.

'Can I get you anything else?'

Ruth shook her head, her eyes still closed. 'Just sit with me for a bit, there's a love.'

Abby drew up a small, upright chair and sat down next to the sofa. She wondered whether she should tell her mother what had happened this afternoon, recount the conversation she had had with Robin Onslow. Could it be right, everything he had said? By the time they had finished their second drink, he had been more than optimistic. All Abby felt was a vague sense of fear. Even if it was all true – and how amazing if it was – she deserved no part of the Maskelyne estate. It would be a mistake. Everyone would know it.

Abby sat there for some twenty minutes, thinking it through, gazing at her mother's tired face. If it was true, it was a mistake right enough, but one Leslie Maskelyne had made himself. He had started it all when he married her mother, and everyone had to accept the consequences. A new sense of wonder began to grow in her. She reached out and stroked her mother's inert hand. All that money. And the house. Abby had no idea exactly what old man Maskelyne had been worth, but it was a great deal more than she herself had ever dreamed of possessing. And it might actually be hers – by accident, but legally hers. She experienced a brief, vaguely guilty thrill of excitement. And then she thought of Stephen. His reaction to such a situation was all too easy to predict. Outrage, disbelief, any glimmer of feeling he might have for her completely extinguished. That was the worst of it. And he would regard her as utterly without any right to anything that belonged to the Maskelyne family. Quite correctly. She had, after all, despite whatever any piece of paper might say, no right at all. The faint excitement within her died.

'No right,' she murmured, testing the words aloud.

Ruth stirred, her hand moving away from Abby's, and she opened her eyes. 'What was that, love'?' Ruth laid a hand on her chest, and breathed deeply, more easily. 'I feel a bit better now.

Thanks for sitting with me.' She tried to sit upright, and Abby moved the cushions to make her more comfortable.

'Maybe you should go to bed,' suggested Abby.

Ruth shook her head. 'I think I'll just stop here for the evening. I'm comfy enough, sitting up.' She sighed. 'I don't want any supper. Maybe I'll just see if there's anything good on television.'

'Mum –' Abby looked intently at her mother. She would tell her. She had to tell someone. Anyway, maybe her mother would know what to do. 'I want to tell you something. It's something really strange, and I don't know what on earth I should do about it.'

Ruth fixed her eyes on her daughter. At least this didn't sound as though it had anything to do with Stephen. 'Go on, then,' she said.

Abby told her. She told her everything that had happened this afternoon, all that Robin had said, how he had fetched his law book, and how convinced he had become that Abby, as things stood, had been left everything by Leslie Maskelyne's piece of paper. Ruth listened in silence, her expression unchanging. Abby finished by saying, 'I know you didn't want anyone knowing about you and Leslie being married, but he's a lawyer, they don't tell people things.' Still her mother said nothing. 'But that's it. That's everything.'

'It can't be right,' said Ruth after a moment. Her voice held all the amazement that her face did not betray. 'He didn't mean to leave you everything. Oh, my Lord. It can't be right.'

'I know,' said Abby. 'But if the law says he has – I mean, what then? What do I do?'

'I don't know.' Then Ruth smiled incredulously, as though she hardly dared to voice her thoughts. 'I suppose – I suppose, you become very rich.'

The words hung in the air, unbelievable, wonderful. Then Abby broke the spell. 'Well, that's the point. Even if everything Robin Onslow says is right, it's not really mine, is it? I mean, it belongs to their family, not to me. It's the Maskelynes', not mine.'

Ruth turned to look at her daughter again, and in both her look and her voice there was something which Abby could not divine, something forceful, mysterious. 'Don't you want it? Wouldn't you like it to be yours?'

'Of course I would!' Abby laughed, but despairingly. 'If I'd won it in the lottery, or on the pools, I'd love to have all that. Who wouldn't? But it's not like that. It's somebody else's, and I'd be taking it away.' She turned to look out of the window. 'Of course I'd like it,' she added more quietly. 'The way things are, the way they're going . . . Think of Chloe . . .'

Ruth felt her blood pressure rising, the increased beating of her heart hard, yet sluggish. She tried to calm herself, but it was difficult. The moment had come, she had to tell Abby now. Everything pointed to it. If this was true, if by marrying her Leslie had unknowingly rendered his will useless and given everything to Abby, then she had to tell her. 'You know,' she said, trying to keep her tone measured, 'it's my turn to tell you something now. Something that may make a difference.' Abby glanced at her mother. She had actually begun to think about Stephen, wondering what he was doing now, and with whom, letting the thought of him fill her with a sweet ache. She didn't really want to think any more about this business. It was probably all nonsense, anyway. You could tell just by looking at Robin Onslow that he wasn't much of a lawyer. Anyway, she had told her mother now. She would decide about it all tomorrow. Maybe. Right now, she was tired.

'What?' she murmured listlessly.

'You asked me once why Leslie left you that money. And I said it was because you were my daughter, and he was fond of me, and wanted to see you right. That was true – in a way. But he did it for another reason.'

Abby gave her mother a quick, guarded glance. 'What other reason?'

Ruth took a deep breath. 'Because you're his daugther. His and mine.' There was silence for several seconds. 'There. That's said.' Ruth's voice was trembling now, and her hands plucked at folds of her cotton dress. She wished she could get up, stand up and leave the room, not wait for what was to follow, but she felt old, old and too weak. She knew she was going to cry, and wondered whether it was in fear or relief. Both, perhaps.

Abby moved her head slightly, as if in negation. When she

spoke, she felt her voice stick in her throat, and had to clear it. 'Oh, Mum . . .' It was all she could manage.

In those faintly uttered words Ruth could hear only what she imagined to be bitter disappointment, her daughter's reproach, the thing she dreaded most. She looked piteously at Abby. 'I'm sorry. Don't hate me, don't think ill of me.' She wept, putting up old, dry hands against the tears that wetted her cheeks.

'Mum, Mum . . . I don't hate you! Don't say that. It's not that . . .' Abby leaned forward and embraced her mother, rocking her heavy body against her own. They sat like that for several minutes. In Abby's mind, the reality of what her mother had told her began to take shape, like a picture coming together, piece by piece. If Leslie Maskelyne was her father, then Stephen was her half-brother. The man she had made love to, whose bed she had shared, whose body she had enjoyed, was her half-brother. What they had done should be disgusting, was maybe even criminal – she had no idea. Her heart and mind felt numb. Whatever he had been, he could be nothing to her now. Yesterday, when he had left her so casually, she had been miserable and uncertain. But at least she had been able to hope. What her mother had told her had changed everything. The pain of this realisation was worse than any of her recent unhappiness.

Ruth tried to calm herself, to stop her tears. 'I couldn't tell you until you were grown up, and when you were, the time somehow never seemed to be right . . .' She closed her eyes again. 'Don't be angry with me. For God's sake, please don't be angry.'

'I'm not angry,' said Abby slowly. She thought of the face in the few photos which she had seen, that of the man she had thought of as her father. He had meant nothing in their lives, Ruth hardly ever referred to him. But he had been a fixed point. To learn now that he was not her real father gave her an odd feeling, like being set suddenly adrift. She gazed at her mother, trying to picture the woman she must have been when all this happened, long ago. Leslie Maskelyne was her father. That was what mattered most to her mother, and she must concentrate on that. It had cost her mother much effort to tell her, and she must speak to her gently. Ruth knew nothing about her and Stephen, and mustn't, ever. God, no. Abby's mind coasted over the things she had been told as a child, about her father – or the man who was not her father – dying in the months before she was born. 'Did it happen after Dad died?'

Ruth nodded. 'He hadn't been dead a month. I felt terrible. Not guilty – well, guilty that I didn't feel guilty . . .' Her voice changed, suddenly taking on a note of intensity, of passion. 'Oh, but you can't imagine how it was. I'd never loved anyone like that in my life. Right from the very first.'

'Why didn't he marry you?' asked Abby, watching her mother's face, trying to imagine her, young and in love. 'Or was he married already?'

Ruth shook her head. 'No, he wasn't married. But there were a lot of reasons why we didn't marry. His reasons, really. He was already engaged to Stephen's mother, for a start. But it was more than that . . .' Her voice trailed away, and the expression in her eyes grew distant.

Abby could guess the reasons. They were probably the same ones that allowed Stephen to want her without loving her, to lie to her without any qualm of conscience, and to leave her feeling cold and afraid while he slipped back to London to his well-dressed, well-educated, middle-class girlfriend. Leslie Maskelyne, the wealthy young man from the big house, must have treated her mother in the same way. Perhaps it ran in the family. The family. Her family, she supposed. Stephen's family. Oh, that hurt. It hurt most of all. She would have given anything not to be part of Stephen's family.

'So, you see,' said Ruth, taking Abby's hand and pressing it between hers, 'you've as much right to anything that belongs to him.' Her voice held a tremulous fierceness. 'When he left you that money, he thought he was being generous. By our lights, he was. But by rights you should have had a quarter of everything, you should have been acknowledged. But he didn't want the rest of his family to know.'

'Why did you go along with that?' She stared wonderingly at her mother. 'That's not like you, to let someone patronise you, after – after abandoning you all that time ago.'

Ruth sighed. 'I suppose I didn't want them knowing, either. Nor you. Anyway, I decided it was all up to him. He was the one who was dying. You make allowances. That's the way he was. The way things were. He thought he was doing good, setting things to rights, marrying me, giving you money. It eased his conscience.' She paused, then added with weary affection, 'Old fool.' She glanced up at her daughter, feeling oddly light-hearted at having unburdened herself without any of the recriminations she had feared. 'I did love him, you know. I couldn't help it. Sometimes you just can't help it.'

'Yes, I know,' said Abby.

'So if this solicitor chap has got it right, I think you should take it.' Ruth's voice was suddenly fierce. 'Take it all. Stephen and the girls have had it easy all their lives. Now it's your turn. He was your father as much as theirs.'

Abby could say nothing. She felt overwhelmed by events, her mind and body drained, listless. She shook her head slowly. 'Oh, Mum, I don't know.' She laughed wearily. 'Everything is like some huge practical joke. Mind you, there would be some justice in it. Robin Onslow told me today that the Maskelynes aren't prepared to pay us a penny on the strength of that document. Just think, if it were all ours now . . .' What a very appropriate piece of retribution for their meanness. Still, no matter what Robin Onslow said, it all seemed to her highly unlikely, the kind of thing you got in novels. She rose and went to the television and switched it on, then handed the remote control to her mother. 'Let's not talk about it any more – any of it. I'm going to see to Chloe.'

As Abby put the remote in her mother's lap, Ruth caught Abby's hand and looked up at her. 'They'll all have to know now, though. They'll know everything about me and Leslie – won't they?'

Abby shook her head. 'I don't know, Mum. I don't know anything, right now.'

Later that evening, when Chloe was asleep, Abby made a pot of tea and some ham sandwiches and took them into the sitting room, where Ruth still lay on the sofa watching television. Abby drew an armchair up next to the sofa and placed a small table between them. They sat in companionable silence, watching *Birds of a*

Feather. When it was over, Ruth slipped her feet to the floor and rubbed at her legs to get the blood flowing.

'Ooh, that's better. No point in putting it off any longer. I have to go to the bathroom. That tea's gone straight to my bladder.' She got up slowly, Abby helping her, and went out, down the little hall and up the steep staircase. In the bathroom, she turned from flushing the lavatory and suddenly felt a fiery tingle that seemed to travel down her left arm. She pulled open the bathroom cabinet and stared inside at the jumble of bottles. Nothing there. Then she remembered – she'd left her pills downstairs in the kitchen. Oh, why did it suddenly seem such a long way down to fetch them? Maybe she should call to Abby. Just as she was closing the cabinet, the pain hit, the most monstrous she had ever known, squeezing her chest with incredible force, so that her mind blazed and her vision blackened. She tried to draw her breath, but it would not come. She wanted to call out to Abby, but everything was very far away. That feeling of incredible remoteness was the last thing Ruth knew, before she fell heavily to the bathroom floor.

Robin had spent most of Monday evening on the phone, tracking down James Lofting, an elderly silk whom he had occasionally instructed, and who shared Robin's penchant for convivial drinks sessions at the completion of cases. He told Lofting the facts of Abby's case as succinctly as he could, gave him his view of the matter so far as his own researches had taken him, and asked Lofting for his opinion.

'I'm afraid I'm asking this strictly as a favour, James – the young lady hasn't got a bean. Not yet, anyway. But it's worth a few drinks next time I'm in town.'

'Happy to help, Robin. Quite an interesting little scenario.' Lofting gazed down at the notes he had taken. 'It's quite unorthodox, of course, and he can't ever have intended this document to operate to dispose of his entire property, but I don't, on the face of it, see why it shouldn't . . . Leave it with me. I'll get back to you in a couple of days.'

When he put the phone down, Robin decided to have a celebratory nightcap. Just one. On the largish side, but just one.

For the first time in a long while, he didn't feel the need to paint his boredom and loneliness with several coats of whisky. Abby's problem had rejuvenated and excited him. And her company. She was a strange girl. On the rough side, certainly, but with an unaffected loveliness and unconscious elegance. The combination was unsettling and quite erotic. He wondered how much this money would change her, if it turned out that it was hers. He poured three fingers of Tesco's own brand De Luxe Scotch Whisky into a tumbler, and sat back in his battered armchair to contemplate this interesting conundrum.

It was Doris who had known what to do. Abby knew nothing about people dying. The only thing she had been able to think of was to call Doris and tell her what had happened. She knelt on the bathroom floor next to her mother, stroking her hand in an unbelieving way, while Doris rang the doctor. Part of her knew and accepted that Ruth was dead, but some other part kept expecting her to wake up. When the doctor came ten minutes later, Abby sat on the closed lid of the toilet and watched him as he examined Ruth's body. He spoke to Abby and Doris as he wrote out the death certificate, but Abby wasn't listening to him. What were they going to do with her? What happened next? She looked so heavy and inert, so pathetic, just lying there on the floor.

'I don't imagine that there's much that can be done tonight,' said the doctor. 'You'll have to ring the funeral directors in the morning.'

'It's Mr Ferris in Sudbury we'll need,' said Doris, with an air of authority. She looked pale and strained, and very shocked, but for someone of Doris's nature it was therapeutic just to be able to make decisions, to organise things.

Abby gazed down at her mother. 'We can't just leave her there,' she said, and then burst into sobs.

Between them they managed to move Ruth's body from the bathroom and along the narrow landing to her bedroom, where they laid her on the worn candlewick bedspread. Doris folded Ruth's slack, withered arms on her breast, and then began to sniffle and weep herself. Abby plucked some tissues from the box near

Ruth's bed and handed them to her, aware that Doris's tears were setting her own off again. Suddenly she felt a tugging at her skirt, and looked down to see Chloe standing on the landing behind her, her thumb in her mouth, glancing round with wonder at the sight of all the people in Granny's bedroom.

Abby wiped her eyes swiftly and picked Chloe up, carrying her back to her room. 'What's happening, Mummy?' asked Chloe, trying to peer back along the landing over Abby's shoulder. 'Why are Auntie Doris and that man in Granny's bedroom?'

'It's just the doctor, love,' said Abby, trying to keep the tremor from her voice. 'He's come to see Granny. She's poorly. Now, let's get you back into bed.'

As she tucked Chloe in, Abby could hear Doris going downstairs with the doctor. He had gone by the time Abby went downstairs. Doris was in the kitchen, her back to Abby as she filled the kettle at the sink.

'Thank you for coming over, Doris. I don't know what I'd have done.' Abby laid a hand on the old woman's shoulders, and Doris immediately began to weep. Abby took the kettle from her and set it on the draining board, turned off the tap, and held Doris in an awkward embrace. Strange, thought Abby, how the adults one respected and feared in childhood gradually, in old age, turned into children, to be helped and pitied.

'She was such a good friend, such a good friend . . .' whimpered Doris. Abby held her, and wondered who there would be to dry her own tears and help her through the coming days.

The next day, as though propelled by the momentum of her grief, Doris virtually took over the business of organising the funeral. She seemed to know what should be done about coffins and head-stones and flowers, and what arrangements to make with the vicar. Abby was happy to be sidelined. She had enough to do with Chloe, and the business of going through her mother's things. Ruth hadn't made a will, so far as she could see, but Abby supposed everything was now hers. At least she could ask Robin to help. She'd find the money to pay him somehow. The cottage and the old Mini were about all Ruth had ever owned.

As the shock of her mother's death receded, Abby felt filled with a sense of inertia. She thought about Stephen constantly, without wanting to, helpless. At the worst and most inappropriate of moments, the recollection of their lovemaking would fill her with a heat of longing. She tried to feel a sense of guilt, but couldn't. The prosaic fact of their shared paternity seemed insignificant in one instant, and then monstrous, overwhelming, the next. Above all, she wanted to see him, simply to look at him and talk to him.

Geraldine Maskelyne called on Wednesday, two days before the funeral was due to take place. She had hesitated before calling, fearing embarrassment following the business with the Owens and her father's money, but felt that some member of the family should offer their sympathy. Abby found it hard to pay attention to the things Geraldine said. She found herself scrutinising Geraldine covertly, looking at her with fresh eyes, and thinking, 'You are my half-sister.' In a dizzying moment, just as Geraldine picked up her sunglasses from the kitchen table and was about to leave, Abby was filled with an insane urge to tell her everything.

'Stephen's in London,' Geraldine was saying. 'I don't suppose he knows about your mother yet. I'll call him this evening. I know he'll be wretched. He was very fond of her. We all were.'

The reckless moment passed. Abby simply smiled and thanked Geraldine for coming. When she had left, Abby wondered why she had been so polite to the woman. It was she, after all, together with her brother and sister, who had refused to give Ruth any money. Maybe they had even hastened her death. This hadn't occurred to Abby until now, and she began to brood upon it.

That evening, she wondered every ten minutes or so whether it was now that Geraldine was speaking to Stephen, telling him, and whether in those moments he was thinking about her, Abby. The memory of their last time together touched her with involuntary longing. Did that make her some kind of monster? She knew she should feel revulsion at what had happened. Desire shouldn't be a part of it, not ever again. Perhaps when she saw him next, things would begin to make new sense and she would feel no more for him than any sister should for a brother. She hoped so. God, how she hoped so.

When she went to bed that night she wept and wept, quietly, her face half pressed into the pillow so that Chloe would not hear, full of guilt that she was crying for Stephen, and not for her mother.

On Thursday night there were distant rumbles of thunder, and everyone wondered if a storm would break, but on the day of the funeral the heat continued. It seemed incongruous to Abby. She knew nothing of funerals, but from what she'd seen on films and TV, they were meant to take place on bleak, wintry days. Instead, everything sparkled in the summer air, even the coffin handles, and the breeze was light, cheerful. She stood by the grave with Doris, and twenty or so other people from the village, and watched as her mother was buried, only half-listening to the vicar. Her grief seemed to have flattened out into depression, undercut by a dull ache of longing whenever she thought of Stephen. She stared at her mother's coffin as it was lowered into its grave, and then glanced over the stone wall at the path that led to the Dips. Her childhood had always seemed to her such a recent, near thing, but now it seemed an impossibly long time ago. Abby had never thought of herself as young or old, had simply let the years wash over her. She stood at her mother's graveside and thought, I am thirty-three. I am an adult. I am alone.

Geraldine had come to the funeral, but not Lydia. Abby told herself that she had not so much as hoped to see Stephen there that day, but she had. Of course she had. But he had stayed away. From her as much as from the funeral, Abby guessed. A recollection of his words and the way he had turned away from her at their last meeting often rose unbidden to her mind, and it did now.

At the end of the service, Geraldine approached her. 'Lydia couldn't come, I'm afraid. But she sent her condolences.'

'That's nice,' said Abby. Her voice was cold. The thought of the money which the Maskelynes had so meanly refused now nagged at her. Geraldine was wearing an elegant two-piece suit in black silk, in which she looked as cool and poised as ever. Abby wished she had been able to find something else in her own wardrobe beyond a black lycra skirt that was too short, and a navy silk shirt.

Still, that was the way it was. Or was it? For the first time in a few days, Abby suddenly thought about Robin Onslow and the document. Her heart seemed to leap into her throat. Imagine, she thought, gazing at Geraldine's carefully composed expression of concern and kindliness, at her triple string of pearls and her diamond earrings, imagine if I were to take it all away from you, all the money that you think is coming to you. Then she thought of Stephen, and could not help asking about him.

'Did you manage to speak to Stephen?'

'Yes – yes, I did. He's dreadfully upset, of course, and sends you his sympathy and best wishes. He's very tied up in some complicated negotiations over a restaurant that he's trying to open, so he couldn't come up for the funeral, I'm afraid.'

'Oh, I didn't expect him to,' said Abby quickly. She glanced back at the graveside. 'I saw the flowers the three of you sent. Thank you. You shouldn't have gone to the expense.'

Geraldine flushed. She glanced at her watch, 'I'm sorry I can't come back with you all, but there's Arabella to see to, you know – my nanny's on holiday, and Peter's holding the fort.'

'That's all right,' said Abby, and watched as Geraldine made her way among the headstones to the church gate, where her Mercedes was parked.

Abby went back to Alma Cottage with Doris and some of the other mourners, and Doris dispensed tea, which everyone was grateful for, and sausage rolls, for which they were not. The gathering was kept mercifully brief, for Abby had to go and collect Chloe from nursery at twelve. When she got back, Doris had finished clearing up.

'There was a phone call while you were out,' said Doris, lifting the last of the saucers from the washing-up bowl. 'A Mr Onslow. He asked you to ring him back. He said you knew the number, but I took it, anyway. There, I'll leave those to drain.' Doris wiped her hands on a tea towel. 'That was a nice service, I thought. I think Ruth would have liked it. Not that she was devout, but she did like a nice service.'

This made Abby smile, and she kissed Doris on the cheek. 'You've been a gem. I couldn't have got through it without you.'

179

'Yes, well . . . An ounce of help is worth a pound of pity, they say.' Doris sniffed back some tears, then briskly untied Ruth's apron and picked up her black straw hat from the dresser. 'You'll be stopping on here for a while, I suppose, to sort things out?'

'I suppose so. I don't really have any plans for the future. I have to think about things.'

'Well . . . I'll still stop by to see how you're getting on, if that's all right. It would seem funny not to, when I think of all the years I've come by regular for my cup of tea.' Her eyes brightened with tears again. 'Right. I'm off. Be good, my girl,' she added, chucking Chloe on her soft cheek.

When Doris had gone, Abby made Chloe some sandwiches and switched on *Sesame Street*. The phone began to ring, and at its sound she felt her heart give its inevitable small leap of hope. She went into the hall, unpinning her blonde hair from its loose knot, and picked up the phone. He hadn't been able to come, so maybe he was ringing now. Maybe he had been thinking about her all the time.

'Hello?'

'Hello, Miss Owen?' asked an unfamiliar female voice.

'Yes?'

'I have Mr Onslow for you. Just a moment.'

She felt the familiar, slithering sense of disappointment within her. Of course it wouldn't have been Stephen. Why did she keep hoping for the impossible?

'Hello, Abby? Robin Onslow here. How are you?' His voice sounded bright and confident.

At least with Robin there was no need for polite dissembling. She sighed. 'Not too great, I'm afraid. My mum died on Monday. The funeral was today. This morning.'

'Oh, God, I'm sorry.' He sounded startled. 'That's terrible. I'm so sorry to hear it.' It was nice, thought Abby – he actually sounded as though he meant it. 'Look, shall I – I mean, would you like me to call back another time?'

'No, no – that's okay,' said Abby. She felt suddenly exhausted, and her calves ached from the heels she had been wearing all morning, her only smart pair of shoes, thankfully black. She

180

slipped them off now, lifted the phone from the table, and slid to the floor, knees up, leaning against the wall.

'The thing is, I thought you might like to know –' his tone slipped irrepressibly from sympathy to enthusiasm '– that I've spoken to counsel about that document of yours.'

'Counsel?'

'A barrister. A specialist in these things. Wills, and so forth.'

'Oh.'

'And it's just as I thought. The marriage revoked Leslie Maskelyne's original will, and that piece of paper he wrote operates as a valid will. In your favour. Provided the signatures of the two witnesses were all in order, it's all yours.'

Abby stared at the banisters opposite, and began to count them, one, two, three . . . In the background, she could hear Big Bird singing a song about sunflowers. 'Everything?'

'Everything,' replied Robin, in a voice of utter and happy certainty. 'Every last penny.'

Chapter Thirteen

Stephen was sprawled on the sofa in his flat, clicking idly and aimlessly through television channels on the remote control. Harriet was curled up a few feet away, reading. She glanced up as the television screen flickered and changed.

'I wish you wouldn't keep hopping about like that. It's quite annoying, actually.'

'I can't concentrate. There's nothing I want to watch.' He yawned and ran his fingers through his hair. 'Christ, I'm bored. I've been bored all day.'

'Then you shouldn't have chucked in your job,' remarked Harriet. 'Anyway, you've got the restaurant to think about.'

'Yeah, but that's all I *can* do. Think. Nothing can get moving until the lawyers finish faffing around with the lease. It's just a case of waiting, waiting.'

The phone rang, and Stephen turned off the television and got up to answer it. At first he didn't recognise Abby's voice. When he realised who it was, his heart sank. This was the last thing he wanted. When he had left her in his bed last weekend, he had intended that to be the finish. She was mature enough, experienced enough, he hoped, to accept in the long run that his silence and his absence meant there was to be nothing more between them. Sure, he'd had some qualms when Lydia had told him that Ruth had died. He'd wondered whether it wouldn't be the decent thing to call, or even go to the funeral. But he had managed to persuade himself that this might send out the wrong signals, and that it would be best just to let it go.

'Abby – this is unexepcted,' he said, trying to suppress his irritation. After an uneasy pause he added, 'I was really cut up about your mother. I hope Gerry told you.'

In Alma Cottage, Abby sat tensely on the edge of Ruth's old sofa, gripping the receiver tightly. She had dragged the phone in from the hallway, not wanting to disturb Chloe, and the cord barely reached into the room. Abby had fought an unhappy battle within herself before ringing Stephen's London number, which she had got from Doris. In the end, desperation had got the better of pride. She had to talk to him. This business of Stephen's father's will, now so certain since Robin Onslow's phone call, seemed to press down on her like some unbearable weight. Maybe if she told Stephen, things would become clearer, and she would know what to do. There was no one else whose help she wanted. For days she had longed to hear his voice, to establish some kind of contact with him, not caring that it might ultimately be pointless.

'Yes,' said Abby. Her voice was strained with nervousness. 'I thought you might ring.'

Stephen sighed, glancing round as Harriet got up from the sofa and went through to the kitchen. He waited until the door had closed, then, keeping his voice low, replied, 'Look, Abby . . . I told you, I'm sorry about your mother. Really. She was very nice to me when we – when we were children. Maybe I should have rung. I don't know. I just didn't – I didn't want you getting the wrong idea.'

'Idea?' echoed Abby. She pressed the fingers of one hand against her forehead, trying to persuade herself that she was just imaginging the hard edge to his voice.

'About us.' He sighed impatiently again. 'Listen, I don't know how you got my number, or why you're calling, and I don't want to be unkind, but –' Harriet came through from the kitchen with two cups of coffee, and he broke off. After a pause, moderating his tone to one of conversational enquiry, he said, 'So, I suppose you'll be going back to London now?' He gave Harriet a covert glance, but she had put down the coffee and resumed her book, apparently not listening.

Abby changed her grip on the receiver, suddenly aware that she had been pressing it uncomfortably close to her ear. She tried to keep her voice level, but the lowness of her tone only added to the urgency in her voice. 'Stephen . . . Stephen I really need to talk to you. Properly. I don't know what I've done, why you're being this way –'

Stephen's voice cut in. 'Tell Mrs Cotterell I won't be coming down to Hemwood for a couple of months. Perhaps she could send any post on here. I hope things work out for you. Bye.'

There was a click on the line, and then silence. Abby set the receiver down slowly. He hadn't even wanted to listen. She should probably be grateful that he hadn't let her make a fool of herself. A dull, almost physical ache seemed to burn within her. She tried, as she stared at her mother's shabby patterned carpet, to think clearly, to analyse the nature of the pain she felt. So much love, so much humiliation, so much – God, yes, anger. Deep, fierce anger. In that moment she saw herself, not as the racked, pathetic person that Stephen had turned her into, but as she had been before she came back to Hemwood – tough, independent, perhaps a little hard where people were concerned. Well, she was still that person. She wasn't going to be used, to be treated like some second-rate commodity. She thought back to the conversation she had had with her mother on the evening she died, remembered the enigmatic look on her face when she had asked Abby whether she didn't want Leslie Maskelyne's money. 'Wouldn't you like it to be yours?' Ruth had said . . .

It *was* hers. In that moment, still smarting from the pain of her humiliating conversation with Stephen, she made her decision. Sod the rest of the Maskelyne family. She was part of it, whether they liked it or not, and she would take whatever was hers. She had nothing else in the world, after all. Stephen and his sisters could whistle for the money. They didn't need it. They were all well off, nicely set up in their own comfortable lives, thanks to the upbringing which their father had given them. And which he had not seen fit to give to her. There was Chloe to think about. The rest of them didn't matter a toss. Somehow, through some weakness which she hadn't thought herself capable of, she'd got herself into an emotional mess over Stephen. Well, she'd get herself out of it. It was just a matter of time. And hardness. She could be just as hard as he had shown himself to be.

Abby took a deep breath and stood up, feeling clearer and stronger in her mind than she had for days. She had told Robin earlier that she wanted to think about things, that she didn't yet know what course of action she was going to take. Well, she'd thought about things now. And Stephen had helped her to decide exactly what she was going to do.

Stephen stood for an uncertain moment by the phone, his back to Harriet. He felt bad. Not guilty, exactly, but fearful. He could tell from Abby's voice what it meant to her, this affair – this stupid thing that he should never have begun. She might not let it go so easily. How in hell had she got his number? God, he hoped she wasn't going to start calling, pestering . . .

He turned to Harriet, frowning, then gave her a swift, sad smile. 'That was Abby.'

'Who?' Harriet looked up from her book.

'Abby – the cleaner at Hemwood.'

'Oh, yes. What did she want?' Harriet studied Stephen's face with quiet interest. She could always tell when he was going through an elaborate performance to conceal his feelings, or some unspoken truth. He always said more than was necessary, spoke when he didn't even have to. Harriet, despite what she had said, remembered Abby very well. She waited, wondering.

'Her mother died. Is that my coffee? Thanks.' Stephen sat down on the sofa. 'The funeral was today.' He sipped his coffee. 'She was a bit upset. I suppose I should have called. Said something.'

'Really?' Harriet sounded surprised.

He glanced at her, then he realised that he had never mentioned to her the friendship that had once existed between himself and Abby. 'I actually knew her mother quite well. Abby and I used to play together when we were little.'

Harriet nodded slowly, her eyes fixed on Stephen's face. 'No wonder she's upset.'

'Actually,' said Stephen, running his hands through his hair,

'I've been thinking . . . Despite what Gerry says, I think I should give her some money. Abby, I mean.' He turned to look at her. 'Don't you think so?'

'Why? Is your conscience troubling you?'

He looked away. What was Harriet guessing? Her face was wearing that alert, clever look. Or perhaps he was just reading too much into what she was saying. Either way, a semblance of candour was the best tactic. 'Well, I'm fond of her. These childhood friendships make you feel – sort of responsible. I don't want to appear to be behaving selfishly.' When he looked at Harriet again, his expression was one of carefully composed frankness.

Harriet put out a hand and stroked his cheek. 'That's nice of you.' And she smiled.

Stephen felt faintly perturbed by the considering look in her eyes. He put his arms around her and drew her towards him, then kissed her. 'I'm a nice guy,' he murmured.

'Are you?' She looked searchingly into his eyes, still smiling.

'Of course I am.' He contemplated her face for a moment, and then said softly, surprisingly, 'In fact, I'm so nice, I think you should marry me.'

'Oh?' Harriet's face betrayed nothing.

'Is that it? Is that all you can say? Oh?'

'Is this a proper proposal?' she murmured.

He kissed her again. 'Yes. Yes, it is. Be Mrs Maskelyne. Be the wife of a famous restaurateur. Live at Hemwood House. Have lots of babies. How's that? Good enough for you?'

She kissed him back for a long moment, very happy, the little mystery of Abby quite forgotten. 'Oh, yes. Yes, indeed.'

Stephen held her, stroked her hair affectionately, grateful for the sudden, safe feeling that all of this gave him. Since he had packed in his job he had been feeling strangely insecure. The imagined pleasures of being a rich, unattached bachelor no longer seemed so attractive. And the thing with Abby had been unsettling. But now she could no longer touch him. He would marry Harriet, and be safe.

Abby went to see Robin Onslow first thing on Monday morning, taking Ruth's marriage certificate with her. For Robin, it was the most intriguing piece of business he had ever undertaken, and he took special pleasure in drafting the letter to Walter Hubbard. When Jackie had typed it up, he read it through twice, signed it, and told Jackie to put a copy on Abby's file – the file which was still so new and thin, but which he guessed would now grow and grow. Depending on how things went, Abigail Owen could well become one of his most important and lucrative clients.

Two days later Stephen rang Walter Hubbard to discuss some business with him. It was a little before ten o'clock, and Walter's secretary was still going through the morning's post. Walter himself was having his morning cup of coffee.

'Good morning, Stephen,' he said. 'By coincidence, I was just about to send you the valuation on Hemwood House, together with a couple of things that need your signature.'

'Oh, right. Good . . .' Stephen's voice was vague, distracted. 'I actually rang to discuss something else with you. I was wondering . . .' He wished he could be more forthright about this, but asking for money was always demeaning, even if it was your own money you were asking for. 'You see, the fact is, I resigned from my job recently. I've got a business project that I want to devote more time to. As you can appreciate, I'm rather in need of funds. Money's not exactly a problem yet, but it could get that way. So I was wondering if there was any possibility of receiving an advance on the estate.'

At the other end of the line, Walter raised his eyebrows. His lips, beneath his thin moustache, were pressed together in a disapproving line. He regarded it as rather rash of Stephen to give up lucrative employment when the estate wasn't yet wound up. Still, it was hardly his place to comment. 'I see. Well . . .' Walter paused, nodding in acknowledgement at his secretary as she laid the more important items of the morning's mail before him. 'Given the very healthy balances presently standing in several of your late father's bank accounts, I think it may be possible to make an interim distribution. I can't give you a present indication as to the amount, of course. That's something I shall have to consider.'

'Thank you,' said Stephen. It irked him even to have to sound grateful. After all, it was his own money, damn it. Still, best to keep the man sweet, since he was going to need a bit of finance for the restaurant project, which was now sailing along smoothly. He hoped this interim distribution was going to be a large one. 'There was something else,' he added. 'You remember that business with the two Owen women, the document that my father wrote?'

'Yes.'

'Well, the mother has died – Ruth Owen – and I'd like to see that the daughter gets some money after all.' He had pondered the matter on and off, ever since Abby's phone call. Thankfully she hadn't called again, but it was always a possibility. Perhaps if he paid a large enough amount, she would get the message and leave him alone. 'I thought – say, twenty thousand.'

Walter reflected. 'Well, I should require the agreement of the other beneficiaries, your sisters –'

'No, I want this to come from my share. There's no need to consult them.'

'I see. Very well . . . It is only one-fifth the amount your father stipulated in the document –'

Stephen thought he'd just about had enough of this, and cut in. 'I think it is quite generous enough. Particularly in view of the fact that I am not legally obliged to pay her a penny.'

'No, of course not,' demurred Walter.

'Fine. I'll look forward to hearing from you about that advance on the estate.'

The conversation ended, and Walter put the phone down and turned to attend to the letters lying before him.

Fifteen minutes later, just as Stephen was contemplating a mid-morning stroll down the Brompton Road in search of ingredients for supper, which he had promised to cook for Harriet, Walter Hubbard rang back. Slightly surprised, Stephen wondered if perhaps he'd come to some snap decision on giving him some money. But Walter's voice had lost its customary cool lawyer's edge; he sounded bemused, almost disturbed.

188

'Stephen, since I last spoke to you I have received a most extraordinary communication. Coincidentally, it concerns the young woman you were speaking of earlier – Abigail Owen.'

Stephen groaned inwardly. This was what he had dreaded. She was upset about what had happened and had decided to get iffy about the money. 'What does she want?' he asked, then added, 'If it's about the money, you might as well write straight back and tell her she can have some. I don't want her pestering me.'

'No, no, the letter isn't from her,' replied Walter. 'It's from her lawyer. What he says is most odd . . . Perhaps I'd better read it to you.' Walter cleared his throat and began to read. *'Dear Sir, we are writing to you with regard to the estate of the late Leslie Maskelyne, of which we understand you have been appointed as one of the executors under a will dated 10th September 1989. We act on behalf of Miss Abigail Owen, who is, as we believe you are aware, one of the parties named in a document dated 18th May 1998 and executed by the late Mr Maskelyne. We believe you are in possession of a copy of this document and will therefore be familiar with its contents. We wish to advise you that a set of circumstances has arisen which leads us, on behalf of our client, to challenge the validity of the late Mr Maskelyne's will –'*

'What!' expostulated Stephen.

'– dated 10th September 1989, in respect of which we understand you have recently obtained a grant of probate. It is our belief and under-standing that, subsequent to the execution of this will, Mr Maskelyne married Mrs Ruth Owen, the mother of our client –'

'I don't believe this!' exclaimed Stephen. He laughed. 'How utterly ridiculous! I've never heard such complete rubbish –'

Walter's voice cut in. 'I think you'd best let me finish.' He continued, *'– the mother of our client, on Friday, 17th May, 1997. We enclose for your attention a copy of the marriage certificate –'*

'Rubbish,' snapped Stephen, interrupting once more. 'What is this document? Look at it and tell me what it says.'

At the other end he could hear the rustling of pages, and then Walter said, 'It's simply a photocopy of a certificate of marriage. It names Leslie Arthur Maskelyne, widower, and Ruth Hilda Florence Owen, widow, as the parties, and . . . let's see . . . married at Colchester Registry Office . . . signed by Joseph Rippingale,

Registrar . . . dated May 17th, 1998. Only a photocopy, of course, but we must presume –'

'We'll presume nothing,' retorted Stephen, trying to fathom what was happening. Why on earth would Abby go to these lengths? Where did she think it was going to get her? It was irrational. 'This is a joke. This is some elaborate attempt to stir up trouble. I know this family. The thing can't possibly be authentic.'

'Possibly. But I doubt if any lawyer would write in this way if he wasn't sure of his ground,' replied Walter cautiously. 'Or at any rate, of the authenticity of the documents he had been given.'

Stephen hesitated. Whenever he got angry, it was usually a reaction to his own fear, or doubt. He let his temper subside, and tried to collect his thoughts. 'But even if there is some truth in this–' he began, then stopped. There couldn't be. It was impossible. Why should his father marry some old biddy like Ruth Owen? *Marry?* Unless, of course, he hadn't been right in the head . . .

'I think you'd better let me finish,' said Walter, and carried on reading. '*As you are doubtless aware, your client's marriage to our client's mother has the effect of revoking the will dated 10th September 1989.*' At this, Stephen sought a chair and sat down on it, listening, a cold feeling creeping through his insides. '*In view of this fact, and in the light of the contents of the document dated May 18th, referred to above, it is our client's contention that this latter document operates as a valid testamentary disposition, and that under it, in the light of the death of the late Mrs Ruth Owen, she is now the sole beneficiary of the late Leslie Maskelyne's estate. We should therefore be grateful if you would confirm your consent to the revocation of the grant of probate which you have obtained in respect of the late Mr Maskelyne's invalid will, and would ask that you kindly forward to these offices all bank statements, share certificates, and other relevant documents, including the title deeds to Hemwood House, in order that a grant of letters of administration may be sought in respect of the testamentary disposition dated May 18th 1998. Yours faithfully, Onslow & Co.*' There was a silence. 'That's it,' said Walter.

Stephen's thought processes felt mired. Even though Walter had just finished reading, Stephen could recollect no clear words, merely a deadly impression of the cold, businesslike tone of the letter and its meaning. Lawyers didn't write like that as a joke. 'What on earth is it all about?' His voice sounded dazed. 'Is she trying to say that she inherits my father's property?'

'In effect – yes.'

There was a long pause as it sank in. 'That's utterly outrageous,' said Stephen, as though he refused even to entertain such a preposterous idea. Then he added, 'It's impossible, surely? I mean –' His thoughts felt confused, and he sought clarity from Walter. 'Look, take me through it. I know this is all just some hideous try-on, but I have to understand it. Just take me through it from the beginning.'

So Walter did. Stephen listened carefully, trying to reassure himself with the 'ifs' and 'maybes'. Clearly the whole thing had to be a piece of nonsense. It was all based on supposition, speculation. 'So, you're saying *if* the marriage was valid, which I don't believe it was. I don't believe it ever happened. Anyway, first of all there's that "if". What next? Oh, yes – the document. They're trying to say that works as a will. Which clearly isn't right. It can't be – can it?'

'Well . . .' Walter's tone was doubtful. 'Without the benefit of some research, I would hesitate to say. I don't have the document immediately to hand. That is something I would have to examine carefully.'

'Well, I'm sorry – it's pretty clear that the whole thing is a set-up,' said Stephen firmly. He spoke with confidence. He had been badly shaken for a few minutes – lawyers' letters were intended to put the frighteners on you – but now that he had worked it through, it seemed quite obvious to him that some utterly unrelated person like Abby couldn't just suddenly lay claim to his father's estate, simply on the basis of a spurious document and a photocopy of a marriage certificate which was almost certainly faked. Even if it was genuine, a marriage of that kind, taking place just three days before his father's death, had to be open to serious challenge.

'That is possible, certainly . . .' The caution in Walter's tone irritated Stephen. The man was supposed to be on their side, wasn't he? Why was he sounding doubtful? Before he could interrupt, Walter went on, 'But it would be wrong of me to give any speculative opinion. I intend to speak to Mr Onslow today. There are facts which require to be ascertained before we can –'

'But you do intend to challenge it, don't you? I mean –'

'Of course,' replied Walter soothingly. 'But first, I must find out a few things. Leave it with me.'

'Well, look,' said Stephen, glancing at his watch, 'I'm going to drive up to Hemwood today. I want this bloody thing sorted out, and quickly.' He hesitated, then said, 'I might as well tell you, Walter, that this woman, Abby, has probably got it in for me in some way. We had a bit of a thing, and I cooled it. This is strictly confidential, you understand. But it may explain it.'

'I see. Well – yes, I'm grateful for your candour. It may be of some significance.' But Stephen could tell from his tone that he didn't really think it was. This, for some reason, frightened him.

'I'll call at your offices around three this afternoon. You'll have spoken to this other lawyer by then, I take it?'

'I would certainly hope so.'

When he put the phone down, Stephen sat mulling it over, going through everything Walter had said, trying to extract crumbs of reassurance. At the recollection of Walter's manner, his disquiet grew. The man had been worried. Was there more to this than Abby just being a vindictive bitch? There couldn't be. Then again . . . He picked up the phone. To allay his fears, and to spread his worry thinner, he rang Geraldine and told her every-thing. He needed to share his outrage, and at the same time seek reassurance. Appalled and disbelieving, but taking encouragement from Stephen's expressed opinion that the whole thing was some kind of a bluff, Geraldine said she would ring Lydia, and that they would meet him at Walter Hubbard's offices that afternoon. When he put the phone down, Stephen felt a little better for the support of his family. But only a little.

Robin rang Abby just after lunch. 'We've got them running scared,' he told her happily. 'I had the old chap Hubbard himself on the phone this morning, very calm and circumspect. But you could tell he was moving like lightning. He couldn't have had the letter half an hour, and he'd already spoken to Stephen Maskelyne.'

Abby felt her stomach dip at the thought of Stephen's likely reaction. She felt momentarily frightened. Well, she had started it now, and there was no going back. With the phone held in the crook of her shoulder, she handed Chloe a Mr Men fromage frais and a teaspoon. 'What did Stephen's lawyer say?'

'Well, first of all he wants to see your mother's marriage certificate.'

'Why?'

'To check that it's the real thing. He knows it must be, of course, but he's got a right to inspect documents. I told him it was in my office, and he was welcome to come and see it any time he wanted. He said he might call round some time today.'

'What else did he say?' She longed to know exactly what Stephen had said, but there was no way of knowing that, yet.

'Not a lot. There was a bit about expressing his clients' astonishment and concern, but that was about it. There's not very much he *can* say at the moment. I'll bet that right now he's got at least two assistant solicitors with their noses stuck in *Williams on Wills* and digging up every relevant authority going, trying to find out exactly where he stands.'

Abby felt buoyed up by Robin's cheerfulness. She mustn't think about Stephen and his sisters. She must think about the money, about her rightful entitlement. That seemed to grow easier with every hour. From being a furtive, doubtful hope, it had grown into pleasurable contemplation. She must not allow herself to feel any guilt. Stephen had felt none. The idea of being a rich woman was very exciting. She couldn't help the way the law decided how things were to be.

'So what will happen now?' She watched as Chloe finished her fromage frais and then wiped her mouth and hands with a damp tea cloth.

'We sit back and wait for the fun to begin,' replied Robin.

'She has the most extraordinary nerve!' was Lydia's expressed view. It was ten past three, and she and Stephen and Geraldine were sitting in Walter Hubbard's room, waiting for him to appear. It was a comfortable room, old-fashioned, with much dark woodwork, long red velvet curtains skirting the bay window, and a chandelier. Its atmosphere was solid and reassuring. On a polished oval table close to Walter's desk stood three cups of tea and a plate of Rich Tea biscuits. Walter's secretary had brought these in earlier, and there they sat, ignored and untasted. The Maskelynes were not there for tea and biscuits.

'I wonder who put her up to it?' said Geraldine. 'She can't have worked out a scheme like this for herself. Must be this lawyer, I suppose.' She sighed. 'I really find the whole thing most distressing – not to mention tiresome. I mean, it's bordering on the tasteless to suggest that Father would marry someone like Ruth Owen when he was practically on his deathbed. Honestly.'

Stephen said nothing. Where the hell was Walter? It was a bit thick to keep them hanging around like this. Lydia got up and walked restlessly over to the window. She was wearing her regulation smart clothes – a calf-length Liberty print skirt, an old Laura Ashley blouse with a ruffled collar, a double string of pearls, and a navy woollen cardigan. It was the outfit she wore to speech days, parents' evenings, church, and on other semi-formal occasions. Geraldine glanced at her, thinking what a frump Lydia always looked. She glanced at her watch, and at that moment Walter came into the room. For a small, spare man in his sixties, he carried an air of surprising energy and vitality.

'Good afternoon to you all,' he said, shaking hands with each in turn. 'I'm so sorry to keep you waiting. I've had to rearrange certain items in my diary to accommodate this – this very pressing problem.' He sat down at his desk.

'Well, just how pressing is it?' demanded Lydia. 'I mean, Stephen's told us about the letter from this lawyer, and the extraordinary claims that Abby Owen is making, but what we want to know is, where do we stand? I mean –'

Walter interrupted, nodding. 'I quite understand your concern. It's a very surprising turn of events, and not one I welcome. We must examine the facts coldly and logically. In the first place, let us deal with the matter of the alleged marriage between your late father and Mrs Owen.'

' "Alleged" is the word,' said Geraldine. 'I certainly don't believe a word of *that*. I saw Father every other day before he died – well, almost – and I would have known if anything was going on. So would Lydia. She was there occasionally, too.'

'What do you mean – occasionally? I went to see Father on a regular basis – you know I did. But I do have two children to look after and a house to run. Anyway, you're forgetting – I already told you that I found out Ruth Owen had been visiting Father on the quiet. So maybe there is something in it.'

Stephen sighed. 'Maybe we should just hear what Walter has to say. What we believe and don't believe isn't important, frankly. Nor how often you two went to see him.'

Lydia thought that was rich, coming from someone who stayed up in London and hardly ever came to see his dying father. But she bit her lip and said nothing.

'Quite,' said Walter, wondering immediately why he had said that. 'As I was saying, the question of your father's marriage is germane to the whole issue. Without that, every aspect of Miss Owen's claim fails entirely. Now, as you know, I have received from Miss Owen's lawyer a photocopy of a certificate of marriage purporting to be that of your father and Mrs Owen.' Walter opened the file on the desk before him, extracted the photocopy attached to Robin's letter and passed it to his clients for their inspection. Geraldine looked at it first, scanning its contents. Lydia, her eyes on her sister's face, noticed a perceptible tension creep into her expression. Geraldine said nothing as she passed the photocopy to Stephen. He, too, examined it, then passed it to Lydia.

'What about it?' Stephen asked Walter, who was sitting watching them all, his elbows on his desk, his back very straight, the tips of both index fingers pressed together against his pursed lower lip.

Lydia passed the document back to Walter. Her face had a tremulous look, and her eyes were large with fear and disbelief.

There was an ominous pause of some seconds before Walter spoke. 'I called Mr Onslow this morning. He says he has the original at his office, and that I am welcome to see it at any time. I intend to go to his office this afternoon to do just that.'

'We're coming, too,' said Geraldine firmly. She was trying to shut her mind to the ghastly implications, should all this be true. Action would help.

'But I am bound to say,' went on Walter, 'that I should be very surprised if it is anything but authentic. I can see nothing in the photocopy to suggest that it might not be.' He waited, looking at each one of them in turn. Nobody spoke, so he went on, 'So I suggest that, for the moment at least, we should discuss the matter on the assumption that the document is genuine.'

'Right,' said Stephen. Driving up at lunchtime, he had already resigned himself to the nightmare possibility that his father had done something as loony as this. For what reasons, God alone knew, but perhaps that much simply had to be accepted. In which case he wanted to get down to brass tacks and find a way round the problem. He was confident that there must be one. 'Let us suppose that Father married Ruth Owen.'

'I simply can't believe that,' moaned Lydia quietly, her eyes wide and tearful.

Stephen ignored her. 'Surely we must be able to challenge it in some way? I mean, don't marriages have to be – to be consum-mated to make them legal? Or binding, or whatever it is? Father was hardly up to that, after all. He was hooked up to an oxygen cylinder, for God's sake.'

Lydia snuffled into a Kleenex at the indelicacy of this, but said nothing.

'Naturally,' said Walter, dipping his head slightly in acknowl-edgement, 'I have considered this point. Non-consummation renders a marriage voidable – that is, capable of being declared void by a court of law, certainly –'

'There you are!' said Geraldine, seizing upon this. 'It doesn't stand as a marriage – isn't that what you're saying?'

Walter sighed. 'No, not quite. It is a little complicated, I'm afraid. You see, a marriage which is voidable still has the effect of revoking the will of either one of the parties. Now, if the marriage were to be declared null and void by a court, the matter would be different. But the parties here are both dead. We could not possibly obtain such a declaration. Besides, a declaration of nullity would probably not have retrospective effect.'

'So – you're saying,' said Stephen slowly, 'that if there was a marriage, it can't be challenged on that basis?'

'I'm very much afraid not,' replied Walter.

'Isn't there *any* way we could say that the marriage was a sham? I mean, there is absolutely no reason on God's earth why my father should have done such a thing at his age, and given the state he was in. Absolutely none,' said Stephen.

Walter hesitated, then said quietly, 'If, as I suspect, the certificate of marriage is genuine, then we must suppose that there was a reason. Now that Mrs Owen is dead, it is one we shall, in all likelihood, never know.'

There was a silence in the room. Then Geraldine, who was looking pale and tight-lipped, said, 'Where does this lawyer have his practice? I think we should all go and see him right now. I'm tired of all this supposition. I want to find out for myself whether this marriage ever took place.'

Chapter Fourteen

R obin was somewhat taken aback when a full contingent of Maskelynes, plus lawyer, turned up at his office at four o'clock. When Jackie informed him of their arrival, he rolled down his shirtsleeves, put on his jacket, ran a quick comb through his hair, and asked her to show them in.

Robin's office was hardly as impressive as Walter Hubbard's. It was cramped and untidy, and through the open window came the sounds of High Street traffic. Robin's recent attempts to reorganise his life had got off to a well-intentioned start, but already his desk was piled with papers, and stacks of files stood at the side of his chair. Geraldine looked around, surprised that anything as bold and outrageous as a challenge to their father's will should have emanated from such seedy premises. She didn't think Abby's lawyer looked up to much, either; he had a stain on his tie and his shirt collar was frayed, so he obviously couldn't be very good.

Robin stood up and greeted them all politely, then offered tea, which was frigidly declined. Walter got straight down to business and asked if they could inspect the marriage certificate. Robin, who had Abby's file ready on his desk, promptly produced it and handed it to Walter. Each of the four of them studied it in turn.

'You can, of course, check with Colchester Registry Office, if you care to,' Robin said, giving them a cheerful, boyish smile. 'The validity of the marriage is not in doubt.'

'Possibly not,' replied Stephen, glowering at Robin, 'but I think you'll find you have a long way to go before you can succeed in any of this.'

Robin inclined his head. 'That's as may be. But I'm tolerably sure of my client's position.' He turned to look at Walter. 'Really, I am.'

Lydia began to say something, but Walter raised his hand in a gentle silencing gesture and said, 'Thank you for your time, Mr Onslow. I don't think there is much more that can be usefully said at this moment. I shall, of course, be in touch with you very shortly. Good afternoon.'

He rose, and the others followed suit. Robin bid them good afternoon and watched as they silently processed from his office.

On the way back to Colchester in Walter's BMW, the atmosphere was gloomy. They drove in silence for some miles, and then Geraldine, who had been twisting the diamond rings on her manicured fingers and staring bleakly at the passing countryside, said wonderingly, 'I can't understand why he did it. Why would Father marry her? Until Lydia mentioned it that night at dinner, I had no idea they even knew one another. And the registry office – I wouldn't have thought Father was capable of making the journey to Colchester in his state of health.'

'I shouldn't think he was,' said Lydia bitterly. 'It probably helped to kill him.'

'Mrs C must have known all about it,' said Stephen. 'She must have known exactly what was going on and said nothing to any of us. I intend to speak to that woman.'

Walter, who was driving speedily along the familiar roads and listening to all this, said, 'I take it that you're referring to your late father's housekeeper? Hmm. I don't think it would be a good idea to antagonise her in any way. She may be important to us.'

'What do you mean?' demanded Stephen.

Walter slowed down at a junction, glancing both ways. 'I think we have to accept that there is little hope, if any, of challenging the validity of the marriage, whatever anyone's views as to the motive behind it. I intend, of course, to seek counsel's opinion on the matter, but I seriously doubt if there is anything we can do.' He pulled away from the junction. 'If that is the case, then it follows,

I'm afraid, that your father's will is revoked by his marriage. It is of no effect. It is as if it never existed.'

'I don't see where Doris Cotterell comes into this. I would have thought we should have a go at her to try and prove that she and Ruth Owen between them coerced him into this marriage,' said Stephen impatiently.

Walter raised his eyebrows. 'I think you would find that extremely hard to prove, even if it were the truth.'

'What about the money?' said Stephen. 'The money he promised Ruth Owen in the document? Doesn't that show you that she was – was possibly blackmailing him in some way?'

'I don't see how that follows. Even if it were the case that she was blackmailing your father, she would hardly wait until after his death – and rely upon a document, at that – to obtain money. And why would he have to marry her? No, I suspect that it was something far simpler and – shall I say? – less mercenary than that.'

Stephen sighed. 'So – what about Mrs Cotterell?'

'Well, she is a witness to the document of May the eighteenth. She and Mr Fowler. If we can challenge the validity of that document in some way, then there is some hope for us.' Walter turned into the lane which led to the car park behind his offices, and slid the car neatly into his parking space. He switched off the engine and continued. 'In such a case, your father would be deemed to have died intestate, and you, as his surviving relatives, would still inherit.'

Stephen realised that the muscles of his neck were tense; he tried consciously to relax. He must cling on to the hope that there was some way out of this nightmare, no matter how slender that hope. The idea of Abby – Abby, of all people – inheriting all their father's wealth, and the house . . . It was insupportable. It was unreal.

'So – what? We talk to Mrs Cotterell. And?'

'We find out the precise circumstances in which this deed was drawn up and witnessed. I think our only hope may be to challenge it on a technicality. But I have to warn you,' added Walter, turning slightly in his seat to glance at each of them in turn, 'that it may be a very small hope.'

*

Doris called at Alma Cottage at half past five to babysit Chloe, so that Abby could do her evening shift at the Fox and Hounds. She changed into her carpet slippers and put her library book on the coffee table near the television for later on.

Chloe was sitting at the kitchen table, cutting out pictures from one of Ruth's old Grattan catalogues to stick in her scrapbook. 'Does she want bathing?' Doris asked Abby.

'If you don't mind,' said Abby.

Chloe looked up morosely at Doris. 'I want Mummy to bath me.'

'Want will be your master, my girl. Come on, let's get some of these stuck in your book,' said Doris, sitting down next to Chloe and sorting through her scraps.

'Can I make you a cup of tea?' asked Abby, pinning up her hair and slipping on her shoes.

'I'll make myself one when I'm done here. You'd best be getting off.'

'I've got a few minutes yet,' said Abby. 'By the way, I meant to ask you – about the cleaning job at Hemwood House. I was wondering whether you need me there every day, now that it's empty. Seems to me it doesn't need anyone more than twice a week, just to keep it clean and tidy.' Whatever Abby thought about Leslie Maskelyne's estate, it had not really occurred to her that the house might belong to her. In her mind, it was still the Maskelynes' property. That was the way it had been all her life.

Doris considered this. 'I dare say you're right. It's fine with me if you just want to go up the odd few days. But it'll mean less money for you.'

Abby shrugged. 'I don't mind. Chloe's school breaks up in a few weeks, so I won't have any mornings free after that. I'll have to give the job up, anyway. Will you be able to find someone else?'

'Oh, I imagine so. I might be able to manage the work on my own, until Stephen decides what he's going to do with the place.' Doris suddenly remembered something. She got up and went to her bag. 'I brought this to show you.' She pulled out a brochure with a picture of a cruise ship on the cover and laid it on the table. Abby came to look over her shoulder as Doris flicked through the pages. 'There,' said Doris happily. 'That's the *Fleur de Lis*, the cruise ship that Eddie and I are going on. As soon as that money comes through, that Mr Maskelyne left me, God rest him, we're booking it. It goes all the way through the Mediterranean. I've always longed to see some of them places.'

Abby felt her heart skip a beat. If all this business went ahead, there would be no legacy for Doris. She hadn't realised this before. No cruise, no new car, no easy retirement. But that was stupid. She could always give Doris the money. Over the past couple of days she had grown quite accustomed to the exciting prospect of being rich. She thought she could handle it very well. Superstition prevented her from making concrete plans, but she liked to daydream. Of course, it might still come to nothing – but Robin seemed completely confident. So now the idea of giving Doris fifty thousand pounds came quite naturally. Then, as she watched as Doris flicked through the pages of her brochure, a doubt crept into Abby's mind. Would Doris want to take money from her? It was quite a different thing from being left a legacy by a grateful employer in recognition of all you had done for him. Quite different. Doris might refuse it. She might regard what Abby was doing as wicked and unjust. Doris had a high regard for the Maskelynes, despite what she said about Stephen and his sisters, and the status of the wealthy family up at the big house was ingrained in her mind, her culture. The same was true for a lot of people in the village. What would they all think of what she was doing? They wouldn't understand all the legal niceties. They would just see Abby stepping in and taking away the Maskelynes' property.

'What do you think?' asked Doris, looking up at her. 'Wouldn't you like to go on a cruise some day? It's always been my dream, I can tell you.'

Abby forced a laugh. 'Chance would be a fine thing. Anyway, I'd better be going. Don't let Chloe eat too many biscuits.' She bent down and stroked her daughter's hair. 'And you mind you clean your teeth. Be good for Auntie Doris, now.'

Chloe swung one leg sullenly and looked up at her mother. 'She's not my auntie. I want Granny to look after me.'

Abby sighed.

'Well, now,' said Doris kindly, 'your granny *is* looking after you. From up in heaven.' Chloe turned back to her scrapbook and said nothing.

'I'll be back about half past eleven,' said Abby. She went out with a sense of depression. There were times when she wished none of this was happening. That everything was as it had once been.

That evening, as Stephen, his sisters and their respective husbands all convened at Geraldine and Peter's house to discuss the disaster which had befallen them, Harriet waited with growing impatience at Stephen's flat. She made herself some coffee, read a magazine, expecting him to walk in at any moment, or the phone to ring. By quarter to nine she was getting annoyed and worried. Where on earth had he got to? They had arranged to meet here some time after seven, and he was meant to be cooking supper. She had been looking forward to a lazy evening. Maybe something had come up to do with the restaurant – but that was unlikely at this time in the evening. Anyway, he would have rung her at her studio to tell her. She went into the kitchen and looked in the fridge. He hadn't even been shopping. She wandered back into the living room. It wasn't the first time that he had stood her up. He was a bit erratic, but she put up with it because it was part of Stephen, and she loved him. But he could be bloody exasperating. Well, she was hungry and cross and she wasn't going to hang around. She would go back to her own place and wait for his apologetic call.

'I just wish Hubbard weren't so damned phlegmatic about it all,' said Stephen. 'He talks as if the whole thing is a *fait accompli*, that there's nothing we can do. I've half a mind to sack him and get someone with a bit more mettle, someone who's prepared to fight it right from the start – the marriage, this bogus will, the lot.'

'To be fair, he did say he was getting counsel's opinion. And he's going to do his best about the document that this lawyer says is a will,' said Geraldine.

'Yes, but it's his *attitude* that gets me. He's so negative. The man has no balls. I mean, I can't afford to let this happen, for Christ's sake!' Stephen felt that his frustration was pushing him to breaking point. If only there was something he could *do*, some action he could take, instead of having to rely on Walter.

'None of us can,' said Geraldine, glancing round her dinner table at everyone's plates. She had rustled up some rack of lamb from the freezer, and had made a rather good Madeira sauce, but no one seemed to be eating much, except for Marcus. Lydia hadn't even touched her food, and she had hardly said a thing so far, which was quite unlike her. She just sat there silently, with that withdrawn look. It was perfectly horrible the way this business was affecting everyone. And she hated to see good food go to waste. She herself thought the whole thing quite appalling. It wasn't just the money she cared about. She and Peter were already nicely off, though it would have paid for a few extra-special holidays and given her a bit of a nest egg. She had even begun to think she might let Peter have some to buy the extra land he wanted. No, it was more than that. It was the idea of an outsider taking away everything that belonged to the family. It simply wasn't right. And Abby Owen – what on earth would someone like Abby do with it all? She thought she knew the answer to that. It didn't bear thinking about.

Geraldine's musings were disturbed by Stephen's response to her last remark. 'Well, Gerry, at least you've got Peter and the farm. And Lydia and Marcus aren't short of a bob or two, either. What have I got? I've jacked in my job at the agency, I've got plans for a restaurant that will now go completely up the spout, whether we see this thing through or not, and I don't imagine I'll have much to live on in a month or two. This does affect me rather more than you and Lydia, frankly. In fact, it's an utter disaster, from my personal point of view.'

'Then I suggest you get another job,' said Geraldine.

Stephen said nothing, and poured himself some more wine.

Lydia sat scarcely listening to any of this. They seemed to have been talking about it for hours, going round in endless circles. There was nothing they could do. Nothing, except wait and see what happened. She didn't think it mattered whether Walter handled it, or some other lawyer. She imagined the result would be the same. Something told her that she knew what that result would be. Abby Owen would, by a sheer twist of fate, inherit all the family property, Stephen would be left on his uppers, Gerry and Peter would have to go on exactly as they were, and she . . . Lydia looked up and across the long oval table at her husband. Marcus had wolfed down his lamb, and now, as he helped himself to more glazed carrots, was eyeing everybody else's plates. He grew fatter and redder every year. It was too much to hope that he would drop down dead of a heart attack tomorrow, though she imagined it would be on the cards one day. But over the last few months she had thought that she wouldn't have to wait that long to be rid of him. She had loved her father, she had not wanted him to die, but the money that she was to receive under his will had been intended as a means of escape. With it, she could take the boys and simply leave, never to set eyes on the porcine face of her husband again, with any luck.

There had been a time, in her naive girlhood, when she would not have believed that it was possible for any woman to start out loving someone, and move in a matter of ten years to the kind of cold contempt and dislike which she now felt for her husband. But then, she hadn't known what it would be like to be married to someone who begrudged every penny he gave you, who only handed out money for clothes and shoes and little luxuries for the boys after exhausting and demeaning arguments. Marcus, who earned more than enough, and who never stinted on clothes for himself or new fast cars, was happy for her to drive around in a beaten-up, second-hand Volvo that was always going wrong. He didn't care that she wore the same dreary clothes month after month or had her hair cut in the most practical fashion so that it didn't need regular sessions at the hairdresser's. How she hated the horrible business of waiting for him to hand out the house-keeping every week, from money kept in a bank account in his sole name, and then having to budget carefully to make it stretch. It was pathetic. It would be one thing if Marcus was a manual labourer on a paltry wage, but he wasn't. He was a stockbroker, and although she was not allowed to know how much he earned, she had a rough idea. They had a nice house, of course, good furniture – anything which was on public show was different. Apart from her.

It hadn't been this way in the beginning. For a year or so after they got married, he had been fairly casual about how much she spent. But gradually he had started to resent it, and started to quiz her, to check receipts and go through the bills from the supermarkets, querying this and that item. And now it was hell – a humiliating, dreary hell from which she had thought she was about to escape. But it seemed the way might be barred to her for ever. For without Father's money, how could she leave? She had qualifications, but what could she do when she had two young boys to look after? She might try to divorce Marcus, but would a court regard his behaviour as unreasonable? Maybe. Maybe not. Anyway, it would not be the existence she had imagined with half a million pounds or so of her own money. Carefully invested, that would have been enough for a happy, carefree life. She stared bleakly at her untouched food and listened as the arguments went on around her.

Harriet climbed the stairs to her studio flat, and was about to pull her keys from her bag, when she saw a figure sitting hunched beside the door. She felt a brief flicker of fear before recognising Charlie. He stood up when he saw her and said hello. She noticed he had a rucksack and a duffle-bag with him.

'Hello, Charlie,' she said, glancing from him to his luggage. 'To what do I owe the pleasure of this late-evening visit?'

Charlie smiled and shrugged diffidently. 'My flatmates have gone off hitching round Europe for the summer. I didn't fancy going – besides, you haven't finished the portrait – and I couldn't afford the rent on my own. The landlord gave me the push.'

Harriet put her key in the lock. 'You do have rights, you know. As a tenant.'

He shrugged again. 'Yeah, well, you don't know my landlord. And it didn't seem worth the hassle. Is it all right if I kip at yours for a couple of days, until I get something sorted out?'

Harriet sighed and opened the door. 'Come on in. Honestly, you are a pain. Still, as long as it's not for too long, yes, you can have the spare bed.'

'Thanks,' said Charlie. 'I'll try to pay you something.'

'Don't,' said Harriet. 'At least this way I'll be able to get started

206

on time in the mornings, without having to wait for you to get here. By the way, how good a cook are you? I'm starving.'

'Excellent,' said Charlie happily.

Stephen rang Walter first thing the next morning, demanding to know what action he was going to take regarding the document. Walter told Stephen that he had spoken to both Mrs Cotterell and Reg Fowler the previous evening, and that they had agreed to come along to his office at two o'clock that afternoon. 'I took the liberty of saying that you would drive them over,' added Walter.

'I don't mind,' said Stephen. 'I just want to find out as soon as possible if we have a leg to stand on. I've been thinking. About that document – couldn't we say that my father's illness was so bad that he couldn't have known what he was doing when he made it out, or married Ruth Owen, come to that? That he wasn't in his right mind?'

'Well,' said Walter, in that cautious tone which so infuriated Stephen, 'I think we might run into difficulties there. Your sisters, who visited him regularly, have never mentioned that his mental faculties were in any way impaired by his illness. I had occasion to speak to him myself about some small piece of business four days before he died, and there was no sign of any problem.'

Stephen wondered to what lengths his sisters might go to preserve their inheritance. Not that far, he thought. 'Well, all right – maybe that's pushing it a bit. But couldn't we say that he was talked into drawing up the document? That Ruth Owen coerced him? He was very ill, and she was clearly making regular visits. Who knows what hold she may have had over him? Mightn't that work?'

'Yes, I have considered the possibility of undue influence,' said Walter. 'It would certainly provide grounds for having the document set aside. But again there are evidential difficulties. We would have to be able to find positive proof of actual coercion, that some sort of force was used which deprived your father of his freedom of action. It is not an easy thing to establish. We should need to furnish a court with particulars of acts which we alleged were instrumental in exercising such influence, together with dates. Which is why much depends upon what Mrs Cotterell and Mr Fowler are able to tell us. I need also to find out particulars of the circumstances in which the document was signed, and so forth. All of that may help. We shall just have to wait and see what they say this afternoon. By the way,' added Walter, 'I should tell you that I discussed the matter of your father's marriage with counsel last night, and again this morning. I'm afraid it's as I thought – we cannot challenge the validity of it. We must consider your father's will as dead.'

'I see,' replied Stephen heavily. Another hope gone. He could hardly believe that any of this was happening. 'Well, thank you. I'll see you this afternoon.'

When he had finished talking to Walter, Stephen wandered out into the gardens. The sun had burned away the early mist, and at half past ten the day was already hot. Stephen had wondered whether Abby still came up to the house to clean in the mornings, and half-hoped she did. It would have been something of a relief just to have told her exactly what he thought of her. But she did not appear.

As he paced round the rose garden, pondering his dilemma, Stephen caught a glimpse of Reg Fowler a hundred yards away, pottering around the yew hedge with a pair of shears. He stood and watched for some moments, thinking of all that Walter had said. Reg probably wouldn't be able to say anything one way or the other about the goings-on at Hemwood House in the weeks before Leslie Maskelyne's death. He wouldn't be able to say whether his employer was pushed or led into doing what he had. But Mrs Cotterell – now, she was a different proposition. She had been there every day. How was she going to feel, he wondered, when she learned that she was to lose her fifty thousand pound legacy, all because Abby Owen was trying on some bogus scheme to take away the Maskelyne estate? He thought he had a pretty good idea of Mrs C's vaguely feudal notions of what was fitting. After hesitating for a moment or two, Stephen went back, locked up the house, and set off through the woods to the village to pay Mrs C a friendly visit.

*

Harriet had slept wretchedly. She had rung Stephen's flat three times the previous night, the last time at eleven thirty, and had then gone to bed. Now she sat at her easel, a cup of coffee standing untasted on a stool close by, trying to summon up the energy and enthusiasm to get on with this portrait. It was nearly finished, and then she would be ready to start setting up the exhibition. Because she was concentrating on Charlie's feet and legs at the moment, she let him read a copy of *Vanity Fair* while she worked, and there he sat, well-rested, sleek and pretty as a cat, occasionally running his fingers through his dark blond hair, yawning and sipping his coffee. He had found a comfortable billet, and this was a cushy job. He glanced up at Harriet as she frowned in concentration over the final details of her picture. She looked as good as ever, very sexy in that big white T-shirt and blue shorts, her feet bare as usual, but her face was tired and angry. He knew all about Stephen and last night. It was his own good fortune that the guy had stood her up, otherwise he'd still be sitting out there on the doorstep. Maybe it was all about to go wrong between her and Stephen. Much as he didn't like to see Harriet hurt, Charlie couldn't help thinking how convenient it was that he would be there to hold her hand if and when it happened. Then again, that was probably wishful thinking.

The phone rang, Harriet jumped, and before she could stop him, Charlie reached out a hand, picked up the phone and said in his best RADA butler's voice, 'Harriet Downing's residence. How may I help you?' A pause. 'Just one moment, I'll see if she's free.' He shook his head sorrowfully as Harriet snatched the receiver from him.

By the time Harriet had finished speaking to her agent, she was in no mood to carry on working. She wanted to know where Stephen was. If he wasn't at his flat, the only other place he might be was Hemwood, but she had tried there twice yesterday evening, and the phone had just rung and rung. Close to tears, she stabbed the numbers on the phone and waited. While she listened to the ringing tone sounding over and over, Stephen was making his way through the Dips to Doris's house.

*

209

Doris was in the middle of making a casserole for her Don's tea that evening. She was by no means the only woman in those parts to have a son in his mid-thirties still living at home, but she was perhaps more attentive to his needs than most. She often wished he'd find a nice girl and settle down, give her some more grandchildren, but as her husband Eddie pointed out, he had no real incentive to leave home, not when he had a mother who cooked him a hot meal every evening and even went to the trouble of putting his boiler suit in the oven to warm on winter mornings. Doris did all this and more as a matter of course, and was already worried what Don would do when she and Eddie were off on their cruise. She'd just have to fill the freezer up, she supposed, though she doubted Don's ability to defrost a shepherd's pie, let alone manage the business of heating it up in the microwave.

Stephen, on inspiration, went round to the back of Doris's house and knocked on the kitchen door, which was ajar. There was something neighbourly and intimate in such an action, and he wanted very much to get off on the right foot with Doris. She shouted to whoever it was to come in, and Stephen entered the kitchen to find her in the middle of slicing mushrooms.

'Good Lord, I thought you were the milk!' exclaimed Doris. 'He always calls on a Tuesday. Come in and sit down, Stephen. I wasn't expecting to see you till after lunch. You know that lawyer of yours called up and asked to see me and Reg Fowler today. I don't know what it's all about, only he said you'd kindly drive us to Colchester. By the way, I hope it's all shipshape up at the house, because Abby's not up there every day.' Doris shovelled the mushrooms into the casserole and wiped her hands on her apron.

'Everything's fine, Mrs C,' said Stephen easily, strolling across and sitting down at Doris's kitchen table. 'Yes, I had to come up unexpectedly. We've run into a bit of a problem about the estate.'

'I thought there was something up,' said Doris. 'Only Mr Hubbard didn't say what it was. Can I get you a cup of tea?'

'That would be lovely.' Stephen sat back and glanced round the shabby, old-fashioned kitchen. Good, he bet Mrs C and her husband couldn't wait to get their hands on that fifty thousand. 'Actually, it's about the estate that I've come to see you. I thought it might be helpful if I explained the problem to you before you see Mr Hubbard. Just so you know what to expect.'

'Well, I'm grateful for that, I must say,' said Doris as she filled the kettle. 'I've been like an ill-sitting hen all morning. I don't like mysteries and I'm not over-fond of lawyers.'

Doris made the tea and brought it over to the table, together with two of her best cups and saucers, then bustled about fetching milk and sugar. Stephen waited until she had poured the tea before beginning.

'I must warn you – it's all rather complicated. But you were with my father more than anyone else before he died, so we're all hoping you can help to shed some light on what happened then. It's to do with Ruth Owen.'

Doris felt a guilty little start of fear. She didn't think there had ever been anything really wrong in Ruth coming to visit Mr Maskelyne, but all the time it was going on, she couldn't help feeling that there was something slightly underhand about it. Leslie Maskelyne had said to her that she wasn't to mention Ruth's visits to the family, and she never had. Not at the time. She'd said something to Lydia later. But while it was going on no one had ever asked any questions. She hadn't actively lied to anyone, but she had been conscious at the time of being an accomplice to some slight deception. 'Ruth?' she asked faintly.

Stephen nodded. 'You know, of course, Mrs C,' he said, pouring milk into his tea in a slow, thin stream, 'that Ruth Owen was visiting my father during the last weeks of his life. I think you mentioned something about it to Lydia not long ago.' When Stephen lifted his eyes to hers, Doris nodded. 'But what you probably didn't know –' Stephen paused for effect as he stirred his tea '– is that three days before he died, my father married Ruth Owen.'

Doris laid a hand on her bosom and stared at him. 'Oh my Lord,' she said. She said nothing for a few seconds, and then repeated it. 'Oh my Lord.'

Stephen watched her closely. It was obvious to him that Doris really had known nothing about it until this moment. She was genuinely shocked. In which case, she had not jointly contrived

211

anything with Ruth. Stephen had suspected that she might have done, ignorant of the effect of such a marriage on his father's will. But if she had been ignorant of the marriage, then she might have only limited knowledge of the circumstances in which his father had come to write his damnable document. That was a pity. Still, there was more that might be done. He added, 'I'm sorry if it's come as a shock to you, Mrs C, but we only found this out very recently, when Abby took the marriage certificate to a lawyer.'

'It must have been that day they went out in her car,' said Doris, her gaze distant as she recalled the events of that Friday. 'They never said where they was going or what they was up to. I thought she might have taken him shopping. Oh, I never thought . . .' She looked at Stephen. 'Perhaps I should have said something – to the girls or you, about her coming to visit, but it wasn't my place.' Her eyes grew damp at the awful thought that she might be partly to blame for whatever had happened, and her voice rushed on. 'Your father asked me not to say. He didn't want you and your sisters to know Ruth was visiting. It hadn't been going on that long. I never even knew they knew one another, not to speak to, until one day he gave me a letter to give to her. And then she started coming up.' Doris drew breath. 'But *married* . . . I can't credit it. I really can't.'

'Don't worry, Mrs C,' said Stephen soothingly. 'You were only doing what my father asked. And you were working for him, after all, not us.' He paused to let this little barb take effect. 'I thought you might be able to shed some light on the reason why my father would marry Ruth Owen, but clearly you can't. That's a pity. But what I must explain to you now may also be a bit of a shock. That marriage, you see, invalidated my father's will.' Doris looked at him blankly. 'It means his will is of no effect.'

Doris took this in. Not unnaturally, her first thought was for her legacy. 'As though it had never been? All the things in it? So – so my legacy, our money . . . We'll not be getting it?'

'I'm afraid it looks that way,' said Stephen, and drank some of his tea, watching her and waiting.

'But what about you and your sisters?' asked Doris, as the implications of these shocking revelations began to grow in her mind.

Stephen shook his head. 'As I said, it's as if he'd never made that will.'

'Then – then what happens?'

'Well, to be brutally frank with you, Mrs C, Abby Owen is trying to lay claim to my late father's estate.'

'Abby?' Doris's eyes widened incredulously. 'How can she do that?'

'She's using a document that my father wrote out the day after he married Ruth Owen. It was intended to act as a codicil to my father's will, to leave Ruth and Abby Owen some money. Quite a lot of money. But if you read it a certain way, it could sound as though he's making Abby his heir.' Doris's eyes were fastened on Stephen's face as she followed all this. 'Your signature is on the document. Yours and Mr Fowler's.'

Doris's hand went to her mouth. 'That's right – he asked us to witness something. I remember – it was the day after he and Ruth went out together. Oh my word. Oh, Stephen, I never thought I was doing wrong – he never showed us what was in it –' Now tears of anxiety and general upset sprang into her eyes, and Stephen laid a hand over hers.

'Now, don't blame yourself. No one else does. You couldn't possibly have known what was in it, or what was going to happen. Don't get in a state.' Doris tried to stop her lips from trembling, and nodded. 'But I want you to listen carefully to me. There is a way of preventing any of this happening. I don't mean that we can do anything about my father's will – the lawyer is looking into it, but it does seem as though that's dead and done with. But there are ways of having that document declared invalid.' Doris, who was hanging intently on Stephen's every word, frowned slightly. 'That means getting a court to say that it's of no effect, and that Abby doesn't have any claim on the estate.'

Doris shook her head. 'She's a wicked girl, to try such a thing. All your father's money, and that lovely house . . . She's no right to any of it. It's yours and the girls', I say.'

Good, thought Stephen. He nodded, then went on, 'As I say, there are ways of getting it declared invalid. If we could show, for instance, that Mrs Owen –' He hesitated. 'I don't like to speak ill of

213

the dead, Mrs C, and I know she was your friend, but this requires a certain bluntness – that Mrs Owen somehow pushed my father into doing all this. After all, she suddenly began to visit my father in May, right out of the blue. They couldn't have known each other more than three weeks, at the outside, yet they get married in secret, and he writes out a document leaving her a hundred thousand pounds. Now, doesn't that strike you as odd?'

Doris looked thoughtful. 'You're right. She never spoke to me about any of it, but it does seem queer. Mind, you never know what's in the past . . . Forgive me saying so, Stephen, but maybe your father had personal reasons for what he did. He liked her coming to see him. He never behaved as though it put him out.'

'Are you quite sure, Doris?' asked Stephen. 'Remember, there's a lot at stake here. As I say, we can't revive my father's will, but if you can help us to get this document declared invalid, I'll make sure you don't lose your legacy. All you have to do is think back, see if you can't remember things that were said, or things she did to maybe make him afraid of her, or that showed she had some kind of hold over him.' Doris glanced away. Stephen went on softly, 'Weren't there conversations? Didn't she say things, tell you how she could get him to do exactly as she wanted, that kind of thing? If you could just remember . . .'

At that moment Doris's husband Eddie walked into the kitchen, the morning paper in his hand. Stephen glanced up at him, and smiled with an effort. Eddie grunted a greeting and went through to the garden. Stephen looked back at Doris. Her face was expressionless. The spell he had woven was broken. He didn't think he could have taken the thing much further, anyway. He would just have to wait and hope.

'Anyway, Doris, you think about what I've said. I thought it might help if you were – well, prepared. To talk to Mr Hubbard this afternoon, that is.' He stood up. 'Thank you for the tea. I hope everything I've told you hasn't upset you too much. I really hate the thought of you and your husband losing that money.' Still Doris said nothing. 'Right. Well, I'll pick you up around half one. All right?'

Doris nodded without looking up. 'All right.'

Chapter Fifteen

It was only when Stephen got back that he began to give any thought to Harriet. In his preoccupation with this disaster he'd forgotten all about their arrangement to meet at his flat the previous evening. He rang her studio, and was disconcerted when a male voice answered. Then he realised that it must be Charlie.

'Is Harriet there?'

After a few seconds, Harriet came on the line. 'Yes?' Her voice was cold.

'It's me. Look, Harriet, I'm really sorry about last night. I had to come up to Hemwood to see Walter Hubbard. There's a bit of a catastrophe looming about the estate.'

Harriet was not impressed by this; she was used to Stephen's glib exaggerations when he was trying to excuse himself. 'Would it have been too much simply to have rung me? You knew where I was. Waiting at your flat.'

'Yes, listen, I know I should have. But we had to have a family conference. It just slipped my mind –'

'*I* slipped your mind, you mean.'

'No, nothing like that. Don't be silly. Look, I've got to stay at Hemwood for the next few days to sort this thing out. Why don't you drive up this afternoon? We could –'

'Stephen, you may be a gentleman of leisure, but other people have to work. I've got a portrait to finish and an exhibition to organise. I'm not going to run around the country after you. I'll see you when you get back to London.' Harriet put the phone down.

'That told him,' said Charlie.

'Oh, belt up,' said Harriet, as she picked up her brushes.

Stephen put the phone down, feeling rather resentful. She hadn't even given him a chance to tell her what was going on. He bet she'd have been a lot more sympathetic if she knew the man she was going to marry might finish up homeless and penniless. Well, at least this way he could concentrate on trying to sort out this hellish situation without any distractions. Not that he was so sure that it could be sorted out. A sick feeling of fear and foreboding had settled upon him, and he sat by the telephone for a long time, staring out of the window.

Reg Fowler came up to the house when he had finished his lunch, and found Stephen in the kitchen, sitting over a cup of coffee and the remains of a bacon sandwich.

Stephen got up as soon as he saw him, impatient to get on with the afternoon's business. 'Right, Reg,' he said, 'let's go and fetch Mrs Cotterell.'

As they drove down to the village, Reg talked more or less incessantly about the gardens at Hemwood House, what needed to be done, the plans he had. Stephen reflected that Reg probably hoped he was going to be kept on by Stephen, if Stephen came to live there. What would he think, Stephen wondered, if in a few months' time he found Abby Owen paying his wages? Probably wouldn't care one way or the other.

When Doris got into the car, Reg's fund of conversation dried up. He had always found Doris intimidating. Doris herself was very quiet all the way there, making only one or two remarks about hedges which had been grubbed up, and the state of the new roundabouts on the Colchester by-pass, which she considered very ugly. Stephen glanced at her a couple of times, wondering how much thinking she had been doing since their conversation this morning, but her face gave nothing away.

In Walter Hubbard's office Doris sat, stiff and formal, on the edge of her seat, handbag on her lap, while Reg slouched comfortably in his chair and glanced at his surroundings with interest. Unlike Doris, he hadn't seen any need to dress up for the visit, and was still in his gardening trousers, boots, and grubby shirt.

'I'm very grateful to you both for coming here this afternoon,' said Walter. 'As I indicated to you on the telephone, we have run into something of a problem concerning the administration of the late Mr Maskelyne's estate. We hope that perhaps you can help us to clear up certain matters.' Walter produced the document of May 18th from the file which lay on his desk, and handed it to Doris. 'Mrs Cotterell, you may not be familiar with the contents of this document, but I think I'm correct in saying that it bears your signature?' Doris scanned the document, looked up at Walter and nodded. Stephen noticed that she seemed quite composed, with none of the nervous anxiety she had shown that morning. Well, she'd had time to get used to the situation. Walter took the document from her and handed it to Reg Fowler. 'And that, Mr Fowler, is your signature also?'

Reg nodded. 'Yes. I remember Mr Maskelyne asking us up to his room to sign it.'

Walter took the document from Reg. 'Good. Now – I want you to think back to that day. Can you describe to me what happened? I mean, as regards the document.'

Reg and Doris glanced at one another, and after a moment's hesitation, Doris said, 'Mr Maskelyne said he had something he wanted me to sign. He asked me if I'd fetch Mr Fowler up, too. I went and found him, and we both went up to Mr Maskelyne's room. Then we signed that piece of paper. Only he folded it over, so that we couldn't see what was written. He said it was private.'

'I see. When you say you signed it, do you mean that Mr Maskelyne had already put his signature to it, before you came into the room?' Stephen caught the sharp note in Walter's voice, and realised that this might be significant.

Again Doris and Reg looked at one another. 'No,' said Doris slowly. 'He waited till we were both there, then he signed it, and then we did.'

'Mrs Cotterell first, then me,' agreed Reg.

'So you saw Mrs Cotterell sign, and she saw you?'

Reg nodded. 'That's right.'

Walter sat back in his seat, tapping the document. He glanced up at Stephen. 'It appears that all the formalities were properly observed. There is no formal attestation clause, but that is not strictly necessary, so long as Mr Fowler and Mrs Cotterell saw your father sign, and signed in the presence of one another.' He gave a sigh.

'But what about the circumstances in which the thing was written? What about –?'

Walter lifted his hand slightly, and Stephen stopped. Walter turned to Reg. 'Thank you, Mr Fowler. You've been most helpful. I wonder if you would be kind enough to wait outside while I discuss something further with Mrs Cotterell? My secretary will see that you have a cup of tea while you're waiting.'

Reg rose, glanced uncertainly at Stephen, and left the room. Walter closed the door and sat down again. 'Mrs Cotterell,' he said, 'There are details involved in this matter which I didn't think it necessary for Mr Fowler to hear, though no doubt he will learn of them in due course. Let me explain our problem to you in full –'

'You don't have to,' interrupted Doris. 'I already know the details. Mr Maskelyne –' She glanced towards Stephen but did not meet his eye. '– explained it all to me this morning. I know all about Ruth and Mr Maskelyne getting married, and about the will, and what Abby Owen is trying to do.'

'I see,' said Walter. His voice was soft and thoughtful. There was a silence, during which Stephen felt the stirrings of apprehension. Maybe Walter didn't approve of him going to see Mrs C. But what harm could it have done? If she'd taken in everything he'd said, it could only help their cause. Doris didn't want to lose that money – of that he was certain. 'In that case,' continued Walter, 'I'd like to ask you some questions about the weeks leading up to Mr Maskelyne's death, if I may. I wonder if you could describe for me the nature of the relationship between Mrs Owen and Mr Maskelyne. It wasn't a long-standing one, was it?'

'Well, I couldn't say for certain,' replied Doris. 'Ruth didn't tell me everything, even though she was my friend. All I know is that he gave me a letter one day to give to her, and that was the start of it.'

'This letter,' said Walter, 'was it written in reply to anything she had written to him?'

'No,' said Doris. 'I don't think so. I remember how surprised she was when I gave it to her. It was the last thing she expected, a letter from him. I was surprised myself. I didn't know they knew one another, not to speak to.'

'And then she began to visit?'

'Yes. Well, first she wrote back to him, and then she came to lunch.'

Walter turned to Stephen and murmured, 'We must have a look through your father's papers at Hemwood and see if we can find Mrs Owen's letter. It may be significant. You never know.'

'Oh, you won't find that,' said Doris. 'I saw him open it. It was just his own letter back, with a date written on the back. He looked at it and then he chucked it in the bin.'

'I see.' Walter sounded disappointed. He paused and then said, 'Mrs Cotterell, can you tell me how things were between Mrs Owen and Mr Maskelyne during the weeks when she paid her visits?' Doris said nothing, though her eyes flickered to Stephen's face. 'For instance,' prompted Walter, 'how did Mr Maskelyne seem to you after the visits? Depressed, anxious?'

To Stephen, the seconds before Doris answered seemed very long.

'I couldn't really say,' replied Doris. Stephen could hear the hesitation in her voice.

'But you were looking after Mr Maskelyne, were you not?' coaxed Walter.

'Yes. Yes, I was.' Doris hesitated again, then took a deep breath and said, 'I think he enjoyed her visits. He was ill, you know – dying – but she seemed to do him good.'

She did not look at Stephen, who turned to stare out of the bay window at the afternoon sky.

'There was nothing strained in their relations?'

'No.'

'Yet I understand that Mrs Owen was careful always to make her visits when other members of the family were not there. Didn't it strike you as suspicious that she didn't want them to know of her relationship with Mr Maskelyne? As though she might have had something to hide?'

'It was him as had something to hide, Mr Hubbard,' replied Doris. Stephen glanced at her sharply. 'It was Mr Maskelyne who planned the days she should come. He didn't want his family interfering.' She met Stephen's gaze. 'I'm sorry, but it has to be said.' Doris looked back at Walter. 'I expect that's why he kept his marriage a secret. He didn't want them making a fuss, which they would have done. I've no idea why he and Ruth got wed, but it was their business, and no one else's. They had their reasons, and I just think it's a shame it's caused all this upset. I don't think they would either of them have wanted that.'

As he gazed at the old woman sitting resolute and upright in her chair before him, Walter felt infinitely discouraged. But in the interests of the estate, he was obliged to press on.

'That's as may be, Mrs Cotterell, but what concerns us is that Mrs Owen may in some way have put pressure on Mr Maskelyne. Particularly as regards the writing of that document. That is why it is so important for us to know the nature of the relationship between the two of them.'

Doris gave a little smile. 'You think anyone could tell Mr Maskelyne what to do? He was his own master, right to the very end. And I'll tell you something else. Even if I don't think it's right what Abby Owen is trying to do, the fear of losing that money Mr Maskelyne left me isn't going to make me say anything other than the truth. There was nothing wrong between Ruth Owen and Mr Maskelyne. I didn't hear what passed between them at those visits, but I know she didn't force him to do anything. Nor to write anything, either.'

'But since you weren't there, Mrs Cotterell, you can't say for certain.'

Doris leaned forward in her chair, her eyes bright. 'Maybe I can't. But there was nobody closer to Mr Maskelyne in those last weeks than I was. Only a pair of nurses that did no more than wash him and stick needles in him. So you won't find anyone to contradict me, will you?' For once, Walter looked stymied. 'Not unless,' added Doris, giving Stephen a glance, 'his family are prepared to say otherwise.'

Stephen got up from his chair and walked to the window.

Walter sat back in his chair, and after an uneasy silence said, 'Thank you, Mrs Cotterell, for being so frank. It was good of you to come this afternoon.'

'Happy to help,' said Doris. 'I won't be needing a lift back,' she added in Stephen's direction. 'I'll take the bus.'

When she had left the room, there was a long silence. At last Walter broke it.

'So you spoke to Mrs Cotterell this morning?'

Stephen, who had been standing staring out of the window, turned round and paced across the room. 'And where was the harm in that?' he demanded. He didn't care how he spoke. He felt bitter and sick at heart.

Walter gazed at the document before him. 'Well, now,' he said thoughtfully, 'who can say?'

'For Christ's sake, man!' burst out Stephen. 'What are we going to do now? Tell me!'

'I very much doubt if there is anything that *can* be done. You heard Mrs Cotterell. We couldn't begin to prove undue influence. There's not a shred of evidence. It appears that there's nothing to prevent the document your father wrote operating as a legal will. It's most unfortunate –'

'Most unfortunate? I'll say it's bloody unfortunate! This thing is going to ruin me completely! The house, my money – the whole lot gone! And you intend to sit there and do nothing, I take it?'

'I understand how frustrated you must feel, but from my point of view as a lawyer, I don't see how I can take this any further. I have yet to obtain counsel's written opinion, of course –'

'We can go to court and fight it! How can it possibly be that Abby Owen should be able to use that idiotic piece of paper to take everything away from me and my family? You've got to fight it! I absolutely insist that you do!'

Walter regarded Stephen sadly. Though he didn't much care for the young man, he had sympathy for him. Stephen had probably spent most of his life in expectation of his father's wealth and property, and it must be hard to see it taken away. Harder still, as a layman, to accept or understand the legal twists of fate which had brought it about.

'Stephen,' he sighed, 'I should be failing in my duty as your solicitor if I were to encourage you in such a step. The proceedings would be costly and protracted, and from my knowledge of the facts, I am bound to say that you would almost certainly lose.'

'I can't believe that you are prepared to let this happen! It's not –' Stephen struggled for words, '– it's not just!' He thrust his hand into his pockets and stalked around the room, then turned and glared at Walter. 'Right from the start your approach to this has been to accept it as though it's a *fait accompli*. You should have been fighting the thing all the way, but instead you've done the opposite! I've half a mind to take this case away from you, and find someone who'll do a proper job for me and my family.'

This sparked anger in Walter's quiet soul. He felt he had had enough of being raged at by this spoilt young man, who had, Walter guessed, even gone so far as to try to persuade Mrs Cotterell to perjure herself on the family's behalf. He had anticipated days ago that this would be Stephen's attitude, if things went against him. He regarded Stephen with equanimity. 'In that case, I suggest you find someone relatively inexpensive.'

They gazed at one another for a long moment, and then Stephen sighed and shook his head. 'I'm sorry. I was out of order. I'm just so . . . I mean, the whole thing is beyond belief. I can't think what to do.'

'I'm sorry,' said Walter. 'I wish I had some solution. I'm still waiting to receive counsel's written opinion, you know. Perhaps that will offer one.'

Stephen nodded. 'Perhaps.' But he doubted it, and he knew Walter did, too. He left the office, too preoccupied to notice Reg sitting in the waiting room, drinking his tea and waiting for his lift back to Hemwood.

Stephen drove out of Colchester with a sick, dead feeling in his heart. This horrible, unbelievable thing was happening, and he was powerless to do anything about it. In spite of what he had said in Walter's office, he didn't think any other lawyer would be prepared to fight the matter. Walter might be infuriatingly mild and cautious, but he was a good lawyer, and Stephen knew that he was probably right when he said that they were bound to lose any case which they might try to bring. So there was nothing to stop Abby claiming the entire estate, every penny of it.

Stephen turned off the dual carriageway and headed at a slower pace towards Gosfield Lake, where he parked the car and set off across the fields bordering the lake, to try and think things out. He hadn't really stopped to consider Abby in all of this, except as a cipher, as a threat to his security and well-being. Now, as he walked, he tried to reflect on what her feelings might be. From what he knew of her, Stephen didn't think she had engineered the whole business. This lawyer of hers, Robin Onslow, had done that. Abby hadn't gone to Onslow in the first place with any idea of robbing Stephen and his sisters of their father's property. She had just gone to see him about the document, hoping to get some money. That had been all she wanted. It was Onslow who had gleaned the facts and seen the possibilities.

At the lakeside, Stephen picked up handfuls of pebbles and chucked them, one by one, into the water, trying to think himself into Abby's mind. She couldn't possibly feel entitled to the property. Perhaps she'd even been reluctant to start this whole business, but had been pushed into it by her lawyer. After all, Onslow, who was nothing more than a small-town hack, stood to gain something. Stephen felt he knew Abby – in an odd, pieced-together way, admittedly, half then, half now – and he didn't think she could really imagine she had a right to Hemwood or the money. She probably even felt afraid and guilty about all of this. But she was angry with Stephen – and with justification, he knew. He'd handled their brief affair badly. He'd let himself get carried away by the unexpected force of his desire for her, and then, when he'd realised it was a mistake, he should have let her down more gently. Then there was the money. They were wrong to have refused to give Abby and her mother anything. No wonder she wanted to get back at him. But to this extent?

223

Stephen walked slowly back from the shore. Maybe it wasn't quite as he imagined. Possibly Abby *was* feeling guilty, but the amount at stake here might well be sufficient to ease her conscience. She was human, after all, as greedy as everyone else. For someone in her circumstances, it was an unbelievable upswing in her fortunes. He remembered what she'd told him of her life since she had left Hemwood, and he imagined that the future which otherwise stretched ahead of her was one of comparative hardship. She needed money badly. But just how much, Stephen wondered, would it take to satisfy her? Probably a good deal less than she presently stood to gain. In the beginning, all she had wanted was the money which his father had left her. Might there not be some way to persuade her out of all this, to demonstrate to her that what she was doing was unprincipled, whatever the legalities? He could offer her twice what his father had intended her to have. Three times, if need be. It would cut a hefty slice out of the estate, but anything was better than seeing it all vanish. Stephen reached his car and paused, turning to look across the lake. He and Abby had come here sometimes on their bikes, long ago. They had been wonderful times. Stephen knew that there were currents of feeling between himself and Abby which it would be easy to play on. However angry she might be with him, he knew that she loved him, and that was worth everything. With care and skill, he might still be able to salvage this situation.

Stephen got into his car, and set off to pay his second visit of the day.

Doris got off the bus in Hemwood, tired and irritable. She had had to wait quarter of an hour at the bus station in Colchester, and her feet were beginning to draw. She'd have to take one of her water tablets as soon as she got in. The bus had been stuffy and crowded with noisy schoolchildren, too, and she could feel one of her heads coming on. Still, there was no way she could have let Stephen drive her back, not after this afternoon. It had given her some satisfaction to see the expression on his face after she had said what she'd said. It paid him back for having the cheek even to suggest that she would be willing to make up lies for the lawyer, to paint Ruth as a villainess who bullied Leslie Maskelyne into all manner of things. And Ruth not dead above a week. Of course, it was a shame about the money – she'd be a liar if she didn't pretend that that hadn't given her a few seconds' pause this morning, when Stephen had come wheedling at her – and she could break her heart when she thought about all the lovely plans she and Eddie had made, but it couldn't be helped. She'd shed a few furtive tears on the bus, but she knew she had done the right thing. It just showed how things could change. No one knew what was ahead of them except the man pushing the wheelbarrow, as her mother used to say. All she really wanted was to sit down with a cup of tea and slip her shoes off, but first she had business to attend to.

Abby was sunbathing in shorts and a bikini top in the back garden, while Chloe and her friend Emily played and splashed in the paddling pool. The back door was propped open, and Abby heard the doorbell as soon as it sounded.

When she answered the door, Doris was on the doorstep, wearing one of her good frocks and carrying a handbag, her face grim.

'Hello, Doris. Come in. I'll get you a glass of lemonade. I was just about to have one myself. You look as though you could do with it.'

'I'm not stopping, thank you,' said Doris, not moving from the doorstep. 'I just came to tell you I won't be able to help you out with your shift at the pub any more. You'll need to find someone else. I don't want anything to do with someone who's carrying on the way you are, taking other folks' property away.' Her voice was stiff, and Abby was taken aback by her tone. Then the penny dropped. Doris must have heard.

'I think I know what this is about,' said Abby, nervously twisting her hair into a long hank between her fingers. 'It's about what's happening with Leslie Maskelyne's will, isn't it? Maybe I should have told you myself. But I want you to know that nothing's going to change about your money. Mr Maskelyne wanted you to have it, and I'll make sure you get it –'

'Oh, I don't care for the money, never you fear,' said Doris, too proud to admit the untruth of this. 'I just think it's criminal that someone like you should think they can walk off with what's not theirs. And don't you tell me it's all legal, and to do with bits of paper and signatures. You know Mr Maskelyne never meant you to have his house and his money. Your lawyer may be able to pull all kinds of tricks, but I know what's right and what's not.' Abby opened her mouth to try to interrupt, but Doris was unstoppable. 'The lawyer showed me that bit of paper he wrote out. I never knew what was in it, but I wouldn't have signed it if I'd known it was going to lead to all this. What do you think your mother would have said to this kind of underhand thing?'

Abby managed to break in. 'I know what she would have said. She would have said I was entitled to what was mine. There's a lot more to this than you'll ever know, Doris. And I never meant to take anything from you. I'll make sure you get your money.'

'I'm not sure that I'd take it,' replied Doris, wishing that there was a way between pride and acceptance.

'I don't care,' said Abby. 'It's yours. If I have to stuff it through your letterbox in envelopes I will.'

'You talk as though that property's already yours to do with as you like, madam! But you know this is wrong. You know it! And what do you think someone like you is going to do with that great big house and that money? Make a fool of yourself, that's all. You weren't born to it, and you know it. There. I'm going now. That's all I came to say.'

She turned and walked away, leaving Abby standing in the doorway. After a few seconds Abby closed the door and went back out to the garden. She sat down, putting her face in her hands, aware that her heart was beating hard. Doris's words had wounded her, mainly because of the truth of them. But what could she do? She had set this thing in motion, and she didn't see how she could stop it now. Anyway, why should she? The property was legally hers, if not morally. That was enough. She must just keep telling herself that. She and Chloe came first, not the Maskelynes. Chloe came over and pulled one of her mother's hands away from her face.

'What's wrong? Are you crying?'

'No,' replied Abby. 'I was thinking.'

'Oh. Can Emily and me have some lemonade?'

Abby sighed and got up. 'Yes. I'll fetch you some.'

She poured out two glasses of lemonade and was about to take them out to the girls when the doorbell rang again. Oh, God, what now?

When Abby opened the door and saw Stephen standing on the step, she was too astonished to do more than stare at him. She could read nothing in his face. He simply stood there, looking at her, swinging his car keys from one finger. She could think of nothing to say. The intensity of her feelings at the sight of him left her lost for words.

Stephen broke the silence. 'I thought we should talk.'

Abby turned away, leaving the door open. He followed her into the house. Abby picked up the glasses of lemonade from the kitchen table and took them out to the girls. She stood in the garden for a few seconds, trying to steel herself against her emotions. She didn't want to feel so unspeakably glad to see him. It was wrong. But how could you suddenly change a whole lifetime's perception of another person? It was one thing to be told that someone was your brother, but when everything you knew and understood about that person was based on an entirely different assumption, adjustment was almost impossible. Reality might change, hard facts about who was who and what was what might change – but feelings were not so easily dealt with. Perhaps there was something unnatural about her. Or perhaps it was just that the heart did not understand truth in the same way as the head did. Either way, she loved him, and she didn't care what he was to her. There were some, she knew, who would consider her utterly damned for thinking and feeling as she did. The fact was, it was beyond her control.

When she went back inside, Stephen was leaning against the kitchen table. Still she could not fathom the look on his face.

'Do you want some lemonade?' she asked, brushing tendrils of hair away from her face.

'Yes. Yes, I'd like some. Thank you.'

Surprised, she poured him a glass, and then sat down at the table, watching as he drank it. She was aware of her own longing, her desire to reach out a hand and simply touch him, feel his skin,

227

brush her fingers against his shirt. Stephen put his empty glass on the draining board and then sat down at the table opposite Abby.

'I've been with my lawyer this morning. And much of yesterday.' Abby said nothing. Stephen looked down at his keys, playing with them. 'It's quite a remarkable stunt that you're trying to pull, Abby. Quite remarkable.'

Abby felt a little hardness creep back into her soul. She reminded herself that Stephen wouldn't even be here, talking to her, if it wasn't for the house and the money. That was all he cared about. Were it not for that, he would have let her well alone. As she looked at him, she understood very well why people said that love was close to hate. 'I'm not pulling any stunt,' replied Abby. 'I'm taking what's mine.'

Stephen smiled faintly. 'Come off it, Abby –' His voice was challenging, friendly. '– you don't really believe that you're entitled to my father's property. Do you?'

What would he say if she told him what Ruth had revealed before she died? If he knew that they shared the same father, would he change his mind, think she had as much right as he did to the Maskelyne property? Something in her longed to tell him outright, so that he wouldn't think of her as a mere chancer, the way Doris did. She knew that was how she must look in his eyes. She could read it in his face as he sat waiting for her to say something. But she couldn't tell him. She didn't want him to know. If she did, then he was lost to her for ever.

Abby looked away. 'I can't help the way things have turned out.'

Stephen detected the stubborn note in her voice. He leaned back in his chair. 'I have to tell you, Abby – this try-on with the document hasn't a hope in hell of working. Naturally the man Onslow has convinced you otherwise, but then he would, wouldn't he?'

'What do you mean?'

Stephen shrugged. 'He's not putting on this show for free. And none of this is going to come cheap for either of us. I might as well tell you that I've instructed my lawyer to fight this all the way. He's quite convinced you haven't got a leg to stand on. Of course, it's going to be long and expensive. I just hope you've thought of how

228

much it's going to cost you at the end of the day.' Stephen was working to keep his tone easy and reasonable.

Abby was filled with momentary doubt. Then she thought of Robin, remembering everything he had said, how sure he was. Stephen had to be bluffing. She lifted her chin slightly. 'Well, that's not really your problem, is it?'

'True. But I don't want to see you end up with a bill for costs you can't pay, and all for nothing. So I'm prepared to do a deal.'

'A deal?'

'Drop this business. Drop it, and I'll see that the estate pays you three hundred thousand. If you want, I'll buy you and your daughter a house, settle you for life. I'm prepared to be generous. You mean a lot to me. We go back a long way. Think of all the things we used to do together. If you go on with this, you're going to wreck everything that was precious between us. Do you want that?'

He was so close, she could have reached across and kissed him. It was the last thing she could do right now. Or ever. But how calculating he was. Even with the scent of him in the air, she was alert to his persuasive abilities. Suddenly the money, all that money, seemed vitally important.

'I'm sorry,' she said, 'but I don't think that would work.'

The quiet firmness of her tone made Stephen's pulse quicken with fear, but he contrived to keep his voice calm. 'What do you mean – work? You just accept the money and get on with your life. No court battles, no legal costs. No bad feelings.' There was a silence of some seconds. Abby stared at the table, avoiding his gaze. 'You don't want any ill feeling between us, do you?' Stephen could feel his own rage running like a current beneath the calm of his voice. He was infuriated that he should have to sit here trying to persuade someone from taking what was his. He wanted to put his hands round her throat and choke her.

Abby looked up. 'No, I don't. But I don't see how I can change the way things are. I'm not a lawyer, but even I can see that there's nothing you can do to turn it all around. Our parents' marriage destroyed your father's will. You haven't got three hundred thousand pounds to give me, Stephen. Or a house.'

The silence that followed seemed to fill the kitchen. Stephen felt too angry to say anything. This was not going as he had intended. What she said was true. Of course it was true. How could he do a deal with her? Christ, there must be some way out of this mess! His sense of helplessness was the worst thing of all. His fists clenched on the tabletop in involuntary frustration.

Abby sat gazing at him, willing him just to get up and leave. She didn't think she could brazen this out much longer. Above all, she couldn't bear the way he was looking at her, with as much hatred as if he wanted to kill her. Unable to help herself, she put out a hand and touched his sleeve, running her hand to his shoulder. Stephen put back his head, his teeth clenched, and groaned. 'God, Abby . . .' Then he looked back at her, filled with a sudden savage desire to hurt her badly. He grabbed her by the shoulders, wanting to shake some sense into her, his fingers biting into her flesh, and she let out a little cry of pain. Hardly knowing what he was doing, he pulled her face towards his by the chin and kissed her, as hard and as roughly as he could, pressing his mouth against hers, dragging her towards him, feeling her initial resistance, then the gratifying slackening of her body and softening of her mouth as she gave in to him. He liked the feeling of her helplessness. It stirred a fierce and hungry desire in him, and he kissed her mouth and throat, dropping one hand from her shoulder and squeezing one breast painfully. He wanted to have her and hurt her all at once.

The sudden sharpness of the pain made Abby push him away from her. She sat back, panting, aching with longing and anger in the same instant. They mustn't do this. It was horrible and mad. He didn't love her. This was just his way of hurting her, marking his rage and frustration.

'My daughter's outside,' she said in a low voice.

Stephen stood up, grabbing his keys from the table. He was seething with violent emotions too confused to let him speak or think rationally. Without saying a word, he left the house. Abby sat alone at the kitchen table, her fingers pressed against her lips, feeling the pain ebbing gradually away.

Chapter Sixteen

Because he could think of nowhere else to go, Stephen drove back to Hemwood and paced around the house, trying to make sense of what was happening. It was impossible, incomprehensible, that things should have changed in this way. The idea that he was to have no money appalled him. He had contrived to build a career of kinds for himself, but it had never been wholehearted. His whole adult life had been spent in the expectation of his father's wealth. Now, for the first time, he had to face what lay ahead without that comforting, cushioning thought. Everything which now happened in his life would have to be as a result of his own endeavours. The idea almost terrified him. Part of him knew that he should get back to London and concentrate on putting his portfolio together, getting another job, but how could he? Contemplating the immediate future seemed an impossibility. He felt like a man in shock.

Stephen's instinct was to tell Harriet everything that had happened, to seek sympathy there, but something prevented him. He knew she wouldn't care if he didn't have the house and money. She would be disappointed for him, but she would love him regardless. Somehow that knowledge was nauseating. He didn't want her pity. And she would still want to marry him. That was the worst thing of all. Marrying Harriet while he had a country house and enough money to afford a life of security and comfort was one thing, but the idea of having to live together in some modest semi, scraping to get by . . . That was unendurable. He might love her, but there were limits. If he had to live on whatever he could earn in advertising, he would prefer to remain a bachelor. She would have to find out at some point, but not yet. There was still too much thinking to be done. Stephen was determined that this should not be the end of it. He couldn't let it happen.

After a while he drove over to Geraldine's and found Lydia there, passing by on the school run. The two sisters were sitting in the farmhouse kitchen, drinking tea, while the boys played outside and Arabella grizzled and dribbled over a rusk in her high chair. Geraldine was smoking, though Stephen thought she had given up a couple of years ago. When Stephen came in they looked up with anxious, hopeful expressions, younger sisters expecting their big brother to provide the solution, know all the answers, as in the past. But as soon as they saw the heavy, haggard expression on Stephen's face, they knew there was no good news. Stephen sat down.

'What happened with Reg and Mrs Cotterell?' asked Geraldine.

'Nothing,' said Stephen. 'They simply witnessed Father's signature to the document. Hubbard says there were no technical irregularities.'

'But what about the undue influence point that we discussed yesterday? Surely Mrs C must have been able to shed some light on what was going on between Father and that woman? There must have been pressure of some kind,' said Lydia.

'Well, if there was, Mrs C isn't saying,' said Stephen. He gritted his teeth and laughed. 'You would think, with fifty thousand at stake, that she might have been more helpful to us. But, no. She is adamant that Father knew exactly what he was doing, that he was happy having Ruth Owen visit him. So.' Stephen raised one hand slowly, clenched his fist until the knuckles were white, and then let it drop uselessly on to the tabletop.

Lydia put her face in her hands. 'God, this is awful,' she muttered.

Geraldine stubbed out her cigarette. 'I cannot believe that Abby is doing this. I simply don't understand her motives.'

'She's doing it,' said Stephen evenly, 'because the law says she can.'

'But she must *know* it's wrong. God knows, one would never grovel, but I can't help thinking we should try appealing to her better nature. It's not as though she couldn't do something about it if she wanted to.'

Lydia lifted her face from her hands. 'You're talking as though we haven't a hope. Walter Hubbard hasn't even got counsel's opinion yet.' She glanced appealingly, hopefully, from brother to sister.

'He hasn't had a written opinion, but he's taken advice over the phone. You know that. What difference is it going to make to see it in writing?' muttered Stephen.

There was a despairing silence in the kitchen. Then Stephen suddenly got up, ramming his chair back awkwardly. 'I can't sit around here. I'm going back to London. I have things to sort out. I'll speak to you both over the next few days.'

He left as abruptly as he had arrived. Lydia and Geraldine sat looking at one another, and then Lydia began to speak, picking up where she had left off. She was telling Geraldine about what she had meant to do with her share of the money, how she had felt about Marcus all these years. It was the closest the two sisters had been in a long time.

'Right,' said Harriet. 'I can't do any more. We'd better regard it as finished.' She sighed and laid down her brushes, wiping her hands down the side of her paint-smeared shirt. Charlie came over to look at the portrait.

'You're right. There is a point beyond which perfection cannot be taken,' he said admiringly.

'If I didn't know how innately modest you were, I might think you were talking about yourself instead of my painting,' said Harriet. 'Either way, it's turned out quite well.' She glanced at her watch. 'I think we both deserve a strong cup of coffee. Be a nice boy and make us one.'

She flung herself into an old wicker chair in a corner of the studio and rubbed at her tired features. Charlie slipped on his jeans and made the coffee. He handed Harriet her mug then went to stand behind her, putting his hands on her shoulders and beginning to massage them. Harriet tensed slightly in surprise, then with a sigh of pleasure she relaxed, closed her eyes, and allowed herself to enjoy the delicious sensation of Charlie's strong fingers easing away the tensions in her neck muscles. She sat there for some minutes in a happy trance. Then Charlie put the tips of his fingers beneath her chin and gently lifted her head back, bringing it to rest against his bare stomach, while the fingers of both hands caressed her throat. Harriet opened her eyes. Against the wall opposite leaned an old mirror, set at such an angle that the first thing Harriet saw was her own reflection. She was instantly, disturbingly struck by the erotic effect of the sight of Charlie's young, naked torso above her face, his slim hands on the bare skin of her neck where he had pushed her shirt back. She glanced away from the mirror and stood up, feeling Charlie's hands slide from her shoulders.

Charlie watched as Harriet crossed the room, flexing her shoulders and neck. After a brief silence Harriet picked up Charlie's shirt and handed it to him.

'I think I'll go out for a bit,' she said casually. 'I need to stock up at the supermarket. I'll find something for you to cook for us tonight.' She slipped on her shoes and combed her hair, then picked up her keys. As she went slowly downstairs to her car, Harriet found herself wondering whether she should have been so accommodating when Charlie had turned up on her doorstep the other night. Although she was sure that the motives behind that gentle massage had been purely friendly and innocent, and much as she loved Stephen, no normal woman could help being acutely aware of Charlie's particular charms. Unless she did something about it, his presence in the flat threatened to become more than a little troubling.

When he got back to London, Stephen drove straight to Harriet's studio. He couldn't face the solitude of his own place, and the restless circling of his thoughts. There might be bills waiting for him, and bank statements, and the last thing he wanted to consider was the sudden awfulness of his financial predicament.

Harriet had given him his own key, and when he went in he was unpleasantly surprised to see Charlie loafing in front of the television with a bottle of Rolling Rock. It had been one thing to have Charlie answer Harriet's phone every time he called, but to find him swigging beer at her place at seven in the evening was a bit much.

'Hi,' said Charlie, who was not entirely pleased to see Stephen.

'Christ, have you taken to living here or something?' asked Stephen rudely.

Charlie grinned. 'Yes, as a matter of fact. Harriet's letting me kip in her spare room until I find somewhere else. My flatmates moved out and I couldn't afford to keep my place on. She's out at the supermarket. Can I get you a beer?'

'No,' said Stephen curtly. 'Thank you.' He threw himself down on the sofa.

Charlie shrugged. 'Okay,' he said, and turned his attention back to the television.

They sat there watching a consumer programme for ten minutes, not speaking, until Harriet came in. When she saw Stephen, she came over and kissed him.

'When did you get here?' she asked. 'You should have rung to tell me you were coming. I'd have got some more food in. Charlie's cooking this evening. He's staying here for a while until he can get fixed up somewhere else.'

'So I understand,' muttered Stephen, glancing at Charlie.

Charlie raised his eyebrows and smiled blandly at Harriet. As she took the shopping into the kitchen she made a surreptitious little beckoning sign to Charlie, and he followed her through.

'I'd take it as a favour if you'd make yourself scarce this evening, Charlie. I don't think Stephen's in the mood for a happy threesome.'

'I'm broke,' said Charlie.

Harriet sighed. 'I paid you just last Friday.' He said nothing. She reached into her purse and took out a twenty-pound note. 'Go on. I'm sure you can make that spin out three or four hours. And while you're chatting to your mates in the pub, try to find somewhere else to live. I think this arrangement has to come to an end very shortly, Charlie.'

Stephen sat on the sofa, chewing his thumbnail, aware that Harriet was getting rid of Charlie for the evening. Fine by him. If he had anything to do with it, Charlie wasn't going to be living here after tonight. He didn't trust Charlie. Far too aware of his own good looks, and uncomfortably close to Harriet in age. His presence made Stephen feel almost middle-aged.

At that moment Harriet emerged from the kitchen with a drink for both of them, and Charlie followed a few seconds later, picking up his jacket. He gave Stephen a smile and said, 'Night.' Stephen said nothing in reply. As the door of the flat slammed, Stephen made his decision. He was not going to tell Harriet. Not yet. Not tonight. There might be something to be gained by keeping quiet for the moment.

She came and snuggled next to him. 'You seem in a particularly foul temper,' she remarked. 'What's this problem with the estate? I'm sorry I wasn't more sympathetic the other day.'

'Oh, I think we're sorting that out. But it's messing up the restaurant project. I'm going to have to slow it down for a while.' How easily and quickly the lies came, thought Stephen. 'On top of which,' he added, 'I don't much like discovering that you're giving houseroom to that artist's tart.'

Harriet giggled. 'What a delightful expression. Come on – it's only Charlie. Harmless, well-meaning.' Into her mind came a sudden, unbidden recollection of the feeling of Charlie's strong fingers kneading her shoulders.

Stephen drank half of his gin-and-tonic. 'You think so? Well, I have other ideas. Anyway, I don't think it's a good idea for him to be living here.'

'Why not?' Harriet put down her drink on the coffee table and yawned.

Stephen put his arm around her and kissed the side of her neck. It took an effort of will to subdue his true feelings at that moment, but he must maintain a façade of semi-normality. He managed a fond smile, then kissed her mouth. 'Because,' he said after a moment, 'I thought it might be an idea if I were to come and live here.' The idea had only just occurred to him, but he knew instantly that it was an inspired one. He still hadn't worked out what he was going to do over the next few weeks, but vague plans were beginning to form in his mind. This way, money would be less of a worry. He had been remarkably profligate over the past few months in expectation of his father's fortune, and now, without a salary, mortgage and bill payments were looming up. He had no reserves on which to draw. This was the ideal solution. Harriet's flat, with its studio, was much larger than his, and what could be a more obvious proposition than living together, now that they were going to be married? As Harriet supposed. He watched her face, waiting.

'Do you know, I was just thinking the other day how absurd it was for us to keep up two separate places,' said Harriet, smiling. 'How soon can you move in?'

'Tomorrow, if you like,' said Stephen. 'I'll put my place on the market straight away.' He kissed her again, aware of a sense of vague intoxication at deceiving her. For this was a deceit, no doubt about it. 'But I don't think I really want Charlie hanging about the place.'

'No,' agreed Harriet. 'Poor old Charlie.' She felt a sense of guilty relief.

Abby lived the next few days in a kind of limbo. It became apparent to her that word had spread in the village about Leslie Maskelyne's estate. She could tell from the curious glances of the other mothers when she went to pick up Chloe, and from the constraint with which Arnold Macey and his wife treated her when she worked her evening stint in the pub. She supposed Doris must have told someone, or possibly Reg, or maybe even the Maskelynes themselves. No one was bold enough or certain enough of the facts to ask her direct questions, but she began to feel uncomfortable and oddly isolated in the community. She had been away too long, knew no one intimately enough to talk to them about it. There was only Robin, on whom she now relied entirely. She spoke to him regularly, getting reports on the progress of the matter. His enthusiasm buoyed her up, carrying her along on its energy.

'It's just a matter of completing the formal procedures now,' he told Abby towards the end of the week. 'Hubbard must have been under a lot of pressure from the Maskelynes to fight this thing, but it looks like he's told them not to waste their time.'

'How do you know?' asked Abby. She couldn't imagine Stephen just sitting back and taking it. Nor his sisters. Then again, maybe they had no choice. It gave her a kind of painful pleasure to be hurting Stephen, in return for the callous way he had treated her. Perhaps he wished now that he'd been a bit more generous in the matter of the money his father – their father – had tried to leave her. If he had, she might not be feeling quite as unscrupulous as she now did.

'Well, when I wrote to Hubbard originally, I asked him to consent to a revocation of the grant of probate of the dud will, and he's agreed. Not that he had much alternative, though he could have made things more difficult if he'd wanted to. I admire that. He's not a time-waster. Mind you, he's refused to hand over any original documents until we get our letters of administration. I've only got copies.'

'So what happens next?'

'Let me see . . . I've made a note of it. This is all new to me, remember. Like being a law student again. Yes – I've got to lodge Hubbard's consent, together with the marriage certificate, and an oath from you as to the value of the estate. You'll have to come into the office to swear that.'

'But I don't know the value of the estate.'

'No, but that's where I'm hoping Mr Hubbard is going to help us again. I'm writing to him this afternoon. I'll be in touch with you next week when I've heard from him.'

When she had put the phone down, Abby wished that she'd had the bottle to ask Robin out for a drink. Or dinner. Just to have someone to talk to. There was no one else. He'd probably only misconstrue it, so maybe it was just as well, but anything would be better than the loneliness of the cottage, and the ache of missing her mother. The pub wasn't exactly company, and the only other person she saw regularly was Margaret, the sixteen-year-old from two doors away who looked after Chloe on the evenings when she was working. There were lonely evenings when the temptation to pack their cases and head back to London was almost too great to resist. But while there was the money to come, she must sit tight. Robin had said that Leslie Maskelyne's estate looked like a straightforward one, so maybe it would only be a matter of weeks. She could wait. And in the meantime, she would ask Robin out next time he rang, and to hell with any wrong conclusions he might jump to.

The following day was a Saturday. Abby was sitting in the kitchen drinking a mug of tea, still in the oversize T-shirt which she wore as a nightdress, when the doorbell rang. With a sigh she went to the front door.

She had not expected this particular visitor. There stood Geraldine, who managed to look as immaculately groomed as ever, even though she was wearing only a sweatshirt and jogging pants, her tawny hair pushed back with a sweatband. In her arms she held a curious assortment of objects – small framed pictures, a piece of Dresden china, and assorted pieces of silverware.

'I have some more in the car,' said Geraldine simply.

'I don't –' began Abby, but Geraldine suddenly thrust the armful of objects towards her, and she was forced to put out her own hands to try and stop them from falling. A candlestick dropped and clanged on the doorstep. 'What is all this?' she gasped.

'They're your things,' said Geraldine. 'Take them inside. I'll fetch the rest.' She turned back to her red Mercedes, which was parked a little way off with its boot open. Abby had no choice but to take the tottering heap of things into the living room and deposit them on Ruth's shabby little coffee table before they fell from her arms. Before she knew it, Geraldine had marched into the front room behind her and set down a large box, apparently stacked with similar items.

'I don't want these!' said Abby.

'Don't you? I don't think either of us has any choice in the matter. They're the things I mistakenly took from my father's house a few weeks ago. Surely you remember? You were stripping the beds at the time. Or possibly scrubbing out the lavatories. I was under the illusion that they belonged to my family, but my lawyer tells me that they belong to you.'

Abby could hear a slight trembling in Geraldine's voice, but she was determined to harden herself against feeling any sympathy for the woman. This was just a bit of play-acting to make her feel bad about everything. Well, it wasn't going to work. She glanced at the box and shrugged.

'I don't want any of it.'

'I see,' replied Geraldine. She could not keep the tremor of anger and misery out of her voice any longer, and her voice rose. 'Maybe you don't want the house. Or our money. But you've gone out of your way to take them. So you might as well have these.'

Abby folded her arms. 'If you came round here wanting to start some kind of scene, as a way to get at me, you're wasting your time.'

Geraldine's breathing grew rapid. It was exactly what she had wanted, hoping to goad Abby into a position of vulnerability. She hadn't expected such a cool response. She stood there in mute frustration for a few seconds, then did the only thing she could think of doing and burst into tears. 'I just don't know how you can live with yourself, Abby!' she raged, between sobs. 'What you're doing is absolutely appalling! It's immoral! Do you know what you've done to our family? You've absolutely destroyed it! Everything that my father worked for, all the things he wanted us to have – you're taking it away! And you know you have no right! Absolutely no right!' With shaking fingers, Geraldine rummaged in the sleeve of her sweatshirt for a tissue, and mopped her eyes.

'I can't help what's happened,' said Abby. The sight of Geraldine's tears did nothing to move her. A week ago she might have felt differently, but Robin had helped her to feel more sure of herself. Besides, why should she feel sorry for the Maskelynes after the way they had behaved over the money? They had probably hastened her mother's death with their selfishness. That, and the knowledge that Leslie Maskelyne was her father, gave her a sense of complete justification.

Geraldine switched tack slightly. She controlled her tears, and took a few deep breaths. 'Yes, Abby, I think you can. I think it's well within your power to undo some of this. You don't realise what you're taking away – my daughter's education, land that my husband had hoped to buy . . . You may look at us and think we're well off, but you're mistaken. We needed that money. And what about Lydia? I don't think you can possibly understand what her share of my father's estate meant to her. She's suffered for years with that husband of hers, and this was her means of gaining some independence.' She paused, wondering if she'd been indiscreet. It was too late now. 'But you've put an end to any hopes of that.'

This startled Abby, though she didn't show it. She herself had had enough of worthless men to know what it meant to be rid of them. She felt a slight pang for Lydia, but let it die away. 'You haven't mentioned Stephen yet,' she remarked.

Geraldine bridled slightly. She felt she'd possibly overdone it by telling Abby about Lydia, so she wasn't going to compound it by going into details of Stephen's jobless, hopeless condition. Let Stephen do his own grovelling. Doing it for herself and Lydia was bad enough. 'Stephen can look after himself. I know he feels about this as we do. We are all suffering horribly.' She shifted stance yet again. 'Look, Abby –' Her tone was still stiff, but had taken on a new, conciliatory note. '– I'm appealing to your better nature. You know very well that everything which has happened is simply a ghastly mistake. My father never meant to leave you all his money –?'

'Only some of it,' remarked Abby.

Geraldine hesitated, faintly taken aback. 'Yes – well . . . perhaps we were not exactly fair about that. Perhaps it was wrong of us. I regret that. But I hope you can see now that none of Father's wishes is being properly observed. This isn't what he would have wanted.' She gazed at Abby's lovely, imperturbable countenance. 'Whatever he intended by marrying your mother, it wasn't this. I'm asking you to search your conscience.'

'Oh, really?' replied Abby. 'You didn't exactly search yours, Geraldine, when my mother was ill, and relying on money from your father to help her have her operation, did you?' She paused, folding her arms and jutting her chin a little. 'You know what? You may find this hard to believe, but I don't give a toss about you and

241

your family. Or Lydia. Or Stephen. I care about myself now, and my daughter.' She glanced down at the box and at the things lying on the coffee table. 'You can either take that lot with you, or I'll stick it all out on the doorstep for the dustmen to take.'

Geraldine was momentarily speechless. She hadn't expected Abby to be quite so ruthless in her attitude. 'You're going to regret this. In one way or another, you will be very, very sorry, Abby,' she said at last, her voice shaking with emotion.

'I doubt it,' replied Abby, as Geraldine stalked past her towards the front door.

When she had gone, Abby stood staring down at the knick-knacks and pieces of silver strewn on the coffee table. She remembered Geraldine coming to Hemwood House to collect them. No doubt they were of sentimental significance to her, but she had been prepared to use them in a theatrical gesture as a means of pricking Abby's conscience. Well, Abby would see that they were returned to her. In fact, she was welcome to the entire contents of the house. They were of no interest to Abby. As to the house – Abby had no idea of the legal position regarding the ownership of that. Was it hers yet, or did she have to wait until Robin got the letters of administration? Stephen had doubtless been staying there last week, when he had come to see her, coming and going just as he pleased. Well, she would make it her business to find out from Robin Onslow on Monday morning just where everyone stood. The Maskelynes were going to have to see that she meant business.

Walter rang Stephen on Monday morning, just as Stephen was packing the last of his clothing before taking it round to Harriet's.

'I thought I should let you know that Oliver Bryce has sent his opinion.' Stephen could tell from the weight in Walter's voice that their worst fears had been confirmed.

'Is there any hope?' asked Stephen.

'None, in Mr Bryce's view. Not without evidence that your father wrote the document under some duress, or as a result of some coercion. I'm afraid we must take it that Miss Owen has become the sole beneficiary of your father's estate. Of course, as Bryce says, it's always open to the family to initiate proceedings in the hope of obtaining some kind of settlement, but there can be no guarantee of the success of such tactics. The matter might be protracted and expensive.' Walter paused for a second. 'Naturally, I don't know this young woman, though you've told me that you and she had some kind of a – a relationship. It may be that she shares the general view that this turn of events is a somewhat unnatural one. If you were to approach her personally, perhaps you and your sisters might be able to prevail upon her to reach a more equitable solution, in the circumstances.'

Stephen gave a short laugh. 'Not much hope of that. But there are certain possibilities that I intend to explore.' Stephen had been doing a considerable amount of thinking over the weekend. He'd had nothing else to do.

'By the way,' went on Walter, who had been trying to prepare the next part of what he had to say with scrupulous diplomacy, 'I feel I should mention the matter of Hemwood House. I know that you have been staying there on a regular basis since your father's death, but – well, I'm afraid that you really must now accept that it's no longer family property.'

'It belongs to her,' said Stephen savagely.

'Yes. Together with the contents. Unless, of course, there are personal items of your own there, in which case I would suggest –'

'Thank you, Walter, for raising the matter,' said Stephen. 'You've made my day.' And he hung up. He sat for some time, thinking this over. Handing over the keys would present him with an ideal opportunity to speak to Abby again. And this time his approach was going to be quite different.

Abby rang Robin that morning to discuss the very same matter.

'Of course it's yours,' Robin told her. 'Just as soon as we get the letters of administration, I'll draw up a deed of transfer. Until then, you can't dispose of it. But it's yours. You can walk in any time you want to.'

'Really?' Abby marvelled at the idea of the house, with its gardens and greenhouses, belonging to her. She still had a set of keys. She might go up one day this week, just to enjoy the pleasure of walking round it, taking possession. She might even do a bit of dusting and hoovering. They were her rooms, hers to keep clean and do with as she liked now. As soon as she had the money, she would arrange for the contents to be taken away and handed over to Lydia and Geraldine. Then she could decide what to do with the place itself. She suddenly remembered her resolution. 'Robin,' she said, 'let's go out to lunch. I'm fed up. I'm lonely. If it weren't for all this business, I don't think I'd still be in Hemwood. I need to talk to someone sane.'

'All right,' said Robin, wondering if this was going to be the start of something promising. 'What about Friday? We could go to that pub where we had a drink. They do fairly decent lunches. Come to the office around one.'

'Okay.' She glanced at her watch. 'I'd better go. I've got to pick up Chloe from school.'

She slipped on her denim bomber jacket and strolled down the High Street towards the nursery. A little knot of mothers had already gathered there, and although a few that Abby knew nodded and smiled at her, it seemed to Abby that there was something guarded about their expressions. Or was she just being paranoid? They all knew about the Maskelyne estate, of course. Doris had told quite a few people about the loss of her legacy, and possibly Geraldine and Lydia had let their own grievances become public knowledge. No doubt Abby was widely regarded as being to blame for everything. Well, when she had her money, she would be off out of here, and sod the lot of them. But in the meantime she had to stay where she was, and just put up with the hostility. She stood a little way off from the other mothers, waiting for the doors of the school to open, and Mrs Cantley's buxom figure to appear.

Even before the door opened, everyone waiting outside could hear the rising wail of a child in the throes of being rebuked. The blend of defiance and self-pity was unmistakable, and each mother instantly sought to identify whether the cry was a familiar one. Abby knew straight away that it was Chloe, and her heart sank. She hated it when Chloe got into trouble at school, which she seemed to do more than most other children. Mrs Cantley opened the door and looked out. Her face was grim and her cheeks flushed. When she caught sight of Abby she beckoned to her and said in stern, ringing tones, 'Might I have a word, please, Mrs Owen?'

The other mothers watched as Abby went into the nursery, flicking back her long hair and jamming her hands in the pockets of her jacket, ready to face the worst.

Mrs Cantley led her to a corner of the nursery well away from the children and the helpers. 'I'm very much afraid to say,' she said in subdued tones, 'that your daughter has gone beyond the limits of what we regard as acceptable behaviour in this school.'

'What has she done?' asked Abby wonderingly. How much damage could one child do with round-tipped scissors or a lump of play dough?

Mrs Cantley took a deep breath and said gravely, 'She has used the "F" word. In my presence. It happened just a few moments ago.'

Abby glanced towards Chloe, who was sitting on the 'thinking' chair, roaring, while the rest of the children gazed at her, round-eyed and awestruck. 'And I have to tell you, Mrs Owen, that I will not have a child in my school who is capable of using such language. It is a disgusting influence on the other children, and is reflective of a most undesirable state of affairs in Chloe's home.'

Abby felt her face redden with anger. She didn't reply to Mrs Cantley, but walked over to Chloe and crouched down, taking Chloe's hot hands in hers.

'Chlo,' she said, waiting as her daughter's sobs and sniffles subsided. 'Chlo, did you say a bad word to Mrs Cantley just now?'

Chloe nodded slowly, miserably, her eyes on her mother's, her little chest rising and falling in the heat of her unhappiness.

'She said "fuck",' volunteered a small boy in clear tones.

'Charles!' exclaimed Mrs Cantley. She glared at Abby. 'This is exactly the kind of thing I am not prepared to tolerate!'

'But Colin told me to say it!' wailed Chloe, beginning to cry again. 'He said he knew a word and if I said it to Mrs Cantley he would give me four Pocahontas stickers!'

Abby glanced up at Mrs Cantley.

'I very much doubt if that is true, Chloe,' said Mrs Cantley. 'You have told fibs about Colin many times in the past, and this, I'm afraid, is the last straw.'

Abby straightened up. 'Don't you think you should at least ask him?' she demanded. 'Instead of accusing my daughter outright?'

Mrs Cantley sought out Colin, a stout blond child, and regarded him gravely. 'Is that true, Colin? Did you tell Chloe Owen to say that word?'

'No, I never.' Colin shook his head and stared back at Mrs Cantley, lying for all he was worth.

'There. I'm afraid that I must ask you not to bring Chloe back to the school, Mrs Owen. I will not have that kind of behaviour. The children in this school are from decent, respectable homes where that kind of language is not customary.'

'Oh, do me a favour!' exclaimed Abby. 'You haven't the first idea which of these children is lying! But because you don't like me, because I'm not a nice middle-class mum with a husband and a Volvo and a couple of labradors, you're going to pick on Chloe, aren't you? Well, I wouldn't let her come back here if it was the last school on God's earth. I've been dying to tell you this for a long time, but this place is a joke, and you're an even bigger one. Come on, Chloe.' She took Chloe's hand and led her out of the school. As she passed the other mothers, she could feel them all staring at her. They must have heard her raising her voice in there, and no doubt they'd find out all about what Chloe had supposedly said. The whispering would go on and on, and she was going to feel even more solitary than she did already. Who was Chloe going to find to play with now? She glanced down at Chloe as they walked.

'Was that true? Did Colin tell you to say that word?'

'Yes.' Chloe looked up, nodding vigorously.

'And did you know it was a naughty word?'

There was a long silence. 'Yes,' said Chloe in a small voice.

'Well, you are daft, aren't you? Fancy doing what some stupid boy tells you to.'

Chloe said nothing, but put her thumb in her mouth. They carried on walking, and as they reached Alma Cottage, Chloe took her thumb out and said, 'Mum, I don't want to stay here now that

246

Granny's gone. Do we have to? Can't we go somewhere else? Somewhere where there's a Burger King?'

Abby sighed as she took out her key. 'We will, love, I promise you. In just a little while.'

Chapter Seventeen

'W hy aren't you doing more with your restaurant scheme? There must be something you could be getting on with, surely,' said Harriet. She was busy trying to organise her exhibition, coming and going between her studio and the gallery, and it vaguely irritated her to see Stephen loafing around reading the paper for hours on end, or watching Sky Sports. It had been a week since he had moved in, and she hadn't realised quite how indolent he could be.

'I told you,' said Stephen irritably, 'I've had to put it on hold for the moment.'

'Why?'

'Just legal stuff. It's being sorted out.'

He looked so morose that she came and sat down next to him on the sofa, and stroked his stubbly cheek with her finger. 'You know, I could do with a break from trying to get this exhibition sorted out, and you're obviously at a loose end. Why don't we go down to Hemwood for a long weekend? We could go and see your sisters, tell them about the wedding, start making some plans.'

There was a fractional hesitation before Stephen spoke. 'I don't think so. I don't really like being at the house, to tell you the truth. Too many associations.' He saw her slightly puzzled frown. 'I tell you what, as soon as your exhibition's finished, I'll take you away for a proper holiday. Anywhere you like. How about that?'

Harriet got up. 'Oh, I don't mind. I was thinking of something

248

more immediate. Anyway . . .' She glanced around. 'Someone's going to be picking these pictures up in an hour or so. Can you make sure they take them down carefully? I've got to go out for a while.'

'Sure,' said Stephen, and flicked through the channels on the remote. When Harriet had left, he switched the television off, walked over to the window and stared down at the street. He couldn't put it off any longer. He would go down to Hemwood tomorrow. What was he going to tell Harriet? He would think of some lie, say he was going off on business for a couple of days, tell her that he and Russell had resuscitated the restaurant thing, but that it was going to be out of town. If what he planned to do came off, he would need some excuse for periodic absences. It wouldn't be difficult. He lied to her with such facility these days that he scarcely knew he was doing it.

Abby's fears about Chloe's friendless state had been unfounded. The other mothers still asked Chloe to come round and play, despite what had happened at the nursery, and Abby was grateful. She wondered if they didn't all secretly feel as she did about Mrs Cantley and were sorry for her. She decided one afternoon when Chloe was round at Emily's to go up to Hemwood House and look round. She was now responsible for its safety, after all.

She walked up through the woods, pausing as she passed the overgrown and dilapidated tennis court. She wondered idly whether she would ever have bothered to have it done up, restored, if it had been her intention to stay at Hemwood. But who would she ever have found to play on it? What people did she know whom she could have invited to the house, to use it and enjoy it in the way it should be used and enjoyed? Wealth took confidence. Thrust upon you suddenly, like a pools winner, it could leave you stranded, unhappy. At moments like this she felt she might be better off just handing it all back to the Maskelynes and going back to her old existence in London. The idea had a kind of savage freedom about it. But she knew that she couldn't. Her life had been touched and changed, and she must see things through. Nothing could ever be as it was.

Abby turned away and passed through the wrought-iron gate into the grounds. To her surprise, she could see Reg Fowler hoeing a distant flower-bed. No one had told him not to, so he was just carrying on, assuming that someone would pay him at some time. Abby realised that that someone would be her. What if he decided to come to her in the next week or so and ask for his wages? She wouldn't have a clue what to do. She carried on towards the house, took her keys from her pocket and let herself in through the back door. Everything was still and silent. The weather over the past two weeks had been very warm, and without open windows to freshen the place, the air was stale and close. Doris had taken her cue, and not set foot up here since the day she had been to Walter Hubbard's office. Abby opened some windows, setting them on their hasps, watching the light breeze billow the curtains. She gazed around, trying to believe that this was her house, but unable to comprehend it. The pictures, the ornaments, the furniture – none of these belonged to her. It didn't matter what any document said. This was the Maskelynes' house.

She went upstairs, trying to imagine what it would be like if she and Chloe were to leave Alma Cottage and come to live here. Not that she had any intention of doing so, but it was interesting to try the idea out. She found it impossible to imagine herself inhabiting any of these splendid rooms. All she had ever done was to move around them in the capacity of a menial, and she couldn't envisage herself having anything to do with them beyond dusting, polishing and cleaning. Even when she had the money, she knew she wouldn't be able to accustom herself to such a place. She wouldn't be comfortable. She wasn't used to it. The best she had ever known, apart from her mother's house, was a flat she had once shared with Chloe's father in Chorleywood, which had had two bedrooms, a big living room, a nice kitchen, and a slice of garden out the back. She had liked that place. Whenever she thought of living in London again, she didn't think much beyond that. Even with the money, she couldn't see herself ever needing more than a nice little semi. What would she do with a big place with a load of rooms?

Abby suddenly heard the sound of a car's engine, and went to the window. She watched in astonishment as Stephen's dark green BMW came into view and then slid out of sight beneath the eaves of the house. She heard the engine being turned off, and then the sound of feet on gravel. Did he know she was here? She waited by the window, her heart thumping painfully, then went quietly out on to the landing and looked down. She saw Stephen let himself in through the front door and walk across the hall, then pause, glancing round. She had no idea what to do or say. Even if she had wanted to, how could she possibly assert herself, tell him that this was her house now and that he had no business here? It was ludicrous. After hesitating for a moment, she went downstairs.

Stephen glanced up, startled. He had come to Hemwood with the intention of seeing Abby, but the last thing he had expected was to find her at the house. On Walter's suggestion he had come to pick up any of his personal belongings that might be lying around, and then he had meant to drive round to Alma Cottage. Seeing her here meant he had to rethink his strategy.

'Hello,' said Abby.

Stephen nodded. 'Hello.'

She watched his face. She had been prepared for him to be outraged, to grow suddenly furious at finding her here, and was ready to retaliate, but he seemed subdued, almost casual. 'So – taken possession already, have you?' he asked. He stepped past her towards the stairs.

'I have to check to see the place is all right,' replied Abby. 'Nobody else is going to.'

'Well, quite. It is yours, after all.' His voice was expressionless. He turned back to look at her, one foot on the bottom stair. 'I just wanted to see if I'd left any of my things lying around from last time. And to have a last look round. You don't mind, do you?'

'No. Go ahead,' said Abby. She had no intention of sounding apologetic, even though she felt awkward and out of place. How well he looked, how effortlessly, heart-stoppingly wonderful. In the intervals when she didn't see him, the longing seemed to diminish, the feelings grew less intense. But all it took was one glimpse of his face and she was back where she started. She waited in the hall until he reappeared with a bag of clothes, trying to think

251

of something to say, but unable to reconcile her emotions with her determination to remain composed.

Stephen stopped at the foot of the stairs. 'I suppose I should apologise for the way I behaved last time I saw you,' he said awkwardly. 'I wasn't quite myself.' He hesitated. 'I'm sure you understand that this has all been a very difficult time for the family.'

'Families do have their difficult times, don't they?' replied Abby. The words sounded harder than she intended, but she meant to give no outward sign of just how much his presence affected her. She might still love him, want him, but the memory of how he and his sisters had treated her mother still remained.

Stephen gazed at her. Was she really as cold as she sounded? It reminded him of the time when he had spoken to her upstairs, after they had kissed. She had seemed remote then, but that appearance had concealed a different kind of truth. As he had since discovered.

He held out his hand. 'I don't think it helps to be hostile. Let's remain friends, at least.'

Abby hesitated, faintly suspicious of the complete change in his manner from their last meeting. Then slowly she put out her hand and let him clasp it. His touch was electrifying, and instantly her resolve weakened. If only he hadn't come here today. So long as he was miles away from her, she felt she could see this thing through. But just the touch of his hand was enough to release in her all the feelings which she had managed to stifle over the past few weeks.

Stephen put out his other hand and stroked Abby's with the tips of his fingers. Abby felt her insides dissolve. 'It's funny,' he said with a sad smile, 'to think how enormously things can change, and how quickly. We didn't ever imagine a day like this when we were little, did we? When we played together, built our forts, climbed all those trees.' He was deliberately touching sensitive, sentimental chords, sure that her strength of will, her determination to remain cold, could not resist.

'No,' said Abby, her voice barely audible. She found she couldn't look at him, was unable to understand how she could feel like this, want him so badly, knowing everything she did. There was a silence, during which the caress of his fingers sent little shocks of pleasure throughout her body.

'You know,' said Stephen suddenly, 'I really wish we could . . . start again. I mean, that Sunday when I left you –' He stopped as though confused.

'What?' said Abby quickly, putting up her other hand to touch his.

'The way I behaved. It was a defence. I felt I was getting in way over my head. I'm a selfish person. I don't like to acknowledge my feelings. And the way I felt about you . . . it seemed too much.'

'What about when I called you after Mum died?' Abby tried to make her voice sound hard, but failed. Disbelief and hope fought for space in her mind.

'Christ, Abby, when you rang, your voice was the one thing I wanted to hear more than anything. But I couldn't let myself – I mean, I wish . . .' He gave a sudden sigh. 'Look, I felt bad about Harriet. Bad about what I'd done. I was frightened by what I felt for you. I didn't know how else to behave. I thought that if I was harsh about it, tried to stop the thing dead in its tracks, then it would be over.' He lifted his eyes to look at her. 'But it's not. It never could be. I just want you to believe that.'

She did not know afterwards whether she had come to him, or he to her. She let him kiss her, closed her eyes to his touch, the closeness and warmth of him. A confused rush of thoughts filled her mind. I have to tell him, she thought. I have to tell him that we can't do this. But she had never felt so powerless, so completely in the grip of emotional forces beyond her control. Then suddenly she pulled away.

'Stephen,' she whispered, 'I can't –'

He put his fingers gently against her mouth. 'Please – don't say it. I'm sorry. I know this was a mistake. I didn't mean this to happen. I just can't help myself.' He took his fingers away and looked at her with regretful eyes.

'Stephen,' said Abby, shaking her head helplessly, 'I don't understand any of this. One minute you behave as though you hate me –'

He interrupted her again. 'Look, look . . . The last time I saw you, I couldn't quite accept what was happening about the estate. I still can't. That's the worst thing – the way it's come between us. After all that's happened, I know there's no way that any relationship could work. I accept that. You don't have to say it. But I couldn't let you go on thinking that I didn't love you. I was a fool to try and pretend to you. I was going to write. The last thing I expected was to find you here today.'

Abby's mind felt blank with panic. 'Why must it come between us?' she asked, her voice breathless and shaky. She had forgotten all about her determination to remain aloof. The only thing that seemed to matter was that he might still want her. She didn't want anything to get in the way of that.

'Why? Oh, Abby, you know why.' He took her face in his hands and kissed her waiting mouth softly, lingeringly. Then he leaned back, stroking her cheek with one finger and regarding her enigmatically. 'Everything is in your hands now.' He moved abruptly away, picked up his things, and headed towards the front door. Abby leaned helplessly against the carved balustrade of the stairs, unable to think of what to say or do. As he reached the door Stephen turned, fumbling in his pocket. He pulled out a pen and scribbled down Harriet's address and phone number and handed it to her. 'I've moved. If you want to reach me, that's my new number.' He leaned forward and kissed her quickly and gently, then went out. Abby stood with the piece of paper between her fingers. She had a mental image of herself rushing out to stop him, to say something to him, but she just stood there, inert, and listened to the sound of him driving away.

Robin watched as Chloe blew bubbles into her glass of lemonade. They were sitting in the back garden of the pub at a picnic table, under the shade of a Heineken umbrella. He hadn't expected Abby to bring her daughter to lunch. He'd been looking forward to this as a cosy twosome.

'I hope you don't mind Chloe coming along,' said Abby, putting out a hand to smooth her daughter's hair. 'We had a bit of a breakdown in relations with her nursery, and I get the feeling that the other mums in the village don't really approve of us. Well, there is one mum who has her over, but I don't want to ask too many favours.' She sighed. 'Actually, I get the feeling the entire village is giving me the cold shoulder.'

'Because of the estate?' asked Robin, nursing his beer, thinking that, like his ex-wife, Abby talked as though children didn't pay attention.

Abby nodded. 'I suppose everyone's heard by now, and that they all think I'm robbing the Maskelynes of what's rightfully theirs.' She stirred her lager with Chloe's discarded straw. 'Sometimes I feel that way myself.' And she told him about Geraldine's visit, and about Stephen's attempt to strike a deal.

'You can't change what's happened, and neither can they,' said Robin. 'The estate is legally yours. If you're feeling some qualms about it, wait until the money comes in and then decide what to do. Give them all a handout.'

'Some days I feel like taking it all, disappearing to the Bahamas and giving them not so much as a backward glance.' She tucked her hair behind her ears and glanced through the pub lunch menu. She passed the menu to Robin and rested her chin on her hands, thinking of the emotional turmoil of the past few days, the number of occasions on which she had picked up the telephone to call Stephen. Each time her nerve had failed her. How could she possibly try to revive something which she knew to be wrong? You couldn't carry on an affair with your half-brother, even if he didn't feel remotely like a blood relative at all. She looked at Chloe. 'What would you like, Chloe? Sausage and chips?'

Chloe nodded, busy with a packet of wax crayons and a colouring book.

'I'll go and order,' said Robin, draining his glass.

When Robin had gone into the pub, Chloe looked up from her colouring. 'He's nice. I like him.'

'Do you?' Abby smiled. The most Robin had done so far to ingratiate himself with Chloe was to look on with forbearance as she took the bottom off the hole puncher and littered his office floor with little round bits of confetti. It amused and interested Abby that, like Abby, her daughter instinctively liked Robin. How safe and pleasant a thing friendship was, compared to the churning uncertainties of love.

Robin reappeared with fresh drinks, and won Chloe over entirely by presenting her with a little paper cocktail umbrella and popping it into her lemonade.

'That should keep her happy for half an hour. Thanks,' said Abby. 'So, any news on the estate?' She had become quite accustomed, over the past weeks, to feeling like a woman of property, getting updates on the progress of her affairs. It gave her a secret, childish delight.

Robin grimaced. 'Some not very good, I'm afraid. We've had a demand from the Inland Revenue for inheritance tax. It's quite a hefty sum, I'm afraid.'

'Can't that be paid once I've got the money, when the estate's wound up?'

'Strangely enough, it doesn't work that way. We won't get the letters of administration to wind the estate up *until* the inheritance tax is paid. Bit of a Catch 22, unfortunately.'

'Well, how much is it?'

Robin coughed. 'A little under two million.'

Abby's eyes widened. 'You're joking!'

'No. That's what the taxman takes. Forty per cent.'

'How are we meant to pay that?'

'Well, the usual form is to take out a bank loan, but with a sum like that . . .' He shrugged. 'I only got the letter this morning, so I haven't had a chance to make any enquiries. But this could hold things up, I'm afraid.'

Abby watched as Chloe carefully crayoned the tail of a tiger in purple and yellow stripes. She didn't want things to be held up. She wanted to get the money and move away from Hemwood. Maybe she should go, anyway. The longer she stayed, the more confused she would grow about Stephen. Leaving the village would solve it. He wouldn't know where she was, even if he wanted to find her, and she could forget about him. That would be for the best.

'Do you know, Robin,' she said at last, looking up at him, 'I don't think I want to hang around while this drags on. I think I might just head back to London, get myself a job and somewhere to stay in the meantime. Till it's sorted out. There's no particular need for me to stick around, is there?'

'None,' said Robin, conscious of the sharp disappointment that her words produced. He had no illusions about himself, knew that Abby would soon have enough money to live a life far beyond his own, but he liked her company, liked their regular conversations. He didn't want her to go. He gazed at her, testing his heart, wondering if he hadn't perhaps fallen in love with her, hoping he hadn't. 'I'll still need you to sign things, but I suppose I can always send them to you.'

'Good,' said Abby, and finished her drink. 'Then the sooner we go, the better. Don't you think so, Chloe?'

Chloe didn't look up, simply nodded.

All week Stephen waited for Abby to call. She *would* call, he was certain. There was always the possibility that Harriet would answer the phone, but the odds were in his favour. He was in most of the day, and Harriet was usually only around in the evenings.

By the time the weekend came and Abby still hadn't rung, Stephen was disconcerted, but only slightly. He had accepted that this was always an outside possibility, and had a second plan of action lined up. He would have preferred not to have to make the next move, but now he had no choice.

When Stephen rang, the day after her lunch with Robin, Abby had begun to pack. She wasn't going to be able to leave till Monday at the earliest, because she had to wait for the furniture clearers to come and empty the cottage, and there were keys to be handed over to estate agents, but just the business of sorting out clothing and getting out suitcases was satisfying. The quiet of the village and the snugness of the cottage had grown oppressive, claustrophobic. She longed for the scent of exhaust fumes, the grey clamour of buildings and endless pavements, the anonymity of London faces. It would mean freedom from everything that pressed in upon her – the Maskelynes, their house, the tormenting thought of Stephen, and all that guilt – and a chance to start afresh.

The telephone hadn't rung for days, and when it did, she paused in the midst of folding Chloe's T-shirts with a sense of premonition. It could be Robin, she told herself. But some sixth sense told her it would be Stephen. She had felt all week as though hooked up to his mind.

'I had to call you,' he said. 'I haven't stopped thinking about you. About us.'

Abby could feel her pulse begin to quicken at the mere sound of his voice, and determined not to be weak. 'Stephen, I think you should know – I'm leaving Hemwood. I'm going back to London.'

Damn, he thought. This was not what he had expected. Clearly he hadn't done quite enough groundwork. 'Abby,' he said, his voice urgent, 'I have to see you. I don't think I can bear it unless I do.'

She hesitated, torn between longing and her knowledge that she had to stop this thing. The easiest way out would simply be just to tell him who she was, what they were to one another, but she couldn't quite take that irrevocable step. She supposed that she could always agree to meet him in London . . . No, that would be fatal. He would inevitably find out where she was living, the affair wouldn't die the sudden death she knew it had to. It could become painful, protracted. His voice broke into her thoughts. 'Abby, you know we can't leave things as they are. You want to see me just as much, don't you?'

Oh, God, how she did. She could see him just once. Just one last time, and then go, cut her ties for ever. 'Yes,' she replied softly. As soon as she said the word, she felt an inner sense of euphoria. She would see him again. She needn't think beyond that. Not right now. It would be enough for the moment.

'I'll drive up tomorrow evening and meet you at the house.'

'All right.'

'And Abby?'

'What?'

'I love you.'

In her haze of happiness, guilt slipped completely away. And she didn't doubt him for a moment.

*

'I thought you'd given up your job at the pub,' said Margaret, dropping her homework folder and pencil case on the kitchen table. Abby had spent the entire day waiting anxiously for Margaret to get back from school so that she could ask her to babysit. There was no one else she could call on, and if Margaret had said she couldn't do it, Abby thought she would have wept.

'I have,' said Abby. 'I'm just going out for a couple of hours. I won't be back late.'

'That's okay,' said Margaret, crouching down on the floor where Chloe was setting up a game of snakes and ladders.

Abby hurried upstairs and went to gaze at herself once more in her mother's old cheval glass. She had spent an hour or so going through her scanty wardrobe, discarding one garment after another. It was madness, she knew, to care so much about this, but she couldn't help it. Even the last fragment of time she had with Stephen was worth taking trouble for. Not that she had anything decent to wear. At last she put on a dress that she had picked up in a second-hand clothes market, an old-fashioned thing the colour of faded roses, with little buttons down the front. The colour looked good against her sun-tanned skin, and the crêpe clung loosely to her body. It was a sensuous dress, but its faint shabbiness had a carelessness that pleased Abby. She didn't want to look as though she had taken too much trouble over what she wore.

She stared at her reflection, pulling back her blonde hair with both hands. 'Why are you doing this?' she murmured aloud. She tested her conscience, but it felt calm and untroubled. She smiled back at her reflection and let her hair fall round her shoulders. All that mattered was this evening. She would worry about tomorrow when it came, as she had always done.

She slipped on her denim jacket and her sandals and went downstairs. 'I'll see you both later,' she said to Margaret and Chloe, then bent to give Chloe a quick kiss.

Cloud that had been building up on the horizon was now drifting across the evening sky, but the air was still and warm as she made her way up the path to the woods. In the pocket of her jacket her fingers curled round the metal of the keys to Hemwood

259

House. My house, she thought to herself. Why was it that she could feel guilty about that, and yet not about the rest of it? Stephen would run a mile from her if he knew the truth. But her conscience lay untroubled. What good would it do for him to know? This was the best way. A clean parting, with nobody hurt. And she would still have this evening to remember.

She came slowly through the fringes of the wood and walked towards the house. Ever since their encounter a week ago, Abby's mind had been relenting. A hard, needy part of her was still determined to cling on to the money which she wanted for Chloe and herself, but the house . . . Why shouldn't she just give Stephen the house, and leave it at that? She didn't want it, after all. Then she could go, and never come back, with her conscience salved. Lydia and Geraldine had their husbands to look after them. She suddenly remembered what Geraldine had said about Lydia trying to escape from her marriage. Poor Lydia, stuck in that hopeless, spiralling trap. Independent once, maybe, but now with small children and the passage of years, unable to strike out and build a new life for herself. Maybe she could give Lydia something . . .

Suddenly all thoughts of Lydia vanished at the sight of Stephen's car standing at the back of the house. He was already there. Abby had thought she might have to wait some time for him – it was only half past seven – but he had got there ahead of her. How much he must want to see her. She felt her heart beginning to beat rapidly, painfully, as she walked up to the back door.

She had no need of her keys. It was open. She went through to the kitchen and stood for a moment. The house seemed utterly silent. Was he in the house at all? she wondered. Perhaps he was outside, wandering around the gardens, and hadn't seen her. She walked slowly through the kitchen and into the hall. Then the faintest of clicking sounds came to her. She walked down the panelled corridor which led from the hall, past the library, to the billiard room. It was a large, dim room, scarcely used, panelled in dark wood and hung with sporting prints. The furniture was shrouded in dust-sheets. Even on that summer evening it had a musty, uninviting atmosphere. Abby saw that Stephen had flung off the big baize cloth which normally covered the table and was now crouched over it in his shirtsleeves, his back towards her, taking careful aim at a red. Abby watched as he took the shot, gazing at the tendons of his arms sliding beneath his skin, the muscles on his back moving as he straightened up. She had never known any man in her life whose sheer physicality had such an effect upon her.

'I didn't expect to find you here so early,' she said.

Stephen turned at the sound of her voice, startled, his face a blank. Then he smiled quickly. 'I've been here since six.' He set his cue against the table's edge and leaned back against its polished rim, appraising her.

Abby walked to the opposite end of the table and gazed directly at him.

'You know I've only come to say goodbye.'

Stephen nodded. 'I know.' There was a long silence, and then he added, 'You look very lovely.' When he moved round the table towards her she felt rooted. Nothing could have moved her from where she stood, waiting. She had thought he might want to talk, but suddenly realised that nothing needed to be said. He put up both hands to touch her neck, his fingers grazing her skin lightly, then dropped them to his sides. 'You could have said goodbye over the phone, you know,' said Stephen. 'If that's all it was.'

Abby nodded, lost in the warmth and steadiness of his gaze. She felt as though she were brimming with feeling, as though it would spill out and suffocate them both. Yet she had no words. Never in her life had she loved like this, and the intensity of the feeling, the powerfulness of the attraction between them, was overwhelming. She longed for him to touch her again.

Sensing this, acutely aware of his own power at that moment, Stephen lifted his hand and ran his fingers down her cheek, so that she shivered and closed her eyes. He smiled, a secret, satisfied smile that held an element of curiosity. He watched her features soften, aware of how her whole body lay open and responsive, waiting for him. The sensuality of it was quite extraordinary. Despite his own watchful calculation, he realised the quickening of his own desire. Potentially beyond any control he might want to exercise. Maybe she wanted that. He would see. His hands touched

261

her breasts very lightly, then he began slowly, gently, to unfasten the buttons of her dress, pushing it open, his fingers tracing patterns of unbearable softness across her skin. He kissed her mouth, delicately, with a reserved lightness. Nothing too fast. No matter how much she wanted him, he must make her wait. This was his game.

Abby was lost. She scarcely had any thought beyond the pleasure of the moment. Everything he did was so slow and gentle. Almost too gentle. She put her hands around his neck to draw him more closely towards her, but he resisted slightly, though the pressure of his hands on her flesh, caressing her breasts and shoulders, pushing aside the thin material of her dress, grew more urgent.

'Why, didn't you just say it then? Why did you come here to say it?' he whispered, his mouth skimming her throat, her face.

'You know why,' muttered Abby. The expression in her eyes was blurred with desire. 'Oh, God, please . . . yes.'

He drew her down on to one of the dust-sheet-covered sofas, unable to control himself any longer, pushing her dress up above her thighs, fumbling at his trousers. There might be more strategy behind this than the first time, but by God, there was just as much pleasure. Whatever he stood to gain, it would be at no cost to himself. None at all.

'It's just the moonlight,' said Stephen, as Abby turned her head at the glimmer of light which stole across the sofa on which they lay, making ghostly the shapes in the room.

'I didn't realise it was so late. I didn't even notice it was getting dark.'

Stephen said nothing, but dropped his head to kiss the hollow of her neck.

Abby let her head fall back at the touch of his mouth. Then she said, 'I'm cold. We've been lying here too long. Hours.'

'Not long enough,' said Stephen. Then he bent and picked her dress up from the floor beside the sofa. She lifted her arms and let him slip it over her head. He sat back and watched her as she fastened the little buttons, one by one. Then she looked up at him,

262

put out a hand to touch his skin. The planes and muscles of his body were silvered by the faint light from beyond the windows. 'You look like a statue,' she said, then bent forward to kiss his chest and run her hands up his arms. 'Get dressed before you freeze.'

Obediently Stephen put on his clothes, then drew her towards him, letting her nestle in the crook of his arm. A drift of cloud eclipsed the moonlight and the room softened into darkness again. Abby laughed. 'We can't see a thing.'

'Hold on.' Stephen got up and made his way to a lamp in a corner of the room, fumbling for the switch. A bright glow suddenly flooded the room. 'Better?' Stephen sat down, drawing her against him.

Abby closed her eyes, enjoying the safety and warmth of his arms around her, the scent of him. 'I have to go soon,' she said. 'I told the babysitter I wouldn't be back late.'

Stephen drew back and looked at her. 'I can't let you go.'

Abby said nothing. This evening had been meant as a goodbye, the last time they were to see one another. How sane and reasonable that had sounded a few hours ago. She forced herself to speak. 'I'll be gone after tomorrow. I think it's the best thing.' She looked away.

'How can you say that?' Stephen put his fingers gently beneath her chin and turned her to look at him. Then he sighed. 'Let's go and have a drink. Then I'll run you back. It's too dark for you to walk home.'

He took her hand and they walked back through the house to the kitchen, switching on lights as they went. Abby sat at the kitchen table, shivering slightly, while Stephen went to find a bottle of wine. She watched as he opened it and poured out two glasses. He held one out to her and she took it.

'To Hemwood,' said Stephen. 'And all its happy years.' And he drank.

'Oh, Stephen . . .' Abby set down her glass and covered her face momentarily. Then she looked up at him. 'Why say something like that? Is it to make me feel bad?'

Stephen stood a few feet away from her, his glass in his hand. He took another drink. 'No,' he said simply, and shook his head. 'I'm facing things as they are.'

'Oh, as they are . . .' Abby gave a deep sigh and sat back in her chair, pushing her hair back with her hands. 'I don't know how they are. I feel so guilty . . .'

'Why?'

'Oh, you know why! I didn't at first. I was so angry with you, so hurt.' He came across and held her, her head against his stomach, for a comforting moment. 'And then there was Mum. I kept thinking what a difference the money might have made. Now . . .'

He crouched down. 'Now you know I love you. I'm sorry you were so hurt. And you mustn't feel guilty. It doesn't matter about the estate.' The muscles in his jaw clenched involuntarily.

'Yes, it does. It's more than just the money. I'm not entirely unprincipled, you know.' She looked away, sipped her wine, wishing there was a way she could tell him why she still felt entitled to take his father's – their father's – money. After letting him make love to her for three whole hours, over and over, how could she? Would he still love her if he knew who she was, what she was to him? She turned to look at him again. 'I wish there was a way round it all.' She put her hand out and laid it against his cheek.

Stephen kissed her fingers. He could feel his heartbeat quicken, wondering if this was too soon. 'There could be a way, you know,' he said. 'If you wanted.' He gazed at her, then kissed her gently. He could tell from her instant, eager responsiveness that there might never be a better moment. He drew away slowly and then asked, 'Why don't you marry me?'

Abby's mind took a sudden, dizzying tumble. 'Marry you?' she repeated, astonished. It was the very last thing she had ever expected to hear him say. It seemed impossible, ludicrous. But that was only in the light of all that she knew. Slowly her mind came to grips with the realisation. Why shouldn't he want to marry her? He knew nothing. As far as Stephen was concerned, he was in love with her. The idea that seemed so impossible to her must seem perfectly obvious to him. That he should want her so much touched her with unbelievable pleasure. Then it faded. For several long seconds she had no idea what to say. If she was to tell him the truth, now was the moment. Abby opened her mouth to speak, filled with a sense of unhappy confusion, knowing that what she was about to say would bring everything to a sudden and horrible end.

And then a dead calm seemed to descend upon her mind. Guilt and uncertainty grew detached, floated away. Why should he ever know? Why should anyone? If there was one thing in the world she wanted, it was to be with Stephen, never to have to leave him. If she were to marry him, it would be that way. She could just say yes, and it would all be so easy. She could share everything with him. Her life, the money – God, how wonderful to have someone who would know what to do with it all, to take that burden away from her. And no more guilt. No one would be robbed of anything. How utterly perfect it would be.

The struggle was only momentary. For Abby, there was no such thing as conscience, in the face of a future with Stephen. What did it matter, anyhow? It wasn't as though they were really brother and sister, not properly. That was all just a wry trick of fate, something in the past that could be forgotten. What mattered was that she and Stephen loved each other and wanted to be together. From the earliest time she could remember, that was the way things had been. Everything else was insignificant, in the end.

Stephen waited, watching her, wondering if he had misjudged his moment – wondering, too, for a sudden instant, whether he was mad, whether this wasn't the hardest way to retrieve his fortune. He saw Abby smile.

'Do you mean that?' she asked.

He did not know what he felt as he returned her smile. 'Of course.'

Chapter Eighteen

'I'm not going to mention it to Gerry and Lydia – not yet,' said Stephen. He and Abby were having breakfast in the kitchen at Hemwood House. Stephen had persuaded her to move in a week ago. As far as he was concerned, it was the most convenient and obvious arrangement. Chloe was sitting on the step at the back door with her dolls and a jam sandwich, as accepting of her new home as she had been of all the others in her brief life. Apart from her bedroom, she rarely ventured into any of the other rooms in the house. She liked to play in and around the kitchen, close to her mother, as though she sensed and shared Abby's awkwardness amongst the fine furniture and precious possessions. It did not occur to her – and Abby had never said as much – that any of these things might belong to them. Chloe did not think of herself or her mother as owning anything much at all, except their clothes, and Chloe her dolls and videos.

'Why not? People have to know some time. It's not going to take people in the village long to work out that I'm living here and not at my mother's. Your sisters are bound to find out sooner or later.'

Stephen finished his coffee. 'Perhaps. But I'd rather tell them about us in my own time. They're still very bitter about the estate.'

'But this is going to solve all that,' said Abby. 'What I have is yours.' She drew Stephen's face towards hers and kissed him.

'Hmm. But not necessarily theirs.' Abby gave him a curious

266

glance, but before she could say anything Stephen looked at his watch. 'I'd better be off.'

'I wish you didn't have to keep going back to London,' said Abby. 'It's strange, being here without you.'

Stephen laughed. 'Abby, I've been back to London once in the past week, and that was only for two nights. Anyway, I told you, I've got business to attend to.'

'Will you take me to it, this new restaurant of yours, once you've got it up and running?' Abby smiled at him admiringly, watching Stephen as he slipped on his jacket and searched for his car keys. It did not for one moment occur to her that Stephen was not in possession of his own private means. That he should have important business ventures to attend to seemed to her the most natural thing in the world.

'Of course.' He bent and kissed her. Abby got up and took the breakfast dishes to the sink. Stephen glanced at her as he checked his wallet.

'You know, at some point you're going to have to get up to London and buy yourself some new clothes. You can afford it, after all. Get one of those people at Harvey Nics to – oh, I don't know, whatever they do. Advise you.'

'You mean the wife of Stephen Maskelyne has to look the part?'

'Something like that. Anyway, I should have thought you'd like to dress decently for a change.'

Abby was stung by this. 'I suppose you'd like me to dress like that old girlfriend of yours, Harriet? The freshly-laundered look, some nice pearls? It's not exactly my style, I'm afraid.'

Stephen's expression underwent a subtle change. Then he smiled and put his arms around her. 'You will always look adorable, whatever you wear. And don't mention Harriet again. She doesn't matter any more. She never really did.'

'Didn't she?'

Stephen shook his head. 'We split up a while ago, you know that. It had been on the rocks for a long time. You're all that matters to me now. I'll see you on Friday evening.' He kissed her again and then went out to the car, almost tripping over Chloe. Aware that Abby was watching him, he bent and ruffled her hair. 'Bye, Chloe,' he said. He still couldn't get used to having this child around the place, but that came with the package, he supposed.

'Bye,' said Chloe, without looking up at him.

Stephen drove down the long, curving driveway with a light sense of relief. The thing was nearly accomplished. But at what cost? Each time he thought of Harriet, it was with a faint, sickening feeling. It wasn't just that he was going to have to let her down in a few weeks' time. That was simply a sad fact of life, an inevitable part of the equation. No, what he had come to realise over the past few days was how much he had come to rely upon her. She knew him, she bolstered his ego, indulged him. He hadn't properly appreciated that until now. But there was no going back. If he didn't want to spend the rest of his life as a hard-up, frustrated advertising hack, he had to do what he could. And that meant marrying Abby. Christ, he was lucky to have been able to pull this off. Things could have been very different. But by the grace of God, she loved him so much that she would do anything for him. There were going to be no problems about the money, once the estate was wound up. He could tell just from talking to Abby that she would be relieved to let him manage everything. The trust which love inspired was nothing short of miraculous. It wasn't the ideal situation, but it was better than most. It wouldn't be too bad in the short term, he reflected, as he drove through Braintree. He would have money, he could turn her into a presentable enough wife, they would lead a life of considerable comfort. He could keep her at Hemwood, and he would always have sufficient excuses for spending time up in London, doing as he liked. He could continue with the restaurant, make a name for himself, and maybe a time would come when he would have enough money of his own to be free of Abby. For now, though, it would have to do.

When Stephen had gone, Abby went upstairs to strip the beds. She had tried hard over the past few days to develop a liking for Hemwood House, to feel the kind of affinity that went with ownership, but somehow it eluded her. It was as though the house were greater than she was, too much for her to possess properly. Had it not been for the idea of sharing it with Stephen, she wouldn't have dreamed of living here. She would get Stephen to teach her about things, about the furniture and porcelain and pictures, and maybe that way she would gradually feel at ease. For the moment she could do no more than dust and hoover and change the beds, wondering if the day would ever come when the place would feel familiar, her own.

But she was happy. No question about that. Unutterably happy. It no longer troubled her that Stephen would never know exactly what they were to one another. It was a piece of knowledge which she had buried deep in her soul, and she was never going to think of it again. She went into their bedroom and began to pull off the sheets. For a brief moment she held Stephen's pillowcase to her face, breathing in the smell of him. She had come to realise over the past week that the love between them was perhaps more intense on her side than on his, but she didn't mind that. In Abby's experience it always had to be like that between two people. In a way it pleased her to feel slightly submissive, after a lifetime of looking out for herself. She didn't mind deferring to him, just as she so often had in childhood. The estate would be nominally hers, of course, but the idea that Stephen would manage everything seemed logical and right. As she thought of this, she suddenly remembered Robin. In the past week of happiness, immersed in Stephen and her plans for their future, she hadn't given him a thought. What if he'd been trying to get in touch with her at Alma Cottage? Feeling a little guilty, she went downstairs to ring him.

Robin had not spent a happy week. He had indeed been trying to get hold of Abby, panicking at the thought that she might have gone back to London without so much as leaving a forwarding address or number. When she rang his office he felt justifiably annoyed, but relieved.

'Where have you been? I've been trying to get hold of you every day.'

Abby laughed. 'I'm sorry. I've moved, temporarily. Well, maybe not temporarily . . . I'm staying at Hemwood House.'

'Well, thanks for letting me know.'

'Don't sound so cross. What did you want to talk to me about?'

Robin glanced at the pile of letters in his in-tray, work which had lain untouched for several days while he concentrated on Abby's affairs. 'I've been trying to sort out this problem with the inheritance tax. It's been a nightmare.' He sighed. 'Still, I've managed to persuade Barclays to lend us the money. Not without some effort, mind you.'

'Oh, well done. You are clever.'

'Hmm. Anyway, we should get the letters of administration in a week or so, and then it's just a question of transferring the money from Maskelyne's bank accounts. He was a thoughtful old boy, simplifying his estate the way he did. Still, I suppose it's easier to sort out your affairs when you know that the end is nigh.'

'I suppose so.'

Robin caught the bright, distracted note in her voice. 'You're sounding very happy, I must say. I suppose it's the thought of becoming a rich woman.'

'Only partly,' said Abby. She couldn't help smiling. 'You won't believe this, but I'm getting married.'

Something inside Robin dropped like a stone. There was a pause while he fought for something appropriate to say. 'Well . . . That's something of a surprise. Anyone I know?'

'I suppose you'll think it a bit strange. I'm marrying Stephen Maskelyne. We've actually known each other for a long time. It just sort of . . . happened.'

Robin just wished he could put the phone down at this point and examine his emotions carefully, work out exactly what it was he felt. For the moment he was totally confused, but something inside him hurt. That much he knew.

'I see. Well, congratulations. Great news.' Robin tried to put a bit of life into his voice, but it didn't quite come off. 'Listen, I'm really glad you called. At least I know where to find you now. I'll be in touch when we've got the letters of administration.'

He put the phone down and sat back, trying to come to terms with this revelation. As far as he'd known, there had been nothing but animosity recently between Abby and the Maskelynes. Still, you never knew. Often a little bit of friction was just what was needed to give that necessary spark. Stephen Maskelyne. He remembered him from the day he'd come to the office with his sisters and their lawyer to look at the marriage certificate. Tall, good-looking bloke, still had all his hair. Lucky bastard. Robin rubbed his hands over his face and sighed. Not that he'd ever really had any serious hopes himself, but . . . Well, as long as she'd been single, it had been nice, somehow. Possibilities were always tantalising, no matter how unlikely. So, ironically, after all this hoo-ha, she was to become Mrs Maskelyne. It did seem a little strange, and rather sudden, considering the way things had been just a few weeks ago. He recalled Stephen's face of thunder as he had sat here in Robin's office, confronting the likelihood of his inheritance vanishing like smoke. And now . . . well, now it would all come back to him. His sisters' share as well. Depending on how far Abby was prepared to relinquish control of her affairs, of course. In Robin's experience, women generally preferred to let someone else manage their money for them, while they got on with the important business of spending it. Abby probably wasn't any different. Very convenient for Stephen, of course . . . Robin tapped his teeth speculatively, wondering whether this turn of events might not have been prompted by base and mercenary motives on Stephen's part. No, that was absurd. No one could make a person marry them, unless they wanted to. But then, if Abby was in love with the guy – and Robin grudgingly recognised that Stephen possessed all those qualities which made women fall in love – it became easy and obvious. Well, if that was what Abby wanted, good luck to her.

Robin pulled one of his files towards him. It was about time he started to catch up on the backlog. And he needed something to take his mind off the small but unmistakable pain in his heart.

'Well, you're certainly being very mysterious about it. The last I knew, you were absolutely set on the place in Chelsea Harbour.' Harriet put down her fork and regarded Stephen thoughtfully. They were lunching together in a small Italian restaurant in Albemarle Street, not far from the gallery where Harriet's exhibition was to be held. Stephen wished Harriet wouldn't ask so many questions about what he'd been doing over the last few days. It wasn't easy on the spur of the moment to fabricate details.

271

'Russell had an analysis done,' replied Stephen smoothly. 'It looks as though that market might already be overcrowded. It's also rather fluid. What I'm really looking for is something with a bit more stability, long-term prospects, regular clientele. That's why we're looking at places outside London.' Stephen glanced at his watch. 'God, is that the time? I'll have to be making a move. I've got a meeting in half an hour. There's a place in Banbury that we might take a look at today, if it seems right. I might be back late tonight.'

'Well, just make sure you're there for my opening tomorrow evening. I need moral support. I want you at the gallery at six thirty sharp.'

Stephen looked momentarily blank. 'Tomorrow? I thought your exhibition opened on the twenty-second.'

'Nope. The fifteenth. I told you ages ago. So I want you there.'

Stephen nodded, trying to look unconcerned. He'd told Abby he would be back tomorrow night. Well, he'd just have to ring her and put it off. Whatever unpleasant surprises he might have in store for Harriet, he couldn't let her down on this one.

'Have no fear, I'll be there.' He leaned across and kissed her, then glanced down at the bill which the waiter had just brought. 'Do you mind taking care of this? I've really got to dash.'

When he left the restaurant, Stephen hailed a cab automatically, as though he actually had a destination, some purpose to his afternoon. He realised, as he climbed in, that he hadn't a clue what to do with his time.

'Where to, mate?' asked the cabbie.

'Harrods,' said Stephen, on impulse. He might not have a great deal of money left, but that was soon to be remedied, and there was always his Harrods card. He would buy Abby something to make up for not being able to get back to Hemwood tomorrow night. And, since it was Harriet's opening, he'd see if he couldn't find something for her as well. After that, he'd ring up Russell and see if he fancied a lad's night out. He'd told Harriet he would be late back because he didn't think he could face the guilt and awkwardness of another evening with her. Lunch had been bad enough. Each lie seemed to spawn another, generating a network of potential conversational snares. But when her exhibition was over, he would really have to break it to her. What would he tell her? Every time he addressed this question, his mind shied away from it. The truth, he supposed. Only that wasn't something which came very easily these days.

After lunch Abby received a phone call from one of the village mothers inviting Chloe over to play that afternoon. It was the second such invitation in four days. Abby wondered wryly whether this sudden upsurge in popularity had anything to do with the fact that she now lived at Hemwood House as its official owner. She had no idea what people made of the fact that Stephen was living there with her, too, if they yet realised, but it was clear that money could work wonders on people's attitudes and perceptions. Chloe from Hemwood House, whose mother had inherited a fortune, was quite a different proposition from Chloe, daughter of a single parent from a dubious background. This woman, Deirdre Lucking – who pronounced her name 'Deirdrah' and had scarcely spoken two words to Abby during Chloe's time at the Rainbow Nursery – now gushed with friendliness.

'They'll have all afternoon to play, and then I'll give them tea. Laura has missed Chloe so much since she left the nursery. What a pity that had to happen. I really think Mrs Cantley is a most undiplomatic woman. To be honest with you, I'm rather glad that this is Laura's last term.'

Abby decided to skirt the issue of Mrs Cantley. 'I'm sure Chloe would love that,' she said. 'What time would you like me to pick her up – about six?'

'Oh, well, you needn't come quite so early. In fact,' said Deirdre, as though struck by inspiration, 'if it's all right with you, we'd be happy to have Chloe sleep over. The girls do so enjoy that, I find. Though not all of them are quite ready for it. Do you think she would like to?'

'I'm sure she would,' said Abby, knowing that Chloe the independent would go anywhere, sleep anywhere, eat anything, with a happy nonchalance born of her itinerant past. She supposed it must now become important for Chloe to keep up friendships with local girls from middle-class families, since these were the people she was going to grow up with. Adjustments had to be made. Abby decided that she would canvass Deirdre Lucking's opinion on the matter of private prep schools when she went to pick Chloe up the next morning.

'That's settled, then. Just pop her pyjamas and toothbrush in a bag and bring her over as soon as you can. Then you can pick her up any time tomorrow morning. I'll go and tell Laura that Chloe's staying the night – she'll be so excited.'

Abby felt faint misgivings as she put the phone down. Was she going to have to socialise with a lot of Deirdre Luckings from now on? She supposed she would. Still, if it benefited Chloe in the long run, it was worth it. Maybe she would turn into one of them, in the end, and then it wouldn't matter.

For now, however, she had the prospect of a brief period of freedom ahead of her. She glanced at her watch. If she dropped Chloe off at the Luckings in the next twenty minutes, she would still have time to catch the train up to London and spend the rest of the afternoon shopping. Now that the money was only a few weeks away, she could afford to spend what was left in her bank account. Stephen's remarks that morning about the state of her clothing had stayed with her, rankling slightly. Well, she could make a start today. Then it struck her that, with Chloe away for the night, she could surprise Stephen by going round to his flat after she'd finished shopping. If he was there, they could go out to dinner somewhere, spend the night together. They could be entirely alone. And if he wasn't there – well, she would just come back to Hemwood. She would see him tomorrow night, anyway. Hoping fervently that she would find him in, she went to search amongst her things for the piece of paper on which he had written his London address.

Stephen got back to Harriet's at five. He hid the silk dressing gown which he had bought for Abby at the back of the wardrobe, and dropped the rest of his purchases on the bed in the spare room. He didn't want to hang around in case Harriet came back. He was due to meet Russell at six for a drink, and then they were going to embark on an evening which, Stephen hoped, would temporarily obliterate all thoughts of Abby and Harriet from his mind. He'd been trying to reach Abby all afternoon on his mobile, to tell her he wouldn't be back tomorrow night. He tried one more time, listening impatiently as the phone rang and rang at the other end, then gave up. He went to shower, changed his shirt, and then left.

An hour later Harriet got back to the flat. She'd had to force herself to leave the gallery. She still had all tomorrow to fiddle and fuss around, if she wanted to. She poured herself a drink and ran a bath, glad that Stephen would be in late. She needed to be on her own, just to unwind and get ready for the opening tomorrow night. She had a good feeling about this exhibition. She felt her work over the past year had been really good. The portrait of Charlie was one of the best things she had done. Poor old Charlie. She'd felt guilty about kicking him out, but at least he'd found somewhere to stay, even if it was just a mattress on someone's floor.

In the bath she closed her eyes and thought about Stephen. He'd been a bit nervy recently. Getting this restaurant off the ground clearly wasn't as easy as he'd thought it would be, but it was good to see him occupied once more, instead of hanging around the place. When the exhibition was over, they would go away for a couple of weeks together, lie in the sun, and plan their wedding.

In the second-floor Ladies' in Debenhams, Abby changed into the new outfit she had bought, and stuffed her old clothes into the carrier bag. Then she went out, washed her hands, combed her hair, and put on fresh make-up. It might all be a complete waste of time, of course. The chances of finding Stephen at his flat were pretty small, given how busy he was, but it was worth a try. She really wanted to surprise him. She shot her reflection a last nervous glance, then set off amongst the thronging crowds of commuters and shoppers for the tube.

When she finally reached South Kensington, it took her half an hour to find the address. The flat in which Stephen lived was part of a large house in a leafy cul-de-sac. Abby paused and glanced up at the windows, then went inside, mounting the stairs to flat number 2, on the second floor. She pressed the bell and waited, listening with rising heart to the sound of footsteps approaching.

The last thing she expected to see, when the door opened, was Harriet.

They stared at one another.

'Abby,' said Harriet, suddenly placing the willowy blonde who stood on the landing. 'We met at Hemwood House, didn't we?'

'That's right,' said Abby slowly.

Harriet wondered why she had come to see Stephen. He hadn't mentioned anything about her. There was an uncomfortable silence, so Harriet said, 'If you've come to see Stephen, I'm afraid he's out this evening.' Abby was looking at her with a questioning, almost vacant look, so she added, 'I don't think he knew you were coming.'

'No. He didn't.' Abby gazed at Harriet. It was as though some intricate piece of theatre had been going on before her eyes all the time, one that she had been unable to see or hear. Only now the curtain was lifting, and the play was revealed. The sudden, shocking clarity of it all turned her cold. Of course he had lied. Lied and lied and lied. He said he had finished with Harriet, but he had been living with her all the time in London. But why? Could it be anything else other than the money? She hadn't realised just how far he would go to get it back.

'I see. Well . . . do you want to come in?' Harriet didn't really feel like asking her in, but she felt she had to, out of politeness.

'Yes, thank you,' said Abby, and stepped inside. She had the dazed look of someone who has woken suddenly from a light sleep. Harriet wondered if the woman was quite right in the head. She closed the door and led Abby through to the living room.

'Would you like a drink? I've got some wine in the fridge.'

Abby nodded, sitting tensely on the sofa in silence as Harriet went into the kitchen.

'Stephen's going to be rather late, I'm afraid,' said Harriet, handing Abby her drink, hoping that Abby didn't intend to wait till Stephen got back. 'He's got his restaurant project up and running again, and he's gone to look at some property with his partner.'

Abby sipped her drink. 'I want to tell you some things,' she said, looking very directly at Harriet.

Harriet sat down in an armchair opposite. She had been right. Abby obviously was a bit peculiar. Maybe it had been a mistake to ask her in. What on earth was she doing up here in London looking for Stephen, anyway? 'Oh?' said Harriet, trying to look bright and interested.

'About Stephen and myself,' said Abby. Harriet sat back and listened.

It was very late when Stephen got back to the flat. He had expected to find Harriet in bed and the flat in darkness, but as he opened the front door he saw the glow of a light from the living room. Maybe she'd fallen asleep waiting up for him. It wouldn't be the first time. But when he came into the room he saw that Harriet was wide awake and sitting in an armchair. She wasn't reading, and the television was turned off. She turned and looked very directly at Stephen, saying nothing, and in that instant Stephen knew that something had happened.

'Hi,' he said casually, slinging his jacket on to the sofa. 'Still up? Sorry I'm so late. Russell and I went for something to eat.'

'I had a visitor this evening,' said Harriet. Her voice was stiff and unnatural, as though she was trying to keep control of herself.

'Oh?' Stephen could feel his pulse quickening. He didn't like the sound of this.

'Your old friend came to see me – Abby Owen.'

Stephen's insides turned cold, but he managed a slight laugh. 'What did she want?' He turned and walked to the drinks cabinet, suddenly, savagely, in need of a drink, despite the amount of wine he had already drunk. This news had sobered him instantly. Jesus, Jesus Christ! Why had she come here? Once again, the bottom seemed to be falling out of his life. It was the last thing in the world he had expected to happen. She had probably blown the whole thing. There was no way she and Harriet could have sat here and not pieced it together. Still, he had to try and ride it out. He slopped some vodka into a glass and knocked it back neat. 'I said, what did she want?' repeated Stephen, unable to keep the desperate anger out of his voice. He turned to Harriet, and saw that she was weeping. She made no sound, but her shoulders shook slightly. Her face was so piteous, so vulnerable, that he felt a spasm of grief and guilt at what he had done. But such feelings were useless now. What mattered most at that moment was to find out the amount of damage that might have been done to his relationship with Abby. So he sat down on the sofa with his drink, waiting.

Gradually Harriet managed to control herself. The fact that Stephen was simply sitting there nursing his drink, that he had made no move towards her, confirmed everything. A cold, dead feeling settled within her.

'How could you do such a thing?' she whispered, her voice breaking. 'How could you let me go on all this time thinking that you loved me, that you wanted to marry me, when you were seeing her, telling her exactly the same thing?'

Stephen stared down at his glass. His mind darted to various options, but he realised after a few seconds that he could not lie his way out of this. Nor bluff. Unpleasant as it was, he had to face it head on.

'What did she tell you?' he asked, looking up at Harriet.

Harriet shook her head slowly, as though in disbelief. 'Everything. About your father's will, about the money and the house, and about what you've been trying to do over the past few weeks.' As she spoke, her misery began to deepen into anger. 'Christ, aren't you even ashamed, Stephen? Do you think you can play around with people for your own ends without caring what happens to them? Abby knows exactly what you were after, now. We both do. You even moved in here just so that you could live off me, and all the time you meant to marry her! Not because you loved her, but because you wanted to get back your father's money! It's pathetic . . .'

He scarcely listened to her words. All he could think of was that he had failed. He had come so close, and he had failed. He let the howling rage that he felt rise to the surface without any restraint. He was even glad that Harriet was there to let him take it out on someone. He got up and suddenly hurled his glass across the room, where it shattered on the wall next to the window. Harriet edged back in her seat as Stephen came to stand over her, shouting at her like someone demented.

'Pathetic? I'll say it's pathetic! My entire life has been destroyed, everything that belonged to me has been taken away! Everything! I've got no money, no job, no fucking hopes left! Don't you think that I would do anything possible to get back what should have been mine? Do you think I want to live my life as some ninth-rate copywriter, trying to keep up with people who have real money, hating them for having everything I should have had, but was cheated out of? Do you?'

Harriet stared up at him, white-faced. Stephen turned away, sick at heart. He sat down again on the sofa, his head bent, running his fingers repeatedly through his hair.

'How can you think that justifies anything?' asked Harriet, her voice shaking. 'You lied to both of us! You were even prepared to go so far as to marry her! In spite of everything you told me, in spite of us –'

Stephen clenched his teeth together. 'She would have done. I could have loved her –'

'The way you could have loved me, if only there'd been enough money?' Harriet began to cry again.

Stephen lifted his head and looked at her. 'That's right. You live in some kind of romantic cocoon, Harriet, where life is about love and loyalty and happy-ever-after. But for me, it's to do with real things, like money and property and security. I have no room for sentiment. I hate to disappoint you, but I'm not one of those wonderful, steadfast people who go on loving in spite of every-thing. I need what I need. And Abby Owen happens to have it.' It came to him again, the enormity of his loss, the futility and humiliation of it all, crashing over him like a wave. What the hell was he going to do now?

Harriet looked at him numbly. She held out her hand. 'I want my keys, Stephen.'

He said nothing for a moment, then slowly took the keys from his pocket. He was trying frantically to rearrange things in his mind. Maybe it wasn't too late to save the situation. Abby was in love with him. She would believe him if he told her she'd got it all wrong, that Harriet had been lying. As he reached the door he turned.

'How long ago did she leave?'

Harriet stared at him in silence, the last vestige of her feeling for him dying away. He was actually going to go after her. She said nothing, waiting as the long seconds ticked by, until Stephen finally left.

Chapter Nineteen

Abby made her way to Liverpool Street, caught the train back to Braintree, then drove from the car park to Hemwood. She did these things automatically, operating on a level of consciousness almost unconnected to her inner mind. Throughout the train journey she gazed unseeingly at the fields and buildings as they flickered past against the fading summer light, and played back over and over the conversation that had taken place with Harriet. It had seemed as unreal then as it did now, conducted with a surface calm, a sort of rigidity of emotion that puzzled her until she realised, later, that the situation had reduced both herself and Harriet to a state of shock. First of all she had asked Harriet if Stephen had told her what had happened about his father's estate. It was clear to Abby already that he hadn't, but she felt she had to deal with this thing logically, or she would go mad. When Harriet had said no, Abby had explained it all carefully to her.

'But he's given up his job,' Harriet had said. 'That means he has no money. How awful for him . . . God, I wish he'd told me.' Then she had looked up at Abby, bewildered. 'But what about the restaurant? How is he able to go on with that?'

'I don't know,' Abby had replied.

'Why should you know? What has it to do with you?' Harriet had demanded angrily. At that moment Abby felt almost sorrier for Harriet than she did for herself. Harriet's face was quite open and wondering. It was the last time she was ever to believe in Stephen in her life.

And then Abby had told her everything. How foolish the telling of that tale had made her appear. For without being able to explain to Harriet how deeply she loved Stephen – and she didn't think anyone would ever be able to understand that – she realised that it made her look immensely gullible. What else had the whole charade been for, if not the money? There could never be any possibility of making Harriet see how it had been between them, how utterly she had believed in Stephen, as she had in childhood, how unspeakably complete it had made her feel to think that he wanted her for the rest of his life. Presumably, thought Abby, as she sat nursing her pain, Harriet had felt the same things, until now. But nothing had been said about that.

When everything had been told, there were no expressions of disbelief or outrage on Harriet's part. She knew from the way Abby spoke that each single word uttered had to be true. She asked some questions, and Abby answered them. Then Abby said, 'I'm sorry about this. I had no intention of hurting anyone. Stephen said that you and he were finished.' What calm words to conceal a cauldron of emotion. But she and Harriet were virtually strangers, and that was the way strangers spoke to one another.

Which was why Harriet could only reply, in the same even tones, 'I don't think you owe me any apology. In fact, I should be grateful to you for letting me know.' Then she had regarded Abby frankly, the pain evident in her eyes. 'I suppose it's just as bad for both of us.' Not a word was said about Stephen, but as they looked at one another, some silent understanding passed between them. But it would have been beyond either of them to express what they felt about him, and what he had done. Why was that? Abby wondered, as she got off the train at Braintree and passed through the ticket barrier. Pride? Sisterhood? Perhaps a little bit of both.

Then she had stood up, handed Harriet her empty glass, and they had said goodbye to one another in a very simple, final way. Abby did not like to speculate now on what Harriet had felt and done after Abby had left, how she reconciled herself to her anger and hurt. It seemed almost prurient. For herself, she did not think there would ever be any way of ridding herself of the weight of her emotions. Perhaps this was some sort of a judgement on her, for keeping from him the thing which she should have told him. At least if she had told him who her real father was, they would all have been spared so much misery. Including Harriet.

As she drove along the dark, winding road to Hemwood, Abby felt as though she were beginning to wake from some long dream. And how painful the waking was. As though happiness, however illusory, had been nothing more than an anaesthetising agent. This was the real world, real and painful, where people betrayed you and cheated you. And they did those things because you *let* them. Because you were stupid. Stupid, stupid. Abby muttered the word over and over as she drove, unaware that tears were slipping over her face until she felt the wetness on her hands as they gripped the wheel.

She was approaching the gates to Hemwood House. For a moment she slowed down. She wiped her cheeks with the back of her hand, hesitating, wondering if she wanted to go back to the house where she had lived with him for such a short time. Then, with a clumsy grinding of the gears, she set the little car speeding up the driveway to the house, feeling for the first time a sense of fierce possessiveness.

How empty it was. She ached for Chloe, to be able to go and kiss her warm, sleeping face and feel some comfort in that. But Chloe was somewhere else, and the place was deathly quiet. She set down her car keys on the hall table and, for the first time, looked at it properly, running her hands over it. This was hers. Not Stephen's, not anybody else's. Hers. She switched on the light for the stairs and went up slowly, looking around as though for the first time. She went from room to room, and in each room she moved among the precious possessions and furniture, touching them all, laying claim to them. Whatever he had done to her, none of this was his, and never could be. It was a source of strength that felt almost like revenge.

But when she went to bed, those feelings drifted away, leaving only an aching unhappiness.

*

At first she thought she was dreaming. Then she realised that she was lying, waking, in the dark, and that the sound of someone calling her name was not her imagination. She sat up, listening. The voice came again, and for a moment she was petrified, until she realised who it was. She fumbled for the bedside light and flicked it on, and saw Stephen standing in the doorway.

There was silence for a long moment, and then Abby said, 'I can't believe you're here.'

He came a little way into the room. His familiar features had taken on a harshness that made her heatbeat quicken.

'I didn't want to wake you,' he said.

'What are you talking about?' she asked, wondering for an instant whether he hadn't spoken to Harriet, whether he had just come straight to Hemwood from wherever he had been. But there was something in his face, a trace of furtive desperation, that told her he knew all that had happened that evening.

He came towards the bed, and she shrank back imperceptibly. Stephen paused, then sat down on the edge of the bed. Abby didn't move. She watched his face. 'Abby,' he said. 'I don't know what lies Harriet told you this evening, but I want you to know that there was nothing between us. Nothing. There hasn't been for ages. When I packed in my job she let me stay with her. It was just to help me out. She's got another boyfriend, Charlie. Ask her. She's been seeing him all the time.' Abby said nothing. He reached out a hand to stroke her arm, and she didn't draw away. 'Abby,' he went on, as though choosing his words with pain and care, continuing the hypnotic movement of his fingers on her skin, 'I couldn't tell you how things really were. You'd never have believed I loved you. I do. I love you desperately. But what would you have thought? You'd have thought I wanted you only for one thing. You would, wouldn't you?' He looked intently at her, willing her to answer. She simply shook her head, and he stopped stroking her arm and gripped it lightly instead. 'Yes, you would,' he went on softly. 'You would have thought I only wanted my father's property. But it's not. It's you I want.' He leaned towards her, and Abby drew back, pulling her arm away.

'Stephen,' she said in a steady voice, wishing she did not find the empty vastness of the house all around them suddenly so frightening, 'I don't believe you –'

'But you must,' insisted Stephen softly, earnestly. 'I had to let you think that the money wasn't important to me. Otherwise we'd be where we are now. With you believing all the lies Harriet told you. You have to understand.'

'Why should Harriet lie to me?' asked Abby. 'She didn't strike me as the kind of girl who tells lies.'

'She's jealous. I ended it. Okay, it was amicable enough, but she can't have liked the idea of me marrying you. When you told her, she made things up on the spur of the moment.'

'She didn't make anything up, Stephen. She didn't say anything about you and her. She didn't have to. I could see for myself how things were. Do you think I'm entirely stupid?'

Stephen's eyes hardened for a moment, and then he put his hand on her neck, stroking her throat with his thumb. 'Abby, it's not true. I love you. I want to marry you. We're going to be together, just the way we always used to be. You and me against the rest of them.'

Abby lifted her chin slightly, but did not move her head away. She could feel his fingers pressing lightly at the back of her neck. 'We can't. Even if I wanted you now, it's not possible.'

He gave a soft little laugh. 'What do you mean – not possible? For us, anything's possible.' He leaned forward again to kiss her, and again she pulled away.

'There's something you might as well know now. I wasn't going to tell you. For as long as I thought you loved me – really loved me – I wasn't going to tell you. But if it takes the truth to make you stop this horrible charade, then –' She did not finish. His fingers were pressing against her neck now, and his thumb had stopped its stroking. For a brief instant she wondered which man he was. Was he just poor, pathetic, weak Stephen, trying desperately to salvage something from the mess he found himself in? Or was he a creature who, once he had lost everything and had begun to cheat and scheme and lie and hurt, would go as far as it took to redress the balance?

She lifted her hand and took his fingers from around her neck. It was quite easy. There was no resistance. He wouldn't have hurt her

285

at all, she didn't think. 'We have the same father,' said Abby. 'My mother and your – our father were lovers. So I couldn't marry you even if I wanted to.' Quite unexpectedly, her eyes blurred, and tears began to slip down her face.

Stephen looked at her as though senseless. He let it all go through his mind for a long moment. 'No,' he said.

'Yes.' Abby nodded.

He swallowed. 'You never told me. You let me sleep with you. Christ! Just yesterday you were willing to –'

'I know,' said Abby, crying helplessly. 'That's how much I loved you –'

She didn't expect him to hit her. Not that hard. The force of it blackened her vision for a moment, then lit it with jagged dots of light. She scrambled back in the bed, trying to get out the other side. Then her hand was on the phone on the bedside table. 'If you do that once more,' she said, her voice shaking, 'I'll call the police.' She didn't believe that she would have time to do any such thing, not before he hurt her very badly. But saying it gave her a sudden savage strength. He was just standing on the other side of the bed, breathing hard, his eyes black and dangerous. 'God, you're a real idiot, Stephen,' she said recklessly. 'If you hadn't put on this act, if you'd just left me alone and got on with your life, I was going to give you this house. You could have done what you liked with it, and I wouldn't have cared. But you've blown that. Now, doesn't that make you feel a bit of a prick?' The side of her face where he had hit her was throbbing.

He stared at her. With her hair round her face, and her features distorted in that childish way, she looked suddenly very much as she used to. Excited, game for anything. He felt something inside him give way.

'Jesus, Abby,' he breathed, 'what have you done to me?' He came slowly round to the other side of the bed, causing her to back away slightly, her hand still on the phone.

She stared at him. 'What have I done to you?'

'You've come into my life from nowhere, and within three months you have destroyed me! Totally destroyed me! Don't you see that?' he shouted.

'I didn't come into your life, Stephen,' replied Abby slowly. As she looked into his eyes, she no longer felt afraid of him. 'I was always there.'

'Oh, God, yes,' he said, and closed his eyes. 'I suppose this was always just waiting to happen, wasn't it?'

Abby was silent for a moment. Then she said, 'I'm not to blame for what's happened. Neither are you. But you've done things to me that I can't forgive, Stephen.'

'I don't want your bloody forgiveness!' he screamed at her. He stared at her in a dull rage, and gradually his breathing grew slower. He ran his fingers through his hair, then pulled his keys from his pocket. 'I just want never to see you in my life again.' Stephen turned and went out. Abby sat in silence on the edge of the bed for a long, long time. After a while, beginning to shiver, she put on her robe and went down to the kitchen, where she sat drinking tea and watching the sun come up behind the trees.

'God, you look awful,' said Charlie sympathetically. He had dropped in to see Harriet an hour before the opening of her exhibition, and found her huddled in her dressing gown, dark shadows beneath her eyes, her face looking pinched and small. 'Well,' he added hastily, 'maybe not that bad.'

'Charlie, I look and feel like hell,' muttered Harriet. She rubbed her hands wearily over her face. 'Still, I have to make an effort.' She got up and went to the bathroom. 'Make me a drink while I have a shower, there's a good lad. And make it a strong one.'

Charlie mixed her a large vodka-and-tonic and one for himself, and waited for her to emerge.

She came out at last, dressed in a red, low-cut dress with a matching jacket, her hair still damp, her make-up bag clutched in one hand, her shoes in the other.

'Where's Stephen?' asked Charlie conversationally.

Harriet began to put on her make-up, using the large mirror leaning against the wall. She stopped to take a long sip of her drink. 'I found out last night that he's been seeing someone else.' As explanations went, it would do. She didn't think she could begin to tell anyone exactly what had happened, not without bursting into the kind of sobbing that had consumed her for hours, on and off, for much of the day.

'God, that's a bit off,' said Charlie. 'I'm sorry.' He chewed his lip. 'Not exactly the best moment for it to happen.'

'No, not exactly.' Harriet brushed mascara on to her lashes, conscious that her hand trembled slightly.

Charlie couldn't think what to say. He'd never much liked Stephen – in fact, he thought him a supercilious twat – but he'd been Harriet's bloke, and it had seemed pretty serious, what with him moving in and everything. But Charlie didn't think for very long about Stephen and his place in or out of Harriet's life. He glanced down at his new jacket, and at the brightly coloured silk shirt beneath it. 'I bought this jacket yesterday. I thought it would be nice to wear something new to your exhibition. You know, look the part.' He sipped his drink and mused. 'Didn't want to wear a tux. If you do that, everyone thinks you're the help.' He flicked at his lapel and sighed. 'Do you think I look all right?'

Harriet paused and glanced in the mirror at his reflection as he lounged decoratively in an armchair. The pain of Stephen might be something she would have to carry round for a very long time, but at least there were some people who would help to make it easier, like Charlie. She smiled. 'Yes, Charlie,' she said. 'You look lovely.'

'Mmm. I thought so, too,' replied Charlie.

Five hours later, the throng in the gallery was beginning to wane. Harriet glanced around, feeling pretty woozy from the amount of champagne she had drunk to dull the ache left by last night. A gratifying number of her pictures were ornamented with little red dots. Everyone had been very complimentary. It had been a bigger success than she had anticipated. From having woken this morning with a sense of dread at the thought of the exhibition, she now realised that it had been something of a blessing. Pretending to be happy did certain things for the morale, even if her face ached from smiling, and it was all a lot better than sitting at home and brooding. There were plenty of days ahead for that.

Charlie came up beside her. 'Max wants to go on to dinner. He's roped in that chap from *Vogue*, and a few others.'

'Oh no,' groaned Harriet. 'Is this something he fixed up in advance? Why didn't you tell me?'

'No, no,' Charlie assured her. 'It's all the spur of the moment.' He gazed at her. 'Do you want to get out of it?'

'Oh, Charlie, yes. Yes, yes, yes. If you can extricate me from this, I will love you for ever.'

A few moments later, Charlie was back at her side. 'Job done. But you'd better go over and be nice as pie to him for a few minutes to make up for it. Shall I get a cab?'

'Please,' said Harriet. She fixed her smile in place and made her way over to the small knot of remaining guests.

Harriet leaned back in the taxi and closed her eyes. 'I just want to curl up in bed and die,' she said.

'You can't,' said Charlie. 'Honour demands that you give me a drink as a reward for my contribution to the success of this evening.'

Harriet opened her eyes. 'Contribution? What contribution?'

'Didn't you see the crowd around my portrait? It sold almost straight away, though I have my doubts about the chap who bought it. He followed me round the gallery for most of the evening.'

The taxi pulled up outside Harriet's flat. 'Come on, then,' she said. 'But just a quick one.'

Harriet knew she shouldn't have any more to drink, but one more glass of wine would stave off the necessity of having to think about Stephen and all that had happened. She poured them both a glass and sat down on the sofa, kicking her shoes off. Charlie put on some music and sat down opposite her in an armchair.

'Oh, this is nice,' she murmured. She sipped her wine, feeling the façade of the evening slip away. She tried to clench her mind like a fist against thoughts of Stephen, but it was impossible. Quite suddenly she began to cry.

'Hey,' said Charlie. He came across and sat down next to her. 'Hey,' he said again gently, and put his arms around her.

Feeling like a small beaten animal in need of shelter, she let him hold her while she wept. 'I'm sorry,' she said at last. 'I shouldn't be crying over that bastard.' She sniffed. 'Oh, Charlie, I've got mascara on your new jacket. I'm sorry.'

'Doesn't matter. I'll send you the dry cleaning bill.' He stroked her tears away with his thumb, hesitated, then kissed her.

After a moment she pulled away. 'Don't, Charlie. I know I've had too much to drink, and I don't want to get any stupider than I already am.' She felt almost alarmed by how easily she responded to him.

'You think I want to take advantage of you, don't you?' he asked, smiling at her. His voice was gentle. 'The trouble with you is, Harriet, that you've never had a very high opinion of me. In your eyes I'm just a failed actor, a bloke out for a good time, the guy who never has any money and jokes around to make people like him.' He stroked back strands of her hair, scrutinising her features. 'While you're the successful artist, the lady in control, the one who doesn't take any nonsense from male models in their underpants who get cheeky with her.' Harriet said nothing, but began to smile. 'Well, I am like that. But then again, I'm not, if you see what I mean. I *do* sit around and worship you, and I *do* harbour all kinds of base intentions towards you. I admit that. But I'm also your friend. And if you're unhappy I'm here to make it better – no, don't get weepy again.' There was another small silence while he rearranged her eyebrows with the tip of his finger. 'You see? I can be an authority figure.' Harriet sniffed and smiled. 'Don't feel threatened. Don't feel that I'm after anything. Just look on me as a sort of brother.'

'A brother.' Harriet nodded.

'A brother with incestuous tendencies,' added Charlie.

'Oh, Charlie . . .' Harriet laughed, and let him kiss her again.

'It doesn't look real.' Abby stared at the cheque. 'Just an enormous amount of money written out in small numbers.'

Robin sat back and clasped his hands behind his head. 'Oh, it's very real. You're a woman of wealth now. I'd advise you to go and bank it straight away. You do have a bank account, don't you?'

'I do,' said Abby, nodding. 'But it's never had anything like this kind of amount in it.'

'Now you can embark on an idle life, you and Mr Maskelyne. When's the wedding, by the way?'

Abby said nothing for a moment. She had spoken to Robin three times in the last four weeks. Each time she had meant to tell him. Each time she had found she couldn't. It was more than she could do to speak Stephen's name. 'That's not happening, I'm afraid,' she said at last.

'Oh? I'm sorry to hear that,' said Robin, his heart lifting. Sorry was the last thing he felt. When Abby said nothing, merely sat staring at the cheque in her hands, he went on, 'I have to say I was rather puzzled when you told me. I mean, I don't want to pry, but –'

'Oh, it's no big secret,' said Abby. 'I was a bit infatuated by him – I suppose I always have been. I should have realised that it was just a way to get back his money. But sometimes you can't always see clearly. Things get in the way.'

'True,' said Robin.

'Anyway, we didn't part on very good terms. It's been rather difficult living at Hemwood House for the last few weeks. I keep expecting him to turn up and –' She stopped. 'Well, anyway, I'm selling the place. I can't live there. I'm going back to London, as planned.' She smiled. 'You must come and see me some time. We can have dinner, and I'll tell you the whole rotten story.' She gazed at Robin. She would be sorry not to have him around. It would have been good to see him sometimes. What would he think when she told him how she and Stephen were related, all that stuff? Because she would tell him eventually, she knew. He probably wouldn't think anything. He wasn't the kind to make judgements.

'I'd like that,' said Robin. 'To tell you the truth, I've been thinking of moving down to the smoke myself, trying to get a partnership in a firm somewhere. It's too much like hard work, going it alone. Now that my wife has taken the children off to wonderful Wales, there's nothing to keep me here. I quite like the idea of starting somewhere new with a clean slate.'

'Well, that's good,' said Abby, surprised at how glad she was to hear this. They needn't lose touch, after all. 'Then I won't have to find another lawyer.' She hesitated. 'Can I –? I mean, after all you've done, I feel I should repay you. Can I give you something to help? There's more than enough here, God knows.' She held up the cheque, looking faintly embarrassed.

'No. That's kind of you, but I couldn't. Just my bill will be enough.' He smiled at her. 'Anyway, you've already helped me.' It was true. From the moment she had first walked into his office, Abby had helped. Her case had given him a new interest in his work, and she herself had made him try to get his life in shape. Just in case.

They smiled at one another, saying nothing for several seconds.

'Well,' said Abby. 'I'd better go and put this in the bank before it vanishes in a puff of smoke.'

'What will you do with it all?' asked Robin. 'If you don't mind my asking.'

'Well, I'll pay Doris her legacy. And Reg Fowler his back wages. And your bill, when I get it. Then Chloe and I will go and stay in some very swanky London hotel until I find us a house with a big garden, and decent schools near by. And then . . .' Abby hesitated, and smiled. 'Then I have certain other plans, which I'll let you know about in due course.' She rose, and leaned across Robin's desk to kiss him softly on either cheek. 'Thank you for everything. There have been moments when I've wished you and I had never gone for a drink in the pub that day, that you'd never worked all this out. But once certain things are set in motion, there's no stopping them.'

'That's very true,' said Robin.

'In fact,' said Abby. 'I think my mother and Leslie Maskelyne set them all in motion a long, long time ago. But I'll tell you about that some other time.'

Doris was peeling potatoes when Abby knocked on the back door, which stood ajar. When she looked round and saw Abby, she put down her knife and wiped her hands on her apron.

'Can I come in?' asked Abby.

'Might as well,' said Doris stiffly. When she saw that Chloe was with Abby, she bent down to give her a little hug. 'I'll see if I haven't got a nice biscuit for you,' she said, straightening up and going to her biscuit tin.

'I won't stop,' said Abby. 'I just came to give you this.'

Doris handed the tin to Chloe and took the envelope from Abby, turning it over in her hand. 'I don't know as I want this,' she said.

'Yes, you do, Doris. Go on, open it.'

Doris opened it and drew out the cheque for fifty thousand pounds.

'I know you don't think any of it's right, this business with the estate,' went on Abby, 'but Mr Maskelyne intended you to have this. And so you must take it. It's what he wanted.'

Doris sighed shakily, her eyes bright with the threat of tears. 'I don't know what's right any more, Abby. But maybe if the Maskelynes had been a bit straighter about the money that old Mr Maskelyne wanted you and Ruth to have in the first place, then maybe things wouldn't have gone against them the way they have.'

'I've sometimes thought that myself,' said Abby. 'Doris, I can't really explain it all to you, but you must believe that not everything about this is unfair. Mum knew that. She told me why. I can't change what's happened, but I'm not going to keep everything for myself, I promise. I'm going to be fair to Lydia and Geraldine and Stephen.'

'Well, that's to your credit,' said Doris. She glanced down at the cheque again. 'Thank you. It means a lot to me and Eddie.'

'I know it does. I hope you'll still have your cruise.'

'Yes. Yes, we will.' She hesitated. 'You won't have a cup of tea?'

'No, thanks. I've got a lot to do this afternoon. Now mind you put that in a safe place. And get it in the bank soon. Come on, Chloe,' she said, taking Chloe's small hand out of the biscuit tin. 'We have to be going.'

'Are you going to be staying on at the house?' asked Doris. She knew that there had been rumours about Stephen living up there with her, but no one had seen him in the village for weeks now. Doris didn't like to ask.

'No. I'm selling the house. We're off back to London tomorrow.'

'Oh, well . . .' Doris nodded vaguely. 'It's been a funny old time, these last few months, hasn't it? Will you be up this way again soon?'

'No, I don't think so,' replied Abby. Not ever, she vowed silently to herself. 'By the way,' she added, 'I wonder if you'd do something for me?'

'What's that?' asked Doris.

Abby took two more envelopes from her pocket. 'Give these letters to Geraldine and Lydia when you see them, would you?' She bent and kissed Doris's cheek. 'Bye.'

'Bye, love,' said Doris. 'You take care of yourself.'

'Did you get one?' Geraldine asked Lydia. On receiving Abby's letter from Doris the next day, she had sped over to see her sister.

'Yes,' said Lydia, putting a mug of coffee in front of Geraldine.

'Well, I couldn't believe it. I just thought it was the most outrageously patronising way of going about things.'

'What did you expect her to do?' asked Lydia mildly. She had a calm, happy look about her, like a woman settled in her purpose. 'She didn't have to give either of us a thing, you know.'

'Well, I'm afraid I disagree. Morally, I don't think a thing has changed. Still . . . The contents of the house and three hundred thousand. It could have been worse. I mean, look at poor Stephen. When Walter Hubbard told me that Abby's solicitor rang him and said Abby was offering to pay Stephen a hundred pounds a week for life, I couldn't believe it! Why doesn't she just pay him a lump sum, and have done with it? God knows, he's going to need it. The last I heard from him, he was ranting on about instructing some people in Gray's Inn, wanting to start proceedings against Abby, and have Reg Fowler and Doris cross-examined in open court.' Geraldine sighed. 'But fancy offering to pay him a sum like that each week. I think it's a most extraordinary thing to do.'

'Perhaps it's her way of making sure that she's never entirely out of his mind,' murmured Lydia.

This was lost on Geraldine. 'Anyway, I'm bitterly upset that she's selling the house. God knows what kind of person will buy it. She could have given it to Stephen, if she didn't want it, instead of that silly monthly arrangement. It would all come to the same thing.'

'I'm perfectly happy with the way she's left things, if you want to know.' Lydia sipped her coffee. Her eyes were fixed on the kitchen dresser, as though she were thinking about something far away.

'Well, how much has she given you?' asked Geraldine.

Lydia glanced at her sister and smiled. 'Enough to be going on with.'